FIRESTAR

Deloran

By David Harrell

ISBN: 0-6153-1359-0
ISBN-13: 978-0-6153135-9-7

I would like to extend special thanks to God who has never failed to inspire and keep me despite my insane moments, and my family for leaving me alone in a good way. Also and/or especially:

My dad for being there, my mom for being an unofficial editor, Robert for enduring my frequent moments of irritability and "quit bugging me" talk, Michael for surviving me, Joe who played alongside the earliest incarnation of Darrio and didn't constantly nag me for buffs, Trish, Naomi, Noreen, Karen, Vivian, Mr. Hollins, and Cheryl.

FIRESTAR

Deloran

"He'll never be one of us. Never has been, never will be."

CHAPTER I
Silent Reward

SO MUCH HAD been lost in the streams of time, but remnants of the old worlds were seared into the new age. Mysteries, secrets, long-forgotten histories, and hard lessons born from the wounds of experience were only some of the elements still lingering from the previous eras. The past held ample examples of tragedy, horror, and death in all of their variations, but there was even after these things a certain period where such knowledge was further bought at the expense of two centuries of conflict. Countless lives had been lost over its course, and the peace had been even more costly. Thus, it was in every respect, even to its victors, a bittersweet ceremony.

The great battles were over, and the entire nation of Salia was energized with festivities. Men drank and sang songs while women danced in sweet intoxication. Children laughed openly in Ambrosia's city streets, and the elders told stories of their former and fading glory. There was a collective rise in spirit due to the recent victory over the Outer Realms who gathered to erase the nation from existence and failed. A great deal of human collateral had been paid into the endeavor, but many of the opposing lives were claimed by a single figure who was made the central focus of the celebration.

He was known throughout the Outer Realms as the Great Destroyer, and five of the six nations that surrounded Salia bore grievous scars from him upon their land and population. The Stony Realm's Crater of Bones was full with the blood of crushed souls, and the Wastes of the Frozen Realm held countless warriors just below the surface of its icy landscape. Entire cities crumbled to ruin in the span of a few moments. Towns were buried and disappeared altogether under the surface of what once were fallow countrysides. Many fell in the shadow of his wake. Fear preceded him while death lingered behind, and there was a creed concerning his encounter that said, "flight on sight," for only a frightening few survived his assaults. Those that lived cursed his name, and it was because of this figure that Salia was preserved.

The campaign was mentioned during the celebration as a collaborative effort by the High Elders, and everyone who participated was given the praise due to them. No one, however, could ignore the critical role bestowed upon their unlikely savior. Despite all of this, and for all that was said, he was not presented to the gathered crowd as a great military figure. He was not honored for his wisdom nor celebrated for his strength. No regard was shown for his intelligence, devotion, or valor. In fact, he was not celebrated due to any merits of his own at all. The adulation given to their hero was no more than a boast directed at Salia's enemies. It was not a festival to sing the praises of their champion. It was a public expression of victory aimed at mocking the Outer Realms.

The silent and supposed hero of Salia sat beside his captain with a bitter frown and a furrowed brow. The two were seated before the crowd while the six High Elders, leaders of the nation, closed their speeches with a decree. From that day forward, Darrio, their champion, would have his name immortalized in a title reflecting his power and nature. His last name would be Deloran, and his title would be Firestar.

The crowd cheered and sang in unison of the glory of Salia and the power of magic. The Outer Realms came together to wipe the nation and its power from the face of the earth, but Darrio, their Firestar, destroyed their enemies and broke their collective wills. Darrio took no pleasure in this, and he crossed his arms in silent defiance. His captain, Seris, also remained quiet but maintained a face of national pride for so long as the ceremony continued. Both resented the play by the High Elders who put on the show to draw attention to Darrio. Both also knew it would only be a matter of time before circumstances worsened.

When the celebration ended, Darrio spat and cursed them for what they did. A foreigner unacquainted with Saline culture would have heard the titles Destroyer, Deloran, and Firestar believing them to be distinct due to their phonetic differences. The new additions to his name would have even seemed to grant Darrio an air of importance and power. Even so, what would have escaped a foreigner, and what did not escape Darrio and Seris, was that Darrio's due acknowledgments were substituted by the patronizing tone. The additions offered little difference in meaning from the Destroyer title which had been placed on him by their enemies. Firestar, Deloran, and the Great Destroyer were synonymous, and their meanings were virtually the same.

Darrio returned to the Hall of Order, Ambrosia's primary military facility, later that evening and went to his quarters. It had been a while since his last return, but when he entered, Darrio saw that nothing had changed. There were still no mirrors in his room, and his bed, nightstand, and adjacent window were in front of him. His work desk was further to the left, near the corner. On the west wall was his dresser, and on the east was a shelf full of books, most of them gifts from Seris. There was also a marked-up map of the known world, but much of the southeast was scribbled out. That particular region of the world still existed, however, much to Darrio's regret.

The world of that time was divided into seven realms with a presiding nation located in each. The Saline Realm and the nation it encompassed were at the center. The country itself came into being when a number of people gathered and used a great and mysterious power known as magic to drive out and destroy the previous inhabitants. These people then set about creating their own laws and customs. Magic, however, was considered an evil practice by the Outer Realms and was cited as an assault on the very laws of creation. Very few outside of the Saline Realm knew how it was prepared and less concerning the details of its execution. Fewer still were interested.

Magic was described in much of the Outer Realms as a defilement of God's language. It was even believed the force was responsible for a terrible event that changed the face of the world. In this sense, it was understood by outsiders to be an age-old sin with a persistent lingering in history despite the best efforts of some to keep it out of the public consciousness. Nevertheless, the people of the Saline Realm embraced the practice wholeheartedly, and it became the way of life in the territory. This was a point of great contention for the Outer Realms that debated endlessly among themselves and even questioned the right of such a nation to exist. In time, Salia grew not only in size but in its mastery and display of magic. This led to a series of terrible skirmishes, two centuries of fighting, and the rise of the Firestar.

Darrio was only a young man in appearance with a dark, brown complexion, wavy black hair, and a bitter temperament. The first trait alone set him apart from the rest of the population. Even so, he was widely recognized and feared more for his abilities than his outer form. Countless days of his early youth were spent wandering alone before his adoption by Seris, and he was, by all appearances, a foreigner to the realm. No one knew where he came from, and his life before Ambrosia, Salia's capital, was unknown. Before the war, Darrio was simply viewed as a strange, anonymous street child with no considerable hope of a better future or promise. After Seris, however, this view slowly changed.

Seris himself was a captain of the Shades, a specialized force trained in stealth and reconnaissance, and he taught Darrio the fundamentals of magic use among other lessons related to life, liberty, and relationships. He was also known among his peers as a shrewd tactician. All but one of the schemes in his military career ended in success, and as Darrio grew in power, even at the latter stages of the war, he was further adopted into Seris' company. The two engaged in many missions together, and Seris lead Darrio directly as the commanding officer. During this time, they suffered many hardships, much of them related to the state of their relationship. Even so, they pressed ahead, both eager to end the war in which they had fought for so long.

Salia was overwhelmed at the start of the Magic War, and though time had given her an opportunity to keep her enemies at bay, Darrio became the key figure of the conflict's turning point. The High Elders had asked for all captains and generals to do everything necessary to ensure the realm's survival, and some even went so far as to lift bans on previously forbidden forms of magic and magic amplification. Seris incorporated some of those practices into his core unit with varying degrees of success. Nevertheless, Darrio's prodigious use of magic was something no one foresaw. Magic was, by its essence, a manipulation of the surrounding forces, and Darrio worked his will of wrath upon Salia's enemies. He became so powerful, even dangerous at times, that Darrio was sent out alone to perform the work of entire legions. Stories returned of his deeds, and while some followed the tales with admiration and gratitude, most listened with astute fear and trembling.

Darrio was placed as the arrowhead during many of the nation's counterattacks, and the Outer Realms suffered grievous and nearly fatal wounds as a result. The Aural Realm then became the final bastion of unified resistance, and the Salians gathered their forces to assault the heavily fortified city of Celeste. What had once been a defensive series of battles became an offensive one, and the fall of the Aural Realm's greatest city was meant to be the final blow against the Saline nation's perceived oppressors.

Darrio was tasked as executioner of the deed, and the capture of the Aural Realm's capital city was given over to him. However, though he stood poised to attack at first, Darrio relented and did nothing. He was urged by his peers and commanded by his officers to continue on and complete the deed, but Darrio, without explanation, merely stood with his face downcast. He had no desire to even look upon the city. Without him, the Salian forces were unable to mount an attack, and they abandoned Celeste to return in victory. The Outer Realms, still too fractured and weak to continue, called all of their remaining forces home. The Magic War had finally ended. The Salians went on to celebrate, and they followed the reverie with reconstruction and planning. Still, while Darrio was largely responsible for the success of Salia's defense, his power and act of rebellion did not go unnoticed, and the High Elders plotted against him.

A few days after the celebration ended, the people of Ambrosia greeted the day with renewed enthusiasm and walked the streets with heads and spirits held high. National pride had never been greater. The city itself was full of gleaming white buildings, elaborate facades, and decorated service structures. Some of these included light fixtures that lined the streets, but all of them were etched with a set of patterns and emblems known as scripts.

Scripts would have appeared to serve as mere decoration to foreigners, but the artisans, a profession whose knowledge of magic was intimate, knew just how much information those patterns contained. Magic was not a form of mysticism to the people of the Saline Realm. It was simply a language whose words and instructions could be encoded onto other things in the form of patterns and shapes.

This was the most basic understanding of magic, and it was hardly a secret that could be kept, but only the artisans were trained to understand the complex rules of its usage. Everyone else simply benefited from their craftsmanship.

Even so, scripts were not made strictly in the form of function, and there were a few aesthetic elements unique to Saline design. The most distinguishing characteristic concerned the use of pointed shapes and circles that followed the contours of other shapes. The circle itself was a powerful symbol to the Salians and represented the star, a highly revered and never-ending source of power. As a result, it was often the central or uniting figure around which all other shapes would orbit. From these simple rules sprang a variety of designs, patterns, and emblems. Many of the clothes were also decorated in this fashion, and everything of practical use was scripted. Even buildings, most notably the Grand Hall, were reinforced with scripts.

The Grand Hall was located at the north end of the city and was the great edifice from which The High Elders conducted their administration. They were a ruling committee composed of six men who oversaw all major affairs pertaining to the Saline Realm. The most seasoned among them was Elder Tiberius, the only one of the original six to have survived the entire term of the Magic War. The others rose to the position after their predecessors were assassinated. It was no secret, then, that Tiberius commanded a great deal of influence over the rest though there was technically no single head of the Saline nation.

As the day continued, the Council of High Elders held a meeting with leaders of the military and civil services to discuss what should be done about the Firestar, but their purpose was clear. Seris was invited among them, and while his presence bothered some, it was not long before someone suggested, on implication, that Seris should be the one to remove their Firestar. Seris answered, "I will not."

"Do you not understand the weight of the situation?" Turil, one of the High Generals, asked. "You've seen the boy and what he's capable of. You know him, and his recently exhibited acts of impatience, recklessness, and untempered focus are—."

"The reason we have won."

"He's fulfilled his role. Even admirably at times, I must admit, but what more is there to gain by his retention? You should release the boy. Perhaps then he can find the peace he needs."

"Is everyone present afraid of his power? Is that why we're here?"

The question sparked outrage among some of the High Generals who argued against Seris and questioned his loyalties, but Elder Tiberius raised his hand to calm the room. "We understand you have a history with the boy, captain, but you should not let this history cloud your judgment."

"With all due respect, my judgment is sound, and you are right in saying I have a history with Darrio. That is why I know he is not the one you should fear."

"We cannot ignore the threat he represents to this nation and the realm as a whole. You yourself submitted the reports of his violence and destruction."

"It was violence conducted against enemies of the realm during a time of war this council authorized."

"And the unprecedented amount of power he possesses in conjunction with his violent temperament does not concern you?" Judas, the second Elder, asked.

"No," Seris replied with stillness. "It does not."

Turil crossed his arms. "Just what, then, would it take to concern you, Seris?"

"It would take an act of God, Turil."

Turil shook his head. "Seris."

"Gods or not," the sixth Elder started, "the Firestar's lack of discipline remains a threat."

"Why not question him, and let him speak for himself?" Seris suggested. "Let him tell you of his intentions before you condemn him as a liability."

"That is hardly purposeful."

"But it is fair," the fifth Elder concluded.

"Agreed," Tiberius said. "Bring him in by this time tomorrow for a private hearing. After that, we shall discuss what to do with him. Does this act sit well with the rest of you?"

"Agreed," and as everyone came into accord with the decision, the meeting ended without further argument.

Darrio himself stood outside of the Grand Hall's entrance awaiting Seris' return from the assembly. He was dressed in the uniform of his station, a shade, and wore a black cloak decorated with the pattern and style of the Saline people. Underneath, he wore a violet outfit with long sleeves and a wrap around the waist. His hands were bare. Beside him were three others in similar dress.

The first was Abaddon, a man of medium physical age with still eyes and strong features. Beside him was the younger and less patient Carsis. Flanking the other side was Tam, a disturbingly silent character in his composure with stilted eyes and an ever-present sense of mania.

"What do you think they're talking about in there?" Carsis asked.

"The Firestar," Abaddon answered.

"It's such a shame the war is over," Tam said in his eerily poetic and wispy tone. "I had hoped to see more dancing of fire and ice."

"You just like the blood," Carsis prodded.

Tam hummed in pleasant agreement. "Yes. I like the blood."

Carsis looked at Darrio with a glimmer of contempt. "What do you think, Firestar?"

Darrio heard the spiteful emphasis of his new title, and he

answered the question with an equal measure of indifference. "I think I don't give a damn."

Tam chuckled. "I like the cold in which you rest, Firestar. Ah, Firestar. It is such a fitting name for you."

"Shut up. I liked it better when you all called me—."

"Be still," Abaddon ordered. "He is returning."

Seris emerged from the Grand Hall with confidence and directed his initial words to Abaddon. "It is done."

"Have you learned anything?"

"Only that they remain as fools." Seris then turned his attention to Darrio. "They would speak with you tomorrow."

"Treachery!" Tam shouted with glee. "They will not permit the Firestar to exist."

Seris shook his head.

"And the drawing of blood?"

"Be still, Tam." Tam complied though he did so only with childlike difficulty.

"What do you want me to do?" Darrio asked.

"Say your peace, but do not hope for tolerance from these hypocrites. They have already decided in their hearts what they will do to you."

Carsis once again glanced scornfully at Darrio. "And what will we do when it happens?"

"Do you trust me?"

"Yes, sir," they answered, but Darrio was silent.

Seris addressed him. "Darrio? Do you trust me?"

Darrio nodded.

"Then when it happens, I will tell you what to do. Until then, attend to your duties."

"Yes, sir," they answered.

"Dismissed."

Turil watched Seris speak with his agents from the upper window of the Grand Hall, and Elder Tiberius stood beside him. "I think I'm beginning to have my doubts," Turil said. "Seris, his shades, even those he's trained…So much has changed since the war started."

"What do you mean? The Shades have performed admirably and with great devotion to the nation's military despite the unique peculiarities he brings to them."

"Yes, but I find his shades somewhat unnerving, the seven he keeps close to him in particular. A few of them have a long history of violence and malevolence, and then there is Abaddon who appears to have no history at all. It makes me wonder what resides in my old friend now that he would continue employing such people and at such close proximity."

"Yet he keeps them under his strictest control."

"Control?" Turil replied. "They practically worship him."

The Elder sighed. "Then tell me, honestly. Do you believe his newfound silences are negligible hearsay, or do you believe the distance is for purposes of treachery?"

Turil closed his eyes and fell into thought, and when the moment passed, he answered, "No. I still don't believe that of him. He's a man of honor and code and of order. He will not respect those he does not deem worthy of respect, but neither will he betray a brother in arms. He is duty-bound. I cannot see him as a traitor."

"But you have your doubts."

"I believe he is becoming guilty of something. Perhaps there is something hidden behind his motives, some purpose to his defense of the boy. He has never acted before without these things. I'm simply unable to see what that entails at the moment."

Another span of silence followed before the Elder asked Turil, "Then why do you think he protects the Firestar aside from his obvious love for the boy?"

"I don't know. That is to say, it is not something I have intimate knowledge of. There is something else to their unspoken bond, that much is certain."

"Do you think this is something that is shared between them, or do you believe it resides in Seris alone?"

Turil shrugged. "I have seen them both separated and of the same mind. I have even witnessed moments of sincerest warmth and instances of mutual cold. Whatever it is, whatever the nature, it is neither simple nor easy to understand, much like every other relationship he's had."

"Then you will keep an eye on them I presume."

"And I will report if I see anything strange."

Tiberius nodded. "Thank you, Turil," and Turil left the Elder to convene with his thoughts.

That night, after several days of rest, Darrio decided to roam the streets and note the expressions he saw, but his reputation preceded him no matter where he went. Most people maintained a certain distance from him and avoided direct eye contact. Others went about their day pretending as if they did not notice him. Despite the large number of people contained in the city, even among his company, Darrio was still alone.

No sooner had he done this did a well-to-do man run down the street in terror. Behind him was his pursuer, a petty thief clothed in dark colors and brandishing a dagger. The well-off man fell at Darrio's feet and begged for help. "He tried to rob me, and now he's trying to kill me!"

The assailant, upon seeing Darrio, stopped in his tracks but could not discern who he was looking at. It was too dark. Nevertheless, Darrio glared back at the man with a cold and icy stare.

The thief felt a chill course through his body and made the decision to run. But as he turned his back to flee, Darrio extended the reach of his will through the road and caused the paving stones at the feet of the assailant to crumble and swirl upward. From there, the particles rose to encompass his waist and solidified once more into a solid block. The thief was trapped.

The victim, pleased with the outcome, taunted his would-be killer. "Ha! You see? Now this is what you deserve! Perhaps now you'll think twice before stealing from me again!"

"Go home," Darrio ordered.

The man's ears heard Darrio's voice, but his mind ignored the order to follow after curiosity. "You sound rather young for a patrolman," but as he took a good look at Darrio, this time with discerning eyes, he gasped in awe and fell away in terror. "By the gods. You're the Firestar!"

The thief cried out upon hearing Darrio's title and grew even more fearful than he had been before. "Oh god! The Firestar?" and he took his dagger and began to chip desperately at the stony restraints.

Indignant over the reactions he received, Darrio asked the man, "What's wrong with you? You asked me for help, didn't you?" But the man paid no heed and scurried away in greater apparent fear of Darrio than the thief who had made an attempt on his life a brief moment earlier. Darrio was irate by this time and approached the thief who was still attempting an anxious escape.

When the man looked over his shoulder to find Darrio approaching, his desperation increased all the more, and he cried, "Gods, help me!"

"Be quiet!" Darrio shouted. "You're under arrest!" but as Darrio extended a hand to take hold of the thief's shoulder, the assailant performed a series of furious swipes to maintain distance between himself and his perception of Darrio as death personified. "Stay still you idiot!"

The thief, still too desperate to be taken by force, made one last swipe at Darrio and then plunged the knife deep into his own chest. Darrio froze, his hand still outstretched, as the man slumped forward and died. He then remained in that state for several moments as tears formed in his eyes and rolled down his cheeks.

Darrio was not known for expressing distress at the death of an enemy or target. There were even people who believed he was incapable of such feelings. In Darrio's mind, however, the war was over, and he hoped upon his return that the people would regard him differently than those who encountered him in the Outer Realms. A soldier commented during their return from Celeste and said, "He'll never be one of us." Darrio overheard this and still hoped. Despite the ceremony, despite the avoidance, and despite his knowledge of the High Elder's distrust of him, Darrio, up to that moment, held on to a small and fragile hope that he would eventually find acceptance. That hope was then extinguished.

Darrio slowly drew his arm back to his side while it simultaneously clenched into a fist. His tears continued to flow while the stony restraint, heated according to Darrio's rage and grief, slowly crept upward to encompass the whole shape of the assailant. Darrio shouted, "You moron!" and the standing structure of the thief was obliterated by a sudden force of wind into a cloud of dust and ash. Afterward, Darrio fell to his knees, wept, and silently cursed the hope he once had.

Seris watched from the background and saw the incident play out from a distance. After he heard Darrio's words, Seris lowered his head and sighed.

Abaddon approached him from behind, looked ahead at Darrio, and then returned his attention to Seris. "After all that has happened, he may never find what he initially sought from this world. Are you aware of this?"

Seris did not reply.

"You must also know that he is sure to be a hindrance to you."

Seris again remained silent.

"Is he really so important to you?"

"He is," Seris answered.

"And is it so different from how you've regarded the rest?"

Seris nodded. "But it is also something you have lost the ability to understand, Abaddon."

"You are mistaken," Abaddon answered. "But what I have lost, you may also lose."

Seris declined to comment.

"I would offer you advice."

"Speak."

"Take joy in what you have while you are still able, for there is no way to return here except by shadow of memory." After Abaddon said these things, he left Seris to watch Darrio sob alone.

The following day, Darrio was brought before the Council of High Elders and Generals to give an assessment of his future plans and aspirations. Seris told him prior to the meeting, "Say your peace and only your peace."

"What if they ask questions?"

"Then answer them, but don't be afraid."

Darrio carefully watched the expressions of all who were present. The Elders showed resolution despite the purpose of the hearing as did the High Generals that were also present. Darrio did not feel he would be listened to. After several moments of murmuring and quiet discussion, Elder Tiberius settled the room into silence and addressed Darrio. "Deloran. Do you know why you are here?"

"I was summoned. You summoned me."

"Aside from this."

"I was told you wanted to learn more about me."

"More importantly, we wish to learn just what your plans are for the future."

"I don't have any plans."

Elder Judas chuckled with disbelief. "Surely you must have aspirations and dreams. Some kind of ambition, perhaps?"

"No," Darrio stated with a twinge. "I don't have anything. No dreams. No ambitions. Just nothing."

The Elders exchanged glances and even appeared to soften in their previous resolution. The third Elder asked once again, "You have nothing, Firestar?"

"Have I done something?" Darrio asked with a hint of agitation. "What am I here for? What do you want?"

Darrio's tone hardened them, and the fourth continued to speak. "We are, for the most part, concerned about your past history and technical progress. In particular, your far-reaching advances in the schools of destruction and manipulation."

"You're concerned about my history?"

"We are," answered the fifth. "During the war, we received a number of extraordinary and disturbing reports about you."

"Like what?"

The sixth lifted a sheet of paper to his eyes. "It says here your singular actions were instrumental in the destruction of multiple enemy cities and encampments that resulted in several new and infamous landmarks. The Hollow Realm's Valley of Death and the Stony Realm's Crater of Bones for example."

"And I was allowed to. So?"

"Are we to understand that you carried out these feats of destruction on your own and without assistance from the others?"

"It's not like I could do it with allies around."

"Why do you say that?" Tiberius asked.

"Do you really need me to answer that? It was too dangerous. They would've been killed." Darrio was blunt in his delivery of the statement which hushed everyone in the room, but he could not bring himself to understand the sentiment as he knew their knowledge concerning the nature of magic was greater than his. Because of this, his level of hostile tension increased all the more. "What the hell are you doing? Why are you making those faces?"

"Firestar," Judas said with great hesitation, "the extent of the destruction to which you readily admit to is…."

"Hard to accept," the fourth Elder finished.

"But you told us to use any means necessary to win, and we did that," Darrio said. "You're the ones who said it was okay to do it. You're the ones who lifted the ban on flesh scripts."

"Are you familiar with the conventions of war?" Tiberius asked.

The question struck a blind spot for Darrio, and he felt vulnerable after hearing it. He could not bring himself to lie, but he knew the truth was sure to incriminate him. He answered, "I am."

"Were you then?"

"I was, but—."

"Then were you aware that some of your actions violated a countless number of those conventions?"

"That's not what you said."

"We are well aware of what we said," stated the fifth, "but at no time did we ask for the explicit and far-reaching devastation you provided, implied or otherwise."

The sixth removed his spectacles. "Quite frankly, our role for most of the war was that of the defender, but as a result of your careless actions, our enemies could very easily cite our counter efforts as acts of genocide. With such an overbearing image of evil, what is there to stop them from gathering their forces and waging a second offensive?"

"A second offensive?" Darrio repeated, and a thinly veiled tone of contempt followed his every word. "How? They're weak. You made sure of that."

"No, you made sure of that."

Darrio shook his head with disbelief. "I can't believe this. Why the hell didn't you say something sooner? Why are you telling me this now?"

"Quite frankly, it wasn't a concern until now," Tiberius answered.

"It wasn't a concern," Darrio repeated flatly. "It wasn't a concern when you needed me as a weapon, but now that you're safe, it's a concern. I wasn't a concern when you needed me to fight your damn war, but now that it's over, I'm a concern."

"Be still, Firestar, and watch your tone."

Darrio became silent, but due to the building frustration and rage, he had bitten his tongue to do so.

"Now, because of your past actions, and according to your own admission, the council must consider you, as strictly a temporary measure, a hazardous asset of the Saline nation, and you are forbidden to practice magic of any type until a final decision is reached on what to do with you."

"What?"

"If you should violate this decree at any time from this moment forward, you will be subject to swift and severe punishment up to and including public execution."

Darrio could feel a new wave of anger pass over him, one which carried an even greater danger than they had known, and while he could yet feel the state of his will slipping, he was able to calm himself just enough for the wave to pass over him without incident. The High Elders, however, did not notice the effort despite the subtle shifts of stone behind them. Darrio remained in place in stunned silence, and he gritted his teeth as he continued to speak. "You... bastards decided on this before I even came in here, didn't you? Why the hell even listen to me?"

"Don't presume to understand and know the will of this council, Firestar. What we do, we do for the greater good of all. You will hear of our final act concerning you in due time, but until then, you are dismissed, and this meeting is adjourned."

Darrio had more that he wanted to say and even greater protests to make against the Elder's treatment of him, but he remembered Seris and decided against it. He left the council chambers bitterly.

Seris waited for him outside, and when the two were clear of anyone who could hear, Darrio expressed his frustration. "Those damn hypocrites! What are they concerned with my history for when Tam and Carsis have records ten times longer than mine?"

"Tam isn't a threat," Seris replied, "and neither is Carsis."

"Not to them, maybe, but neither am I. Why does everyone keep treating me like one? I haven't done anything," Darrio sputtered. "Why does everyone keep treating me like this? I haven't done anything."

"Stop it, Darrio. Men, all men regardless of position, fear either what they cannot kill or what they do not understand. The refusal of these men to open their eyes and see what they do not know is foolishness on their part, not yours."

"Then what am I supposed to do this time? What are they going to do to me?"

"They will look for further reasons to charge you, and if they cannot find one, they will attempt to create one."

"And if that doesn't work?"

"Then they will try to kill you."

Darrio fell silent but remained visibly upset.

"Be still, Darrio, and mind your state."

Darrio purposefully breathed to calm himself and shook his head several times in the process.

Seris saw the risen particles around Darrio's feet fall back to the ground and sighed. "For now, you must continue to submit yourself to the council's wishes." Seris then drew out a pair of metal restraints etched with an illuminated and intricate pattern of scripts. The pattern was divided into three rows. "Put these on."

Darrio looked at them and answered, "No."

"Darrio."

"Those are for criminals. I didn't do anything."

"If you don't put them on, they will use it as a reason."

"Do they expect me to wear those and still operate as a shade?" Seris nodded.

"Then to hell with them!"

"Why do you insist on making this hard for me?"

Darrio stared long and hard at the restraints. They were purposefully crafted to suppress the will of anyone forced to wear them. This would effectively disable the wearer's ability to use magic, and once attached, they could only be removed by a set of key phrases known only to the lockmaster who crafted them. Darrio resented the treatment with every fiber of his being, but his regard for Seris was greater. Darrio hesitantly extended his wrists while Seris placed the restraints. Once clasped, Darrio reacted with a pained expression as a portion of his being forcefully collapsed and came under restraint. His breathing became shallow and hard.

Seris pitied him. "Look at me, Darrio."

Darrio winced but looked up.

"Give no thought to what these fools would do to you. Give no thought to what anyone would do to you."

"Why?"

"In doing so, you give them power and control. Do not consider their actions against you. Think only of what you will do."

Darrio saw many things in Seris. There was wisdom, ambition, wrath, compassion, and a certain emotion he felt had long been denied to him. He accepted Seris' words and softly replied, "Yes, sir."

Several days passed since Darrio's questioning, and with his power suppressed, the Elders hoped to trap Darrio by having him assigned to difficult and solitary tasks. Most of them took place in the city where the Elders could keep watch, but a few extended beyond the borders and into neighboring areas and regions. Seris protested and asked that Darrio at least be provided with assistance, but the Elders refused to honor the requests. Seris then provided help to Darrio in secret and relayed his support through other agents in his service. He used only those he could trust, however, and relied heavily on his own loyal group of shades.

Aside from the other shades under Seris' command, there were seven, including Darrio, whose loyalties were to Seris first and others second. The Seven Shades of Seris, as they were called, also included Abaddon, Tam, and Carsis. The other three were away conducting operations in the Outer Realms. Among them was Lon, the cunning strategist of the group, who had been temporarily stationed in the Hollow Realm. He was due to return. The others, Talim and Eloi, were settling trade disputes in the Silent Realm. Darrio considered this to be for the best, however. There was no one among the unit he was close with, and though he often fought alongside them, Darrio did not consider any of them his friends.

As Darrio completed task after task, he eventually discovered he was capable of performing small feats of magic despite the iron's influence over him. Abaddon credited the phenomenon to Darrio's strength of will. Seris, however, advised Darrio against such usage even in the face of great risk lest the Elders discover the infraction and use it against him. Meanwhile, Seris continued to stand against the Council of Elders and protest their unusual use of Darrio's station.

Shades were typically used for stealth and reconnaissance operations, traveled in pairs, and served support roles in open combat.

They were trained to be agile, silent, and efficient in the use of close-range weapons and were often used to sneak behind enemy lines and carry out assassinations. As a result of the heavy emphasis on stealth, they were well versed in magic of the manipulation and illusionary schools but were far less capable in the school of destruction, a domain normally reserved for the long-ranged caster units. They were not as physically rigorous as the close-combat centered adepts either, but their role as spies and stealth units was invaluable to the nation's military. However, the shades who trained under Seris shared several unique and, to some, unnerving characteristics.

First, Seris had a tendency to work with those considered unfit for military duty. This trend began as a voluntary gesture that he hoped to use as a point of argument against those who outranked him. When his efforts bore fruit, however, he was not given the recognition he sought. Instead, the High Generals of the time nursed a grudge against him and made it a habit of theirs to refer undesirables to his unit. Many of these cases were noted for their lack of obedience and destructive temperaments, but rather than curse his superiors and resign as they hoped would be the case, Seris instead took the men and bent them to his will. Most were broken in the process, and their characters were rebuilt until Seris' authority and command were ingrained into their being. Many who served under him gave thanks for his training, but those that did not were disciplined by the ones who revered him.

Despite all of this, the High Elders, and Turil especially, found Seris' program strange and unconventional though no one could argue with his results. He did not limit their training to stealth and illusion though they remained a large part of his regiment. Seris taught on a wide variety of subjects and techniques from all four schools of magic. This was on top of what would have normally been received from other leaders of his kind. There were detailed lessons on the environment for the school of manipulation, illustrative psychoanalysis techniques for illusion, hands-on medicine and instruction on bodily systems for restoration, and discussion on the nature of elements and their use in combat for destruction. His teachings were ongoing, and those under his command never stopped learning from him as he too learned from them. Indeed, his method of instruction was even further removed from the rote method practiced by the majority of the other generals and captains in that he would often participate in his own demonstrations, sometimes at great peril. Some considered him partially insane and as unfit for command as those he trained were unfit for duty, but many things had been said about him, and he ignored them all. His teachings gave flexibility to the Shades, and many thanked him after implementing his techniques on the field of battle.

The High Generals, however, discovered something which had been another point of contention between Seris and his superiors. Some of the men he disciplined showed loyalties that were primarily to Seris and Seris alone. There were several cases in which a soldier transferred from Seris' company only to refuse recognition of his new leadership as a legitimate authority. Seris was heavily criticized, and an investigation was conducted into his methods, but no fault was found. Afterward, Seris explicitly instructed everyone to obey whoever was put over them, but even in this, they did so only as a favor to the captain. Seris and his forces were therefore considered an especially delicate matter. Despite his rank, few dared to give him orders that would directly contradict his personal aims. Even the High Elders expressed, to Seris directly, that they would feel no remorse at his dissolution, but removing him and his influences would have weakened the nation, and this knowledge forced everyone involved into a state of abject tolerance.

Eventually, the Elders became impatient with Darrio's successes, and though they suspected Seris of assisting in this, they could not bring themselves to confront him and plotted against Darrio all the more. Instead, they settled on taking a more direct approach by sending their Firestar on an unusual escort mission.

Under normal circumstances, sending a shade to perform the work of a caster or adept would have been considered most unusual, but since the shade being sent was not only one of Seris' but also the Firestar, very few gave the situation a second thought. However, fewer still outside the Council of High Elders and Generals knew that his magic had been restrained since his irons were well concealed underneath the sleeves of his cloak. This fact did not seem to bother the one Darrio was tasked with protecting nor did anything else.

The man in question was a merchant named Sam, and he was, by all appearances, a happy and good-natured fellow. He was also talkative, a trait Darrio found especially annoying, and the hours he spent with the man seemed to stretch themselves into days. They were on their way to the neighboring town southeast of Ambrosia called Silesia. Sam intended to replenish a portion of his stock there and resell it in Ambrosia, but it was a three-day trek across fields and forest, and Darrio was counting the moments.

On the night of the first day, the two set up camp on the edge of a forest. Darrio could not help but listen to Sam's chatter as they ate. He could barely stand it. "My wife!" Sam said. "That wife of mine. Wonderful woman, really, but sometimes she can just be so…umph! You know what I mean? And man, let me tell you, my children can be the same way. The youngest, his name's Matthew. That boy's got such a spirit in him. You'd swear he were an angel sometimes, you know? You're awfully quiet. I don't think I know many people as quiet as you. And you know what? You're not such a bad guy. I mean, there're lots of bad guys out there with a cleaner reputation than yours, no offense, but you're not so bad, you know? I thought, you know, as a heavy magic user that you'd be as stiff as everyone else, but you're not so bad. Not that I approve of magic, mind you."

"Don't you ever shut up?" Darrio hoped the display of his aggravation would lessen the audible noise clouding his mind.

Sam, however, took little notice of Darrio's discontent. "No, I don't think so. Nobody's asked me to anyway. Say, you don't think people actually get bored with my stories, do you? I mean, I know I can go on for a while, but I think they're pretty exciting, you know? My customers don't complain. Oh! Let me tell you about this one regular of mine. She's a dandy of a woman but kind of slow."

Darrio sighed as Sam prattled on, but the ceaseless stream of words was eventually interrupted by frequent yawns. Sam decided to rest much to Darrio's relief.

"Well, it's been nice talking to you," Sam finished, "but I've got to hit the hay. Going to be a long day once we get to Silesia, and, oh man, you're going to love it when you get there. Nice people, kind of slow, and I don't know that they've heard of you, oddly enough. They don't talk about you there as opposed to everywhere else I go. I should tell you about this one town. Now they just can't stop talking about you."

"Go to sleep!" Darrio ordered, but Sam bowed cheerfully and nodded off only to snore loudly afterward. Darrio groaned and looked towards heaven. "Why do you make people like this?"

Darrio remained awake and kept watch over the surroundings as he continued to remember Seris' warning about the Elders, but as he did, his mind began to wander, and he recalled an old memory. In it, he could hear a mob in the background and the frightened patter of bleeding young feet as a boy fled with his mother from an advancing crowd. He felt the full tension of an uncertain situation in an uncertain time, and the hairs on the back of his neck stood on end. At the end of it all, Darrio sat and watched as the troubled memory replayed itself in his mind's eye, and he relived, in that very moment, the scene of his father's death.

"Damn it," Darrio uttered. Old and troubled memories had resurfaced since his entry into the Aural Realm, but he hoped they would stop after his departure. They caused him enough trouble before, but after several instances of their return, one of which stayed his hand at Celeste, he doubted the memories would ever leave.

A rustling in the bushes returned Darrio to the present, and after he took a moment to reenter a state of total awareness, Darrio prepared himself for defense and approached the area cautiously. It was dark. Even with the moon overhead and the campfire behind him, Darrio's eyes had difficulty adjusting. He then felt an unusually cold gust of wind press against his right cheek. He relaxed and looked upward. "What the hell do you think you're doing, Tam?"

Tam, who was perched overhead on the branch of a tree, looked down and laughed. "How perceptive of you, Firestar. How did you know it was me?"

"You're the only idiot who purposely gives away his position."

"Do I?"

"Front is back, back is front, left is down, down is left, up is right, and right—."

"Is up!" Tam shouted happily. He then dropped and landed on his feet beside Darrio. "If I were here to kill you, it would have been my blood on this bush. But then you are sealed, so perhaps not?" Darrio sighed while Tam looked over at Sam and tilted his head. "Is he today's threat? How boring. Surely worms and not thoughts crawl their minds in order to attach you to such a thing." Tam then gasped with excitement. "Or maybe they mean to destroy you with tedium!" His mood then cooled, and he tilted his head once more. "Would that work on others? I will have to ask Lon when he returns."

Darrio could barely stand Tam's presence, and he became

impatient. The two had shared heated confrontations in the past. "What…the hell…do you want?"

Tam hummed. "I came, though only in passing, to tell you that an enemy trails you."

"An assassin?"

"Maybe. Maybe not. He is surely skilled in illusion and hides his meaning well. I cannot smell his blood. Maybe he has none."

"How strong is he?"

Tam hummed again with thought, and his eyes widened with surprised revelation. "I do not know!"

Tam was a keen hunter and could discern a man's feelings, scent, and affinities with magic better than anyone known, but when he confessed to not knowing the stalker's level of power, Darrio believed the enemy was either weak, close, or otherwise inhuman. With this understanding, Darrio continued. "So…will you be looking out for him?"

Tam shook his head. "Another task requires my attention."

"What is it?"

"Will you note this?"

Darrio nodded and awaited the next statement.

"I will be the one to set your power free and watch the binding shackles fall from your wrist."

Darrio nodded his head in understanding and told Tam to leave. As Tam faded into the night and cover of the trees, Darrio returned to the camp where Sam remained blissfully asleep despite the volume of their conversation. "You really are strange," Darrio said, and his eyes carefully surveyed their eastern side.

The Shades adopted a code of communication using key words to denote the direction of a target or goal when it was suspected that an enemy was near. The statement that initialized this form of communication was the question, "Will you note this?" The direction was then deciphered by taking the last lingering sound of each key word and combining them into a single sound. The words were always placed at the end of a statement or, in Tam's case, just before a conjunction, and because Tam's key words were "free" and "wrist" respectively, Darrio knew to watch his eastern side, but there was still another side to their communication out of which Darrio learned a number of things.

First, due again to Tam's nature as a hunter, Darrio believed the tracker to be a scout and of little concern as a direct threat. Those who specialized in illusionary techniques usually traveled with as few burdens as possible and knew very few, if any, direct combat skills. Because of this, such people were used almost exclusively as spies though Darrio did not see any reason to believe whatever was tailing him was another shade. Tam would have mentioned something of the sort. Second, illusionary magic was primarily used to deceive the senses, but it was largely ineffective against those with strong wills or an understanding of its signs. Tam, being of such a strong, if not demented, temperament was practically immune as were most of Seris' shades. Nothing less than a master would have been able to evade Tam's field of detection, and nothing less than lifeless material would have been able to escape his powers of perception. Whatever was following was either capable of silencing all emotion or simply had no feelings whatsoever. Still, with all of this in mind, Darrio decided he could not afford to underestimate such a creature, and he did not rest but kept watch the entire night.

When morning came, Sam arose and immediately began to speak. "Oh man, what a night! I had the strangest dream, though. Thought I smelled blood too. Was someone here?" Before Darrio could answer, Sam continued. "Anyway, I dreamed of this huge city made entirely out of crates. Crates! And these weren't like medium-sized, ordinary crates but huge, towering crates that people lived and worked in! And there were boats all over the place just floating in the air! Amazing, right? And what's more, I saw you there, and there were these two soldiers standing next to you. Or maybe they were ex-soldiers. I think they were ex-soldiers."

Darrio was not a morning person, and the lack of sleep only exasperated his deteriorated mood. "For the love of God. Are you ready to go or not?"

Sam answered completely unaffected by Darrio's attitude. "I think so. Everything's together, right? Yeah. Man, this will be great. Seriously, though. You're going to love Silesia. There isn't a man alive who wouldn't love Silesia. That's some town. My town actually. I was born there, you know. Mother and father both raised me. Quiet folks. Don't know why they didn't talk more. I should visit them more but busy, busy, busy, you know?"

Darrio sighed, but the two continued their trek into the second day and came upon an outcropping of rocks and a cave. Darrio thought it would be best for them to set their second day of camp inside the mouth of the cave, and when Sam went to sleep, Darrio quietly set a trap at the entrance. He then set out to locate his pursuer.

As Darrio moved, he carefully watched the area for signs of occupancy, but the dark made it a near-impossible task. As he cursed himself, Darrio came upon a tree that was marked up with a message. When Darrio examined the markings more closely, he found the words etched into the bark simply read, "Behind you."

Another gust of wind pressed against Darrio's head. "Damn it, Tam," Darrio said as he spun around, but standing before him was a shadowy figure.

It was little more than a silhouette but resembled a solid man with long hair. All of its features were draped in darkness, and it stood in total silence and stillness.

"Who are you?"

The figure did not respond but advanced slowly with an outstretched arm. As it approached, seemingly blind, Darrio stepped around it, evaded all of its frail attempts to touch him, and examined it. It was a wispy thing, had depth and form, but was more vaporous than solid. Darrio noted that it would take little pressure or injury to make it dissipate, and he considered it harmless, albeit strange. It was clearly the result of magic but not of any kind he had seen before.

There were seven known elements of magic though only five were studied and taught in detail. These were earth, fire, water, wind, and thunder. Wind magic was also referred to as air magic by some while thunder was sometimes called lightning. The term pairs for these respective elements were used interchangeably. What remained, light and dark, were understood as lost elements since no one at the time had an understanding of their components and lacked the ability to control them. Though Darrio understood this, he knew the entity before him was not the result of any element he had encountered before. There was also no one with a high enough understanding of the craft to produce separate, enduring, and standalone entities. This meant the shadowy form was created with knowledge even higher than Salia's finest artisans in addition to being a display of one of the lost elements, namely dark magic.

Just as Darrio came upon this realization, the shadow opened its eyes like a veil, and out of them came a piercing yellow light. It turned and looked directly at Darrio, which caught him by surprise, and it latched its hand onto Darrio's left wrist.

At once, Darrio felt himself strained with a familiar feeling. The shadow's touch had the same effect as the irons he wore though it was greatly amplified, but the longer it held on, the closer Darrio felt to death. Darrio reached underneath his cloak to draw the first of two crescent-edged blades and severed the figure's hand. This caused the entire shadow to dissolve. Darrio then gasped for air and relief as he fought to clear his head and stay conscious, but after he regained his bearing, he saw a great number of like-featured silhouettes rise out of the ground around him. Their yellow eyes pierced through the darkness. Darrio was surrounded, and he cursed as he drew his second weapon. He was well trained in the use of them but preferred evasion and magic. With the enemy's numbers and the first shadow's grasp eliminating the use of what little magic he could access, Darrio found he had no choice but to rely on his blades.

Darrio searched for an opening and identified a thin spot in the formation while the silhouettes slowly advanced. A shadow then reached out to him from behind. Darrio turned with a piercing attack aimed at the wrist, and the figure dissolved. He wasted no time in his attacks. Though Darrio knew any significant force would cause the shadows to fall away, he attacked vitals and critical sections out of routine. He moved forward with slashes and thrusts, targeted throats, hearts, wrists, and every other point that would have either killed or severely injured enemies of flesh and blood. The thought entered Darrio's mind of how Tam would have enjoyed such a situation, particularly the hypothetical mess he would have made, but Darrio forced the image out of his mind. He hated Tam.

The shadows were everywhere and endless in coming. For every one that Darrio collapsed, another rose ahead of him, and this made Darrio cry out in frustration. He pressed ahead, cursed repeatedly in rising tones, and pushed himself faster and harder through the endless hands that reached for his open face. When Darrio came to a wall made up of the creatures, he crossed his blades and leaped through the obstruction, cutting away as he did so, and he emerged on the other side with trails of dark vapor tracing his path. The dark cluster of shadows disintegrated behind him, and when Darrio turned, all became quiet and still. Before he could give further thought to the situation, Darrio remembered Sam and quickly returned to the camp.

The trap had been sprung, but there was no victim nearby. Darrio then reentered the cave and found a man similar in shape and features to the shadows but quite solid. He was standing over Sam, who was still asleep, with a serrated blade directed at the merchant's neck. He was poised to strike. Without hesitation, Darrio targeted the assassin and launched his right blade at the man who, after hearing the disturbance, turned just as the weapon entered his flesh. He fell quickly and quietly much to Darrio's surprise. The enemy showed no pain, no surprise, nor any other emotion. His eyes, face, movements, and mannerisms were mere voids of expression. Sam, despite all of this, continued to sleep peacefully.

Darrio approached the body. The assassin's hair was long and dark, his face was fair and defined, and his complexion was clear and smooth. There was not a blemish to be found on him, and yet he was clearly no native of the Saline Realm. His clothes bore none of the traditional patterns and designs worn by the Saline people, and while they were etched with scripts, they were far more intricate than anything Darrio had seen. They even appeared to be organic, living, much like the scripts of a generally forbidden form.

The overall theme was of water, and there were many droplet shapes inherent on the clothing. Darrio removed his dagger from the body, cleansed it, and pulled the corpse deeper into the bowel of the cave. There he searched it, but aside from the assassin's dagger, he found nothing else of practical use. Darrio then cut off a portion of the assassin's pattern and stored it away under his cloak. He was unlikely to encounter more enemies like this, and he figured, at least temporarily, that it would be safe enough to sleep, but he kept an audible distance from Sam whose snoring masked every other sound of the night.

The following morning, Sam arose feeling well-rested and energetic. "Man, I had a great night! No dreams, no nightmares, nothing to interrupt or ruin things. It was, quite possibly, the greatest night of my life. Perfect sleep! How about you?"

Darrio lifted his head but answered with a silent glare.

"Not great, huh? That's okay. Today's the day we enter Silesia. I'm so excited, oh man! Great people. Great food. The place is just great. You're going to love it, I'm sure."

"What are you selling anyway?"

"You know. Knickknacks, books, materials. Everyday stuff. Interested? I've got so many good things in store. Even got some of them for sale."

"Then why did you request an escort?"

"For...robbers?"

Darrio stared, crossed his arms, and tilted his head.

"You're not buying it are you?"

"No, I'm not."

"Well," Sam chuckled, "I don't know if I should tell you."

"Is it illegal?"

"Oh, no! Heaven's no. It's nothing like that. It's just... how do I put this? There are...certain people who don't like me very much."

"I can imagine."

"Huh?"

"Nothing," Darrio said as he shook his head. "So what happened? Did you rip someone off?"

Sam laughed. "No, nothing like that, and if you don't already know, you probably don't need to. I tell my wife that all the time. Lovely woman but very nosy. You should meet her. And my kids! Have I told you about Matthew yet?"

"Alright, alright. I get it," Darrio said. "Just don't talk so much. If you do that, I'll ask fewer questions. Alright?"

"Sure, but man, I've still got so much to tell you about the town."

Darrio groaned and continued with Sam for the rest of the journey, but he hardly listened to anything Sam had to say. His mind was preoccupied with the mysterious assassin, the pattern, and the powers of dark magic. The only situation in Darrio's mind that made sense was that the assassin had been sent by the High Elders, but there were many questions that arose from the theory in addition to ones raised by the events themselves. Who was the man? Why was he capable of using one of the forgotten elements? Where did he come from? If he were truly a foreigner, why assist the Elders? Where did he gain his knowledge of magic? Were there others with even greater understandings of magic than the artisans of the Saline Realm? How? Question upon question rose in Darrio's mind, but since they only served to disorient him, he put them to rest until more time could be devoted to them.

Sam and Darrio entered Silesia in the middle of the third day, and Darrio initially viewed it as a homely and modest town with homely and modest people. The houses were made of wood capped with thatch roofs, and they were largely unremarkable while the streets were simple paths of well-traveled dirt. The people were dressed in plain clothes of solid fabrics and colors and bore no elaborate patterns or designs. If Darrio had not known he was still in the Saline Realm, he might have mistaken it for a village of the Aural Realm. There were only two wells to draw water from, and they were used for bathing, cooking, and gardening. Sounds of bleating and children's laughter hung in the air, but it was still a quiet place.

As Sam and Darrio walked down the street, Darrio looked around and noted the expressions of the people as they passed by. Unlike the majority of those he encountered in Ambrosia, the eyes he met in Silesia were, more often than not, warm and pleasant. He was not met with fear or feigned indifference though no one had announced who he was. Most of the people there were content to go about their own business without being bothered by the everyday happenings of a national celebrity even when the celebrity in question was one as infamous as the Firestar.

Darrio watched a boy run down the street. He was chasing a girl with a stick. Both had wide grins on their faces and squealed with laughter. Darrio tried to recall the last time he felt as happy and free as the two children but was met with frustration and discouragement. With all that occurred in the years of his existence, he found little to be happy about. Even in what peace and security he had, he took little comfort.

Sam breathed deep and exhaled loudly. "Smell that air. You get that? It's untouched. Unmolested. Just full of the God-given good stuff. I told you Silesia was great, didn't I?"

"It's okay," Darrio replied. His tone was subdued. "No one uses magic here, huh?"

"Nope."

"Why?"

"I guess it's because we manage well enough without it. There's only been about two or three users here, but it doesn't last long. They usually get bored and leave. Most of us just like doing things the old-fashioned way, you know? Nothing beats food by the fire of your own making, they say. Ever had food cooked by magic? Tastes odd. Nope, these are simple people who like simple things in simple ways. Can't stand a whole lot of complication. Just simple fun, simple work, and simple food. Oh, speaking of food, you've got to try this dish by Aunt May. I tell you, you haven't lived till you've had Aunt May's cooking."

"Who?"

"Aunt May. She cooks the best meals, let me tell you. Even has Matthew in on the deal. I think he wants to be a cook. Can you believe it? That boy of mine loves to cook. And my other son, Jeremy, he's quite the hunter. I think their skills go hand in hand come to think of it. Jeremy hunts, and Mathew cooks. It's crazy, isn't it? And that's not the best part. I love to eat! Isn't that great?" Sam laughed, but Darrio gave him a strange look. "Say. Maybe you should stay for a while."

"I don't think so."

"Why not? You can go, meet the locals, introduce yourself. I mean, we haven't traveled that long together, but you sure don't strike me as the Firestar I've heard stories about."

"Then you don't know me."

Sam retorted. "You know what my father always told me? He told me, 'Son! Titles and names don't make the man; the man makes his own name and title!' He wasn't the most reputable man, though, so… anyway. People call you the Firestar and have this notion of you. So what? Doesn't mean you have to act it. You ask me, I think you should just go out there and show the people who you really are. I think they'd like you. Heck, you might even make a few friends."

"Friends?" Darrio found the concept partially funny though in a condescending and cynical way. "You have no idea what some people would like to do to me."

"What? Here? Or maybe you mean the Outer Realms."

"Anywhere."

"Look, man. The war's over. So it wasn't in your best interest to make a good first impression. Doesn't mean things can't change now. You never know. You could actually go out and do a lot of good in the world. I don't know about this whole magic thing, but uh…yeah."

"How are you so damn naive?"

"Huh? I don't think I'm naive, but who knows. I sure as heck haven't lost my peace of mind. Come on, man, seriously! You should consider what I'm telling you. It's going to take some time to finish my business anyway, so as long as we're here, you might as well stretch your legs and meet the local folk."

Darrio groaned. He hated socializing, even more so with people he didn't know.

"What's it really going to hurt?"

"Fine," Darrio answered, "but don't take too long."

"Fair deal. We'll head back, say, midday tomorrow?"

"Alright."

"Good, and cheer up! You're in Silesia, remember? Relax! I'll have a quick word with the wife and kids and then get started on that business of mine. See you tomorrow."

Darrio found Sam annoying and greatly so, but for a moment, he wished Sam would stay with him even if only to keep him company, but Sam departed, and Darrio said nothing. Instead, he immediately conjured up several excuses, both real and imagined, as to why he would and could not meet anyone, but just as he settled on the whimsical, "I didn't want to," he shook his head. No matter what excuse he decided on, Darrio felt he needed to at least move from his spot and attempt conversation, even if indirectly, with at least one person before opting out. He did not have to go far.

Darrio took a few steps towards Aunt May's Eatery, but a young boy, the same one Darrio had seen brandishing the stick earlier, sped around the corner and ran blindly into Darrio. Darrio remained still while the boy bounced off.

The child quickly apologized. "I'm sorry!"

"It's alright."

"Are you okay? I haven't seen you around here before."

"I'm not from here."

The boy's eyes widened with excitement. "Oh! Are you here on some kind of business?"

"Huh?"

"You're a salesman, aren't you? Your clothes...."

Darrio looked over his attire but could not see the resemblance and did not have the heart to explain it. He simply answered, "No. I'm not a salesman."

The boy returned to his feet. "So where are you from, mister?"

"Ambrosia."

"Is it far?"

"You've never heard of it?"

"No."

The boy was clearly innocent and unspoiled by the world. So far as Darrio could tell, the town was the only thing the boy knew. "What's your name, kid?"

"Tim."

"Do you know a place where I can sleep?"

"No, but my mom does. I'll go ask her." The boy sped off but slid to a stop and turned around. "What's your name?"

"Darrio."

Tim gasped in response. "What?" Darrio had given his name without thought and immediately regretted it, but Tim reacted with excitement. "That's a great name! I wish I had a name like that."

Darrio relaxed.

"So do you have a last name? What is it? I bet it's even better than the first one. Tell me."

Darrio felt he risked enough by giving the boy his first name but realized the point was altogether moot. No one, aside from Seris, referred to him outside of his title. This was even true of those in his company though he had been called something else before Firestar. Nevertheless, he knew better than to give his last name. "Don't worry about it."

"Aw, okay," and Tim sped off.

Darrio waited a while and had the distinct feeling he was being watched. A healthy dose of paranoia had saved his life on more than one occasion during the Magic War, and he did not trust the High

Elders. It was because of their decisions that he participated in the war in the first place, and Darrio did not believe their aims were to his benefit. Even so, Darrio questioned whether or not he was being irrational. His encounter with the mysterious user of dark magic would have normally been justification enough, but Silesia was a peaceful place, and it did not seem likely that anything terrible would happen there. The air was soothing, the sky accommodating, and all of creation appeared to be at peace. Darrio then remembered all of the villages and cities he encountered in the Outer Realms and mumbled to himself, "Yeah. I bet they felt the same way too."

Tim returned. "There's a place around the corner. I'll show you." Darrio followed the boy to a meager inn of simple accommodations. "It's probably not as fancy as what you're used to, but it's a place, right? I thought you'd like it."

Darrio had slept in far worse conditions. "This is fine. Thanks."

"Take care, Sir Darrio."

Darrio checked in and immediately went to his room. There was a pub on the ground floor, but Darrio could never bring himself to drink. Instead, he sat on the rented bed, put out the lights, and peered out of the window. The sun was setting, and the people were heading inside for the day. It was a simple life in Silesia, and so far as Darrio could see, it was a happy one as well. Everyone got along despite the occasional oddities, and they went about their day with fewer cares than those in the big cities. In Darrio's mind, the atmosphere of the place was a cross between Celeste and a village far east of Ambrosia called Aria. "Damn village," Darrio mumbled, and he pushed the image of Aria out of his mind.

Darrio then remembered a particular period in his early childhood when safety had been the least of his concerns. It was a time long before the unification of the Outer Realms and before the start of the Magic War. He had a wide-eyed curiosity about the inner workings of everything, and his father, a man named Dimitri, encouraged him in it.

Dimitri was a wood cutter, a carpenter, and a clockmaker, and Darrio remembered spending many afternoons watching his father work. His young, big eyes were often leveled with the workbench while his black hair was left to sway unkempt in the wind. Darrio frequently asked questions, the most common being, "What's that?"

"That," Dimitri answered with a smile, "is a cog."

"What's a gog?"

Dimitri laughed and explained how all parts of the clock worked together in tandem to keep the exact time. Darrio did not understand any of it, but he would sit amazed at the amount of knowledge his father possessed. Darrio knew his father's posturing and intellectual indulgences were for Darrio's sake and growth, but he could not help but be frustrated at times by his own inability to comprehend what his father was saying. He had even cried at times, and his father comforted him. "Don't worry, Darrio. You'll understand when you get older."

"How come I can't understand now?"

Dimitri then smiled with gentle accommodation and answered, "Every good thing comes in its own time, son. Truth, wisdom, understanding, everything. You'll just have to wait and be patient."

"Why did you have to die like that?" Darrio mumbled in the darkness of his room. "I don't understand it."

Darrio remembered running with his mother from a crowd of determined accusers and self-appointed executioners. His father was hurrying the two along, but for every moment he checked the rear, and with increasing frequency, the closer the mob came. Reasoning with them already failed in the moments prior to the event, and Dimitri had long given up the practices of his previous life. There would be no hope for Darrio and his mother had events continued in such a manner. Just as the family was crossing over another impasse, Dimitri turned to face his pursuers.

Darrio's mother looked back, and when she saw that her husband had stopped, she asked "What are you doing, Dimitri?"

"Keep going."

"We're not leaving without you."

The crowd approached and brandished torches, rope, and other implements of harm. Dimitri mouthed a second and silent plea to run before turning his attention to the mob. "Please, stop this."

"Get out of the way, Dimitri," ordered a man from the crowd, "and stop aiding her. She has to pay for what she's done."

"This is insane. Why are you treating us like this?"

"Nobody's blaming you," said a woman. "She's the one who chose the path of the devil's magic. She might have even tainted the boy. She's deceived you, Dimitri!"

"Emilia isn't a witch. I've known her for almost my entire life. She would never get involved with such things. Neither of us would!"

A man brandishing a pitchfork stepped forward. "Enough, Dimitri! Step aside, or we'll be forced to deal with you too!"

Dimitri turned to his wife and son. Sorrow filled his eyes, his face convulsed with grief, and his body started to buckle. Emilia, equally burdened by sadness and conflict of heart, tugged on Darrio and slowly inched away.

"Dimitri!" the man called again. "Move!"

"Run. Emelia, run. Darrio, run! Run! Run!" Dimitri's final command stretched itself in time as did the moment of the mob's intolerance, and the man behind Dimitri plunged a pitchfork through the back of Darrio's father.

Darrio's eyes widened, his emotions sank, and his heart bled in sorrowful agony. His mouth exhaled an angry shout while his mother pulled him away to greater safety. The moment was forever seared into Darrio's consciousness, and his cry hung long on the horizon. It was a simultaneous howl of abject mourning over his father's death and an utter condemnation for the people who killed him.

Darrio sat alone in the dark room of the inn and pointed his gaze southeast. The sun had set. "I should've killed you all when I had the chance," and as Darrio remembered, he fell back into bed. Tears rolled down his face. "You bastards," he sobbed, and Darrio turned over to bury his face in the pillow. His heart and mind still bled with that painful memory despite all efforts to keep it contained and despite all of the years that passed since. Darrio shivered, his muscles tensed, and he felt as if his life were draining away, but for all the pain and resentment he felt, the resultant was anger, hatred, and frustration. His head remained on that pillow for the rest of the night. "I should've killed you all," he finally said, and it rained heavily as he slept.

CHAPTER 2
Happenstance

HAD IT NOT been for the previous night's unusual precipitation, the people of Silesia would have risen to another dry and earthy extension of the season. Nevertheless, the morning was peaceful as it had always been for the town, and the citizens slowly stretched and emerged from their homes to greet the new day. There was talk in the streets as men greeted women with an overall sense of satisfaction and contentment.

Darrio awoke early with many hours to spend before he and Sam were scheduled to leave. Sleep had done much to bury the sensations he felt from the previous night, but he was still in no mood for happy expressions and spirited chats. Instead, he momentarily left the town and crossed the eastern field into a region of trees to practice his craft.

To Darrio's relief, the draining effects of dark magic were temporary, so he continued to test the limitations of his power. While he was busy raising a clump of dead leaves on the wind, a figure silently approached from behind. Darrio released the leaves. "Unless you're here to get yourself killed, don't sneak up on me like that." Darrio turned to find another shade standing before him. He did not recognize the man. "Who the hell are you?"

"Arthis," the shade replied.

"And what are you doing here?"

"How's the client?"

"The merchant? He's fine."

"Good."

Arthis shifted uncomfortably, and Darrio found it difficult to discern whether or not he was a threat. His eyes appeared innocent, but the nervous movement denoted either hesitation concerning an action or lack of confidence. Both could have been faked. "Did the Elders send you?"

Arthis nodded. "I'm doing a progress report."

"How long have you been following me?"

"I just started today."

Darrio did not believe him. "You sure you weren't waiting here for me?"

"Waiting?" Arthis repeated with confusion. "Waiting for what?"

"If you're doing a progress report, why aren't you still watching me? Why are you talking to me?"

"Well…what you were doing. It's supposed to be illegal for you, isn't it?"

Darrio cursed himself for setting up such an obvious excuse.

"You realize I'm under obligation to report this, right?"

Darrio sighed and slumped down on a nearby log while his mind mulled over the signs of paranoia again. "Yeah. Whatever."

"How was the trip?"

"So-so."

"Any stories?"

"Nothing you'd believe."

"Try me."

Darrio was in no mood for social interaction, but he continued on hoping the ordeal would end sooner. "I was attacked."

"By who?"

"I don't know. Some assassin with skill in dark magic."

"Dark magic?"

Darrio explained what happened to him and included details concerning the assassin's dagger and pattern.

Arthis was both amazed and disturbed. "You still have the restraints on, don't you?"

Darrio lifted his wrists together so Arthis could see the irons. "Damn things aren't helping me at all."

"How did you manage to get out of that situation and defeat that darkness user with your will suppressed and bound like that?"

"I already told you. I surprised him. Were you even listening?"

"That doesn't sound possible," and Arthis shifted back.

This made Darrio anxious. "Stop that."

"Stop what?"

"Stop moving like you're scared of me."

"Why shouldn't I?" and he continued the sentiment with a diminished tone. "Maybe the Elders were right about you."

Darrio stood to his feet. "What the hell are you here for? I know it's not for some damn progress report."

Arthis stood still, and the innocence in his eyes faded. In its place was a cold, determined stare.

Darrio glared. "You're here to kill me, aren't you?"

"I had to be sure."

"Sure of what?"

"That you really are the threat they made you out to be."

"Moron," Darrio said as he drew his weapons.

Arthis drew a single short sword from underneath his cloak and held it with one hand. With the other, he produced a ball of fire and suspended it over his palm. "It looks like you're only able to perform small feats of manipulation magic."

"So?"

"So you're not going to win this fight, Firestar, even if you were trained by Seris." Arthis launched the first attack by shooting forth his ball of fire, but Darrio ducked the motion, and the attack struck the tree behind him and engulfed it in intense flames. It crumbled soon after. When Darrio looked up again, Arthis had advanced on him and was poised for a horizontal swipe. Darrio deflected the attack with his right weapon and thrust forward with the other, but Arthis lifted his free hand and sustained Darrio's attack with a repelling force of thunder magic. Darrio cursed him, and Arthis grunted. "You're taking this personally, aren't you?"

"Yeah."

"Why?"

"Because you spoke to me."

The two separated and took a moment to assess each other's abilities and weaknesses. Arthis was proficient with destruction magic, particularly so in the fire element, and as he prepared for the next assault, he used it to heat his weapon. In the meantime, Darrio felt a forward attack was not to his advantage and decided to go on the defensive and wait for an opening. He was not altogether successful, and despite his best attempts to evade and parry the heated sting of Arthis' blade, he was unable to come through the battle unscathed. Arthis showed no restraint in his use of magic despite Darrio's handicap and performed whatever he could to keep Darrio occupied and under pressure. When Darrio separated, Arthis unleashed a volley of fire darts. When Darrio was close, Arthis shifted the ground beneath Darrio's feet and attempted to end things with a quick strike to the vitals. Darrio, however, was quick and versatile in his recoveries, and he actively learned from the battle.

There was a method to how Arthis conducted his movements. He was primarily an opportunist who sought leverage on the field and foe, a passive stance in Darrio's opinion. If he did not see anything to gain in a motion or element, he did not use it. Darrio reasoned several ways he could have died had Arthis practiced other elements in addition to fire, but he was not about to make suggestions. Arthis would not give Darrio a single opening or moment of respite unless he felt the advantage was his. In this, Darrio made his plan.

It was late in the fight, and the ground shifted uncontrollably beneath Darrio, but instead of moving to new ground, he feigned injury, fell to his back, and let his crescent daggers slip from his hand. Arthis stopped his attack to evaluate Darrio's condition, but since he appeared defenseless, Arthis approached slowly. "You know, for all intents and purposes, this was an even match."

"Even?" Darrio scoffed still playing his role as the defeated. "You call this even?"

"Come on, Firestar. Had you been capable of more, I wouldn't have stood a chance." Arthis stood over Darrio and pointed his blade to strike. "I guess today's my lucky day."

"You cocky bastard." Arthis advanced to finish Darrio with a strike to the neck, but as he descended, Darrio conjured up an explosion of dry dirt from the ground which produced a cloud of dust and debris. Arthis was blinded. Darrio then kicked out his opponent's feet, caught the falling weapon, and struck the shade on his left wrist while forcing him to the ground. There, with Arthis outstretched, Darrio pounced on top of him and stood.

When the dust finally settled, Arthis opened his eyes to find Darrio towering over him with one foot clamped down over the bleeding wrist. With utter surprise, Arthis shouted, "How the hell did you—?"

Darrio held the blade in reverse and directed the point of it towards Arthis. There was a cold stare in his eyes. "You said the High Elders sent you, right?"

Arthis, still dumbfounded by the result of the battle, did not answer, and Darrio slowly ground his right foot into the still-open wrist wound. Arthis cried out, "Right! Right!"

"Is there anyone else with you?"

"No."

"Are you lying to me?"

"No, I swear!"

"Good."

"You're…you're not going to kill me, are you?"

Darrio did not answer.

"I was only doing my duty. It was nothing personal. Are you really going to kill me for that?"

"No. Not for that."

"Then what?"

Darrio looked upon Arthis, and his eyes waxed cold. "Because you spoke to me."

Arthis gasped, and his eyes widened. "Wait. Don't—!"

Darrio knelt down and swiftly plunged the blade into Arthis' chest. Arthis sputtered blood, and his body trembled, all of which were preludes to his certain and painful death. Darrio remained stationary through all of this and watched until everything became still again. He then rose, left the blade behind, and looked towards the town. The children had emerged to play at the entrance. Their innocence in the sunlight aroused feelings of envy within Darrio, and he felt hung once more between despondency and hope. Darrio felt no regret in the actions he took against Arthis though. He defended himself against an enemy. If there was anyone to blame, it was the High Elders.

Darrio retrieved his weapons and used what power he had with manipulation magic to bury the corpse before returning to the inn. He intended to pass the time in solitude until midday approached so he and Sam could return to Ambrosia, but as he waited, Darrio recalled the first of his memories with Seris. It was the day they met.

Darrio had left his early childhood behind, but he was without his mother, and he roamed the streets of Ambrosia hungry and alone. He then came upon a silver-haired captain, Seris, who just came off duty and was prepared to go home and study. Clutched to his side was a loaf of bread. When Darrio saw this, he decided to steal the bread and run, but when he reached out his hand, Seris spun around and took hold of Darrio's wrist. Darrio struggled to pull away and shouted in both anger and fear. "Let me go!"

"You were going to steal from me."

"I was hungry!"

"And this is how you get your food?"

Darrio had a small dagger concealed underneath his shirt. Without thinking, he drew the blade from its hiding place and swung at the captain in an effort to get free. Seris remained still despite Darrio's motions even while the knife bit into his arm. Seris looked at the wound, looked back at Darrio, and released him.

Darrio fell to the ground stricken by what he had done, and he could only stare at Seris with wide-eyed shock.

Seris, however, straightened up and took little notice of the damage or the blood running down his arm. With his eyes transfixed on Darrio, Seris waved his other hand towards the wound, and the knife was ejected from his arm. It then clattered against the stones while Seris' wound closed and healed. Seris then said, "You're fairly angry for one so young."

"I...I just wanted something to eat."

"If you had asked, I would have given you the bread, but since you did not ask," Seris said as he slowly approached, "and instead chose to attack me."

Darrio crawled backward to maintain his distance but stopped when he saw Seris' eyes. They were quiet, peaceful, and there was no malice in them.

Seris extended the hand of his once-wounded arm. "Come, and you will eat under my roof instead."

Darrio left his room in the present and entered the town square to look for Sam. There he found the merchant in the process of selling shoes to an elderly couple. Darrio approached and grabbed Sam by the arm. "Come on."

"Hey, ouch! That hurts. What's the hurry, man? The day's still young, and I haven't even—."

"This isn't a suggestion you idiot. We've got to go now."

Darrio's statement wounded Sam much to Darrio's surprise, and Sam meekly replied, "Yeah. Sure. Okay."

The trek back to Ambrosia was largely silent between them and entirely without incident, but there was a minor quake on the second day. Darrio thought nothing of it. On the third day, as Sam and Darrio spotted Ambrosia on the horizon, two casters and three adepts approached their position and impeded their return. The commanding adept addressed Darrio. "Firestar? You've been ordered to come with us."

"What for?"

"To stand trial before the High Elders." The casters and other two adepts took escort positions beside Sam. "We'll take the merchant."

Darrio shook his head. "But I have a report to make."

"Doesn't matter. You're coming with us. Now."

Darrio saw no alternatives, not without being harassed as a fugitive for the rest of his life, so he complied with the order.

Ambrosia was in a state of partial ruin. Many of the high buildings displayed impact damage and scorch marks while the smaller establishments were full of burn holes and broken glass. The main road was littered with rubble and had been turned upward in places. The Grand Hall exhibited the most extensive damage, and Darrio surmised that it was the target, but when he asked what had occurred, he was met with irritated silence. No one wanted to speak with him.

Seris was near the front entrance of the Grand Hall when Darrio arrived, but he was despondent, his eyes locked deep in thought.

When Darrio saw him, he asked, "What happened?"

Seris said nothing.

Darrio was then brought before the Council of High Elders and Generals who were agitated and even anxious at Darrio's presence.

Turil was absent. Darrio asked, "What the hell is going on around here? Why did you bring me here? What are you trying me for?"

"Do you believe you can make fools of this council, Firestar?" Tiberius asked.

"What are you talking about?"

"Why did you attack us?"

"Attack?" Darrio was incensed and brandished the shackles on his wrists. "How the hell can I attack with these on you idiots?"

"You still retain some ability with magic even with those shackles on, do you not?"

Darrio quieted. "Who told you that?"

"Answer the question."

Arthis was dead, and if he had been telling the truth, he would not have been able to send word of Darrio's infraction. There was also no one else who knew of Darrio's retained abilities except Seris, Tam, Abaddon, and Carsis. It did not seem possible, at least at first, that any of them would betray another member of the unit. Carsis, however, was extremely jealous of Darrio and actively craved the attention Seris gave to him. Tiberius loudly cleared his throat, and Darrio answered, "A little."

"And you did not report this?"

"You were sending me on all of these solitary missions. If I had said something, all you would've done is made me weaker. That would've killed me."

"Are you implying something of us?"

"I'm not implying anything," he said bitterly.

"Then watch your insinuations," Elder Judas warned.

Darrio sighed. "Just…tell me what happened. Why am I on trial? What are you accusing me of? What did I do?"

The Elders exchanged glances and spoke. "We were attacked, quite frankly, and under a hailstorm of fire, ice, and an earthquake."

"The prison doors were shaken apart," the third continued. "There were reports of criminals falling out with madness babbling on and on about time, catastrophe, and Salia's doom."

"And it appeared to us a great feat of magic possible only with your level of manipulative and destructive mastery."

"But I'm not an illusionist," Darrio declared.

"So we've heard, but we also heard that your powers were completely suppressed. I see no reason to believe there is not more you haven't told us."

"Shortly thereafter we received word of your return and sent for you," finished the fourth.

"But I'm still not capable of all that," Darrio said. "Not with these shackles on."

"Then until we find out who the culprit is, those shackles will remain," Tiberius replied.

"Figures."

"So what do you have to say about this?"

"Me? I think you're all a bunch of stupid, cowardly hypocrites."

"About the attack, Firestar!"

Darrio's statement struck a nerve, and while he noted it, Darrio decided against pressing further. "I say I was just doing my job, got attacked, and made it to my destination. Then I got attacked again, returned home, and was brought here to stand trial in front of a group of cowering ingrates for something I didn't even do."

"You were attacked twice?" Judas questioned.

"Don't play dumb. The second guy said you were the ones who sent him, and I don't know where you managed to find a user of dark magic, but I know our encounter wasn't a damn accident or a coincidence."

The sixth Elder sputtered. "Dark magic? What dark magic? Where is this coming from?"

"He's obviously lying," the third Elder stated. "Dark is a lost element along with light. There is no one, and I mean no one, who knows how to control them."

Darrio spoke through gritted teeth. "I know...what I saw," and he pulled the assassin's dagger from underneath his cloak and threw it in front of the council's desk. The pattern remained attached to the hilt.

The fourth Elder forced a gust upon the weapon which caused the items to rise up and land in front of him. As he examined the blade, the cloth, and their markings, his eyes widened. The scripts writhed in the open light. "This is impossible. Look at this!" The items were passed along the table, and each Elder looked at the scripts in awe. "Where did you get these things, Firestar?"

"From the first assassin, I just told you. You mean to tell me you didn't send him?"

"These scripts...this is an understanding of magic far beyond what we know. Our finest artisans don't even come close to...and this is an assassin's blade?"

Darrio was frustrated and sighed. "Yes. An assassin. Dark magic. Tried to kill me."

"How did you subdue him?"

Darrio relayed his encounter with the assassin and the accompanying effects of dark magic, but as he finished, the remaining life in the Elders' faces drained away.

"How did you subdue him without magic?"

Darrio groaned. "You're not even listening to me!"

The Elders whispered among themselves in frightened tones while Darrio waited. During the process, he wondered just how they managed to reach such high positions but figured it was not so much according to ability but connection.

When they finished their talks, the fifth Elder spoke. "We've decided to defer all suspicion of you, temporarily, in light of this new…development."

"Fine."

"But will you swear to this council that you were not the cause of these attacks? That everything you have just told us is true?"

Darrio shook his head. "Everything I just told you is true, but no. I'm not going to swear."

The fifth glanced over at Tiberius who nodded. "Very well. You're free to go. We'll summon you again when you are needed," and Darrio was released.

Seris continued to wait for Darrio outside of the Grand Hall's entrance. He was still troubled and deep in thought.

Abaddon was beside him and asked, "Is there a reason for your continued silence?"

"Silence?"

"You appear concerned. Is it the Firestar?"

"Darrio does not concern me at the moment."

"Then what is it?"

"It is nothing."

Darrio emerged alone, but the events and questions raised by the day still weighed heavily on his mind. "It doesn't make sense."

Seris heard Darrio's voice and turned. "What happened? Have they released you?"

Darrio nodded. "But they're confused. I'm confused. Does anyone know what's going on?"

"No."

Abaddon noticed the tears in Darrio's clothes and asked, "Did you finish your objective?"

"Huh?" Darrio looked down. "Oh. Yeah. The merchant's safe. Talkative little bastard."

"But you were attacked."

"Twice. I surprised the first one, but the second one took some work. Would've killed him sooner had I been thinking," and Darrio sighed. "Now the Elders are going to keep an even closer watch on me. Any idea who told them about my retention with magic?"

"No," Seris answered, "but his timing was unfortunate." He then asked Darrio and Abaddon to follow him. "So you were targeted. Did you identify the attackers?"

"Sort of. The first wasn't really after me and wasn't even from around here, but the second guy was a shade."

"What was his name?"

"Arthis."

Seris nodded. "Did you discover anything else?"

"Not really, but...do you know anything about dark magic?"

"It is lost art," Abaddon answered.

"The first assassin was using it."

Seris and Abaddon slowed, and Abaddon asked, "You encountered a user of dark magic?"

"Yeah. Turns out he was after the merchant, don't know why, but the Elders didn't send him. If it's such a lost art, how do you think he got it?"

"There is no way to know," Seris replied. "Since he is dead, the secrets he carried have died with him."

"Well, I still can't believe the Elders tried to assassinate me like that. Line of duty is one thing, but this...."

"I told you they would."

"And then they had the nerve to put me on trial."

"The trial is not yet over. They may not attempt more direct actions against you, but they may use you to discover who attacked the city."

"So what should I do?"

"Follow their orders," Seris replied, "and trust me."

Darrio was placed on light duty over the following week while the High Elders and High Generals continued their investigations. During this time, Darrio secretly honed his restricted abilities under Seris' supervision in the Hall of Order.

During one such practice, Carsis approached to watch Darrio just as Seris left to speak with Abaddon over an organization matter. Once they were gone, Carsis glared for a while and said, "I still don't get it. What makes you so special?"

"Try asking someone who cares," Darrio answered.

"He goes through all that trouble, takes all that criticism, and you just sit there like there's nothing going on. Why? What did you do to him? What the hell have you got that I don't?"

"A brain?" Darrio offered as he launched another fire dart. "And I already told you, I don't care."

"Don't think you're better than me because you're not. If I even had half the power you had, I would've wiped that city and a dozen others like it. It's not fair that he should suffer just because you decided to act stupid."

Darrio stopped and turned a glaring eye to Carsis. "Do you have something you want to say to me?"

Carsis straightened up and answered, "Yeah. I do."

"Then say it."

"I don't like the way he looks at you or the way he talks to you or the way he's always trying to protect you. There're a million other people in this world who could use his attention, but you're the only one he wants to treat like a s—...."

"No. Say it."

"No," Carsis replied as he shook his head. "No, I'm not going to say it because you don't deserve it, any of it. And you sure as hell don't deserve him."

Darrio formed a small flare in his right hand, shot it toward Carsis, and caused it to explode in a blinding flash. Carsis was dazed by the attack, and in the meantime, Darrio drew a blade and pressed Carsis against the wall with his left arm. Darrio's face was flush with anger, and his eyes, for but a second, flickered between their natural color and red. "If you've got anything else to say, say it now."

Carsis chuckled and reveled in Darrio's anguish. "I don't know. Seems like I've made my point."

"Was it you?"

"Was what me?"

Darrio did not answer.

Carsis thought for a moment and laughed. "What are you, stupid? What makes you think I'd tell the Elders about your little secret?"

"Are you saying you didn't?"

"Don't be an idiot. I wouldn't do that. Not to him. Not again."

Darrio paused and answered, "If I find out you're lying to me, don't think for a second that I'll hesitate to—."

"Darrio!" Seris called from behind. "What are you doing?"

Darrio looked quickly at Seris, then Carsis, and released him. "Nothing," Darrio answered. "It's nothing."

"I told you two to stop fighting."

"We didn't get that far," Darrio answered as he put away his weapon, and he turned once again to Carsis.

It had not been the first time Carsis stoked the fires of Darrio's anger. He had used bitter words and taunts in the past for no other reason than to harm Darrio. Talim characterized this early relationship as a kind of sibling rivalry, but little had improved since that time. There were fewer arguments, fights, and threats of death between them, but Carsis still hated Darrio, and Darrio wanted nothing to do with Carsis. Despite all of this, Carsis knew to avoid pricking the rims of Darrio's patience. While he could harm him up to a point, there was still a line even he would not cross. This threshold was partly responsible for Darrio's infamy in the world, but it was not necessarily an unusual phenomenon and was known by the Salians as a state limit.

Due to its method of implementation, primarily in select numbers of the Saline military, there was an inherent side effect to magic's use which resulted in the creation of the state limit. This was an emotional barrier of will that could only be crossed in one of two ways. The first was a great and sustained use of magic over a short period of time. The second was referred to as triggering. In this, an event, memory, or person would cause the subject to enter an emotional state that was in accord with a consistent pattern of action or thought. When this limit was crossed or triggered, the subject would transition to a different state, and the will was given over to the total abandon of desire. The only sign of its crossing, besides an apparent change of temperament, was a change in eye color. This was not a problem common among the general population of Salia. The methods which created the limit were banned for civilians. It was more prevalent among the Adepts, Shades, and Casters because of the amplification methods that were allowed during the Magic War.

Darrio's most common trigger was anger though his limit was further from his normal state than the average person. The binding effect of the Elder's shackles, however, pushed the boundary back even more. Carsis crossed what had previously been a point of no return, but the shackles provided a new buffer of safety for him. This fact, as he realized it, only annoyed Darrio all the more, and he stepped away from Carsis and uttered, "You idiot."

The courtyard was the center stage of activities in the Hall of Order, and there were many servicemen training and exchanging experiences in the area. Darrio retreated into this place and headed to his quarters on the western side of the grounds.

Lon was present and had just returned from his station in the Hollow Realm. He was speaking with Tam. "Interesting. I had not thought to use such a technique."

Tam replied, "I've found it most effective on lesser minds. It would not work on you, of course. Did I not try something to this effect on you once?"

Lon smiled with warm recollection. "Ah, yes. You did."

"You saw right through it. My methods are as glass," Tam said in mourning, but his demeanor changed when he took notice of Darrio. "Firestar!"

Lon also diverted his attention to address Darrio in a clear, concise tone. "Tam told me of your recent title change. He also told me the High Elders are giving you much in the way of trouble."

"Yeah," Darrio replied.

"If I were you, I would tell them nothing. Silence is the most potent weapon you have against their assessment of you."

"It makes an effective poison also," Tam chimed.

"You mustn't give them reason to believe you are their enemy."

"I know," Darrio replied.

"Rather, you should smile and nod, let them have their peace, but in all things, give them nothing."

Tam gasped, and a grin crept across his face. "But do you not act the same when targeting an enemy's throat?"

"Indeed. I only said he mustn't appear to them as an enemy. I never said he should not regard them as such. They tried to kill him after all."

Tam's face glowed with admiration, and he laughed. "You see? This is why I like you! Mind like a blade, ever thirsty…like mine."

Lon nodded in total agreement with Tam and proceeded to address Darrio once more. "Smile and nod and be kind to your enemies. Then, when their throat is exposed, you may strike cleanly and effectively. Captain Seris has been most cunning in this."

"And when do you think he will move to strike? I am getting most anxious with all this peace."

"Patience is the companion of silence, my friend, and a kill in this manner requires stillness and planning. In many ways, I find this more gratifying than any other method of execution, but then, I am also biased. He will tell us when we are ready, Tam."

"I've got to go," Darrio said. He was not at all comfortable with the conversation they were having nor was he settled in the tone in which they were having it. There was an expanse separating their courteous mannerisms and speech from the cold and darkened grounds of their hearts and actions. What connected them, Darrio wondered, God only knew, but this bridge was far longer in Lon than it was in Tam.

Lon was known among Seris' shades as the Kind Killer, and his reputation as a cunning assassin, albeit a polite one, was well documented. He had on several occasions set elaborate traps for his prey that would, in many ways, play out in the most brutal of fashions. Greater steps meant greater risks, and the more people involved in his snares, which likewise increased the risk of failure, the more gratifying a successful execution was for him. Darrio saw the matter as a sick and demented pleasure though Lon cited the acts as an art form. Many of his deadly manipulations were subtle, sometimes simple, and consistently in good spirit. The target and players, as Lon called them, were often unaware of the triggers set up around them, and Lon prided himself on the invisible destruction of his targets. Assassinations were carried out under his guidance which had never been understood as assassinations. He was a man who dedicated his mind to the craft of death by manipulation. Tam, in all respects, was his confidant. They would often exchange techniques and practices used on the field from stalking and torture to strikes and execution. Darrio took nothing from anything they said, however, and made it his daily goal to keep as much distance from the two as possible.

Lon smiled at Darrio with closed lips and calculating eyes. "Peace be with you then, Firestar, except where such peace be inappropriate, of course."

Darrio left the courtyard somewhat unnerved by the shrewd glint in Lon's eye. His character and close association with Tam was enough, but Darrio also knew Lon to be mischievous and hoped he would not find himself in one of Lon's lesser traps.

As Darrio continued his retreat, he turned a corner and was ejected backward by the standing frame of the muscular Talim. He was a beast of a man and was great in height, physique, and features. Many did not believe he would succeed as a shade and stated his body type was better suited to adept work. Nevertheless, he had taken well to magic of the illusionary school and used it often in his negotiation work. Where negotiation was not an option, he used his powers to terrorize and dominate in an unrestrained attempt to destroy the will of his target. His body, though he worked hard for the shape, served no better purpose in most cases. It was still a tool he used against the mind. The most obvious application was in the realm of intimidation, but it also served him in the elevation of status in the eyes of the people he dealt with. To friends, he was tall, strong, and attractive. To enemies, he was giant, monstrous, and bold. If Talim's form was not enough to deter an attacker, he would allow his magic to finish the task. He was such a strong manipulator of the will and senses that many of his foes committed suicide before him. Tam was jealous of this. "Ho, little Firestar!" Talim bellowed. "If I knew you were coming, I would have stepped out of the way."

"I'll bet."

"How goes the struggle?"

"What?"

"The Elders, boy! The Elders! The others tell me they've been troubling you."

"Why is everyone talking about this?" Darrio mumbled.

"Hm? What did you say? I can't hear you when you talk in such low tones."

"I'll be fine," Darrio answered.

"Good, good. Then I should make my report. Take care, Firestar."

Talim was a man of few words when it became necessary, and he carried an air of authority wherever he went. Abaddon, however, was the second in command. In the past, Talim challenged Abaddon in conflicts disguised as sparring matches in the spirit of jest, but time after time, he was met with utter defeat. Abaddon's understanding of magic far exceeded the years of training and practice held by the others of his unit, but it was a power he rarely used offensively. Talim, still, was undeterred and determined in his own mind that he would surpass Abaddon. Since the closing battles of the Magic War, however, Abaddon brushed aside all of Talim's proposals saying, "I no longer have time to play with you."

Darrio finally entered his quarters believing he was safe and alone, but behind him, standing silent in the dark, was the diminutive form of Eloi. When Darrio turned, unable to detect Eloi's presence, he cried aloud in surprise. It took all of his will to restrain himself, and he asked in anger, "What the hell are you doing in here?"

Eloi was soft-spoken, even more so than Tam, and was mild in his manner, movement, and appearance. His eyes were large and appeared translucent in the night, and his skin, while pale, still glowed with life. Despite this, his emotional expressions were feigned, and there was nothing to be felt behind any of his words. Some thought of him as a lifeless puppet who was animated by an empty will. Eloi stood unmoved by the emotions of others. Judgments, then, would only be met with an insincere smile and an empty gesture. "I wanted to say hi," he said, and a stark moment of silence passed between them. "Hi."

Eloi made Darrio uncomfortable. He would often creep around the grounds and silently observe the others, especially Darrio and Seris. Even Tam had trouble detecting Eloi's presence, yet another trait Tam desired. He would speak most often with Carsis and Talim on the occasions where Eloi spoke, but his words were otherwise few. No one could tell how he felt, if he was feeling anything at all, and no one could decipher what he was thinking at any one point. When asked, however, Eloi would answer, and he was honest to a fault. Talim was enraged with him when he asked on one occasion why Eloi was staring at him, and Eloi replied, "Because you are ugly to me." Talim chased Eloi into the adjacent room, but as soon as his line of sight was broken, Eloi was gone. There was no teleportation magic in existence though some attempted it with fatal results, but Eloi's state of rapid movement and concealment kept the speculation of such possibilities alive.

"Get...the hell...out," Darrio ordered.

Eloi silently opened the door, and after this, he turned, smiled, and bowed his head to Darrio. All were artificial and empty gestures. "Bye," he said, and after he shut the door, Darrio sighed. He was finally alone though his mind continued to wander.

Each Shade of Seris had a particular set of eccentricities and seemed to personify a certain trait. Carsis was jealous. Talim was ambitious. Eloi was envious. Lon was cunning. Tam was mad. Darrio was full of wrath, and Abaddon, ever still and collected in his mannerisms, had become the living embodiment of control. They all had their own separate histories, lives, and experiences, and some held stories of times before the war. Nevertheless, while Darrio believed these traits probably reflected Seris to some degree, he did not believe the parallels were too close or endangering. Despite this, even if Seris turned out to be a devil in Darrio's eyes, he resolved himself to service. There was no one else he knew to follow in life save one, but Darrio knew so little about Him and was not inclined to trust anyone he did not know.

There then came a day when Darrio was off duty, and he went about his business in a brown cloak and homely attire so as not to draw attention. His irons were hidden by the sleeves of his garment, and his weapons were equally concealed. He would not go anywhere defenseless and had never done so in the past, but the events of the time made being armed even more pertinent.

The unexplained attack on the city served as fertile ground for a wave of rumors and speculation citing Darrio as the primary suspect. There had already been enough fear given his name and title, but talks of him being an imminent threat to the realm only exacerbated things. There was nothing Darrio could do to stem the tide of such opinions nor would he bring himself to try. He grew under Seris' care among the people and knew their fears and concerns, not all of which were unfounded, and that premise placed him in an ever-defensive posture.

There were also many kinds of people who made up Ambrosia's citizenry, and some of them hated everything Darrio represented. Even worse, the most malicious of them would have shown little to no hesitation in challenging him. Had his condition been made public, there would have been no end to the line of opponents not including those who would venture in from the Outer Realms. On one hand, this would have been a good thing for the Elders. Darrio would eventually tire in such a case. On the other hand, Salia was already hated as a nation and would be hard-pressed to keep her enemies from expanding their efforts after killing her Firestar. An act such as that would have greatly emboldened all of them. It was because of this potential situation that Darrio's condition was kept secret at all.

As Darrio made his rounds, most of the people who recognized him either sneered or stepped away. Children were forced to maintain a certain distance by concerned parents and family members.

Whispers passed around him like a condemning wind. Even the merchants went so far as to shelter their goods. Some refused him service, and as Darrio's frustration increased, so did the negative perceptions surrounding him.

After a while of this, Darrio became discouraged and angry at the people, and he made his way to the western exit to escape their stares and talks. On the way, he saw Sam who was walking down the street.

Sam spotted Darrio and greeted him. "How's it going, Firestar?"

It was the only cheerful response Darrio received that day, but he responded with dismal abandon. "Fine, I guess."

"Heck of a week, huh?"

"Yeah…but you don't think I—?"

Sam lifted a hand in silence. "I've heard the rumors and all the blah, blah, blah. You don't even have to ask. I don't."

Darrio relaxed. "Good." A moment of silence then passed between them, and Sam's eyes shifted to the ground around them. He was not his usual, talkative self. "What's going on?" Darrio asked. "Are you alright?"

"Huh? Oh yeah, I'm fine. I think. It's just been rough since I got back, you know? These guys have been watching me from dawn to dusk, and for the life of me, I can't figure out why. It's beginning to give me the creeps."

"What guys?"

"Oh, it's nothing. Don't worry about it."

For a moment, Darrio felt the need to press the issue and discover what was going on. There was obviously something Sam was not telling him, and given his overly cheerful demeanor, it was likely more grave than he put on. "What about the family? How are they?"

Sam smiled. "They were okay. Said they missed me, but…I told them it'll be just a little longer, and then I'm back for good.

"Why?"

"Why what?"

"Why aren't you with your family?"

Sam's demeanor changed, and he moved about awkwardly. "It's kind of a long story. I don't know."

"Tell me," Darrio urged.

Sam's eyes scoured the area for an escape but found none. He sighed. "Well, shortly after marrying Tira, my wife, my father died."

"Oh."

"He didn't have much to begin with, see, and he couldn't afford to leave an inheritance, not a positive one anyway, so he got involved in some…uh…helpful trouble? I'll just put it that way. So the only thing left of him now is this load of debt that I've got to pay, and sometimes they don't make it easy, you know? Sometimes, it's just downright hard."

"Do you really have to pay them?"

"It's not like I've got much of a choice in the matter," Sam chuckled, but this concealing expression was failing him. He continued on with exaggerated strength, "But no worries! My debts will get paid soon enough, and then I'll be able to move on with my life. I'll go home to Silesia, eat Aunt May's cooking, and things will be alright. Did you get a chance to eat at Aunt May's? Her cooking's the best, right? I told you about my son too, didn't I? Matthew? Remember him?"

Darrio shook his head. "Don't do that."

"Eh? Do what?"

"That talking thing. You don't have to pretend around me."

Sam, initially confused, was then struck by Darrio's keen eye and momentary openness. Sam had encountered many types of people in his day. Some were merchants, men of renown, women of influence, and most, if not all, hid behind a particular mask. It would take on a variety of different shapes and forms, but the result was always the same. No one was able to see the real person that hid beneath. It had become such a normal custom to play upon the title and image given by others that few people, even the actors themselves, knew who they really were. Sam viewed such things as acts of deceit and had little respect for their dishonesty and frivolous talk. Sam then realized he had become no better than them. When he looked at Darrio, Sam caught a glimpse of the hurting individual behind the temperament and anger. There was a person behind the title of Firestar and a human in the Great Destroyer. Not only did Sam see these things, but he also found himself challenged by Darrio's assertion. Sam too wore a mask, and it was a mask of words. This flash of insight took place in the span of a peculiar moment, and when it passed, Sam spoke again. "Firestar?"

"What?"

"What's your name? Your real name."

"Deloran."

"No," Sam replied. "Your first name."

Darrio hesitated. "Why do you want to know my name?"

"Come on. Don't tell me you're going to start hiding now."

Darrio thought twice about answering and then a third time and a fourth. It was his turn to be challenged, and he decided to meet it. "Darrio."

"Darrio," Sam repeated, and after getting a sense of the name, he smiled and straightened up. "Nice to meet you, Darrio. My name is Sam." Sam extended his hand, and Darrio hesitated but shook it. Sam then said, "And from now on, no matter where you go, this'll be one friend you can count on, no matter what."

Darrio sputtered. He had never expected such a thing, and tears welled up from the corner of his eyes. Despite all attempts to restrain himself, he could not keep them from falling. "Why are you being so nice to me?"

"Why? Because I want to, that's why."

Darrio struggled to gather his thoughts and recollect himself. He remembered his surroundings and the eyes of potential enemies hiding in the dark and wiped his eyes. Darrio then composed himself as best as he could and answered, "Thank you."

The two faced each other in that moment with warm openness, and for a moment, nothing was said. Sam then broke the silence and said, "So...you going to buy something from me or what?"

Darrio could not help but laugh, and it felt good to do so.

When their business was finished, Sam saw Darrio off at Ambrosia's western gate. "Don't be a stranger now, you hear me?"

Darrio nodded and wandered out into the field where he felt not only happiness but hope.

After a few minutes of walking with no particular direction in mind, Darrio decided to settle down and lay in the grass. He was prone to doing such things to clear his mind and empty his spirit. He then let his eyes survey the expanse above him. Clouds dotted the sky and floated by gracefully while the calm breeze of the wind settled over his cheeks and calmed his nerves. It was a relaxed moment, and he felt a sense of peace settle over him and sighed. "Why did you make me? Why did you put me here?"

Darrio looked beside him and noticed a pair of terras some distance away. They were four-legged creatures with short stubby tails, dark brown coats, and a pair of short curved horns. The males had larger horns than the females. They appeared to be frolicking but aggressively, and as Darrio watched them, he remembered an exchange of words between him and Seris.

Seris had asked him, "And what do you want to do with your life?"

"I don't know," Darrio had answered. "I just want to help people. Protect them, I guess."

Seris had smiled.

The animals ran into the woods and disappeared. "I still want to help people," Darrio said aloud. "That's what I want to do, but…." His thoughts were interrupted.

The terra's shrill death cry echoed to Darrio from the woods, but Darrio, though curious, thought twice about investigating. He did not think he would find anything of great consequence, and if he did, the Elders were sure to use it to their advantage. Even so, he was duty-bound much like Seris, and he rose to his feet and stepped towards the source of the commotion.

The woods were unnaturally dark despite the clearance overhead, and Darrio spotted the fallen terras. Their eyes were opened wide with panic, and there were bruises on the pelts. Tracks also showed that they initially wandered out from the darkened core of the woods. Surrounding them were two more dead creatures with several more still ahead. Many bore signs of damage. After seeing this, Darrio surmised that the animals fought each other, but there was only one predator among them, and even it died in a state of fear. Darrio's attention then turned to the center of the woods and the darkness ahead. Something had occurred there, and he drew his weapons and entered with caution.

The light appeared to fade behind Darrio as he moved. Illusionary magic could have supplied a similar effect by dimming the vision of a target, but that would have meant someone had Darrio in sight. Furthermore, Darrio was not showing any symptoms of such manipulation. His breathing remained steady, his senses oriented, there was no feeling of dread or fear, no change in his sense of temperature, no trick of his eye, no shadowing of his mind, nothing. There was only a sense of heaviness and a distinct impression that Darrio had once again been weakened, an effect of dark magic. The air was full of it, and the further Darrio went, the more he could feel and see. Had it not been for his will, Darrio felt he would have ended up much like the creatures behind him. His shackles also reacted, but this fact escaped his attention.

Darrio pressed forward. The darkness was like a cold mist that increased in density the further he progressed. In time, it even became hard to breathe, and Darrio felt that if he did not reach the end soon, he would eventually drown. Movement became a tiresome struggle, his lungs ached for clear, clean air, and it was as if he no longer traversed across land but through an omnipresent field of water. Darrio finally came to the end of the field and stumbled to the ground like a fish coming out of a lake. It would take time to adjust.

Darrio surveyed the area. He was on the outer edge of a large clearing that acted as a bubble of security from the surrounding darkness. Six figures were dressed similarly to the assassin Darrio encountered, and they stood in a circular formation at the center. However, the three closest to Darrio bore a separate pattern from the other three and were characterized by the flame-like shapes etched into their clothes. The others took on the shape of dew drops. Darrio hid himself among a collection of brush and bramble and remained quiet. The six, though, were unaware of the new presence among them as they were already involved in a heated debate.

The one counted first, a man bearing a fire pattern and closest to Darrio's position, was speaking to another man bearing the water pattern. "But you knew better, Treos! You knew not to send Sheol on such a mission, and now he is dead! What else must he pay in your arrogance?"

"I keep telling you, it was not arrogance," Treos, the furthest from Darrio's position, answered. "Even with Sheol's terrible history, no one could have foreseen what happened."

"Regardless, you should have known the master would not have agreed to such action. Not only have you jeopardized his affairs, but now the rest of us will be held suspect as well. Think about this.

Think of what your actions mean for the rest of us."

"I understand well, Sephor, and I understood then. The only thing you fail to understand, however, is that we are working towards the same goal. I do not know why I was given this edict, but I do know it is for the higher cause towards which we are both working."

"Then I find both your messenger and methods suspect."

"And I find you to be a hypocrite. These foolish people and their High Elders think they have an understanding of magic, and they do not. If fortune favors us, they will view the demonstration as an example of their persistent and ongoing ignorance."

"They needed no further demonstration, Treos. They are mocked already by Sheol's murderer. What do they call him now? The Firestar?"

"Surpassed by a foreigner," said the woman among the water bearers. "Shameful."

"Foreign or not," Treos continued, "shamed or not, they still parade about in pride, high on the victory given to them by their champion and bane. They shall feel the presence of true magic soon enough, and the master will thank us for what we have done."

"You mustn't say such things," Sephor said. "He was quite clear on the remnant's silence. You think he will praise you for following this new revelation? I say he will punish you. You, Sheol, and all of the others were defying his direct will when you orchestrated this. And, Elea."

The woman raised her head.

"I am especially surprised by you."

Elea replied with great restraint. "You know nothing, Sephor."

"Mind your state, Elea," Treos advised. "Be still."

Elea calmed, but the glare did not leave her eyes.

"We would never dare to endanger the master or his plans, Sephor. You must know this."

Sephor did not answer.

"You must also come to understand that all of this is part of the greater will."

"I cannot believe that."

"You must."

The bramble Darrio was in was full of thorns that scraped across his face as he breathed and kept his footing. He did not understand why he chose such a spot for concealment until then, but the consequences became all too clear when a thistle found its way toward his nose and pricked him. He sneezed.

The second man of the water bearers picked up on the sound and spotted Darrio's face from among the brush and bush. The two met eye to eye. "There's a spy among us!"

"Shit," Darrio grumbled, and he leaped back into the misty wall of darkness.

"After him," Treos ordered.

Darrio was unable to set snares, traps, or any other obstacles without the aid of magic, and the waters only hindered his movements. Despite this, self-preservation proved a great motivator, and he pressed ahead on the rush it provided him. The pursuers entered the field and followed behind. There was no struggle for them. Instead, they swam through the waters with the ease of fish and rose high into the air to gain a better vantage point of attack. Darrio drew his weapons and moved evasively. The pursuers descended on him and struck for his head like pecking birds of prey, but Darrio deflected the blows and pushed himself forward. The air grew thinner and thinner as the chase continued. Movement became easier as did breathing, and Darrio's head cleared. The hunters were unable to remain in flight. As they approached the edge of the woods, the dark users continued on the ground closely behind Darrio's position and were nearly in reaching distance of his cloak. Then, when Darrio finally emerged into the fullness of the light of the field, the enemy stopped.

Darrio still continued on for a time, but when he saw the chase had ended, he turned. His pursuers stood disgruntled at the edge of the woods. They were unwilling to follow and reveal themselves. Instead, they grumbled and returned to the mist, and they disappeared once more into the darkness.

Darrio recalled a number of ways in which his demise could have been assured during the chase and wondered why none of them were employed. For people so skilled in dark magic, they were surely capable of using more than one element and school. A shifting of the ground, a well-targeted bolt of thunder, or a turning of the air would have been more than enough to ground him for the length of time needed to accomplish the task, yet none of this was done. There was another dimension to dark magic that was not yet apparent.

Darrio quickly returned to Ambrosia and entered the Hall of Order. On the way, he brushed past Talim, Eloi, and Abaddon, and though Darrio said nothing, the three did not miss the urgency on Darrio's face. "What frightens the boy, so?" Talim wondered.

"He is not scared," said Eloi. "Nothing frightens Firestar."

"What would you call it then?"

"Concern of duty."

"Ha!" Talim barked. "What does that even mean?"

Eloi looked up at Talim and frowned, but his tone was vacant. "You are dense today."

Darrio entered Seris' office exhausted from the sprint, and he took a moment to catch his breath.

Seris looked up in concern. "Darrio? What's wrong? Has something happened?"

"I saw them. In the woods. They were there."

"Be still, Darrio. Who did you see? What was there?"

Darrio panted. "There was a gathering. A group of them. All were using dark magic. They were talking about some plan and master. They were the ones who attacked Ambrosia."

Seris stood. "Where did you see them?"

"The woods across the plains, past the western gate."

"Show me." Darrio led Seris back to the site, and it had been hastily abandoned. There were breaks in the branches and scattered footprints, all evidence of Darrio's escape. The animal corpses also remained, but the darkness was gone. The air remained dense with moisture. "It has been a dry day," Seris commented. "Why is the air so heavy here?"

"Because of the dark magic. It was acting like a cloud, and they were swimming through it when they chased me. I couldn't do anything in it."

"They did not use shadows like before?"

"No."

"Perhaps it requires a different set of skills."

"What are we going to do?"

Seris gave the situation some thought and answered, "We'll present these findings to the Council of Elders and see how they react."

"I don't want to enter that chamber again."

"I know."

Seris and Darrio returned to the Hall of Order where Abaddon was ordered to gather the others together. When all seven shades were present, Seris briefed them on Darrio's developments, dark magic, and the next steps he planned to take.

"The concealed and gripping stress of darkness," Tam mused. "It sounds like such a wonderful tool. I wish it were not a lost element. Then I too could learn it."

"Me too," Eloi repeated.

"What do you need the dark element for?" Carsis replied. "You can't even use magic."

"I know."

"But it seems to be a thing we could all benefit from," Talim said.

"We are not here to discuss the supposed benefits of dark magic," Abaddon finished.

"Indeed," Seris continued. "I will call an emergency meeting with the Council of High Generals and Elders to discuss what should be done. All of you may be called to assist with the task. Therefore, all of you must become familiar with the dangers you will face should you encounter one of these dark element users."

"Bah," Talim protested. "If they should cross me, I shall merely send them into a delusion from which there is no awakening."

"How are you going to do that," Darrio questioned, "if you're unable to use magic?"

Talim was unable to answer, and Seris continued. "The first user Darrio fought was able to produce figures of shadow and vapor. They were weak and dissipated at the slightest impact, but they remained dangerous."

"If one of them had managed to catch me, even one, I would have been finished."

"But they were still only shadows, mere forms of men, and you cannot cast illusion techniques on a thing which has no senses. Keep this fact in mind. You may have to rely on your physical training in order to combat these enemies."

"No problem," Carsis said. "If they're anything like illusionists and casters, I'll just shred them to pieces."

Darrio shook his head. "It won't be that easy. The group I met was arguing, so they weren't able to find me until it was too late. I don't think they'll make that same mistake again."

"What were they arguing about?" Abaddon asked.

"I don't know. It was something about their master, some new revelation, and some plan. There were two groups there. It looked like they were having some differences."

"I see."

"So we'll be quiet and sneak up on them," Carsis said.

"No," Abaddon replied. "The field of darkness Darrio entered behaves much like a field of waters. Any of them skilled in the art of detection could pick up on the subtle vibrations in this field to detect you. If you find the air to be unusually heavy, even if you are silent, every movement you make will relay your position. Even your heartbeat may act as a beacon. Consider yourself found in this case."

"And until we can determine the extent of their abilities," Seris said, "assume all of them share the same skills."

"How bothersome," Tam sighed.

"Perhaps we should look to it as a challenge, Tam," Lon replied.

Eloi turned to Talim. "You will have to use your physical strength this time."

"Do you doubt me, small one?"

"Yes."

Seris spoke. "I trust everyone understands the potential threat we may face?"

"Yes, sir," they said in unison.

"Then return to your duties. I will call for each of you as needed. Abaddon?"

"Yes?"

"I would speak with you privately."

Everyone, with the exception of Abaddon, filed out of Seris' office. Lon and Tam moved to the courtyard to discuss the potential uses of dark magic in interrogation and torture. The other shades, casters, and adepts were careful to maintain their distance. Carsis returned to the training area to hone his combat skills and prepare for the trials ahead. Talim entered the library to refresh his knowledge of illusionary magic's effects on the mentally ill and vacant, and Eloi slipped away in silence. He was not seen for the rest of the day.

Darrio, however, returned to his quarters to meditate on the day's course of events. There were many unanswered questions still lingering in his mind and a standing implication of greater things to come. Whether these things were good or bad, he could not be certain, but this did not worry him. His only concern was whether or not he would be ready. "I want to help," Darrio mumbled. He then closed his eyes and fell to sleep.

CHAPTER 3
A Dying Wish

As DARRIO STOOD before the Council of High Elders and Generals, he once again explained everything he had seen while Seris stood beside him. Turil was also present and studied both with an eye of intense scrutiny. As Darrio spoke, the Elders became visibly anxious, and there were whispers among the High Generals on the possible identities of the intruders. Turil ignored such talk.

One general proposed the men of darkness, then dubbed as shadow casters, were advanced alchemists from the Silent Realm. During the Magic War, alchemists were vital in the creation of compound-based weaponry, poisons, antidotes, and other effectual supplements. Their potions and chemicals had a wide range of effects and were even seen as a close rival to restoration and illusionary magic, but the process was admittedly crude and required time for maximum effectiveness. It was said that since the war, alchemists and chemists were extending their craft to further compete with magic, but disagreements between the two camps slowed their progress. Despite being a realm associated with intellectual pursuits, the nation of Taurus, which occupied the region, had proven itself to be more than formidable.

Another suggested the enemies were disgruntled Firans from the Burning Realm. They were no strangers to open conflict and were experts in the use of fire, smoke, and ash. They were also renowned for their fine metalwork and armaments. The warriors of Fira, in fact, were such fierce fighters that close combat was avoided with them at all costs. Thus, instead of adepts, casters were the primary force reckoned against the fine steel of their shields and weapons which were highly prized. Fira's Legion, however, developed little in the way of long-ranged units, and the national tribes were constantly fighting due to their apparent love of conflict. Granted, the battles were being fought over the air with words, boasts, and challenges, but this fact made the possibility of the Shadow Caster's association with the Burning Realm equally unlikely. The nation was simply too divided to launch a successful attack.

Talk then drifted to the Hollow Realm. The bowmen and fighters who hailed from that region were known for their accuracy, agility, and speed, and a good hunter, armed or not, was a dangerous enemy. There had been many successful attempts to assassinate the Council of Elders and Generals using the Hollow Realm's Hunters during the war. Greater achievements were had among the lesser-ranked captains. Nevertheless, the Shades were even rivals when matched with hunters but only by a slim margin. Magic, by its nature, was a manipulative force on the environment, and the denizens of the Hollow Realm were naturally adaptive. For all of the powers and gifts granted to the people of other nations, the Hollow Realm's proved to be the most dangerous to Salia's well-being. Had it not been for Elder Tiberius, the hunter assassinations alone would have plunged the Saline Realm into civil unrest.

Darrio's ears twitched over the discussion of the Outer Realms, and he responded, "I said they were using dark magic. It wasn't chemical, it wasn't alchemy, it wasn't smoke, and it sure as hell wasn't a hunter's shadow. Are any of you listening?"

"We heard you," Turil answered, "and your story is fantastic. Unfortunately, that makes it equally difficult to believe."

"What's so hard to believe about what I said?"

"You're the only one who bore witness to these events, correct?"

"So?"

"Did you see what he describes, Captain Seris?"

Seris first looked at Darrio and then at Turil before replying. "No. I did not."

"But I brought back the knife and the pattern from the first assassin who attacked me," Darrio said. "I gave them to the Elders. You must have seen it."

"I did see it, but there was nothing to discern from them."

"What are you talking about?"

Turil traded glances with Elder Tiberius who then spoke. "I gave the dagger and cloth to our top artisan, and she informed me the blade was useless as an empowered item. The scripts contained in the patterns, however complex, were missing several keys which made the overall arrangement a meaningless collection of symbols and commands. They gave the edge and his garments no finer properties than that of a rag and a cooking knife."

"A child could have thrown it together," Turil said.

Turil's insinuation was beginning to wear on Darrio's nerve, but before he could protest, Seris countered. "Darrio learned the name of the second assassin during the encounter with him."

"He does not sound like a good assassin then."

"His name was Arthis."

The name sent a jolt through Turil's face.

"Was this man not a promising shade under Captain Palim?"

Turil paused. "He was."

"Then you knew of his death."

"I was not told of the cause."

"Palim is your subordinate, and he did not tell you the cause of his death? Did you ask him, Turil?"

"Are you implying something of me, Seris?"

"I insinuate no more against you than you do against my subordinate." That statement then became Seris' warning to Turil. For every implication or attack made against Darrio, Seris would return the favor in kind.

Regardless of their difference in rank, Seris and Turil still viewed each other as equals and shared an old air of friendship, but certain choices and time itself had caused their paths to diverge. Their relationship then was different from what it had been. Even so, Turil still viewed Seris as a man of honor and deep conviction. Thus, the sudden, albeit veiled, hostility perplexed him. They shared many secrets between them and were intimately privy to each other's thinking processes and mannerisms. It was held as a mutual sentiment that one would never raise a hand against the other. While it was normal in the past for the two to think alike and share the same feelings, they had become sharply divided on matters concerning Darrio. Therefore, in a manner shared only between him and Seris, Turil impressed his sentiments using a little-known method of illusion, and he asked, "Why are you doing this, Seris?"

Seris responded through the channel with equal silence and answered, "Because he is mine."

"Turil," Tiberius probed. "Have you nothing to say?"

Turil watched Darrio as he stood beside Seris with a confused look on his face. Darrio was still young by Turil's reckoning despite the passage of time, but relative age aside, he saw nothing overtly remarkable and worth protecting at the expense of a nation, continued peace, and an old friendship. He was the Firestar, Deloran, the Great Destroyer, and a clear danger to the realm and possibly everyone around him. Turil watched Darrio, but he did not understand. Nevertheless, he kept his peace. "I have nothing to say. I will simply continue to investigate the matter until the truth reveals itself."

"As will I," Seris stated.

The Elders were visibly unsatisfied with the declaration, especially Tiberius. "Then until matters find a way to reveal themselves, and as we still have no concrete understanding of these men or their intentions, I formally move for Seris and his shades to find these shadow casters and capture one of them if possible."

"Agreed," Judas motioned.

The other Elders did likewise as did the Council of Generals, Turil included. "So be it."

"So be it," Tiberius ended. "Captain Seris? I am placing you under the supervision of General Turil. You will report your findings to him. Understood?"

Seris looked at Turil and nodded. "Understood."

"General Turil? Captain Seris seeks the identity of Salia's enemies and the plan of which they spoke under the direct order of this council. He is to be given no other orders that would interfere with this mission. Is this understood?"

"Yes, sir."

"Then this meeting is adjourned. Dismissed."

Seris and Darrio stood their ground as the High Elders and Generals filed out of the chamber, but Turil remained in his seat. When everyone had gone and the door was closed, Seris spoke. "Do you have something to say, Turil?"

Turil's hands were clasped together and held in front of his mouth. His eyes were still engaged in fervent study, but he replied, "I know that I don't understand, but time has not been given the opportunity to cloud me." To Darrio, Turil asked, "I'm aware of the history you two share, but in your own words, what is your affection to this man?"

Darrio was caught off guard by the question and stumbled in giving an answer.

Seris interceded. "Why are you asking him this?"

"You insisted he be allowed to speak for himself, Seris. Let him speak for himself now." Turil then returned his attention to Darrio and stated, "Answer the question, please."

"He's...," Darrio started, "he's my captain."

"Is that all?"

Darrio glanced over at Seris, and a great number of associations sprang to his mind. He was not only his captain but a trainer, teacher, provider, defender, friend, and a host of other titles, but Darrio did not utter these things. Such words, though locked away in his mind, swelled with equal measures of pain, warmth, and regret in his heart. Instead, he said in a definitive tone, "He's my captain." Darrio then faced Turil. "That's it. That's all."

"Seris? I ask you the same question."

Seris remained quiet for a moment but spoke as Darrio had. "He is my subordinate. Nothing more."

"So you say." Turil stood and walked slowly towards the door, but Seris and Darrio were uncomfortably still. Just as Turil was about to leave, he turned. "You will begin your assignment tomorrow. I suggest getting some rest."

"We will."

Turil heard but did not respond. Instead, he left, and the sound of the door closing behind him echoed throughout the empty chamber.

"Darrio," Seris began.

"I meant what I said."

Seris paused and spoke with equal resolution. "As did I." The two said nothing to each other for the remainder of the day.

The following morning began like any other, and Eloi hung upside down with hands and feet clung to the ceiling of Darrio's room like an insect. He snuck into the chamber to observe Darrio's peacefulness in sleep. Eloi envied such peace. His own mind often swirled with questions as he probed the great mysteries of the world and life. His heart, however, was quite empty and devoid of all meaningful sentiment. At times, he even forgot he was alive. As such, he had taken many opportunities to remind and reassure himself of his own existence. The observation and imitation of others, while primary, was only a single aspect of this.

Darrio was only half covered at the time due to it being a warm season, and Eloi traced the scripts of Salia that were etched into the brown skin of Darrio's chest. It was known as a flesh script and was one of the primary amplification techniques that were banned prior to the war. The scripts of the Saline Realm were normally embedded on the surface of nonliving things. The effect was magnified, however, when placed on the surface of living entities. One of the many traits unique to flesh scripts was their ability to grow. This allowed the user to mature in power and mastery beyond the limitations of the original print. This was also considered the most dangerous aspect of the scripts because magic drew directly from the spiritual will of the host.

Salians recognized two wills at work in the soul of man. These were the spiritual will and the will of desire. The spiritual will, governed by the affairs of both heart and mind, was associated with love, moderation, and goodwill. The will of desire, governed by mind and body, was normally attributed to passion, want, and selfishness. The mind then stood as the great mediator between the spiritual will and the will of desire. Spiritual will was regarded as the higher of the two. However, magic's drain on the spiritual will reduced both the governance of heart and mind over the body. The result was the creation of state limits. The often-used phrase "be still" was not only a gesture of peace among the Salians but also a call to mind one's own state as well as the state of others. Thus, state limits and the conflicts of will were nothing to be trifled with in Saline culture.

Eloi had seen Darrio's flesh scripts on several occasions in the past, and each time he noticed a certain measure of growth and change. Most of the smaller designs were hard, sharp, and revolved around a central form. There were many of these formations on his body. Yet, in an area centered near Darrio's heart, there was a new, rounded figure that stood out from the rest. Flesh scripts were known to take on the emotional characteristics of the host and served as an accurate measure of power, but there was no one who had a greater or more elaborate display of flesh scripts than Darrio.

While Eloi pondered this and became lost in thought, Darrio stirred and awoke from his sleep. The first thing he saw was Eloi staring down at him with big, reflective eyes, and seized with embarrassment and surprise, he shouted.

Eloi, however, remained still. "Hi."

"What the hell are you doing?"

"I was watching you sleep."

"Again? Why? Why do you keep doing that?"

"You are peaceful when you sleep. Every other time you are angry. And violent."

"Idiot! Moron!"

Darrio grabbed a history book given to him by Seris when he was younger and launched it at Eloi who promptly scampered across the ceiling through the door. Eloi then spun around, his head dangling just above the entryway, and he looked back at Darrio. "See? You are angry now." Eloi pulled his head back once more just as Darrio's blade embedded itself into the wall behind him. He did not return.

"Stay away from me, Eloi! Do you hear me?" Darrio then recoiled from a sudden pain in his skull. Eloi had given him a headache. After taking a moment to regain his bearings, Darrio swung his legs over the side of the bed and groaned. The scripts which enveloped him had grown to cover an expanse between the base of his neck to the height of his knees. From his shoulders, they continued down his arms and ended halfway down his forearms. The entire pattern revolved around two central shapes on his back and a single one on his chest. The single exception was the softened shape Eloi noticed. It remained outside the conventions of its surroundings.

When his head finally cleared, Darrio took a moment to examine the state of his pattern. It was brief, and he did not see the anomaly.

He then got dressed, armed himself, and removed his second dagger from the wall.

It was an especially sunny day. After leaving the Hall of Order grounds, Darrio stepped onto the main street. As soon as he did this, he heard a voice call out his name.

It was Sam. "Hey, Darrio!"

Darrio was unused to hearing his first name from the mouth of others and was uneasy about answering at first. Nevertheless, Darrio responded, but his tone was tired. "Hey."

"What's up? Looks like you're in for a busy day or something."

"I've got a mission to worry about later on, but they're not going to call me for a few hours."

"Then why are you up now?"

"Stupid Eloi was watching me sleep again, and he…." Darrio stopped. He realized he had been talking to Sam about a person he was not familiar with. "I forgot. You don't even know who he is."

"Sounds like a strange guy. Black sheep of the group?"

"Not really." As far as Darrio was concerned, every member of his unit was a black sheep, himself included. "I mean, I don't work with normal people. Tam's insane, Lon's no different, Talim thinks he's better than everyone else, Abaddon's too damn quiet, and Carsis is…I don't know what he is, but he's a jackass. And then there's Eloi who's just…creepy. He's always watching people and in my room, and he just gets on my damn nerves."

"Wow," Sam replied half breathless. "Is there any other reason you don't like the guy, or is he just one of those types you can't get along with?"

"He's just one of those types, I guess."

"You know, I met someone like that once. Guy didn't have to say anything, but something about him just didn't vibe with me. Got under my skin, you know? I smiled and kept up the chatter, he was a customer after all, but I'd feel something like a sigh every time I saw him. Know what I mean?"

Darrio nodded. It was nice to have someone to talk to even if he felt the topics were mundane and ultimately pointless. Sam provided Darrio with a nondestructive release for his aggression and frustration. Before the war ended, the only thing Darrio knew to do with his emotions was to turn them towards methods of attack much like he had done to Eloi. "Maybe I shouldn't have thrown my weapon at him."

"Come again?"

"Nothing. It's nothing," and Darrio felt overexposed.

"I probably didn't hear you right anyway. Oh man, look at the time. I've got to keep moving. Money don't make itself, you know. See you around, Darrio."

"See you." Darrio felt better after talking to Sam, but he could not help but wonder how long it would last. Sam was certainly a nice guy and a good person so far as Darrio could tell, but experience taught him that such people did not last long, not around him. He prayed this would not be the case with Sam.

Darrio once again made a routine patrol of the city and then left to be alone in the western fields. There, he thought about his father and the sentiments of his mother. "You can't be angry forever," she said, but that had been so long ago.

"What a quiet place to spend your time, Firestar."

Darrio saw Tam standing behind him and said, "What's it to you?"

"Me? It is nothing. All are mere resting places for the dead. Captain and General are ready to brief us on our mission. They've sent me to rally everyone."

"Did you find Eloi?"

"No. He is as hidden as the shadows as always, but why do you ask, I wonder?"

"No reason." Darrio stood to his feet. "Let's get this over with."

Darrio returned with Tam to the Hall of Order where Turil was prepared to brief each of the shades on their tasks in his office. Eloi was the last of them to arrive, and he crawled in from the ceiling and dropped to his feet between Carsis and Talim. Darrio glanced over and caught Eloi's eye, and upon doing so, he nodded apologetically. Eloi gasped but said nothing in reply.

When Turil saw that everyone was present, he started. "Since the attack, our agents have reported a rise in suspicious activity by what we can only assume was initiated by the Shadow Casters. I trust Captain Seris has already briefed you on some of the dangers you may be faced with."

"I have," Seris answered.

"Good. Then you shall all be divided into pairs, and each of you will investigate a different site for information regarding these men of darkness. This is strictly a gathering mission. You are not to engage with them under any circumstances."

"Are you kidding?" Carsis asked. "They attacked us. I think we should hunt them all down and cut them to pieces."

"That would defeat the purpose of the gathering, and besides, the council specifically asked that one of them be captured alive. To be assured of that, we need to know how they move and where they meet. Of course, the ultimate question concerns their identities and how they came to gain an affinity for dark magic in the first place, but that's getting ahead of ourselves."

"Then we have a problem," Talim interjected. "You said we would be broken into two-man teams, and there are only seven of us here. Do you presume to say one of us is going alone?"

Turil shifted uncomfortably. "Yes, unfortunately, and the council has decided it should be the Firestar."

"Figures," Darrio mumbled.

Seris sighed. "Tam and Abaddon. You two will go to Allinea. Fires have been appearing sporadically around the city, and you are to find out why."

"Abaddon?" Tam questioned. "Why him? He is already as a dead man, and Lon is so much more interesting."

"It is so the two of you can stay on task. Remember your assignment, Tam."

Tam's eyes glittered with inspired understanding. He nodded respectfully. "Yes...very well, sir. I understand."

Turil noted the change of tone in Tam's voice but said nothing.

Seris continued, "Talim and Eloi will investigate the valleys in the North. We know the area to house bandits and marauders, but many of them were found dead recently. No one has claimed responsibility. Find out why."

"Curses," Talim groaned.

"Yay," Eloi replied, but he was unenthused.

"Team three will be made up of Lon and Carsis. You two will head to Ceria."

"Damn," Carsis grumbled.

Lon's eyebrow rose with curiosity. "You still don't like me?"

"No, but it's not even that. With you around, I won't get the chance to shred anything much less know what you're thinking."

Lon was flattered and smiled. "Then I'll be sure to incorporate you into my plans as well. Don't worry. You'll have your fair share of sheep to slaughter."

"This is a gathering," Turil reminded them. "We need information, not corpses."

"Lastly," Seris continued, "Darrio. You will be entering Esea to investigate the strange disappearances of some of the city's citizens."

"Who's missing?" Darrio asked.

"Mostly women and children, but there have been no demands for their return, and there have been no kidnappings from the prominent families. That is all we know."

Turil watched Darrio's face for signs of a reaction. He had read the terrifying reports of Darrio's actions and even met with a few of the survivors. Darrio was said to be cold, emotionless, and little more than a roaming beast with an empty lust for destruction. From the Ash Dunes of the Burning Realm to the Wastes of the Frozen Realm, Darrio was hated far and wide for many reasons. All were born out of fear. The High Elders repeatedly reinforced this idea in their secret talks with the Council of High Generals. Nothing short of the Firestar's destruction would suffice so far as their goals were concerned. Turil, however, had promised before the entire council that he would look into the matter until the truth revealed itself. Until Darrio committed an act of barbarity before his own eyes, or else under his direction, Turil would reserve his judgment.

Darrio lowered his head in silent contemplation and furrowed his brow in the process. The mention of women and children had been a concern to him. Turil knew well the dangers of relying on outer appearances, but Darrio's simple expression sparked a flame of doubt in his mind. Turil decided then he would test what he learned against its scrutinizing light. "Everyone should make the necessary preparations and head out before nightfall," he said. "No later than this. Understood?"

"Understood," they replied.

"Dismissed." Darrio and Seris trailed behind the others as they filed out of the chamber, but Turil called out to them. "I have something to say to you two."

"What is it?" Seris asked.

"I wanted to apologize." The remark caught Darrio off guard, and Turil noted this as well. "All I've had to go on lately are reports and hearsay. You have changed so much over the years, and time has separated me from my last impression of you. Still, I should not have judged you solely on that, not with what my eyes have seen. I hope you will forgive me."

Darrio lowered his head. The groan of his indecision was barely audible, but after a moment of contemplation, he replied. "Okay."

"That is all. Good luck on your mission."

Darrio left quietly, but Seris remained. He was studying Turil.

"What is it, Seris?"

"Has your mind also changed that you are willing to give him the benefit of the doubt?"

Turil smiled. "I suppose it has."

"Then you will judge fairly."

Turil was taken aback by the statement and nearly took it as an insult. "I have not changed that much, Seris. You should know me better than that."

Seris focused on the statement and nodded. "You are right."

Turil smiled. "Of course, I'm right."

Seris responded in kind but with a glint in his eye that Turil did not recognize. "I will take my leave then."

When Seris was gone, Turil fell back into his seat. At his desk was an artist's rendering of the two framed in gold. In it, he and Seris were standing in front of a tree. Their swords were drawn and pointed into the ground in front of them. Turil was grinning as was usual for him, but Seris' face contained a thinly veiled smirk. They stood side by side as combatants, companions, and friends. The caption underneath the picture read, "Captain Seris (Left) and Captain Turil (Right): Battle of Horus." Turil sighed. "My friend. What has happened to you?"

The day edged on, and as the sun was setting, Darrio set out in haste for Esea which was located southwest of Ambrosia. It was normally a short journey as it was no greater in distance from the capital than Silesia, but the difficult terrain extended the travel time. Darrio's tardiness in departure only compounded the problem. If his magic had not been restricted, Darrio would have simply leaped from place to place and forced the wind currents to carry him like the other shades. Unfortunately, he was limited to running, walking, and, after a short while, crawling to reach his destination.

Eventually, Darrio came to a steep hillside that he would have to climb. To traverse around it would only make the journey longer, and the Elders would demand even greater swiftness of him. Darrio placed his hands on the rocks and climbed. "Damn Elders," he groaned. "Damn shackles." Darrio slipped and slid several feet down the steep hill's face but regained his footing soon afterward and latched on to the neck of a young plant. "And damn this." Darrio formed a step in the hill by way of manipulation magic and firmly placed his foot on top of it. He then proceeded to do this for the rest of the way up. The steps crumbled back into dirt and dust as he left them behind. When he reached the top, Darrio looked and saw the whole realm stretched out around him. Ambrosia sat like a figurine on the field, and Darrio imagined himself plucking the city from its foundation and tossing it into the air only to watch it crumble and fall into pieces on the way down. It was not out of the bounds of reason so far as magic was concerned, but on a practical level, it was a nearly impossible task even for him.

Darrio looked ahead. Esea was still nowhere to be seen, and this only made the journey appear longer. As Darrio sighed, he looked to his right and found a small camp situated at the base of the cliff. There were five large tents, a caravan, fire, and sounds of song, dance, and merriment. It would have been a small diversion to see what the occasion was for, and Darrio was hungry, so he slid down the hillside and made his way to the camp.

Around the fire were three dancers of modest attire, one male and two female. Surrounding them was a circle of other men and women who sang in unison with the dancer's movements. Darrio crept quietly into the camp and attempted to listen. The people sang, "Oli, oli, oli, oli. Greatest realm of truest blue. There is nothing in this world we would not conjure just for you. Oli, oli, oli, oli. Heart for all the wills of gods. The fires faint, the waters churn, the earth turns over, they are gone. Enemies consumed in all the wrath of all the finest stars. Salia, we sing your praises even when our bones are gone. All the stars converge upon this holy ground of magic's touch. Magic Realm of word and gods, our blessed land we love so much."

"Enjoying the song, boy?" A knife slipped under Darrio's throat, and the man attached had a sinister grin on his face. "You'd better start talking fast because I'm of the mind to cut you right here, right now. What do you say to that?"

Darrio made no sudden moves but displayed a complete lack of fear. Instead, he answered, "I say if you're going to successfully sneak up on a shade, you better not talk to him or you'll be dead before you finish the first sentence."

The smile and resolve quickly melted off of the knifeman's face. His skin paled, and he stammered, "A s-s-shade?" He then withdrew, put away his weapon, and fell to his knees. "I'm sorry. I didn't realize you were a military man. I didn't even mean anything by it, honest. I only do that to scare away bandits."

Darrio sighed. "Just tell me what's going on here?"

"Just dance and song, kind sir. We're a troupe of performers, you see, and my name is Thom, the Sword Dancer."

"Sword Dancer?"

"I've learned a great deal about the element of air, and I use it in my performances. I juggle and dance and entertain the people with different feats of air magic and blades. It's quite difficult to manipulate a sword with just the wind, you see, but with years of intense study and practice, I've come to—."

"Yeah, okay," Darrio interrupted. "You don't have to do that."

"I'm sorry, but if I may ask, are we under investigation? Is that why you're here?"

To tell Thom he was simply there out of curiosity and hunger would have made Darrio feel foolish, so he kept silent and tried to think of another excuse.

Thom, however, took it to mean something else entirely. "I knew it! That new guy's been nothing but trouble. Curse him! I told Herod we shouldn't have taken him in."

"What new guy?"

"His name's Shadow Song. We picked him up a few days ago. He said he was seeking passage and volunteered to join our troupe as a form of payment, but I told Herod, our ringleader, that the guy smelled like trouble. I've got a good nose, you see, dealing with the wind and all, and Herod lets him join anyway and tries to incorporate him into our show. But I tell you, that man is a living oddity. He never smiles or frowns or laughs or anything. There's just something not right about that. Why, I think it's just plain wrong. When I pinch you, you're supposed to feel something, damn it!"

"Calm down."

"Sorry. Really, the only thing he does well is sing and with a heart to boot though he loses it every other moment of the day."

"Can I meet him?"

"Sure! By all means!" and Thom led Darrio to the fire. The song and dance stopped as he stepped onto the scene, and all eyes were fixed on him. There was an older man seated on the bench dressed in violet, and he was crowned with a large and black top hat. Thom addressed him. "Ringmaster Herod. There's a military guy here to investigate that stranger we picked up."

"Is that so?" Herod questioned. "Then would you mind telling me what kind of charges Shadow Song is accused of?"

"There are no charges," Darrio replied, "but Ambrosia was attacked recently, and I just want to interview him to see if he knows anything. Thom said he only showed up a few days ago."

Herod mumbled to himself and then replied, "Well, if Shadow Song will submit to being questioned, so be it. Where are you, Shadow Song?"

There were many faces in the circle surrounding Darrio. Some were sad, some were upset, some were curious, and others were skeptical. There was a single face of calm, though, that stood out among the others. It was not worried or anxious nor was it excited. It was simply there, and this face belonged to the man Thom had mentioned. Shadow Song rose to his feet, and with a still tone devoid of all emotion, he spoke. "I am here, and I will submit myself to whatever it is you demand of me."

He was a tall man with long dark hair, but his eyes were empty. There was no light of life in them. He was also covered from head to toe in tattered brown garments.

"You should probably talk in one of the tents," Herod suggested.

"Indeed." Shadow Song led the way to the tent furthest away from the fire, and the song resumed behind them. When the two were alone, "What is it you wish to speak about?"

"Do you know anything about the attack on Ambrosia recently?"

"No."

Darrio nodded but decided to ask an even stranger question to catch Shadow Song off guard. "Well, do you know anything about dark magic?"

"Yes," but Shadow Song's tone did not change.

Darrio did not expect to receive such honesty, and for a moment, he did not know what else to say. "Then…you're one of the shadow casters I'm looking for, right?"

"Is that what you're calling us?"

"You're not even denying it."

"Why would I?"

Darrio was unsure how to answer. "Well, if you're not called shadow casters, what do you call yourselves?"

"A remnant."

"Of what, and how do you know dark magic?"

Shadow Song looked through the crack of the tent's entryway. There was a foot in view. "Thom is listening. I will not speak with him around."

"Idiot," Darrio huffed. When Darrio emerged, Thom fell back. "What do you think you're doing? This is a private investigation."

"I apologize!" Thom replied, kicking away. "I'll leave, I'll leave!"

After Thom shuffled off, Darrio reentered the tent. "Moron." But when Darrio faced Shadow Song again, he found his eyes were illuminated with a yellow light, and it was in fact not Shadow Song at all but merely a shadow. The back of the tent had been cut open, and the real figure was running. Darrio forgot about the shadow and stepped forward to pursue, but the figure took hold of Darrio and started to drain him. It then spoke with a terrifying voice that did not echo with a single tone but with a variety, and it was embedded with every negative emotion known to man. Darrio quickly drew his weapon and struck the figure in the arm. The shadow dissipated into a fine mist, and Darrio took a moment to recover his strength. The voice had shaken him, and he felt it reverberating throughout his being. It brought with it dread, sadness, lust, pride, hatred, envy, and every association of emotion. Despite all this, Darrio felt a particular feeling rise to become dominant. It was fear and not of the unknown but of Darrio. Darrio winced. "You bastard!"

Shadow Song sped away from the camp, but when he peered over his shoulder, he found Darrio trailing behind him in ardent pursuit.

"Get back here, you moron!" he shouted.

Shadow Song paid no heed to Darrio's command and leaped high into the air. He then forced the air against his body which carried him up and over the oncoming cliffs. In a single bound, the winds lifted him over the natural obstacle, and he disappeared over the other side. Darrio stopped and let his hands dangle beside him. The weight of his shackles had never been more apparent, and he cursed aloud in a fit of anger.

Thom approached swiftly from behind and fell to his knees from exhaustion. "That guy...I knew he was trouble, but what was that sound? I've never heard anything like it."

Darrio did not answer but instead turned and returned to the camp and spoke with Herod. There was no celebrating and no song when he arrived. Everyone had been shaken by the shadow's cry even more than Darrio had been. Darrio initially stood before Herod without saying a word, but after a moment he asked, "How long have you known about him?"

"He was...an unusual man to be sure, but I tell you the truth! We did not know about this attack you spoke of! He never even mentioned such a thing!"

"And how many users of dark magic have you come across in your travels?"

"Dark magic? None."

"Then why didn't you say anything?"

"He seemed an okay sort."

Darrio sighed.

"What is he?" Thom asked.

"My new target, and now I need your help to catch up with him."

"Herod? It's the least we can do."

Herod agreed and directed everyone in the camp to immediately gather their belongings and move. "Where are we going?"

"Esea."

"What? We just came from there," Thom complained.

"You did?"

"It's where we picked up the stranger in the first place."

"What was he doing there?"

"I don't know. Something about a cleansing, but he wouldn't say any more than that."

Darrio was unfamiliar with cleansing rituals, but the simple description was ominous to him. When all of the people gathered their belongings, the caravan moved briskly around the hills and towards the fields. There was yet a wooded crossing and a river to pass, but the caravan was much faster than traveling by foot, and the troupe fed him for his troubles.

As the night drew on, Darrio became tired and fell asleep, and his hands slipped out from underneath his cloak. Thom took notice of Darrio's irons and informed Herod. "Do you see that, Herod?"

"I see it."

"What does it mean?"

Herod stared long and hard at the shackles but said nothing. After a day's travel, the camp settled to rest on the edge of the wooded crossing. Darrio sat beside Herod and Thom while the people drank and talked around the fire. Herod spoke. "So tell me. From where do you hail?"

"Ambrosia," Darrio answered.

"Ambrosia? That's quite a city."

Darrio dismissed the sentiment and spoke in kind. "Yeah."

"You look fairly young for a shade, though."

"You know what they say about appearances, right?"

Herod nodded. "But I've never understood the desire to prolong one's appearance of youth for so long. Is this sort of thing encouraged in the service?"

"No. There's a prime stage they encourage everyone to reach, but it isn't mandatory."

"Then why haven't you advanced?"

Darrio looked at Herod and answered, "I don't feel like it."

"Are...are you joking, or are you serious?"

Darrio did not answer.

"I wonder if it's anything like my father," Thom said. "He remained in the same physical state as you for a long time before allowing his body to age. I think it was a whole cycle."

"Why?"

"I don't know. He said he was holding on to something, but I don't know what it was."

"It was probably a memory," Herod said. "People will do that sometimes, but I don't want you to misunderstand. I'm not against people extending their lives. Even I'm older than I can remember. I just don't see the point in prolonging youth, is all."

Darrio shrugged. "Could have something to do with how the body's set up to react."

"Or maybe it's a spiritual thing," Thom said, "so they feel like they're learning as much as they possibly can before moving on to the next stage. At least, it makes sense for the initial cycle. Speaking of which, what season are you in right now? I'm in the second."

"That's a personal question."

"Well, it's not the fourth, is it? Your eyes...I mean, you don't look that tired. Are you in the third? Couldn't be the first."

"What did I just say?"

"Bah," Herod interrupted. "All this talk of stages and seasons. It seems to me age was better reckoned in years. The ancients were brighter at least in that sense. How long would you say you've been on this earth? By that standard, I mean."

"You're not going to give up on my age, are you?"

Herod smiled. "If you will not answer that, then will you at least tell me what you are holding on to?"

"I'm not holding on to anything," Darrio sighed. "Let's just leave it at that."

The following morning, the people packed up and prepared to move through the woods. Herod cited the move as necessary due to the need to reach their destination quickly. The caravan was then carefully disassembled, and the people moved ahead. As they progressed forward, Darrio kept an eye out for strange sights and sounds. Someone then shouted, "Ringmaster! You better have a look at this!"

Darrio moved to the front with Herod and Thom. Before them was a line of shadows in the form of Shadow Song and a misty dome of darkness behind them. The mist rose several feet into the air with its peak reaching the top of the trees.

"What in the heavens is that?" Herod muttered.

"It's a barricade," Thom said. "They're barring us."

"All I wanted was something to eat," Darrio said under his breath. "Stay here."

Darrio drew his weapons and approached cautiously. The shadows were silent, their eyes were shut, and their wispy forms flowed in the wind like grass. As Darrio drew closer, the eyes of the shadows opened, but their mouths remained shut. Instead, the ones directly in front of Darrio parted and stepped to the side. Darrio was allowed entry, but despite this, he remained on his guard and stepped through the cold and murky wall.

The dark mist of the dome was even denser than the mist he traveled through in the western woods of Ambrosia. It was difficult to press ahead as well, and Darrio held his breath the entire way to prevent suffocation. He emerged on the end of a small clearing. Near the center was a single intense flame that hovered alone in the air. It was the only light source for the area. Shadow Song stood alone in the middle of the clearing. His tattered garments were gone. In their place was the garb typical of the shadow casters Darrio spotted in the woods, and his bore the pattern of fire.

As soon as Darrio came through, Shadow Song spoke. "Why do you persist in following me?"

Darrio was cold and wet, and the environment made him increasingly tired. "You didn't answer my question."

"Question?"

"How can you use dark magic?"

Shadow Song paused and answered, "It was an acquired art."

"Acquired?"

"Would you like to attain it?"

Darrio gave no thought to acquiring the dark element himself, but an echo of refusal rose from within him and emerged from his mouth. "No." The tone was not his own.

Shadow Song recoiled. "That voice….Who was that?"

Darrio, oblivious to what had just come out of him, spoke normally. "What are you talking about?"

Shadow Song observed the air around him for openings in the dome of darkness but found none. "I suppose there really is no limit to the places He can go."

"Who are you people?"

Shadow Song leveled his eyes with Darrio. "My name is Ashtoreth, and we are all that remain of the prior worlds."

"Worlds?" Darrio heard a commotion through the watered barrier. It was the sound of wailing and slaughter. When Darrio stepped forward to investigate, slates of stone rose from the ground and crept along the surface of the dark until they converged into a knot above.

"I will not let you disrupt the cleansing."

Darrio turned, the fire went out, and Ashtoreth's words echoed throughout the cold, darkened air. "Prepare yourself."

The haunted shrieks of the shadows outside and the howling cries of their victims intensified the stress within the darkened atmosphere. The air was cold and heavy with moisture, and the dark made Darrio uneasy. He was sure Ashtoreth would be alerted by the vibrations in the air to his every move, and his heart, beating hard as it was, was like a beacon amid the thick, soupy air.

Darrio attempted to calm himself and turn the situation to his advantage. He ignored the screams and listened for other sounds like steps in the dust, the rustling of cloth, and even the drawing of a sword. Darrio listened for anything that would alert him to Ashtoreth's direction and course of action, but there was nothing.

"Are you moving?" Darrio asked. It was a simple bait attempt to get Ashtoreth into talking, but there was no response. The elements of circumstance were well placed to strain his mind and undermine his will. There was a foreboding sense of doom around him, and Darrio had seen lesser men crumble under lighter conditions. Darrio, however, was an unwilling host and refused to give service to death.

With weapons still drawn, Darrio tapped the blades together and attempted to form a picture of his surroundings from the echo. He only attempted it once before and with marginal success. His life was in greater peril, however, and he hoped the results would extend beyond marginal. Darrio moved forward and felt for any changes in the space. His natural senses, heightened in the pitch blackness, took in every sensation of every moment. Had Ashtoreth attempted a close-quartered attack, Darrio would have been able to detect him and react. Long-ranged attacks were another matter.

Ashtoreth uttered a sudden command in an indecipherable tongue, but it echoed with omnipresence, and there was no way to tell where it came from. Darrio then heard a grinding of dust and stone to his left and felt a sharp object coming in his direction. He stepped back just as a thin string of earth scratched his cheek and pierced the ground under him. Darrio touched the earthen spear which had grown in diameter before settling with the girth of a sword handle. It had become a single extension from the ground to the dome's inner shell. Darrio knew then Ashtoreth had no intention of moving and was simply going to kill him using the environment itself. In that sense, Darrio believed he was close to Ashtoreth, but he could not be sure of how close. He took another step forward, another command was given, and the ground trembled beneath him. Darrio leaped back, and another set of spears, three of them in quick succession, formed and shot upward in the space he once occupied. They were measured and spaced apart to contain Darrio had he still been between them, and they grew in girth and twisted together to form a makeshift column of solid rock. Everything between them was crushed, and Darrio knew that Ashtoreth was close.

Darrio stepped further away and noticed the air grew lighter as he did so. He learned from this that Ashtoreth's range of detection, despite the air's heaviness, was limited. Darrio tested this by tapping the inner wall with his hand, and there were no results. He then picked up a stone and threw it in the direction of the pillar. A slab of rock descended and flattened it upon Ashtoreth's command. A plan was forming in Darrio's mind, but he strafed around the outer perimeter and continued his observations.

In the meantime, the outside commotion continued to deliver chilling screams and fevered cries. Darrio wondered if Thom was using his skill as a sword dancer to defend against Ashtoreth's shadows. If that were the case, he figured, the battle should have been over by then, but the shouts of withering souls continued on. If there was any hope of helping the people outside, Darrio knew he would either have to secure an escape or end the battle with Ashtoreth, and escape was the least practical option.

Darrio put away his weapons, grabbed a handful of heavy stones, and started to run around the perimeter. For each completed circuit, he inched in closer in a spiral path meant to lead right to Ashtoreth's position. Ashtoreth spoke, and the attacks against Darrio were few while he remained on the outer edges, but they increased in intensity as he moved in closer and closer. Great, earthen spears thrust themselves toward Darrio from every direction, but his speed and senses allowed him to evade all of the incoming attacks. Darrio would even pause every so often to throw one of the stones in Ashtoreth's perceived direction. The distraction succeeded in surprising Ashtoreth, and it confirmed the position he occupied. Despite this, Darrio continued his run to increase the strain on Ashtoreth's mind.

After a while of this, Darrio was left with a single stone, but Ashtoreth commanded, and the ground shifted once more. Three wide and concentric circles of rock rose to crush whoever was on top against the ceiling. The outer ring, the one Darrio was on, was the first to move. The second and third, delayed in time, were also on the rise. There would be no access to Ashtoreth if Darrio could not get inside before the rings reached their peak, so he leaped from the first ring to the second and jumped into the center of the third. Before he landed, however, Darrio threw his remaining rock ahead of him. Ashtoreth heard the sound and swung in its direction with a sword. Darrio then landed and tackled Ashtoreth from behind. With Darrio's foe to the ground, he drew his dagger and thrust it into the heart. The surroundings, stone and shadow alike, immediately crumbled, and streams of light flowed through the cracks of the shell, but Ashtoreth was still alive, and the destruction was not complete.

Ashtoreth struggled to his feet. Blood spilled from his mortal wound. He was unable to heal it because of the darkness, and he sputtered a curse as he stood. "All that you have gained will amount to nothing, and all that you love will be taken from you. So long as you live and so long as you pursue, your life will be defined by misery and woe."

Darrio was incensed by Ashtoreth's curse, and he rushed forward and pressed the wound with the blunt end of his first dagger. He then forced the second into Ashtoreth's bowel and pushed him back while in full sprint. Their bodies crashed through the weakened shell, and Ashtoreth rested next to a frozen tree. There, he lifted his eyes to the heavens but died without peace in absolute silence.

With his enemy beaten, Darrio looked around but saw no better of a sight than the sounds he heard before. The bodies of the troupe members were scattered along with the caravan's debris. Their corpses remained intact, but they were drained of all life. The horrified expressions of pain and anguish were ever present on their dry, dead faces. It was a cruel signpost for the manner in which they died. What shadows remained dissipated at Ashtoreth's death. There was but one survivor, Thom, who stood alone in the midst of the decay with two swords still suspended around him. When he saw Darrio, he collapsed, and his weapons fell lifelessly to the ground.

Darrio approached, silent and sullen, and he knelt before the sobbing Thom. He was unsure of what to say and did not think he would be of comfort. Nevertheless, Darrio asked, "Are you okay?"

Thom shook his head in disbelief. "Okay? Am I okay? Everyone I've ever cared about is dead! My friends, my family, everyone! And you're asking if I'm okay? No! No, I'm not okay!"

Darrio stepped away. There was nothing he could say, but as he stored his weapons underneath his cloak, Thom caught another glimpse of the irons around Darrio's wrists.

"Wait a minute," Thom said, and he stood. "Wait...just a minute."

"What?"

Thom looked Darrio over with a scrutinizing glare. "Young looking shade...dark skin...and I wondered why they would bind you, but…I think…I know who you are now. You're that damn Firestar everyone keeps talking about, aren't you?"

Darrio shook his head and stepped back. "No."

"You're lying."

"But I'm not—."

Thom rushed forward and shoved Darrio to the ground, but Darrio did not retaliate. Thom was not an enemy. "Get the hell out of here!"

"But I didn't mean to—."

"Get out!" Thom spat and kicked debris in Darrio's direction, and afterward, he stooped forward and grabbed a handful of stones. He launched each one hard and unceremoniously in slow succession. "Get the hell out of here! Go!"

Darrio stood to his feet and tried again to plead with Thom, but the next stone struck Darrio in the face.

As he recoiled in pain, Thom shouted all the more. "Get out of here you bastard! You…damned monster! Get the hell away from me!" Darrio then fled with a lessened will and heavy heart while Thom shouted behind him, "If I ever see you again, I'll kill you!"

Darrio emerged on the other side of the woods alone and crushed by Thom's scorn. He fell to his knees and pounded the dirt while uttering in repetition a curse on himself and his circumstances. Then, after a moment of bitter weeping, Darrio shouted his frustrations into the air. The resulting cry echoed across the horizon, frightening the surrounding birds and animals that happened to be nearby. The wind too appeared to wail with him and carried his anguish in a single whisper across the fields and into Seris' office.

Seris peered out of the window and scanned the southwestern horizon. The breeze unsettled him.

Abaddon, who was seated across from him, asked, "Is there something wrong?"

Seris remained in a distracted gaze, but after a moment, he sighed and returned his awareness to the room. "It is nothing."

"Then why have you asked about my family?"

"Curiosity. I know so little about you."

"And there is little that bears repeating."

"Tell me of your desires then."

"I do not concern myself with desires, save one. Everything else is meaningless."

"Then to what do you strive for?"

"That single passion and a degree of certainty."

"Certainty?"

"There are only a few certainties in this life, and death is among the elect. Everything that is uncertain brings chaos and confusion. Even life is an uncertain thing."

"Is such a thing enough for a nation?"

"Are you seeking my counsel?"

Seris nodded.

"Many things are required to meet the needs of a people, but such a list is inexhaustible. Save that a man become like God, there is no possibility to rule as such. By my experience, however, I have seen manipulation, distraction, direction, and control prove more practical in the maintenance of men."

"But what of benevolence and mercy?"

"The mere appearance of these is enough for most."

"You have not answered my question."

Abaddon replied. "Benevolence in parts and mercy in parts."

Seris was quiet, and his eyes roamed the room while his mind mulled over the spoken words.

"To what does the world gain by having a leader who cannot detach from a weakness of heart? It is better to be hated in part than to be loved by all, for all those who love become complacent and presumptuous. It is better to be feared than to be respected, for those who fear are the most susceptible to your control. The nations of men are not maintained on good will but on control, fear, margins of kindness, and a degree of certainty."

"Certainty," Seris mused, and after another moment of silence, he asked, "What became of your family, Abaddon?"

"They have returned to the dust."

"Did you have any siblings?"

"Two brothers. They endured many hardships with me."

"And what became of them?"

Abaddon peered through the window, and with a sense of empty calm and detachment, he said, "The three of us have gone our separate ways. As of now, they are no more."

CHAPTER 4
Derelict Dreams

DARRIO FOUND RESPITE at a nearby river where he allowed his body to collapse beside the shallow embankment. The surrounding rocks gave him a place to rest, and the water was cool, clear, and accommodating. A calm, soothing air rested over the area, and it was just enough to ease Darrio's burden. Just below the surface was a school of fish. They moved eagerly downstream to reach their spawning grounds, and beyond this river was another line of trees, a field of grass, and Darrio's destination, Esea.

Darrio cupped his hands and leaned forward to take from the river, but as he was drinking, he saw his face on the surface of the water. To others, the view would have been no more than a surface image, but Darrio saw reflections of his inner self in the face. He hated the view. He already displayed an ardent aversion to mirrors, and the sight of his face became an ever-growing source of discontent. Darrio spared little time in thinking about why he felt this way. Instead, he picked up a stone and hurled it at the surface of the river. The fish fled at the sudden disruption, but because of the river's ceaseless flow, the image remained. Darrio diverted his eyes and chose instead to think of something else, and he sighed to himself as he crossed over to the other side.

When Darrio entered the city, the first things he noticed were the merchant stands lining the narrow, cobblestone streets. Their wares ranged from food to weapons, and among them were a plethora of empowered goods that included consumables and garments. The owners of these stands boasted of the many effects and qualities of their items to sell their goods. One was said to make the wearer more beautiful while another advertised the rapid healing attributes of a line of scarves. Garments of elemental powers were also present, and a line of fire hats, developed specifically for cooks, were among the most popular items. The streets of the district were often crowded with buyers, and Darrio did his best to maneuver through them. In the meantime, the advertising call of merchants inundated his senses.

"Hey, there! Boy! Need more pants? You can really impress the ladies with these!"

"No, thanks," Darrio answered.

"Sir? Sir! In need of a weapon? I've got the finest blades on the market! I'll even give you a discount!"

"I'm fine."

"Oh, wow! Are you military? How would you like a cloak of invisibility? I swear, it's real!"

"What?" It was the only call that snagged Darrio's attention even if only for a brief moment, but when he further considered the offer, he shook his head and moved on. Invisibility, like teleportation, was a largely impossible feat. Even the Shades, which specialized in concealment, could not make themselves vanish in plain sight. It was believed the only true method of invisibility required manipulation of the light element. Everything else was an imitation born from the school of illusion.

After passing through the streets, Darrio entered the city square which was the central hub for all of Esea's activities. To the north was the temple district. There, the people of Esea would visit, worship, and burn incense at the variety of shrines, worship houses, and temples. There were a few market stands associated with such things in the area, but they were generally frowned upon and overlooked. This was true for all such areas in the Saline Realm. The east side, the one that Darrio entered through, was known as the market district. From there came the buzzing and murmur of commerce. It was the busiest section of the city by far given the hundreds of stands, sellers, and buyers. After this was the southern district which was mostly a collection of houses catering to the rich who built their fortunes in the market. Theirs was a life of luxury, expenditure, and, in Darrio's opinion, waste. For everyone else, there was the eastern district. It was neither poor nor extravagant. There were no homes for the poor.

The city square also housed its own number of services and stands. The most prominent of these were situated on the outer edge. Among them were an inn and two bars, and the inner portion of the square contained a grouping of premium stands trading in rare goods and oddities. Of the two bars, Darrio entered the Bottom's Up Tavern in hopes he would discover information related to his mission.

It was loud and boisterous inside due to the overwhelming chatter concerning the latest in local news. There was also a joyous melody in the air that the musicians played with enthusiasm. Darrio assumed it was either a celebratory song or a festival was soon to take place. In any case, he ignored it. He chose instead to listen to the chatter for any words that would stick out to him concerning his task.

Only a few people took notice of him, but his presence did little to dampen their spirits. Shades were rarely used in overtly public missions, so only a few people recognized who he was. Even then, those that did only glanced and turned away. This was just fine for Darrio. He did not like chatter or small talk and only wanted to do his duty and leave. Darrio hated bars, took no pleasure in revelry, and did not drink. These were well-known facts among the Shades and some of the many counted against him.

The bartender had been watching Darrio from the moment he stepped through the door. He recognized the uniform and thought the station would bring with it a healthy sum of money. The minutes Darrio stood without buying though felt like hours to the bartender, and he became impatient and worried about Darrio's presence deterring future customers. After a while of waiting, he called out to Darrio and said, "So! You just going to stand there all day, or do you fancy a drink? I've got some good stock back here if you're interested. It'd do wonders to wipe that frown off your face."

"I'm not thirsty," Darrio replied.

"Well, you sure didn't come in here for nothing. What can I do you for?"

Darrio was unable to pick up anything among the chatter, so he sighed and made his way to the counter. "I'm trying to find out about the disappearances in this city. Do you know anything about that?"

"What? Say again? I can't hear you in all this ruckus."

Darrio leaned forward and spoke louder. "I said I'm here on investigation. Do you know anything about the missing people?"

"I still can't hear you, boy. Maybe you should go and look someplace else."

Darrio felt the bartender was being evasive, but instead of leaving, he continued to press. "Are you telling me you don't know anything about the missing people? You haven't seen or heard anything?"

"If you can't talk any louder then you're going to have to ask someone else."

"Stop acting like you're deaf. Some of the missing were women and children. If you know something, tell me."

"I can't help you, boy. Your voice is just too damn soft."

By this time, Darrio was incensed and frustrated at the bartender's dodging. It was unclear to him whether or not he was an accessory or simply afraid of reprisals. Either way, in Darrio's mind, it did not justify the impediment of his mission. Darrio drew one of his blades and thrust it deep into the table. The festivities then stopped, and all eyes rested on him. "I'm only going to say this one more time. After that, I'm done being nice. What do you know about the missing people? Don't make me ask this again."

"Oh. Here for the lost, eh? Should have said so. Well, come closer. I can only say this once."

Darrio leaned forward and listened.

"Quite frankly, I don't give a damn where they went."

Darrio pulled back. "Excuse me?"

"And you won't find many around here who do."

"Then what the hell did you waste my time for?"

"I don't need to serve your kind around here. You people don't even run this city. If you want answers, go to the temple district. Otherwise, quit bothering us."

Darrio pulled his weapon out of the table but forced it deeper in a position closer to the bartender's hand. "You don't seem to understand what country you live in. I don't give a damn who you're connected to around here, and I don't give a shit about their interests. If I go and don't find anything at the temple district, I'm coming back here, dragging your ass outside, and I will force something out of your mouth. Do you understand me?"

The bartender looked down at his hand. Darrio's blade was less than an inch away. "Yeah, sure," he answered.

Darrio then removed his weapon from the table, returned it to its sheath, and left in silence.

The bartender, after overcoming his unease, roused the crowd into resuming their activities. Afterward, he motioned for one of his stewards to approach him. "Go and tell Valeria what happened. I've got a bad feeling about this guy."

The temple district was largely silent, but the chanting of its practitioners and laymen was ever-present. Darrio passed over several shrines, and each one was dedicated to a particular entity or deity. One was associated with rain, another with hills, one with conflict, and another with valleys. At the forefront of the religious activities was a temple devoted to the god attributed with the creation and knowledge of magic, and he was referred to as Magnus, the god of control. "The highest star," preached the Low Priest of the temple. "The one from which all power is born. Out of him came the knowledge to set us all free. Free from the bondage and whims of circumstance. Free to perfect and master ourselves and our environment. The forms of magic we see today are but pale comparisons to their former glory. Truly, there will come a day when this glory will be restored, and with it, there will come a cleansing flood of power and fire."

Among the layman was a single young man wearing a white shirt, a red collar, and a single white glove on his left hand. His hair was also white though he appeared only a few years older than Darrio. His eyes were calm as he studied the priest, and there was a peaceful air around him. To Darrio, the young man almost seemed to glow. After listening to the message, he turned to Darrio and asked, "Do you believe in what that man was talking about just now?"

"Who? Me?"

"Yes."

"I don't know him," Darrio said.

"Neither do I. Can I help you with something? I couldn't help but notice. You look as if you're lost."

"I'm looking for the people who've gone missing around here."

"Then you should probably make your way to the shrine of light. It's just down the road. See?"

Darrio peered ahead to find an open shrine located in a distant corner. It had a simple altar fixed with a cross on the front, but it was housed in a crudely constructed room of white stones. The front of the shrine was an open archway that led out to a small enclosure of dying grass with two rows of old, donated pews. There were two men still at the site who were dressed in white. "I see it," Darrio replied, but when he returned to face the man and thank him for the direction, all he found was an empty space. Darrio felt he would have detected any sudden movements from the young man, but he found no signs of hurry, and no one else in the area noticed the sudden change. The man was simply there one moment and gone the next.

Darrio left the temple of Magnus confused but continued on to the shrine of light. On closer inspection, it appeared to be a largely abandoned corner of the city. Among the lesser shrines, which dotted the area, were visible signs of neglect such as cracks and cobwebs. Offerings from days gone by still sat in the open sun with no one around to remove them. The lesser shrines were all deserted.

In the midst of this, the two men at the shrine of light were kneeling in front of the altar to mourn their unfortunate situation. "Dear God, why have you forsaken this place? Why have you let this happen? They mock your name and hedge us in. Your enemies surround us on every corner. Will you not act? Will you not do something? Please, Lord, tell us what is happening."

"Yes, Lord, something. Please," the other finished.

Darrio recognized them as foreigners from the Aural Realm due to their familiar accents, and his initial reaction was one of contempt. Nevertheless, he was hesitant to interrupt. It was not at all unusual for wandering preachers of faith to travel from other nations to spread word of their beliefs to others, but most ceased all interaction with the Saline Realm due to the war. Missionaries, as they were called in the Aural Realm, however, were well known for their persistence and stubbornness, but Darrio held no grudge against such people. When it appeared as if they were done, Darrio spoke. "Excuse me."

The men turned and faced Darrio with frightened expressions and downcast eyes. "Yes? How can we help you?"

"I'm conducting an investigation in the city and just wanted to ask a few questions."

"What is this about?"

"There's been reports of people missing. Some of them were

women and children, and I was told I could find what I'm looking for by coming here."

The men were fearful and suspicious of Darrio, and one of them asked, "But what are they to you that you were sent to find them?"

Darrio was in no mood for another round of deflections due to his altercation with the bartender, and he already held an underlying grievance against them because of where they came from. "It's my job, alright?" he snapped. "Are you going to help me or not?"

The two men exchanged glances before nodding in mutual agreement. "Okay. We will help you."

"Good. Now start by telling me what you know."

"It's just as you said," the first one said, "but the people were targeted as members of our gathering. Others have been taken too, but most of them visited here at one point or another."

"We're a simple community," continued the second. "We don't ask for much, only to be left alone and unhindered in our faith."

"But some of the other priests and businesses have come against us and pushed our shrine to the city's border wall."

"Which limits our exposure. Not many people wander this far back, you see."

"So our gathering has been getting smaller and smaller."

"And this is on top of the kidnappings."

"One at a time," Darrio groaned. "You're giving me a headache.

"We apologize," they answered simultaneously.

"Why do you think your group is being targeted?"

"Because they hate us!" shouted the second.

"Peace, my brother," said the first, and when he was assured the other was calm, he continued. "It is because they hate us. We have professed and encouraged belief in one god, but the faith is regarded as extreme here. Some call us heretics."

"Can you at least tell me where they were taken?"

"The fields northwest of the city…I think. I caught one of the kidnappers in the act, and he flew off in that direction."

"Why didn't you ask for help?"

"We did, but no one cared. No one helped us"

"Besides," the second added, "we have no defense against your magic arts, and if we should die, there will be no one to continue the teachings here."

Darrio first viewed them as cowards who were using their responsibilities as an excuse to cover their fear but felt a concession had to be made in this case due to the circumstances. The initial thought made him feel guilty. "Alright," he replied. "I'll look into it."

"You will?"

Darrio nodded. "If I find anything, I'll tell you, but stay here until I get back." Darrio then turned to leave but was only halfway down the road when he turned back and shouted a parting message to the men of light. "But for God's sake, stop being so damn fearful! You're missionaries, and it's annoying!"

The words struck a chord with the two men, and the sentiment, though gentler in tone, echoed in the spirit of their souls. They shivered and faced the shrine. "Was that…His answer to us?"

"It would seem so."

"Who was he? He felt…familiar somehow."

"Perhaps he is someone we should know. We will find out in time. In any case, we still have work to do. Come. Let us get back to the task at hand."

Darrio left Esea and traveled into the western fields to search for the people, but after a long and fruitless expedition, the day ended and the night came. Exhausted and hungry, Darrio leaned upon a single tree and readied himself to return for a time at an inn.

"Hey. Genius." On the other side was a young man with the same features as the one Darrio spoke to at the temple of Magnus, but his clothes were black, as was his hair, and he wore a single black glove on his right hand. His arms were crossed.

"Where did you come from?" Darrio asked.

"Not important."

"Are you an assassin? Did the Elders send you?"

"You wish." He then uncrossed his arms and pointed north. "Over there. That's what you're looking for, isn't it?"

Darrio looked ahead. There was a thin stream of smoke in the distance. It was coming from a camp. It had not been visible before.

"You'd better hurry."

When Darrio looked back, he found the supplier of his help was gone, and this, again, confused him. "What the hell," he mumbled, but a woman's scream recaptured his attention, and Darrio ran in haste towards the site.

The body of a young woman fell lifelessly to the ground. Around her were three standing shadow casters bearing a water pattern and five subjects who were bound and gagged. Among them was a single child, a girl. "Still failure," said the shadow caster closest to her.

"Come on, Bacchus. We're exposed now, and we only have five of them left."

"I'm aware of that," he snapped. "Someone's interfering with us. I'm sure of it."

"In any case, we'll have no choice but to look elsewhere at this rate. Our pool of potential subjects has dwindled, and the master will be upset with us if we report to him empty-handed. Again."

"Be still, Varis. There are still other methods we've yet to employ." The third of them suddenly faced south. "What is it?"

"Someone's coming."

"Hold him."

Darrio was fast approaching the camp and drew his weapons along the way. The third shadow caster met him and prepared to bar his progress, but Darrio showed no signs of stopping. The caster then manipulated the ground beneath Darrio's feet to become soft and muddy, slowing his progress. Darrio threw his right blade which flew towards his target in a circular motion. The caster ducked the attack, but with his attention momentarily diverted, Darrio gathered what little power was available and recalled the dagger with a manipulated form of thunder magic. The weapon jerked back towards the unaware caster and pierced his back. Darrio then moved towards the stunned enemy who fell to his knees and decapitated him with a single stroke.

Varis watched the skirmish from a distance, but after Darrio drew his weapon from the back of the victim, Varis became consumed with fear. "He's still coming, Bacchus."

"What?"

"We won't be able to move all of the subjects in time."

"Damn it all." Bacchus surveyed the subjects. "We'll have to start over. Kill them."

Varis drew his sword and approached the first subject who was oblivious to the surroundings and locked in apparent delusion. "A shame," and Varis struck.

Darrio moved his legs as fast as he could but knew his chances of reaching the camp in time were slim at best. He looked ahead to find Varis cutting down the kidnapped subjects. Three of them had fallen, and the fourth was the next to die. The last of the five, the little girl, sat fearful and quiet as Varis stood over her. This sight of senseless murder, particularly of innocents, and Darrio's standing desire to protect them activated something within him. The shackles that bound him were insufficient in suppressing his burgeoning will, and Darrio, triggered by his frustration, slipped into his state limit.

The sudden shift in winds alerted Varis that a change had occurred, and he stayed his hand out of dread. Bacchus, too, felt the shift and turned to see what occurred, but nothing prepared him for what he was soon to witness.

Darrio stormed towards the camp with a trail of dust and pebbles that were caught up in the aura of his power. His eyes had turned red, the shackles on his wrists trembled, and the inscriptions glowed intensely. His face was contorted with expressions of hatred, and when Varis turned, the sight filled him with both awe and terror.

Bacchus called out to him. "Run, you fool!"

Darrio heard, and in his next step, he summoned a slab of rock to propel him toward the camp and his new target. Varis turned his back to escape, but Darrio landed nearby, and the momentum carried him sliding towards Varis who he slashed across the back. Varis spun around, agonized by the cut, but Darrio followed up with a quick series of slashes to the knees, stomach, and chest. After this, he assaulted Varis with multiple thrusts, but Varis was suspended in the field of Darrio's aura and unable to defend himself. Darrio finished his flurry with a blow to the face using the end of his right weapon, and after this, he set his weapons beside him and expelled the blood from the surface of his blades to the earth.

Varis fell lifelessly to the ground bleeding and mangled while Bacchus stood in wide-eyed horror. "Varis!"

Darrio heard the cry of Bacchus and turned to his new target while Bacchus took one last glimpse at Varis' body and turned to flee. Darrio then took the sword of Varis and threw it towards Bacchus, but with the same form of magic he used prior to recall his own blade, he caused the spinning weapon to accelerate mid-flight. The blade overtook Bacchus completely severing his right arm, and as he cried aloud in pain, Darrio moved forward to end him. He stopped, however, when the surviving girl screamed, and her cry caused him to fall from his state limit. He was temporarily dazed and overcome with an intense headache. Bacchus, in the meantime, took the opportunity to pick himself up, and he fled into the night leaving his right arm behind.

The girl continued to shout and shuffle across the ground as if being chased by an unseen assailant, but when Darrio regained his senses, he tended to the girl. "Stay still," he said. "I'm going to cut you free."

"No!" she protested. "Please don't eat me! Don't eat me!"

"Nobody's going to eat you. Be still." Darrio cut the bonds from the girl's wrist, but she slapped him and immediately tried to fight him off. "Stop that! Be still, damn it!" Darrio then took a moment to remove the girl's blindfold, but her eyes were shut. "I'm not your enemy, alright? Look at me."

But the girl's eyes remained shut.

"Look at me!"

The girl's body remained rigid, but she slowly opened her eyes to Darrio. They were clouded over and white. She was blind. "Please don't eat me," she pleaded, and tears streamed down her face. "I don't want to die. Please don't eat me." The girl then curled up into a fearful ball, closed her eyes, and would say no more.

Darrio picked her up and carried her back to Esea. He left the others behind.

At the shrine of light, the two men examined her. "What's wrong with her?"

"It's a conscious nightmare, an illusionary technique."

"Can't you do something about it?"

Darrio shook his head. "I'm not an illusionist, but as long as no one reinforces it, the effect should wear off on its own." The girl whimpered quietly. "Just talk to her. Let her know it isn't real."

"What happened to the others?"

"I couldn't make it in time."

Darrio turned to leave, but the second of the two men called out to him. "I want to thank you for what you've done. I know you tried, and you didn't have to—."

"Don't," Darrio interrupted. "Just...don't."

The man silenced.

"I'll need to speak with her when she's well."

"I understand. We'll be expecting you then."

Darrio left the shrine of light and wandered into the streets. People bumped into him as they brushed by on their daily errands, and the marketplace continued with the buzz and chatter of commerce. The whole matter made Darrio sick to his stomach, and he turned his attentions inward to shield himself. He then attempted to leave to release his frustrations and escape the confining atmosphere, but there were three men waiting for him by Esea's exit gate dressed in long, yellow robes. As Darrio approached, they drew near, and the tallest of them addressed Darrio. "Are you the one who was asking questions this morning?"

"Get out of my way," Darrio replied in a detached tone. "I'm not in the mood." Darrio tried to walk around them, but the three barred his every attempt and movement. "Do you want me to fix that walking problem of yours?"

"Somebody wants to speak with you."

"I don't care about that. Move."

The leading man stepped forward but stopped when Darrio placed a hand on the handle of his weapon.

"I meant away from me."

The man then stepped back, looked ahead, and nodded to a fourth man who snuck behind Darrio and promptly knocked him out.

Darrio woke again in a dimly lit cellar surrounded by three men. Among them was a woman of moderate age in an elegant robe and a sash over both of her shoulders. "How's our boy now? Is he awake?" Darrio groaned which reassured the woman of his consciousness. "Good. I hope my disciples weren't too rough with you. I have questions for you, Firestar."

"What the hell is this? Who are you?"

"My name is Valeria, High Priestess in the Order of Magnus and overseer of his temple here."

"Magnus," Darrio repeated. He was still suffering from the pain of his blow, and his mind was clouded.

"How hard did you hit him?" Valeria asked the tall man.

"Sorry, Mistress."

"Yes, Magnus," she said returning to Darrio. "God of all magic, master of control, purveyor of the great mysteries. Surely you of all people must have frequented his temple in Ambrosia."

Darrio shook his head. "Once. Not what I was looking for."

Valeria was flustered by the response and sputtered in her speech. "Wha-what do you mean you've only visited once? You mean to tell me you don't follow in the service of Magnus?"

Darrio shook his head.

"Then who, of all the gods, could you possibly adhere to?"

"First of all," Darrio replied, "there's only one I even care enough to recognize, and second, even if I knew His name, I wouldn't tell you. It's personal."

Valeria's mouth fell open, and for a moment, she was speechless. "I don't believe this," she uttered as she carefully took a seat. "The Firestar's...a heretic? This doesn't make any sense."

"What the hell did you bring me here for?"

"Aside from your snooping, the High Elders called in a favor. Asked me to keep an eye on you while you conduct your affairs in my city. Can't say I respect them much. Crotchety old men who think very little of worship or the old ways. Politicians, all of them."

"So what does that make you?"

"Me? I'm a lot of things, Firestar, and primarily a believer in every sense of the word. I feel magic was given to us for a higher purpose, far beyond the conventions of convenience, military, and…commerce. When Magnus bestowed this gift upon us, he meant it for something more. In fact, it's my personal belief that the degraded use of such a wondrous gift should be treated as heresy, but such is not doctrine, so I have little authority to enforce it. But can you imagine what magic's inception must have been like? It must surely have been a time when magic flourished as an art beyond all arts. Glorious," she said with longing. "Simply glorious," and she sighed. "It's tragic to think of all the knowledge that was lost in the Great Catastrophe."

"What catastrophe?"

"You mean you don't know? Seriously, Firestar. Have you been taught nothing?"

"Are you going to answer me or not?"

Valeria groaned. "Now you listen. In the beginning, soon after the world was made, Magnus descended to the earth and bestowed upon us mortals the knowledge of magic, control, and self-governance. It was his words and his teachings, in fact, that propelled the first world into an era of unprecedented prosperity."

"The first world," Darrio uttered, and he recalled a statement made by Ashtoreth.

"The world as it was when magic first came to us. Soon after, there was war on the earth, and these wars, fought with magic powers far beyond us now, changed the whole face of creation. We know this transition as the Great Cleansing. That event ended the first world. The second world saw magic spread even further throughout the earth, although, sadly, a great deal of that knowledge has been lost."

"Then what?"

"Then came another transition known as the Great Catastrophe, and the knowledge of magic was nearly extinguished. A wall of fire rushed out over the whole earth and devoured all traces of magic's potential. Some say it was the work of two particularly mischievous demons, but I believe it was an orchestrated attempt by one of the other gods to eliminate the gift Magnus had so graciously given us."

"So the age we're in counts as the third world."

Valeria nodded. "And we, the disciples of Magnus, wait for the day when magic returns to its former glory when the word was spoken and pure and power came out of it like a roaring river. It will come with a cleansing fire, and the power of truth will flourish like the wildflowers of the field. It will be like a paradise, and the world will finally be as one," she sighed. "But it's neither known when such a time as that will come nor the conditions from which it may come."

"So what does all this have to do with you kidnapping me?"

"Were my boys too rough on you? I thought one such as yourself would have been used to such treatment."

"Maybe from enemy soldiers, criminals, and people who hate me, but I never thought I'd be taken by a cult."

"Cult?" she repeated with disgust. "Did you just call us a cult?"

"What do you expect me to say? You kidnapped me, I don't like you, and I don't care about all this Magnus stuff."

"You ignorant, uninformed fool! Wrath of Magnus or not, you're a fiend, and let's get one thing straight here. We are not a cult. We are a well-founded, formally recognized, and organized religion with temples located throughout the Saline Realm. And to be honest, I expected more from you, Firestar. I heard you could be curt and hard-hearted, but I never imagined you would be so disrespectful."

"It's hard to respect someone who snatches you from the street and doesn't give a straight answer to any of your damn questions."

"Details. And for one so young, even if only by appearance, you should take better care to mind your tongue. Such language is unbecoming of your image."

"Details," Darrio mocked. "For one so old, I would've expected better manners."

"Why you wretched little bastard. Cut him loose!" The men did as ordered, and Darrio was freed, but Valeria continued. "I warn you, Firestar. Nothing happens in this city without my knowing about it, especially as it pertains to matters in the temple district."

"So what? Is that why you kidnapped me? Because you're stupid if you think I scare that easily."

"No. I did it because I knew that I could and to keep you aware. Of me, primarily."

"I'll keep that in mind," Darrio sneered, but after a moment of silence, he impatiently asked, "Can I leave now?"

"Of course you can. Are you mocking me again?"

"No, I'm minding my manners. You're supposed to do that, especially with your elders."

"Get out of here, Firestar! Go! Get out!" As soon as Darrio made his exit, Valeria vented her frustration. "Impetuous, undermining creature! I'm younger than he is! How dare he?"

"What should we do, Mistress?" asked a disciple.

"Watch him, and as soon as that girl wakes up, tell me."

"Yes, Mistress."

Darrio emerged from the temple of Magnus, but the sun had already set, so he decided to rest for the night at one of Esea's inns. While there, he recounted the events of the day and tried to connect what he learned from Valeria with the words spoken by Ashtoreth. The implications made little sense to him.

Ashtoreth had spoken of prior worlds and how he and the Shadow Casters were all that remained of them. It was not beyond the realm of reason to believe such a thing. The restorative schools of magic would have been more than enough to prolong their lives for that long. The reason for such a thing was still elusive as was their purpose which was of primary importance. Furthermore, for a people who stayed hidden for so long, Darrio could not understand why they would choose to reveal themselves then though it did not appear as if it were altogether voluntary. He remembered the dispute between the two factions present at the meeting in the woods, those bearing the water pattern and those bearing the fire pattern. The Water Bearers, as Darrio decided to identify them, appeared to be more overt in their dealings while less was known about the Fire Bearers. There was also nothing known about the master they mentioned. He then remembered Turil's orders to capture and not engage the Shadow Casters. Since the start of the mission, he had killed three of them and severed the arm of a fourth who then escaped. Thus far, it was not going well.

The following morning, Darrio revisited the temple of light to see how the girl was doing, and the two men brought her out to him. "She's a little shaken but altogether fine. Are you sure this is a good time, though?"

"What's her name?"

"Saria."

Darrio knelt down. "Saria? I need to know who those men were. Do you know what they were after?"

"Them?" she asked looking back at the disciples of light. "Nothing. They were nice to me. They're always nice to me."

"Not them. The shadow men. The people who took you. Do you know what they were after?"

Saria shook her head in confusion.

"Do you even know what I'm talking about?"

She once again shook her head.

Darrio looked towards the men of light. "She doesn't remember?"

"No."

"Remember what?" Saria asked.

"You were kidnapped," Darrio replied. "There were three men in black clothes, and I'm trying to find out who they are."

The girl took a moment to think, and a fearful expression came over her face. "Where's my sister?"

"Who?"

"She was with me when I went to sleep. Is she okay?"

Darrio recalled seeing a young woman who was among the dead at the camp. He was unsure of how to respond. "I don't think you want to know." Saria reached out her hands and traced the features on Darrio's face. He immediately responded with a twitch and recoiled from her touch, but when she pressed forward, Darrio allowed the tiny fingers to press against his cheek and forehead. Her initial response was one of confusion and wonderment, but this soon changed into pity and grief. When it appeared as if she discovered what she was looking for, she pulled away. Tears fell from her eyes.

Darrio stepped back and felt a profound sense of pity for the girl. He tried to think of something that was both calm and reassuring, but nothing came to him. "I have to go," he said. "There's still one of them out there."

"You're going after him?" asked one of the men.

Darrio nodded. "And when I find him, I'll…," but Darrio paused and remembered Saria's presence. "When I find him…I'll make him talk," and with that, Darrio left.

In the meantime, Turil was discussing an arrangement with Seris on the outskirts of Ambrosia for a series of secret incursions into the Outer Realms. "No one could know about this, of course," Turil said. "The Elders would surely object."

"You're speaking to a captain of shades, Turil. I'm well aware of my position."

"I did not ask you to do this because of position."

"Then why did you ask me?"

"Because I still consider you to be an ally and a friend. I know you have no great regard for the class and rank of others, Seris. I know you too well, at least in this regard."

"And yet I serve."

"You serve the realm."

The two fell into silence, but Seris decided to probe once again. "Why are you doing this, Turil? This is unexpected, even for you."

Turil was silent, and he carefully mulled over what he wanted to say. "The Elders, they are…obsessed with the boy."

"Darrio?"

"He is all they ask about. There are still a great number of serious threats to the realm, but they worry so much over the boy's nature that they cannot see the danger such fear poses. I believe if they are pushed once more, their mania concerning the Firestar will be total."

"And what kind of dangers are you talking about? What do you perceive, Turil?"

"There is a force behind the Shadow Casters' actions, something I believe is not merely isolated to this realm. I'm afraid I have no proof for this statement, but I can feel it in my bones, and the Elders will not spare much beyond necessity due to their fear over what the Firestar may do."

"I have said countless times that Darrio is not a threat."

"And countless times have they discarded your claim. Their minds are clouded, Seris. They cannot see, and in the meantime, Salia's enemies draw closer. I have even read reports of factions from the Outer Realms who are trying to surpass our arts of magic. We already have knowledge of the alchemists in the Silent Realm, but there are even greater enemies who would gladly lease such knowledge to others, others who would offer no hesitation in using it to harm us."

"I have not heard nor read of such reports."

"They are privy only to generals, Seris. If you had heard, I would be greatly concerned."

"And these factions you speak of. They are outside of this realm?"

"Outside and waiting though some of them have already reached across our borders. You remember the charges against Lon."

"I remember, but if what you say is true, then they are scattered and disorganized. Whatever threat they pose is minimal."

"Not as long as the Elder's eyes remain fixed, and even if I am unable to change their minds, I will be damned if I do not do all that I can to protect everything we've lived and fought for."

"Then on this point, we are agreed."

"Then you will join me?"

Seris locked eyes with Turil and confirmed with a nod. "But first, you must answer a question of mine."

"What is it?"

"What do you know concerning Arthis and his attack on Darrio?"

Turil sighed. "I did not send the order. It was given directly to him by one of the Elders."

"Which one?"

"Elder Tiberius though Elder Judas also played a role."

"And how do you know this?"

"They told me of the action themselves but only after the Firestar's trial. They hoped I would not make a public spectacle of the case. They asked me to understand and to trust them."

"But you do not."

"Like you, I have come to trust in the potential of Salia. Not so much the men who govern it."

"I see," Seris replied, and he continued in silent thought.

"You are...still with me, are you not?"

Seris returned his eyes to Turil. "To the end, my friend."

"To the end," Turil repeated, and he smiled. "I assure you, Seris. We will do good things for this realm, and in time, virtue will rise once again."

"Yes, Turil, virtue. And then order, peace, and a degree of

certainty." Turil nodded in agreement though he was unaware of what Seris meant. Nonetheless, Turil decided to treat Seris to a drink to celebrate, and the two returned to the city.

Back in the fields northwest of Esea, Darrio arrived at the campsite where he discovered the severed arm of Bacchus laying in the grass several feet away. He also turned to where the corpses were and took a brief moment to bury them for Saria's sake. Darrio then tracked a trail of blood that led him in a northwestern direction. The trail went cold after an hour, but Darrio continued down the general path knowing his prey would have sought additional medical attention. Restoration magic would have been enough to seal the wound provided the enemy had the stillness of mind to do so, but additional treatment would be necessary to avoid the more long-term complications.

Eventually, Darrio came upon a small, humble village with an inn and a modest temple. As he entered, a boy spotted him and cried out, "Another one! Another one!" The men of the village immediately took up arms and surrounded Darrio with pitchforks and various other tools with threatening gestures and glares.

Darrio remained still. "What are you doing?"

"Put your weapons down," said a man of relatively good standing. "Can't you see he's military?" He approached from behind the crowd and was dressed in a white robe that was tied off at the waist. His button-down top contained a stiff collar that completely encircled his neck, and there was a red emblem on the front that signified his position as a Saline doctor.

Darrio judged him to be a respectable man who held sizable influence over the village's residents, but he also knew appearances to be deceiving.

"I'm sorry," the doctor apologized. "After what happened with our last guest, the people here have been a bit uppity lately."

"Uppity," Darrio repeated, and he shrugged off the defenders as they backed down and went back to their labor. "Right."

"I presume you're here about the man who came by recently."

"Was he wearing a black robe?"

"With a strange set of tear-shaped insignias, yes."

"What can you tell me about him?"

"Can we talk about this in my office?"

Darrio nodded and followed the doctor. The village itself was much smaller than Silesia and was composed of only a handful of houses. Aside from the buildings already mentioned, there was little else concerning an overt sense of commerce or industry. It was a simple place where people traded and helped each other for the common good. It reminded Darrio of home, albeit, a much smaller version.

When he entered the doctor's home, a house furnished with books and other intellectual material, the doctor asked Darrio to have a seat at the center table. He then asked, "Drink?"

"What?"

"Would you like a drink?"

"Water's fine," and Darrio sat.

The doctor graciously obliged and took a seat across from Darrio. "So, that man. Strange fellow. When he stumbled into town and someone alerted me to his condition, I saw a person who was missing an arm and a good portion of his will."

"And how's that?"

"He said his brother had been killed recently in an experiment they were conducting."

"Experiment?"

The doctor nodded. "He claimed to be a student of creation. A scientist, he said, but I've never heard of the title before."

"Neither have I. Any idea what he meant?"

"No, but he said it with a great deal of pride. You would have thought he were an artisan by the way he spoke."

"So what happened to him?"

"I patched him up. He had only enough presence of mind to seal the wound though not to treat it. I healed his arm well enough and paid for his stay at the inn. I initially felt sorry for the fellow."

"But something happened."

"The following morning he started asking people what they knew about the light and no one could tell what he was talking about. He then decided to sport a demonstration by enveloping the village in a veil of darkness. Everyone grew ill, but fortunately, there were no serious complications. There were stomach aches, isolated fits of madness, and curious pangs of guilt, but all of these symptoms were mild at best. He then noted us all as useless and fled west."

"How long ago was this?"

"Yesterday." Darrio stood. "Leaving so soon?"

"I've got to catch up with him."

"I was hoping you could tell me what he did first."

"I'll tell you later," Darrio replied, and he left. He took no time to make any more observations and left the village behind in a full westward sprint. However, his travel would inevitably lead him into the Steaming Grove, a thin but dark stretch of trees that lined Salia's western border with the Burning Realm. As Darrio approached, he spotted a dark-robed figure and drew his weapons. "Son of a bitch!"

Bacchus, still weary from his altercations, spun around upon hearing Darrio's exclamation and cursed. He then sped up his retreat and entered the grove.

Darrio's initial steps into the grove were hard and fast, but he quickly slowed himself to a careful walk. The borders had been contentious areas during the war and were often set with traps. The ones in the grove, however, were a particularly interconnected combination of snares from the Burning, Saline, and Hollow realms. One careless step had left a man blind, impaled, dismembered, and incinerated, but there were even more terrifying effects to be wary of.

Bacchus also was aware of the grove's condition, and he stepped carefully through the brush while examining every leaf and shape in sight. He had an immeasurable sum of knowledge concerning scripted traps and knew enough about the other realms' methods to know what to look for. He was thus capable of clearly identifying what areas had not been disturbed, what markings constituted real scripts of substantial harm, and what scripts were fake ones meant to direct the ignorant into a trap.

Darrio, however, was not as knowledgeable about such things. Though he tried his best to remain cautious, his foot was caught in a hunter's snare, and his body was lifted high into the air by a length of rope attached to his foot. Darrio cursed his luck in aggravation, but this utterance triggered a pair of sound-activated scripts, part of a separate but overlapping trap, which were scribbled onto two sheets of paper. These papers were wrapped separately on a stretch of rope that held back two suspended stumps of wood that were ready to swing in and crush whatever was between them. Once activated, the scripts caused the papers to burn away and eat through the ropes, and the wooden stumps swung in to converge on Darrio's head. "Shit!" Darrio immediately curled up as the two wooden ends met, and with a single slice, he cut himself down and planted his feet on top of the suspended logs. He figured it would be safer to track Bacchus from the heights than on the ground. There were simply too many ways to die on the surface.

Darrio spotted Bacchus several feet ahead of him. He was looking back at the commotion, and upon seeing Darrio bearing down on him in the safety of the canopy, Bacchus groaned and quickened his pace. Darrio leaped where he could to keep up, but when he came to the end of the grove, he stopped. Stretched out before him were the blistering, arid lands of the Burning Realm. The sky was overcast with dark clouds but was emblazoned with an array of orange hues from the setting sun. The blackened earth stretched before Darrio like a carpet of cracked coal, and though it was a land he came across before, the view still managed to capture his attention. The next moment, however, focused him on a different matter.

Bacchus cleared the grove and continued his sprint across the barren fields, but when he once again turned to check his assailant, he found that Darrio was not pursuing.

Darrio looked down on Bacchus with contempt because he was unable to continue. The shackles of Salia not only restricted Darrio's will, but they also kept him bound within the borders of the Saline Realm. Though he tried with all the strength he could muster, the binding agent of the bonds constricted his muscles, and he was unable to move beyond the trees. After a third attempt, a shock was sent through Darrio's body that nearly toppled him from his perch.

Darrio cursed, and Bacchus smiled with relief and laughed, taunting Darrio in the process. "This is only the beginning, Firestar! You will pay for what you've done!"

Darrio stood in place hating the circumstances of the moment, and when he finally committed his will to leave, he did so with repetitive cursing. He left the grove and gave the earth periodic kicks of frustration. His hands were clenched though he opened them occasionally only to clench them again. He continued in this manner all the way back to the small village of Ebon, the place he had left, and at the end of the road was the doctor who was waiting for Darrio's return.

Darrio saw the doctor and hung his head in shame, but the doctor approached with an accommodating smile and said, "It's been a long day. You'll rest in my home tonight."

Darrio tossed and turned the entire night, and nightmares of his failures swirled in his mind. "Not strong enough," he heard in his own voice, and his father's death played out again in front of him. He then saw his mother tied to a stake. "Not smart enough," and her body transformed into a shrieking flame. He then saw Bacchus taunting him in the distance, and Saria was near Darrio and crying. Her hands were dirty, she was covered in soot, and Darrio heard, "Not fast enough, not smart enough, not close enough, not strong enough!"

"Shut up!" Darrio screamed as he awoke. "Shut up! Shut up! Shut the hell up!"

The doctor rushed through the door and asked, "What's happening? What's wrong?"

Darrio was in the doctor's guest room, and after taking a minute to regain his senses, a feeling of shame came over him. He desperately tried to hide by steeling himself, and answered, "Nothing," and he shook his head and feigned a headache. "It was just a dream."

"Oh," the doctor replied. He was unable to find signs of physical injury, brief as the observation was, and concluded that it was just as Darrio said. There was a sneaking suspicion in the back of his mind that things were not as they seemed, but against his better judgment, and always allowing himself the consideration that he could be wrong, he brushed off the notion. "I'll return to bed then." Still. "Are you sure?"

"I'm fine," Darrio lied.

The doctor was convinced, again unable to see signs of physical distress, and returned to bed.

When he was gone, Darrio promptly buried what he was feeling. "Shut up," he whispered to himself. "It doesn't matter anyway." It was a painful endeavor, and though his heart ached and his body rebelled against him, he eventually became still enough to sleep.

The following morning, the doctor prepared breakfast and placed it on the table. Darrio emerged from the guest room famished and ready to eat anything. When he saw the food that was prepared for him, he asked, "Is that for me?" The doctor nodded, and Darrio picked up a fork and ate. While he proceeded to shovel food into his mouth, the doctor sat across from him and observed. Darrio took notice and paused for a moment to breathe before asking, "What are you looking at me for?"

"You're the Firestar, aren't you?"

Darrio looked away and whispered, "God, why?" He then returned to the doctor. "You poisoned the food, didn't you?"

"What?" the doctor gasped. "No, of course not."

"Was it the drink then?"

"I'm a doctor. I don't poison people. Why would I do that?"

"I'm the Firestar," Darrio said as he returned to eating. "The only people who've cared enough to realize that were either afraid of me or wanted me dead."

"That sounds most unpleasant."

"Most of the time, it's both."

"Is this normal for you then?"

Darrio dropped his fork. "Is there a point to this, or do you plan to keep sticking me with questions? I'm not a damn corpse, you know."

"I'm sorry. I just…I've been rude. I haven't even given you my name yet."

"I don't need to know your name," Darrio said as he picked up his fork. "You'll disappear like all the rest anyway." After realizing what he just said, Darrio cursed and soon after silenced himself.

After a long, quiet, and awkward pause, the doctor shifted in his seat and said, "I'm much better at healing the body of my patients. I don't fare so well when it comes to their souls and minds, so you may not take this well from a doctor like me. Still, if you would allow, I would offer some words of advice."

Darrio sighed. "What is it?"

"Failure isn't always a bad thing. Sometimes, it is okay to fail."

These were hard words for Darrio to accept. "It's...okay?"

"I'm a doctor. I do the best that I can in every endeavor to ease suffering and save lives, but in the years I've been in practice, I've had to come to some hard realizations, one of which is that I cannot save everyone. It's simply not within my power to do so."

"So...what do you do when someone dies?"

The doctor sighed. "I go and take part in the grieving process. This is a small village, so perhaps doctors are unable to do this in the big city, but I mourn with the patient's family, I pray, we all pray, and I help them as they learn to let go of the loved ones they've lost. We all lose something or someone at some point, but when we refuse to let go, all sorts of problems can develop whether physical or mental."

Darrio was silent for a moment after, but when he finished the last of his breakfast, he uttered, "You're full of it."

The doctor chuckled and rose to take Darrio's plate. "I'm at peace, Sir Deloran, and my patients and their families are at peace. That is all I care about."

As the doctor proceeded to the kitchen, Darrio asked, "So, what is your name?"

"My name is Ron."

"And did the man who was here before say anything else?"

"He said only that he was a scientist in search of the light."

"Scientist. Light," Darrio said, committing the words to memory, and when it was done, he stood.

"Leaving so soon?"

"I've got a report to make."

"I see."

Darrio headed to the door and placed a hand on the knob, but before he left, he paused. "Doctor Ron?"

"Yes?"

"Thanks. You know, for the food and the room and everything."

Doctor Ron smiled. "You're very welcome, Sir Deloran. Feel free to come by anytime."

Darrio left and headed south towards Esea, and as he walked, he thought hard about what he would say to Saria but could think of nothing. His entire mission had been a failure in his mind. There was no one apprehended for questioning. Instead, there had been a lot of fighting, local disturbances, and a great deal of questions left unanswered. On the other hand, Darrio did glean a title from one of the shadow casters and a clue as to what they were searching for. He did not believe it would be of much consolation, however. After the sun set, Darrio rested in the upper branches of a tree and gazed into the clear, star-filled sky.

Stars were considered the height of power in the Saline Realm, and they were highly respected. To have one's name or title attached to one was generally regarded as a great sign of respect. If an element were also tied to the symbol, it was seen as a sign of the bearer's disposition. As water was spoken of with respect to life, the greatest healer of Saline recollection was referred to as a Waterstar. The most distinguished defender of the realm, someone whose resilience and strength proved invaluable to the people, was referred to as an Earthstar. Such titles were exceedingly rare in Salia's history and were only given to three figures prior to Darrio. None of them had been duplicated. Of all these titles, however, Firestar was set within a category of its own. Fire was sometimes associated with purification and cleansing but was most often used in the context of destruction. Depending on one's view of this, to be labeled the Firestar was either a blessing or a curse. Translated into the dialect of the surrounding realms, its meaning would have been understood as referring to a person with, "the immense power to destroy."

Darrio recalled his conversation with Valeria which triggered a memory of his first visit to the temple of Magnus. He was only a child at the time and had just entered Ambrosia alone. He was dirty, tired, heartbroken, and alone. With a single knife of foreign design on his person, he roamed the streets looking for food, but just as he had done in places prior, he at first asked the citizens before resorting to theft. There then came a particularly hungry and tiresome day when Darrio ventured into the temple of Magnus, ignorant of what was inside.

There were laymen of the temple sitting in tightly packed rows listening to the high priest as he gave his teaching on magic and the god of magic, Magnus. Magnus, he had stated, was understood to be the highest of all stars. The Firestar represented his wrath, the Waterstar represented his mercy, the Earthstar represented his resilience and strength, and the Windstar represented his ability to enact change. These stars were collectively referred to as the Four Pillars of Magnus. "There is an essence of each star within all of us," said the priest. "We are all made up of stars, and the stars of Magnus are what define our personalities, who we are. It stands to reason, then, that all of us are children of Magnus."

There was a small mention of an unnamed creator-god for the formation of man, the earth, and the heavens, but this mention came only in the context of establishing a shell for creation. Salians were polytheistic and believed the shell, the material form of all existence, began as an empty, lifeless husk that numerous other gods filled with power and life. Darrio, however, had been raised by his parents to believe differently though he could not always reconcile his understanding of the matter. Despite the multiple-personality-centered philosophy of Saline thought, Darrio believed a single god presided over the whole affair of creation and existence. He had been taught many things about Him such as His traits of mercy, forgiveness, justice, and fatherhood. God, however, was such a good and distant figure in Darrio's mind that he could not reasonably fathom coming close to Him. Though he would speak his mind to God during moments of compulsion, and though Darrio regarded Him with respect, he had been unable to draw close because of an overwhelming fear that stemmed directly from his self-identity. Darrio, as he saw himself, was simply not good enough.

Magnus, then, appeared to be a viable alternative to what he knew. However, while Magnus was credited with the establishment of magic, he offered nothing else beyond it. He was said to have given man control over his life, even the state of his own existence, and that nothing would be impossible for him. With magic, there was nothing outside of man's reach, but under this condition, man was essentially alone. This kind of isolation, which Darrio came to identify with for far too long, was not something he was willing to accept. He chose instead to believe in the God of his parents, whether He damned him or not, in the knowledge that he would at least have someone to turn to when he was alone. He knew of nowhere else to go and told himself, "It is better to die than to fade. Better to die than to be alone." He had not returned to the temple since.

The following day, Darrio completed his return trip to Esea, and Valeria stood in wait. "I'm glad to see you've returned, Firestar."

"Were you waiting for me?"

"In a way. How was your trip?"

"What trip?"

"You left to chase after that shadow caster, didn't you? Did you uncover anything?"

"How did you—?"

"I told you. Nothing happens in this city without my knowing about it. That means nothing."

Darrio did not trust Valeria, nor did he trust her interest in the investigation, but because of her connection to the High Elders,

Darrio felt he could only hold back so much. He sighed.

"So, tell me," Valeria continued. "What did you find?"

"Nothing," Darrio answered. "I took off his arm, but he crossed over into the Burning Realm. A witness said the man called himself a scientist, but beyond that, your guess is as good as mine."

"A scientist?" she repeated with surprise. "Scientist, scientist."

"Do you know something?"

"No, and be quiet. I'm trying to concentrate."

Darrio rolled his eyes and crossed his arms, and he wondered how long he would suffer Valeria's presence.

"I wonder what tasks that position entails," she uttered. "Perhaps I should ask him."

"Ask who?"

"Ask who what? Oh, there you go bothering me again, and now I've lost my train of thought. Never you mind what I mean, Firestar. I have work to do." Valeria then left Darrio and shuffled her way to the temple library.

"Hag," Darrio breathed, and he doubted whether Valeria would even remember to report his findings to the High Elders, but that was of no concern to him. Saria was at the forefront of his mind.

There was a small gathering at the temple of light, and the head priest was finishing his sermon. When he was done, Saria stood, and her ears perked up as she listened to the echoes around her. She then turned her face towards Darrio, and when the group dispersed, Darrio approached. Saria looked up at Darrio with her empty, blind eyes and frowned. "You didn't find him, did you?"

"I couldn't catch him," Darrio replied. "He escaped into the...I mean, there's nothing else I can do. I'm sorry."

Saria lowered her head and was silent for a while before going through a series of heavy and rapid sighs. "So...she's really gone?"

Darrio remained silent, and Saria fell into tears.

Darrio summoned a mental image of Bacchus and marked him as a target. He knew there was no practical way to pursue the man, but Darrio decided he would hunt down the scientist and deliver his blade at the earliest opportunity. "Is there anyone else around here that can take care of you?"

Saria shook her head.

"No one?"

"She was the only one," Saria replied.

Darrio was at a loss. He had little experience interacting with children and was never sure of how best to respond particularly when it came to sensitive situations. They were already fragile according to his mind, and the last thing he wanted to do was damage them. Saria continued to weep, and Darrio, ignorant of how else to handle the situation, told her to stop crying.

"What?"

"Stop crying."

Saria tried her best to comply, but the tears continued. "I'm sorry," she replied.

"Don't apologize."

"I'm sorry."

"You didn't do anything."

"I'm sorry."

Darrio found that he was getting nowhere and decided it best to keep quiet while he devised another approach. For a time, the two simply stood without saying a word. Darrio then asked, "Is there a home or shelter you can go to?"

"No," Saria replied.

"Did you and your sister have anything?"

Saria shook her head. They were among the unfortunate poor of Esea and were ignored by the more affluent portion of the city. They were primarily responsible for their own survival and caretaking.

Everyone else, according to their own standards, was simply too busy to lend a hand. Merchants had wares to stock and inventory to maintain, and the buyers had their own businesses to attend to. As such, the poor were an invisible class in the city's hierarchy, and no one cared to help them even when approached.

By vice or virtue, the men and women of Esea made their fortunes and found helping the poor to be an unnecessary drain of their funds. Instead, they would encourage, or rather demand, that the poor help themselves but did not extend the resources to do so. The more Darrio saw concerning this side of the city, the more he came to despise it. It was not as if such conditions did not exist in Ambrosia or any other city he visited, but the dejected faces and exclusionary air of Esea's affluent bothered him. He had been in similar situations before, and he hated them for it. "So there's no one left to take care of you? Is that right?"

Saria nodded but said, "I mean…no. God takes care of me. That's what my sister said. She said even if something happens, God will take care of me." Darrio sighed and shook his head, but Saria, hearing his motions, was hurt by this. "Wha…why did you do that?"

"Do what?"

"You did this," and she ended with an exasperated sigh. "You don't believe me?"

"I believe you," Darrio replied. "I just…it's complicated."

"How?" she asked. Her crying had stopped, and her attention was drawn to Darrio. "Did something happen to you?"

"A lot of things happened to me," Darrio grumbled.

Saria was worried. "Are you mad?"

"Mad?"

"At Him."

"No, I'm not mad! What do I have to be mad about?"

"But if you're not mad, why are you yelling?"

Darrio had no answer to the question, and he forgot himself and mumbled, "Stupid kid."

Saria once again broke into tears. "You think I'm stupid?"

"Shit. I mean, damn! I mean…." Darrio shut his mouth. When he was calm enough to speak again, he knelt down. "Look. You're not stupid. I've just…I've got a lot of…it's not you, it's me. Okay?"

Saria slowly regained her composure but continued to sniffle and would not look in Darrio's direction.

Darrio sighed. "Are you hungry? Do you want something to eat?"

Saria nodded.

"Let's get something to eat." Darrio could not understand why he was going to such great lengths for the girl. He figured it was because she was a child, but as they located a place to eat, Darrio watched her. She had a ravenous appetite and enjoyed whatever attention was given to her. When a well-meaning man attempted to offer a shot of humor, she chuckled, but a careless comment revealed a hatred for teasing. She would make a clicking noise every so often with her tongue while facing Darrio's direction, and then she would smile a second later. After three iterations of this, Darrio realized that she had been checking to make sure he was still present. It was then that Darrio finally understood the growing attachment he was having for Saria. She reminded him of himself.

When they finished eating, Darrio decided to retire for the night, but Saria protested. "You're not going to leave me, are you?"

"I have to go eventually. I have a report to make."

"Can I come with you?"

"Are you kidding me?" Saria recoiled from Darrio's careless expression for which he quickly apologized. "It's dangerous. There's a lot of…it's not safe for people like you to travel with me."

"You're only saying that because I'm blind."

"I'm saying that because you're innocent," Darrio snapped. "I'm telling you this for your own good. You're better off with someone else like the priests at the shrine."

"Why are you saying that?" she sobbed. "You could protect me. We could be friends."

Darrio sighed and stood to his feet. "You're not safe with me."

"Please don't leave," she begged. "I don't want to be alone."

The words struck a still-open wound in Darrio's heart, and he immediately recalled the feelings of loneliness he had when he was a child. Though it was alleviated to some degree by Seris and a passive belief in God, Darrio's heart still ached at times for something more in his relationships. There were dangers in being associated with him, but Darrio knew what damage an aching and lonesome heart could pose to a person. It was something he would not wish upon anyone, more so for the little girl he was coming to know.

"I'm going to bed," Darrio said on his way to the exit door, but Saria remained silent. "Are you coming or not?"

Saria gasped happily and jumped to her feet. She then took Darrio by the hand and followed him through the door. That night, as she slept underneath Darrio's cloak, Darrio stood by the window and looked into the night sky.

There were only a few clouds, and the moon hung among the stars. Darrio sighed as he placed his hands flat on the windowsill. He thought back to his own time of innocence, a moment far removed from the events of the Magic War, and he remembered how simple things were for him and the peaceful serenity he once took for granted. He remembered his father, his mother, his former home, and all that he could recall of those former times. He then remembered the moments and events that shattered all that he loved. He remembered the teasing, the suspicion, the chaos, the jealousy, the fear, and every vice that was expelled upon him growing up. He then remembered and recalled in great detail the contrasts between his previous life and his current one. When he finished thinking about these things, he lifted his gaze and let it fall to the dry and dusty earth. His hands were clenched, his chest was tight, and with a disparaged whisper, he declared, "I'm not mad."

CHAPTER 5
Emergence

EAGERNESS BESTED PATIENCE as Valeria stood outside of the inn's front door. She had been tapping her foot impatiently against the dusty ground and was accompanied by three disciples who were equally restless but tired. "Are you sure he came to this location?" Valeria asked.

"Yes, ma'am," a disciple replied.

"Why take her here?"

"Perhaps he knows something."

Valeria scoffed. "He didn't even know who Magnus was. On the other hand, if he does know something or comes to know something, it could complicate things."

"I'm sure he knows nothing, Mistress."

"Are you sure? I seem to recall you being sure of another situation that just happened to turn out badly. Are you sure you're sure?"

The disciple, shamed, turned his face in silence, and Valeria returned her attention to the inn and shouted. "I'm done waiting for you, Firestar! I know you're in there, so come out this instant!"

Darrio was awakened from his restful stint on the hardwood floor by Valeria's call, and he grumbled. "The hell?"

"Firestar? I know you can hear me!"

Darrio made his way to the window, but when he saw Valeria, he groaned and lifted the pane. "What do you want you old hag?"

"Do you have the girl with you?"

"Saria?"

Saria had been stirring from the noise and answered, "What?"

"Bring her here," Valeria commanded.

"Why?" Darrio asked.

"Why? Because I said so, or would you rather I tell the Elders of your insubordination because that can be arranged as well."

"Insubo—? What does that have to do with anything? I don't answer to you."

"What's happening?" Saria asked.

"Be still."

"I'm through playing games with you, Firestar," Valeria said. "Either bring her out here, or we're coming in."

Darrio stepped away from the window and took a moment to observe Saria. Aside from her blindness, there was nothing remarkable about her. She was an ordinary girl and poor on top of it. It made no sense for a high priestess of Magnus to want her. For Darrio, it was a clear sign that something was wrong. "Get up, Saria," he told her. "We're leaving."

"Why?"

Darrio did not answer but instead sent a force through the bed that propelled Saria into the air. Saria screamed, and Darrio caught her mid-flight and set her on her feet. "Look. I don't have time to explain this to you," he said as he took Saria's hand. "Just stay close to me, okay?"

Valeria tapped her foot against the road as she waited impatiently for a response. "I don't think he's going to cooperate."

Darrio emerged a moment later with Saria clutched tightly to his left sleeve. His right arm dangled beside him.

"So you've decided to be reasonable, have you?"

"What do want with her?"

"I want to question her. See what she knows about these men of darkness and their plans."

"That's my job."

"Your job? Wasn't it also your job to capture one? Alive?"

"How do you know?"

"Don't dodge the question, Firestar. You had a duty to do, and you failed to carry it out."

"I did what I had to."

"And I'm doing what I have to. Now. Hand her over."

Darrio observed Valeria's motions. She was uncomfortable, agitated, and anxious. Darrio suspected there was some other motivation beyond what she was telling him, and he promptly refused. "No."

"Oh, come now, Firestar. What use is she to you? She can't fight, she's blind, and the girl has no affinity for magic whatsoever."

"I don't care. She's coming with me."

This declaration caused Saria to gasp with renewed excitement, and her face looked upwards with an expression of admiration.

Valeria took note of Saria's reaction and rolled her eyes. "Oh please. Her? With you? You can't be serious."

"I am. Now get out of the way."

"You're not in a position to make requests."

"I wasn't asking."

Just then, the more observant of Valeria's disciples noticed a trembling coming from the wrist area beneath Darrio's right sleeve and a light that emanated from the shackle hidden underneath. He then looked down to find thin locks of stone circling around his ankles and the ankles of the rest of his group, Valeria included. "Mistress!" he cried.

Valeria diverted her gaze to the disciple and then towards the ground where she discovered that during their exchange, Darrio manipulated the earth beneath them to hold her and the others in place. "You little bastard."

Darrio turned to Saria. "Come on," and Saria climbed onto his back. When she was secure, Darrio darted past the clergy of Magnus.

Valeria shouted. "Come back here!"

As the two moved along and bumped into various merchants and shoppers, Saria cried, "Why are we running? What do they want with me?"

"Hush," Darrio said just before running into his fifth merchant stand. It was not long before Valeria and her disciples arrived to chase him from behind. The streets were crowded with early buyers, and Darrio overturned stands in his haste to break through. This helped him in a few cases to slow his pursuers but hindered him greatly in others. When he finally cleared the buzz of the commercial district, he once again summoned what power he had available to spring forward with small, quick-rising slabs of earth. He then used air magic to cushion his landings. The latter action was for Saria's sake.

By the time Valeria reached the edge of Esea, Darrio was disappearing into the horizon, and Valeria grunted in her frustration.

Her disciples trailed behind her and struggled to catch their breath. One of them fell to the ground. "What now, Mistress?"

"Now?" she replied in anger. "Now it's personal."

When Darrio was convinced they were no longer being followed, he stopped and took a moment to rest at the familiar river he crossed before his arrival to the city. "I shouldn't have been able to do that," and he took a moment to check his restraints. The shaking ceased, and the light that once emanated from the scripts dimmed but continued to glow. It was clear to him the seal imposed on him was weakening, but he did not know how or why.

Saria slid off of Darrio's back and sat down. "Where are we? I smell water."

"We're safe for now. Get something to drink."

Saria maneuvered her way to the river and drank. When she was satisfied, she shifted into silence but soon became restless. "Are you mad at me, Sir Firestar?"

"Why would I be ma—? Wait. What did you call me?"

"That lady called you Firestar. That's your name, isn't it?"

Darrio was unsure of how to answer, but when he paused to think, he saw his reflection in the river. "Yeah, sure," he answered in a dismissive tone. "Why not?"

"What does it mean?"

"Don't worry about it," Darrio said as he returned to his feet. He looked towards Ambrosia's direction and recounted the distance they would need to travel. It would take longer for him to return with Saria in tow, and the overall route he took was unsuitable for a child. However, a long detour would have been no safer. It was not uncommon for travelers to be robbed while engaging in long trips. Merchants on extended business journeys routinely hired protection for just that reason. "Are you finished?"

"Yes."

"Then let's go."

Darrio and Saria headed east on their return trek across Salia's landscape to Ambrosia. When they reached the stretch of forest where Darrio faced Ashtoreth, however, Darrio decided a detour would be necessary. Though Saria was blind, she could see well enough using her other senses which were heightened, and Darrio believed taking her to an open grave with all of its odors would have only made things worse for her. Instead, they moved further south to a main road that would take them to a small city south of Ambrosia called Lumineth.

When night fell, Darrio picked a clearing off of the road for the two to rest. He gathered wood, set a fire, and gave Saria his cloak to sleep under. As they warmed themselves, Darrio thought about the possible reactions he would receive from Seris and the others. Seris, he believed, would likely be curious to know why Darrio returned with a blind girl. The others were likely to see little to no value in her except for Eloi and Talim who expressed some fondness for children in the past. Tam and Lon were largely indifferent. Carsis could not stand them.

"Sir Firestar?" Saria said.

"What is it?"

"Promise you won't be mad."

The request was an odd one to Darrio, and he started to wonder if it would become a pattern, but it was too early to tell. He sighed. "I promise I won't be mad."

Saria hesitated due to Darrio's tone. She could not tell if he was annoyed or tired. Regardless, she continued. "The day the men kidnapped me, I had a nightmare."

"So you did remember something."

"Are you mad?"

Darrio shook his head. "No. What did you dream about?"

"I was alone in my room, and there was a shadow monster outside my window, and the shadow monster kept saying he wanted the light, but I knew that meant he was going to eat me, and I didn't want to be eaten."

"Then what happened?"

"Then he broke into my room and started chasing me, and then I woke up, but I don't remember how."

"If it was after the light, why do you think it wanted to eat you?"

"I don't know. Do you think...do you think that's what they want to do?"

"What?"

"Make shadow monsters that can eat people."

Darrio chuckled. "No, Saria. I don't think that's the plan."

"I hope not. That monster was scary."

"Get some sleep."

Saria settled down to rest while Darrio leaned back to think about

Saria's dream. It was common for illusionists to leave traces of themselves and their intentions within the delusions they created. Because of this, it was rare for criminals to operate in the school of illusion and go unpunished given the emotional signature they would leave on the victim.

The emotional signature, much like the will of desire concerning state limits, was a defining impression of the illusionist's heart. Those with good intentions would leave behind impressions of peace and love. Those with malicious tendencies left a signature marked by fear, anger, or some other emotional and psychological malady. The worst of illusionists would leave such a marked impression of themselves that details of their identity, such as their name, or other traceable elements, such as their location, could be recalled from the victim's mind. A good illusionist, by contrast, was characterized as collected and careful. Such people were often emotionally subdued to leave little, if any, impression behind. There was still reason to worry since an illusionist of the latter sort, lacking empathy, could go too far and irrevocably injure a mind. As a result, illusionary magic had proven itself to be among the most damaging of schools so far as long-term effects were concerned while also carrying the greatest risk. Talim, however, was counted among the best illusionists despite his overbearing character. Not only was he capable of masking all traceable elements behind psychological walls and traps, but he would do so while purposefully leaving a strong impression. He was certainly capable of subtlety, but such gentleness was only practiced in negotiations. In battle, Talim made his presence known. In fact, as Darrio remembered all this, he decided Talim would be the best person to interview Saria to find any traceable elements related to the shadow caster who subdued her.

The following morning, Darrio and Saria continued their trek and happened upon a middle-aged and rugged man with an overly pleasant demeanor and tattered clothes. He was standing alone on the side of the road as if he were waiting. When the man saw Darrio, he approached and asked for money. Darrio refused.

"Why?"

"Because you're a thief."

"I beg your pardon?"

"You're too strong and healthy to be poor. If you were, you'd be in the city where there're more people to ask."

"But I get a lot of exer—."

"And there's no place to buy food out here. We're a long way from the nearest city."

"Well, there you go. That's how I—."

"And I know there're at least two other people watching here you moron. One of them is an illusionist, a terrible one, and you're hiding a scripted knife underneath your shirt. Those aren't cheap. Did you think I was stupid or something?"

The man cast his eyes to the ground and crossed his arms to think. "I suppose there's no way for me to wiggle out of this one," he sighed. "But who are you? The only people I've seen with that kind of detection range are—."

"None of your business. Get out of the way."

"I don't think so. For all we know, you could be a hired agent." The thief then signaled to a group of five others who were hiding among the surrounding brush. They took up positions around Darrio and Saria and drew their weapons.

"Stay close to me, Saria," and after Saria clung to Darrio's cloak, he continued. "I'm only going to say this one more time. Get the hell out of the way."

"Excuse me? We're the ones with the advantage here. Not you."

"You don't have any damn advantage," Darrio said as he drew his blades. He then decided not to kill with Saria in the vicinity and reversed the direction of his weapons. The thieves prepared themselves for battle, no one yet willing to make the first move, but Darrio took this moment to examine not only their dispositions but their stances as well.

All of them stood calm and were in defensive postures which Darrio counted as strange given their superior numbers. A second observation also revealed an apparent level of training that was unusual for petty thieves. Each of them had their eyes fixed on Darrio and stood in a certain spot. Darrio soon realized their formation took on the shape of a perfect hexagon. These two facts, along with the scripted weapons they brandished, made it obvious to Darrio that these men were not simply after food or money. "Who are you people?" he asked, but no one answered.

There were many forms of magic deemed forbidden by the Council of Elders, and most of them fell within the category of amplification. Magic was a dangerous tool when used in overabundance, and the various techniques of amplification only multiplied the risk. Flesh scripts, which were only lifted for soldiers of the Saline military, were among the most potent forms of amplification, but it was still only one of many. Another form, called geo amplification, called for the even positioning of its casters to a predefined shape or formation. Different formations offered different benefits depending on the number of positions needed for the formation and the type of magic being used. It also had the added benefit of reducing the drain on each member's spiritual will. It was so significant that state limits were rarely reached when using the technique. The more members needed for the formation, the greater the power with a reduced necessity of will from each member. Unfortunately, this form of amplification required a great deal of coordination on the part of its participants. If a single person were out of place, the effect would either be diminished or dissipate completely.

Darrio knew this much about the form they were using, but he was still unfamiliar with the finer details of geo amplification. As such, he was not sure what benefit the hexagonal formation would provide to the thieves. He did not wish to find out either.

Darrio initiated the attack by sending a concentric force of dust toward the thieves to blind them. After this, he followed up with a burst of fire darts that targeted four of the six positions. In response, the thieves spread out simultaneously, and each one sidestepped in unison. The darts flew through the gaps in their formation, and their relative positions remained the same.

When the dust cleared, no one moved, and no one said a word. Darrio's curiosity then got the best of him, for he had not seen such coordination in a while. "Where did you people train?" he asked.

"What?"

"Your formation, your stances. I can tell you're more than thieves, so who are you?"

"Don't tell him anything," said one of the others. "This guy already knows too much."

"I know because I'm a shade," Darrio replied.

"A shade," repeated a thief. "You mean you're military?"

"Can't you tell?"

"Never seen a shade before. Heard they're used for spy missions and such."

"You're kind of young looking for that high of a position, aren't you?" questioned another.

Darrio sighed and relaxed his stance but was careful to keep the shackles on his wrists hidden. "You really don't know who you're dealing with, do you? My name is Darrio Deloran, the Firestar if that means anything to you."

This declaration caused most of them to tremble. "Wait. You don't mean…? Oh, shit. We've really stepped in it this time."

"Like hell we have," said another. "The Firestar wouldn't be down here escorting some little girl down the road. I think he's lying."

"I don't know. That cloak, those eyes, and how many people have you seen with skin that dark?"

"So…maybe he's a foreigner. Yeah. He could be a hunter from the Hollow Realm for all we know."

"He doesn't talk like a foreigner. He speaks the language and everything. No accent."

"And hunters don't know magic," said another. "Besides, what would a hunter be doing in this country?"

"My illusion did not work on him," stated another.

"Your illusion doesn't work on anyone, Artemis. So…okay, let's say he is the Firestar. What's he doing here?"

"I wouldn't know, Deco."

"Hey," Deco said as he turned again to Darrio. "What are you doing here?"

Darrio shook his head and groaned. "It's none of your damn business what I'm doing here, but just this once, I'll forget what I saw, and your names, if you all stop talking and get the hell out of my way."

"This is serious. If he is the Firestar, he's well within his duty to kill us all. We could've been dead by now."

"Uh-huh," Darrio added. "That would've been a good excuse. And here I was about to end you just for being in the way."

"What stopped you then?"

A cold, heartless glint appeared in Darrio's eyes, and with lifeless detachment, he answered, "Curiosity."

"I'm convinced," said the man in tattered clothes. "Our apologies, Firestar. We'll just be on our way and quickly."

After this, the six men fled to the east and did not turn back, and when they were gone, Saria tugged on Darrio's cloak. "Sir Firestar?"

"Huh?"

"Were you really going to do those things you said you would do?"

Darrio shook his head and answered, "No."

Saria relaxed, albeit slightly, and the two continued on.

Night fell once again on their travels, and Darrio set up camp beside the road. Once they were settled, Saria asked again. "Why were they scared of you?"

"What are you talking about?"

"When you told them your name, they got scared. Why?"

Darrio was unsure how to answer the question and took several moments to think about what he would say. "I'm just...I'm not liked by most people."

"Why?"

"I'm just not."

"But why?"

"I'm just not."

Saria fell silent but soon crawled over to Darrio's position and placed her hands on his face.

"What are you doing?"

Saria said nothing and continued to apply pressure at various points around Darrio's face. When she was done, she sat down. "You're mad."

"So what? A guy can't be mad about something?"

"You're mad at yourself."

Darrio huffed, and Saria recoiled. "Now what's wrong?" he asked.

"I'm sorry."

"I didn't say anything."

"I felt it though."

Saria was afraid which annoyed Darrio all the more though the hostility was not towards her but himself. "Seems like I can't do anything right lately," Darrio mumbled as he stood.

"Where are you going? You're not going to leave me, are you?"

"What?" Darrio could not help but be confused. In his own eyes, he was harmful to her, yet Saria still wanted him around. Had Darrio been placed in a similar situation, he would have been glad to see the disparaging party leave. Darrio sat back down and watched her.

Saria could not see, but she was clearly a sensate and was aware of every move Darrio made and every pause that he took. Darrio could not feel something, it seemed, without her knowing, and when she pressed her fingers against Darrio's face, Darrio realized she was reading him. He did not understand the mechanics behind her abilities or how someone so young had been capable of attaining them. He could only sit and wonder about the personality that attached her to him. "Why are you staring at me?" she said.

"I don't get it. Why are you putting up with me?"

"Huh?"

"I just hurt you. Why do you still want me around?"

Saria was confused and not used to such pointed questions. For a moment, her eyes wandered as she looked inside for an answer. Finally, she said, "Where else will I go?"

Saria's response penetrated Darrio's heart. He did not consider himself worthy of such an answer nor did he believe himself capable of taking care of her. He hastily came to the conclusion that he had to find a more suitable place for her, a place where she could grow and live a normal life. The residual process of reinforcing this decision, however, only made the wound of her words worse for him. Even so, Darrio concluded that this course of action was for the best. In his own mind, he could never suffice as her guardian.

Saria, as if responding to his sentiments, crawled back to Darrio and said, "Promise you'll never leave me, Sir Firestar."

"What?"

"Promise me."

Darrio felt his-short lived resolution dissolve. "But I'm not—."

"Promise me? Please?"

Darrio then felt Saria had become something more to him than a lonely little girl he found in Esea. He likened the feeling to what he could only imagine was sibling affection though it frightened him. He was afraid of allowing his heart to attach because of what he thought it would mean. He tried to block it and rationalize every reason as to why he should maintain the distance, but the thoughts of his mind slowly fell to the wayside. Darrio was a killer, and she was a child. She was innocent. He was not. Darrio formed a list of contrasts in this regard after deciding beforehand that the two could not be reconciled. He could not protect her. He would not. He was unsuitable, and yet his heart ignored him.

"Promise me," Saria repeated.

Darrio's chest writhed in conflict. He looked at Saria and into her pleading, faded eyes and once again found traces of himself within her. After considering the effects of his own loneliness, he pondered what effects they would have on Saria, and after this brief consideration, his mind abandoned all further argument. His pain was eased, and his heart softened, swelled with a new and foreign rest. Darrio then sighed and strained out his answer. "I promise. I won't leave you."

"Thank you."

"But you've got to do something for me."

"What is it?"

"Don't call me Firestar. Not anymore. It's Darrio."

Saria smiled. "Okay, Sir Darrio," and the two rested for the night.

When morning came, Darrio figured they were about halfway to their destination with still more treacherous ground to cover. He normally despised escort missions, but Saria's whistling offered a pleasant distraction to the still-nagging mysteries and demands of his assignment. There were so many unanswered questions that rose over the course of his mission, and more seemed to appear at regular intervals. Nevertheless, Darrio decided to take things one step at a time. There would be time to ponder these things later. His most pressing matter was getting Saria to Lumineth and from there to Ambrosia.

Two more days passed largely without incident, and Saria asked more and more daring questions of Darrio. Darrio was not able to answer all of her queries. Some of the subjects were too difficult to discuss, and he had forgotten many of the pleasures of his past. This latter fact saddened Saria. Questions that dealt with his anger, however, or any hint towards his underlying insecurities were either met with stubborn refusal or feigned ignorance. It was clear Saria was trying to help him for what help a child like her could offer, but while Darrio was able to detect this, he continued to stay on guard for her sake.

On the final night before they entered Lumineth, Darrio was up to keep watch over the camp when he heard a rustling in the bushes behind them. The thief who greeted them before, the one who was polite and dressed in tattered clothes, emerged. "What are you doing here?" Darrio asked.

"I'm sorry, Firestar. I didn't mean to intrude, but—."

"Did you think you'd have a better chance against me at night?"

"What? No, it's nothing like that. It's just…well, one of us has been following you, and—."

"Excuse me?"

"It's not what you think!"

"Quiet down."

The thief looked at Saria and lowered his voice. "Who is she?"

"None of your business."

"Right, right. Anyway, the reason we were following you was to see if you were heading to Lumineth, and it looks like you're headed that way."

"So? What's it to you?"

"You haven't heard anything concerning that place or what's been happening there, have you?"

"No."

"Good," the man sighed in relief. "Then please do not go there."

"Why?"

"It's unsafe. Trust me. Just give it a few days."

"You attacked me, and now you want me to trust you?"

"We were only defending ourselves. Really. I know how this must look, but—," another rustling caught his attention.

"Forum? Get over here! They're coming back!"

"A moment," he replied. "I'm sorry. I have to go. Please, heed my warning. Just for a few days." Forum then rejoined his comrades and fled even further to the east.

Darrio returned to camp to consider what Forum told him and had in mind to enter the city anyway, but he had a greater responsibility to keep Saria safe. On that note, it was hard for him to think of an excuse as to why they would not be able to enter the city just yet. There were no suitable distractions he could think of to keep them occupied for the next three days. There was nothing appropriate for a girl her age at least. Even so, Darrio knew he would have to think of something even if it was just to stave off the restlessness both he and Saria would feel if they remained stationary.

When the sun rose again, Saria was the first to rise as she was awakened by the heat of the light. She then crawled over to the place where Darrio slept and rolled him back and forth to rouse him from his sleep.

Darrio was groggy. "What the...?"

"It's morning," Saria said. "Time to wake up. You said we would be going to Lumineth today."

"We can't go," Darrio replied still drowsy. "Too early," and he laid his head back down to sleep.

"But you said," she whined.

Darrio sighed. He knew there would be no way to satisfy her until he rose. He thus sat up and said, "Look. It's too early for us to go in right now. There's something going on in there, and we have to wait for it to pass."

"What is it?"

"I don't know."

"Then how do you know we have to wait?"

It was a good question but one Darrio did not feel like answering. "I just know, all right? And the best thing we can do right now is just rest up and wait." Darrio then fell back and tried to return to sleep. After a moment of silence, Saria thumped his chest. "What the he—...what are you doing?"

"I'm bored."

"Go back to sleep," Darrio replied, but as soon as he closed his eyes again, Saria thumped his chest a second time. "Now what?"

"I can't sleep."

"Then stay up. Look at the clouds or something." Once again Darrio rested his head, and Saria thumped him a third time. Darrio groaned. "What?"

"How am I supposed to look at the clouds?"

Darrio sighed once again and shut his eyes, but just as Saria was about to thump his chest for the fourth time, he quickly extended an arm and grabbed her by the wrist. "We'll do something, okay? Just give me a minute." Darrio then released her, and Saria sat in wait.

Darrio forgot nearly all of the childhood games he used to play as most of them were solitary. Instead, he would often busy himself with questions and puzzles while tinkering with his father's tools. For a while, under Seris' care, he even thought of being an artisan, but circumstances steered him in a completely different direction. His only application for problem solving and analysis came from how best to efficiently kill his enemies. He then realized, in that sense, that he did in fact share something in common with Lon and Tam. "Okay," he said purposefully disrupting his thoughts. "I've got an idea. Let's go find something."

"Find what?"

"A stick and a stone."

"For what?"

"You'll see." Darrio and Saria roamed the field looking for ideal samples. Saria would grab a stone and rub her fingers over the surface. Then she would present the stone to Darrio for approval, but he would often refuse. When he did accept one, he would then say, "One more," and the search would continue. The same thing occurred when it came to the sticks. The two searched, and Darrio decided what would be suitable and what would not. When they gathered seven stones and seven sticks to Darrio's satisfaction, they returned to their camp and sat down.

"Now what?"

"Now take three of the sticks and three of the stones, and I'm going to take three."

"Okay," Saria answered, and she took her share. "Now what?"

"So we've got one stick left and one stone left. What do you want? The stick or the stone?"

Saria took a moment to think about her choice before coming to a decision. "The stick."

"Alright."

"No, wait! Never mind. I'll take the stone."

"Okay."

"Wait, wait! Um…um…."

"Saria, pick one."

"Um…never mind. You pick."

Darrio sighed. "I'm taking the stone."

"Then I'll take the stick."

Each took their item and Saria asked, "So I've got four sticks and three stones."

"And I've got three sticks and four stones."

"What do we do with them?"

"I don't know. I didn't get past this part."

"Sir Darrio!"

"Well, it kept you occupied, didn't it?"

"I'm picking the next game." Saria then goaded Darrio into games of hide and seek, of which she was a remarkable seeker, and various clapping games. When night fell, both were equally tired and rested by the fire of their camp. The sticks and stones were still on the ground, and Saria arranged hers in various shapes which she felt with her hands. "Sir Darrio?"

"Yeah?"

"Why did you pick the stone?"

"Because I wanted to."

"Why?"

"I don't know."

"All of the stones you threw away had a crack in them, and all of the sticks you threw away had more than three branches. You only kept the ones that had three or less, and you only kept the stones that didn't have any cracks. Was that on purpose?"

"I guess so, but I wasn't thinking about it."

"But why did you pick that way?"

Darrio knew why. Cracked stones signified weakness while sticks with too many branches signified two things to him. On one hand, the branches were like a measure of one's relationships. More branches meant more relationships, and Darrio preferred to keep his to a minimum. A great number of branches also represented a great dependency on others. Where most people would simply see a stick and a stone, Darrio would see aspects of his own character. Even so, he knew he was projecting a great deal of himself into the activities, but he would not tell the details to Saria. "I like smooth stones," he said at last.

"And the sticks?"

"It's easier that way."

"What do you mean?"

Darrio had slipped. "I mean...it's easier to hold them."

"Oh."

"Get some sleep." Saria rolled over. In the meantime, Darrio looked skyward and saw that the moon was full. He then wondered how long he would continue to lie as he had been doing, and a feeling of anxiety and dread came over him. He looked over at Saria, and the thought of Sam entered his mind followed by the recollection of Valeria's face and the face of Ashtoreth. The clouds then covered the moon and all was dark. Darrio did not believe in omens and thought those who did were overly superstitious. However, the event which then transpired, personal and subject to interpretation as it was, rattled his senses.

That night, Darrio dreamed he was running through the darkened and ruined streets of Ambrosia. The sky was enveloped in a blanket of dark clouds, and a storm was approaching quickly from behind. He then came upon a black tower at the edge of the city and proceeded up a flight of stairs to the top. There, he emerged on the edge of a clearing, and there were four pillars of separate colors holding up the ceiling. The pillars were brown, blue, green, and red, and they were evenly spaced apart. There was also a total absence of walls to shield Darrio from the elements.

Seris stood in the center wearing the traditional uniform of a Saline captain. When Darrio approached, a wall of fire rose between them, and when it subsided, Seris was dressed in a new uniform. It was still the dress of a captain but was adorned with medals usually reserved for generals, but one of the medals was damaged, and there was a spot where another was torn away. Seris was also wearing a crimson cape that flowed but was drenched with blood.

The new Seris then extended his left hand and summoned a creeping cast of blue crystal to emerge from the ground around Darrio's feet. Darrio was restrained and struggled to pull free, but Seris approached and drew his sword. Darrio looked up into the cold and blind eyes of Seris, and there was a darkness that swirled on their outer rims. Seris then pulled his sword back and uttered, "My son," before plunging the sword deep into Darrio's chest. Blood flowed from Darrio's wounds and hands, and he collapsed to the ground while the world around him grew darker. He then saw Seris look down on him and say, "Why have you forsaken me?"

Darrio awoke with fear and trembling. It was just before sunrise, and Saria rose after him. "What's wrong? What happened?"

"Nothing," Darrio replied. "Nothing. I just had a bad dream."

"Was it about shadow monsters?"

Darrio shook his head but refused to speak on the matter any further. The dream left a strong and ominous impression, but the meaning completely eluded him.

After they ate, Darrio looked once again at the sticks and stones still set on the dirt and said, "I've got an idea now."

"What?"

Darrio took the sticks and set them in a row, each one parallel to the others. He then took the stones and placed the first one at the top of the first stick, the second at the bottom of the second stick, and he placed the rest of the stones down in this alternating pattern. "We're going to play a game."

"How does it work?"

"You get one move on each turn, and you can only do one of three things. You can either take a stick, move a stone, or put a stick back down, but you can only take a stick if there's no stone above it, and you can only move a stone if there's no stick above it. And you can only put a stick down if it ends with a stone above it, and even when you do that, the opponent can't touch that stick for one turn. So I have three stones on my side, so I can take one of those three sticks, but I can't move the stones because the sticks are in the way."

"Okay."

"And you can only push a stone forward. You can't pull it back, and you can't move the same stone on your turn that your opponent moved on the previous turn. Do you got all that?"

Saria nodded. "I guess. So how do you win?"

"You win when all of the stones are on the opponent's side."

"Okay," but after running a few rounds of Darrio's improvised game, Saria began to complain. "I can't win."

"Nobody can win like this," Darrio said, and he took a moment to think. The dream still weighed heavily on his mind. There was a certain tone to it, a warning, but working on the game allowed him to divert his thoughts. "Okay. You can put down as many sticks as you have in a single turn, but you can still only move one stone at a time. You can only move the ones on your side and only if there's no stick in the way."

"Okay," and the two tried the game again, but after another set of rounds, Darrio realized that so long as they played evenly, there was still no way for either side to advance. "This isn't fun," Saria said.

"Okay, well, let's try this. You can move as many stones as you have sticks in addition to the move you already get to make, and your turn ends when you've made the moves you want, but you can still only pick up one stick per turn, and you can't move stones that your opponent just moved."

"What about the stick you pick up on your turn? Can you put that down too?"

"Um…yes." The two tried the game one more time but found the same problem remained. Darrio then came to see something in his makeshift game. "I think I know what the problem is."

"What is it?"

"Most games break down on a curve. It's like a battle. Somebody loses something or something happens so that one side gets weaker or gains the advantage, but that can't happen here."

"So…what now?"

Darrio looked over the placement of the sticks and stones. "Okay. New rule. You can only move stones on your side and only if they weren't moved by your opponent on the previous turn and if there's no stick in the way. You can pick up one stick per turn, and you get one stone move per turn, but you can get more moves with every stick you have. The new rule is you can force a stone to hold a position for the rest of the game, but you have to sacrifice a stick to do it."

"Sacrifice?"

Darrio nodded. "And you can't sacrifice a stick you just picked up. You have to wait a turn before you can sacrifice it."

"Okay."

"Player with the most stones on the other side wins." Darrio and Saria tried the game one more time with the new rule set, and victory ended in Darrio's hand. He was surprised. "It worked."

"Aw…I lost."

It was the first time Darrio managed to construct something enjoyable that actually functioned, and despite it being a simple game, the accomplishment filled him with a sense of pride. It excited him so much, in fact, that he immediately began to set his mind on how he could improve the game, but Saria protested.

"I want to play something else."

"What? But we just started. Two more."

"But it's boring."

Darrio faced the pieces of his newly-created game and was about to insist on one more round, but he sighed and decided to let it go. "Okay, fine."

"Let's go exploring."

"But there's nothing around here."

"Let's look anyway. Maybe we can find a snake or something."

Darrio allowed Saria to take the lead but was careful to steer her in directions that would lead them away from the city. After roaming for what seemed like hours, the sun began to set, and Darrio suggested heading back to camp, but Saria insisted on searching for just another moment. Her nose then picked up on the scent of roast. "Do you smell that?"

"Smell what?"

"It's coming from over there."

The two continued on and found a camp situated far east of their own. Sitting around it were the six thieves. "Stay here, Saria."

"You're leaving me alone?"

"I'll be back. Just stay still."

Saria did as told while Darrio advanced. He crept along the grass, remained silent as he did so, and when he was within earshot of the camp, he listened.

"It's only a matter of time before they catch us, Forum."

"Relax, Deco. This will all blow over soon."

"Blow over? He caught us in the act. We have no defense against that kind of testimony."

"We don't need a defense. All we need is proof of justification."

Deco sighed. "We haven't had a decent meal in weeks."

"That's right," said another. "It's not that I mind so much what we're eating, but I'd like to go home and see the wife eventually."

"Mine's probably worried sick," said the fourth.

"Mine ain't," said the fifth.

"You're not even married," Deco replied.

"Well, that's just the point, then, isn't it? How am I supposed to find a woman while we're hiding out here?"

"Didn't we all swear an oath?" Forum asked. "We saw this coming. We all knew what it meant."

"I know, I know," Deco said. "But that doesn't make things any easier. I mean, couldn't we get support from some of the other shrine priests? Maybe they'll help."

"They won't."

"Why not?"

"They're small, unorganized, and generally apathetic. They'll fall apart at the first sign of a major conflict."

"How about Valeria? She might be able to—."

"No."

"Are you still nursing a grudge against her? Every time I mention her, you've got something negative to say."

"It's not a grudge. I just know her. She isn't going to help."

"Then we're stuck."

"Stuck," Artemis repeated, "and all but one of us will die."

"Shut up and eat your gruffon, Artemis," Deco said. "I don't care what you see. It's not over until it's over."

Darrio slipped away unnoticed and took Saria with him back to the camp. Once there, she asked, "Did you find anything?"

"We're going to the city tomorrow."

"I thought we had to wait another day."

"Things have changed," and after Darrio said this, he looked at his game, sighed, and abandoned the pieces.

After their rest, Darrio and Saria rose the following morning and entered the city of Lumineth. The disciples and acolytes of Magnus were out in force on the narrow streets, and a relatively few number of casters and adepts were with them. The citizens moved about in a hurried and weary manner, and Darrio saw that some were being harassed. Darrio addressed the nearest adept captain and asked him, "What's going on here?"

The adept turned to Darrio and was surprised to see a shade present. "What are you doing here? Who's the girl?"

"Never mind that. What's going on with the city?"

"It's under martial law."

"Why?"

"The local priest found six of his acolytes practicing forbidden forms of magic and says they were plotting against the realm."

"Then why are there so many of them out here and so few of you? This is beyond temple law."

"The Elders have ordered the High Generals to place major sections of our forces on hold, so we're a little thin right now."

"Why did they do that?"

"You'd have to ask them. I'm just following orders."

Darrio took a moment to speculate but decided to let it rest. "Is there anything I can do?"

"You could assist us with the questioning. The disciples started well before we did, and now the community is unresponsive. If there's anything you can do, we'd appreciate it, but if your mission takes priority, we'll understand."

"I'll see what I can do."

"Thanks."

"Come on, Saria."

Darrio and Saria progressed further into the city, but their destination was the temple of Magnus. On the way, Darrio witnessed many acts of harassment on the part of the acolytes. People were wantonly taken aside and barraged with a series of questions, some of which were irrelevant to the investigation. Of these were loyalty and affiliation questions whose sole purpose was to determine whether or not someone was a heretic or not. Saria commented on the sense of fear that permeated the air. "Everyone's so tired and afraid."

"I can see that."

When they reached the temple grounds, they found three disciples in long robes standing over two citizens, one man and one woman, who had been placed on their knees. "Where are they hiding?" asked the first disciple.

"We don't know," the man answered.

"You're the brother-in-law, aren't you?" and the disciple turned to the woman. "You don't know where your husband is located?"

"You asked us about this last week, and we told you the same thing we're telling you now. Why do you keep bothering us?"

"One of you knows something."

"That's enough," Darrio said.

The man and woman turned around, and upon seeing Darrio's cloak and insignia, they stood. The disciples also took notice of Darrio's station but said nothing.

"You two. Go home."

The man and the woman sighed with relief and left.

After a long moment of silence, the first disciple said, "What did you do that for?"

"Who's the high priest of this temple?"

"Master Derenger."

"Where is he?"

"He's inside."

"Then let me through." The disciples looked at one another but parted ways to allow Darrio passage inside.

High Priest Derenger stood facing away from the door and was gazing upon a tall statue that had the form of a man holding an orb of light in one hand and an orb of darkness in the other. It was meant to represent Magnus. Darrio then spoke, and his voice echoed across the empty, cavernous room, "I need to talk to you."

Derenger turned to face Darrio and smiled. His hair and beard were orange in color, and his face was square and chiseled. He was pleased to have a visitor. "What do you wish to discuss with me?"

"How do you expect to get anything done when you're treating the people like this?"

"You were sent to aid us then?"

"No. I stopped here for supplies."

"I see."

"But you're not going to get the people's support like this."

"I don't need their support. I need their compliance. These are dangerous times, and the men we seek are equally dangerous."

"Why? What did they do?"

"I found them in the act of performing certain amplification rites, geo amplification and geo magia to be more precise."

"Geo magia?" Darrio knew of the practice. It was adopted by the Casters and to a lesser degree by the Adepts. Shades, however, were never trained in its usage. They usually worked alone or in pairs, so geo magia was deemed to be of little use to them.

"I'll assume by the puzzled look on your face that you don't know what I mean."

"I've heard of it. I just don't remember the details."

"I'm sure," Derenger replied with a smirk. "Geo magia is a style of magic that uses the inherent and arcane powers of pattern, position, and shape to achieve an enhanced or altered effect. It is very deep, very strict, and if used correctly, very dangerous."

"And you need to know something about geo amplification for it to work, don't you?"

Derenger nodded. "Can you imagine it? A significant increase in power and intensity with a reduced necessity of will."

"And what school does it tend towards?"

"All of them. It is a neutral style, equally applicable to all four schools of magic."

Darrio considered the possibilities of incorporating geo magia into his style of fighting, but his station prevented any practical pursuit. The ban was lifted for Adepts and Casters, but it remained for everyone else. Even so, legalities aside, Darrio was still only one person, and geo magia, so far as he knew, required at least three people to be effective. Something told him, however, that this was not the case. Nevertheless, he dropped the issue as something he would have to revisit later but only for the sake of increasing his own understanding about the topic. After this, Darrio focused his attention on something which had been distracting him since he first entered the temple.

Nevertheless, Derenger continued to speak. "I heard certain members of Salia's military have been impressed with flesh scripts. I understand such things are still forbidden for civilians, correct?"

"Hm? What's your point?"

"No point. I'm simply curious as to what it must be like. All that power…and the toll it must take."

"You get used to it."

"But at what cost?"

Darrio fell silent. His eyes were fixed on a dark corner beside the statue, but he soon returned his attention to Derenger. "I heard the six acolytes were plotting against the realm. What's that about?"

"One of them is a star watcher, a seer. He said the world was due to transition into a new age, one largely separated from the influence of magic."

"A world without magic?"

"We have a belief that the world will someday transition through a point in time known as the Great Cleansing, and after this point, magic will be restored to the glory it once had after the world was first made."

"I'm familiar with that already. Get to the point."

"Before the transition, or so the seer said, the image of Magnus would descend from the air and be stricken by a man with blood-soaked hands. Salia would burn under a tarnished fire, and the new age would be marked by rapid progress and tyranny. These same men then took it upon themselves to combat the changes of which we and the entire realm are apparently agents."

"He said we're causing it to happen?"

Derenger nodded. "You can see now why they are so dangerous. Heretical thoughts of such a scale combined with power of equal measure makes for a significant threat."

Darrio considered telling the priest what he knew about the men, their whereabouts in particular, but decided against it. Instead, he would attempt to talk with the men to obtain their side of the story. There was still his curiosity over geo magia tugging on the back of his mind as well, but he refused to entertain it at the moment. "If I should run into them, what do I need to watch out for?"

"There are two illusionists, a healer, and the other three cross schools between manipulation and destruction."

"And when did they leave?"

"Two weeks ago."

"Thanks," Darrio answered. "That's all I needed to know."

As Darrio took Saria by the hand and turned to face the door, Derenger said, "If you do happen to see them, I hope you'll give them my regards."

"What regards?"

"A courteous 'goodbye' as you see them off to hell. That is all."
Darrio did not answer and left without a word, but after he was gone,
Derenger smiled. "Such a kind young man."

"Yes," said another man whose form remained hidden, but his
voice emanated from the shadows beside the statue.

"Do you believe he will be a problem?"

"He was never the problem."

"Then what of the heretics and the Elders?"

"No."

"You are confident then?"

"You don't believe me?"

"I believe you. Your appearance just seems out of the ordinary.
Normally, he sends only a single messenger."

"These are extraordinary times," and out of the shadows stepped a
prominent shadow caster with a heavily scripted hood drawn over his
head. Strands of raven-colored hair draped out of the darkness of his
cloak and hung over his chest. However, he bore neither the patterns
of fire nor water. Instead, it was a design of curves and lines which
signified the wind. "The Great Cleansing is upon us, and the world is
soon to transition. The master has made his intentions very clear."

"What of the seer?"

"The wrath of Magnus will come upon the seer. In the meantime,
we still have work to do." The shadow caster drew a scroll from
underneath his cloak and handed it to Derenger. "See to it that Valeria
receives this."

"I will."

"And as the others have warned you, so will I. All involved are to
be kept silent. If any of you should speak, even to others like us of us,
you will be killed."

Derenger nodded. "I would like to ask you a question, if I may."

"What is it?"

"You and those with you are the last remnants of the old worlds. I must know. What was it like?"

"Are you referring to the state of magic?"

Derenger nodded.

"In the beginning, it was not called magic. As for what it was like, it is something which I cannot describe."

Derenger frowned. "I see."

"There is one more thing you should know."

"Yes?"

"We are not the only remnant. There remains a pair of lingering elements which are playing out their influence in this world. They are meddlers, and you must be aware of them."

"What are they?"

"They are Night and Day."

Derenger was puzzled. "Do you mean the sun and the moon or perhaps the seasons?"

The shadow caster shook his head. "I meant what I said. Their resistances are subtle, and their methods are discreet. To tell you anything further is beyond the realm of momentary relevance. You need only be aware of their existence and know that we do not go unhindered."

"Then I shall keep an open eye."

"Your eyes will not help you. Again, I say this only so you are aware. The warning remains as before. You have your task."

Derenger nodded, and the shadow caster retreated into the dark where a gust of wind signaled his leave.

CHAPTER 6
Solstice

SARIA WAS CONFUSED by Darrio's explanation and asked, "So...why aren't we in the city, again?"

"It's not safe," Darrio answered. The two had returned to camp after securing supplies for the last leg of their journey. Under normal circumstances, Darrio would have remained to find a free agent he could send to Ambrosia to alert the High Generals of his acquisition and tell the High Elders of his impending return. He did not want to undergo another trial because of their suspicion. However, given the city's state of investigation and his own transgression in not reporting the whereabouts of the dissident acolytes, he did not think it best to stay for long. More importantly, Darrio detected a second presence within the temple.

While he was almost sure the subject was a shadow caster, he had no sense of what he was capable of or what his intentions were. From the moment Darrio set foot within the temple, he felt a thin stream of cold pass over his head. This was already unusual given the season they were in. Even so, Darrio first thought the breeze could have come through a fracture in the wall or an open window. The stream was constant, though, and followed a certain rhythm. There were three hard gusts followed by two soft gusts in an even tempo. He carried a very different sense from the others Darrio encountered, and from the moment Darrio entered the temple, it was clear the shadow caster was trying to attract his attention. There was no telling why, so Darrio thought it best to err on the side of caution.

As the day transitioned to night, Darrio encouraged Saria to rest. "We're leaving early tomorrow, and there's still a few days left before we reach Ambrosia."

"But I'm not sleepy."

"Yes, you are."

"No, I'm not."

Darrio looked at Saria and placed a hand on her head. "Yes, you are." Saria was about to protest, but her eyes drooped, and her head lowered. She fell over into sleep, and Darrio covered her with his cloak. He had little skill with illusionary magic and felt some apprehension in using what he did know to subdue Saria into sleep. Nevertheless, he felt it necessary to keep her safe while he went to question the six men. Darrio first moved Saria and the camp to a spot further south and settled them near a bundle of trees that grew beside a crop of stones. He then went to find the other camp.

The six men were once again sitting around the fire and complaining about their misfortune. Darrio, however, made no attempt to remain hidden and approached in full view of everyone. Forum was the first to notice, and he quickly grew nervous.

Darrio stood before them with his arms crossed. His expression was one of cold annoyance. "Somebody needs to tell me exactly what's going on around here."

"What do you mean?"

"I talked to your high priest, and he said you were the enemy."

"We're not the enemy!" Deco protested.

"Then somebody is lying to me, and I hate being lied to. Now we can either do this the easy way, you tell me the truth, or we can do this the hard way."

"What's the hard way?"

Darrio tilted his head. "Do you really want to ask that question?"

Artemis sighed and motioned for Darrio to sit. "Please."

"Are you insane, Artemis?" Deco asked.

"I am not, but our lives are short, and for what remains, I hope to do some good by aiding the Firestar in whatever he needs."

"Stop saying things like that!"

Darrio took a seat beside Forum and across from Artemis, but Deco shifted away.

"I'm not sitting next to you."

Darrio narrowed his eyes but said nothing.

Artemis spoke. "You want to know what is happening? You want to know who we are and what we are doing?"

Darrio nodded.

"We are the acolytes who have denounced the beliefs of Magnus."

"Why?"

"There is a conspiracy written in the stars. I read of a world, both past and future, where Magnus was nowhere to be found, and when I read of these things, I was disparaged."

"I heard you were making plans against the nation."

Forum was in the process of eating but nearly choked on the accusation. "We may be disillusioned, but we're not traitors. If anything, it's the priesthood that's treacherous, not us."

"How?"

"There's a new kind of movement going on among the high priests and priestesses."

"One they used to call blasphemous," Deco added.

"What kind of movement?" Darrio asked.

"They seek to control the lost elements of light and dark," Artemis answered. Darrio slipped into thought, but Artemis continued. "We believe light and dark are the elements of creation. Everything we see was formed out of the waters of darkness, but the light gives creation its life. The dark conceals while the light reveals. The dark holds form, and the light opens it up. Both are in unison, cyclical, harmonic. The light is greater, but the darkness was first."

Darrio was momentarily distracted from his line of thinking and turned to Forum. "What is he saying?"

Artemis sighed. "What I am saying is this. To grasp the powers of light and dark is to grasp the reigns of creation itself. Magic on its own is a manipulation, but light and dark, used in tandem, allows for more direct control."

"Then you should've said so," but Darrio felt a movement in his spirit that disagreed with the assessment of Artemis. He was unsure of what it was about since he knew nothing about the lost elements aside from what he experienced and learned through hearsay.

"Don't mind him," Deco laughed. "Even Forum doesn't get him all the time. Hell, I can't even understand half of what he's saying, and that's only during the half of time when I'm actually listening."

"The half of—? What? You're not making any sense either."

Artemis smiled. "You see now what it is like, Deco?"

"Well, at least I don't speak in riddles."

"Please," Forum interrupted. "The truth of the matter is that we're not your enemy. Artemis has only told us what he's seen, and we have no intention of assaulting the realm. But we do mean to defend our families and ourselves from the plans and advances of the priesthood. They would not do well with that power, and if it means we must practice forbidden forms of magic to do so, then so be it."

Darrio returned to his stream of thought while the others looked on, silently hoping he would believe them. Deco was holding his breath. "Alright," Darrio said.

"Alright?" Deco questioned. "What's alright? What do you mean by alright?"

"I'm a shade, so I can't get involved in temple matters, which is what this really is, but if we find out the High Priest lied in his request for help, the generals will probably focus their attention on the priesthood, not you."

"So…where does that leave us?"

"Nowhere. Look, I can't do anything except report what you told me when I get to Ambrosia. In the meantime, I'd suggest you all go home, get your families, and get as far away from here as possible. The priests are free to punish you however they want when it comes to doctrine, but until it becomes a national matter, there's nothing else I can do."

"I'm just glad you believe us," Forum said.

"Don't thank me yet. If I find out you were lying to me, you better pray they don't send me after you because I'm not nice when it comes to enemy targets. At all."

"I believe you."

"Then let me ask you one more thing."

"What is it?"

"Geo magia. Does it always need more than two people to work?"

The six men exchanged glances, all of them puzzled. "Why would you be interested in geo magia?"

"It's just a question. Are you going to answer it or not?"

"No," Artemis replied.

"No, as in you're not going to answer?"

"No, as in it does not require more than one person. It's possible to perform geo magia provided you have enough points of focus which are equally distanced from your relative position, but this all depends on the circumstances. There are many laws regarding it."

"But it's possible."

"Yes."

"That's all I wanted to know." Darrio then stood to his feet and left them.

"I don't care how young he looks," Deco said. "That guy's scary."

"Indeed," Artemis said as he leaned back to peer into the star-filled sky. Though relaxed at first, his eyes then widened.

"What? What do you see now?"

"I see the Firestar."

"And?"

"His shadow. He is the trigger that will end the world, and it will not be a cleansing, but a catastrophe."

"Th…that's it. I don't want to hear any more oracles from you."

Artemis turned to Deco and frowned. "Ingrate."

As Darrio proceeded further away from the men, his mind analyzed the potential of what he learned. He could not imagine a situation where anyone would benefit from the centralization of power, and he was particularly wary of Valeria though the thought of her triggered a connection. He remembered the dream told to him by Saria and recalled what little he knew of the Shadow Caster's plan. It seemed they were trying to acquire the light element, but Darrio still could not see the overall purpose of the task. Nevertheless, he imagined their intentions could not be good since they already attacked the realm once. Also in consideration was Valeria's behavior towards Saria, the only survivor of Bacchus' experiments. After seeing the parallel between the movement of the priesthood and the movement of the Shadow Casters, Darrio cursed, and he later uttered, "Damn that old hag."

When Darrio returned to the new site of the camp, he saw that his cloak was still lying in the grass, but when he lifted it up, Saria was nowhere to be found. He searched around the rocks and the immediate area and was still unable to find her, but the grass was tall in that area. There were breaks in the plants, and Darrio was able to trace out a thin trail. On closer inspection, he saw a pair of footprints that were leaving the scene. They were headed south.

A great distance away from the camp was a single shadow caster who led Saria by the hand across the field. Saria, though her blind eyes were open, was silent and oblivious to her surroundings. She was still asleep. The shadow caster, a female water bearer, had a hood drawn over her head that hid her face under the cover of darkness. As they walked, she hummed a strange and soothing melody into the wind. When she finished, she spoke. "Bacchus, you brute. He was a fool to leave you behind, wasn't he? But we'll see what the master has to say about you. Who knows? Perhaps…perhaps he will even let me keep you."

Saria was silent.

"I believe you would understand why we've done this. You are such a trusting young thing, aren't you? But you must be careful. You cannot put your trust in just any man who happens by. Such is the way to heartache." Still another moment of silence passed, and the shadow caster sighed with pangs of sadness. "My love. You promised we would find a cure for this curse. Please let the path we've taken be the right one."

Darrio was quickly advancing from the rear. He had a single blade drawn, but the rustling he made alerted the shadow caster to his rapid approach. She pulled Saria further down the field and then lifted the child into her arms for a full sprint into the approaching woods. Darrio paused on the edge of where they entered. The area was dense with trees and brush and was likewise difficult to traverse. This would have made it additionally difficult for Darrio if he had to face off against dark magic, and the realization of all this made him curse. Nevertheless, Darrio entered, and while careful, he maintained a steady and quickened pace.

The shadow caster, try as she might, was slowed significantly by having to carry Saria, but she was unwilling to let go. Another rustling signaled Darrio's approach. The shadow caster gently set Saria down and turned just as Darrio emerged and tackled her to the ground. The two fell back as Darrio raised his blade to strike, but the hood of the woman fell off due to the shock of the fall, and her face was revealed. Darrio immediately recognized her as the one referred to as Elea by the others during their meeting west of Ambrosia. Darrio then opted to stay his hand, but Elea raised hers instead.

A forceful burst of thunder launched Darrio back and to the ground, and his body slid across the foliage and into a bush. He slowly pulled himself back to his feet while Elea did the same and prepared for battle. She extended her arms from underneath her cloak and raised her hands as if they were blades. Her forearms were adorned with a pair of black, solid armlets, one at the center and one covering the wrist, and each armlet was inscribed with a pair of parallel patterns and a series of accent shapes between them. It was obvious to Darrio that the armlets were heavily scripted, but there was no way to know what effect they would have. There was also a pair of flesh scripts inscribed in black on her arms that were similar in design to the armlets and her attire. Darrio first checked himself for injuries and then addressed her. "Where do you think you're going with Saria?"

"She's of no relevance to you, so of what business is it yours?"

"She's my business, and that makes her relevant. Give her back."

"No," Elea replied in defiance.

"You people were going to kill her last time."

"I was not with them."

Darrio recognized distress in her response, but this only served to puzzle him. "Then what are you taking her for?"

Elea said nothing at first as she diverted her eyes in search of an alternative answer, but after doing so, she could find no suitable excuse. She looked upon the sleeping Saria, and her eyes turned desperate. She tensed her arms and said, "I want her."

Darrio still could not understand her sentiment, but as he stepped forward, Elea advanced. She led her attacks with her right arm and kept her left arm close to her body for defense. When she attempted to strike a blow to Darrio's face, he ducked and tried to counterattack with a horizontal slash across her stomach. Elea, with her left hand, summoned a repelling barrier that kept the blade at bay. Her repel then turned into a forceful action that spun Darrio in circles. Darrio took advantage of the momentum to perform a sweeping kick, and Elea fell to the ground, but she immediately rolled away just as Darrio thrust his dagger into the space she once occupied.

Darrio followed after her with spikes of earth which he summoned from the ground behind her. The first two missed, and the third grazed her shoulder. Elea could feel the rumbling of the fourth upon her. She placed her hand on the ground and caused the spot to become hot, soft, and muddy which effectively nullified the attack. When she looked up, Darrio was upon her once again and was about to thrust his blade into her. Elea raised her arm for protection, and the steel from Darrio's weapon landed on her upper armlet, but it did not slide forward because of a strong attractive force that Darrio tried to pull away from. He also noticed the blow caused the armlet to greatly increase in density. This hardening on impact was apparently an effect of the scripts inscribed on the metal. Elea then spoke a word that Darrio did not understand, and a strong repelling force came from the armlet against him. Darrio fell back several feet.

"Your weapons are useless, and your magic is weak," Elea panted.

"So?" Darrio replied.

"So give up and leave us alone."

"I'm not going anywhere without Saria," Darrio replied as he straightened up. "And you're not going anywhere either," and Darrio drew his second weapon.

Elea stepped back. "What are you doing? I just said your weapons are useless."

"Then what are you afraid of?"

Elea paused and hesitated to answer. "Either you've devised a scheme to defeat me, or you're insane. Neither is beneficial to me."

Darrio leaned forward in preparation for a full charge. "Then shut up, defend, and prepare to find out. I can't use you if you're dead."

Elea was dumbfounded by what appeared to be Darrio's lack of concern, but as he charged forward, she once again took on a defensive stance. Darrio, however, changed his movements. Rather than thrust and stab to strike at her vitals, he swung his blades at the top of her head and aimed at the furthest reach of her arms. Elea moved gracefully and dodged and deflected every blow. She thought it strange Darrio was not going for any debilitating strikes but counted it towards the foolishness of youth.

Darrio then made two simultaneous strikes against Elea from both her left and right sides. She blocked them both and spoke the word she used earlier to make them fly apart. Darrio, however, let the weapons escape from his hand, and when they traveled a significant distance, he recalled them to converge once again on Elea's position. Elea stepped back just as the weapons crossed each other, and Darrio once again recalled them to her new position.

"Bastard," Elea grunted, and she ducked. The two weapons continued on and embedded themselves into a tree. When she rose again, Darrio had already advanced.

Darrio was not as skilled in hand-to-hand combat as he was with his weapons, but his style of unarmed fighting used magic as a heavy supplement to his movements. Restricted as he was in its use, he was still more than capable of carrying himself against Elea's movements, and Elea had to be ever watchful for Darrio's blades which he would recall on occasion to throw her off. Darrio then found an opening as she deflected another blow from his flying weapons, and the force pushed her arm back. Darrio then summoned both of them at once to strike her armlets. As she deflected them, Darrio circled around, grabbed her by the arms, and banged the armlets together. As a result of the scripts, the two became attracted and fused together. Elea was rendered helpless and fell to the ground as a result.

Before she could speak again, Darrio warned her. "Your repel script uses too much force. Use that command again, and you'll tear your damn arms off."

"I was not going to say the command."

"Then what were you going to say?"

"I hate you."

Darrio shook his head. "You should be grateful," he replied as he retrieved his weapons. "I already killed three of you, and if it weren't for my mission, you'd be dead too."

"What mission? What are you talking about?"

"You're coming to Ambrosia with me."

Elea was clearly flustered by the prospect. "You can't take me there. I can't go."

"Why not?"

"I...," but after a brief moment, Elea closed her mouth.

Darrio huffed. "I don't give a damn anyway. You're coming whether you like it or not." He then focused his attention on Saria and knelt in front of her. "Saria? Wake up."

Saria slowly recovered from her waking dream, and after getting a sense of the new environment, she asked, "Where are we? This isn't the camp." Saria then detected the presence of Elea. "Who's there?"

"That's the person who kidnapped you."

"You...caught her?"

Darrio nodded, "And she's coming with us."

"Why?"

"It's part of my mission, Saria, but don't worry. I won't let her hurt you."

Saria pointed her face in Elea's direction. "I'm sorry, Sir Darrio."

"Stop apologizing. It's not your fault. Now stay still." Darrio made a final examination of Saria but found no wounds or injuries. "Are you sure you're okay?"

"I'm fine."

"Good. Come on."

Saria climbed onto Darrio's back, and once she was secure, Darrio marched to Elea and forced her to her feet. "Move."

The three left the woods silently and returned to the camp where Darrio said they should rest given the events of the night. Darrio further secured Elea's restraints by binding her wrists with fabrics cut from the sleeves of her garment. "How do you expect me to sleep in this position?" she asked.

"Your problem, not mine."

Elea uttered a curse against him in the same language she used to issue the repel command. Darrio ignored it but noticed that the language was unlike any he heard before. The words themselves seemed to have organic, even living, traits when she spoke them, but he could not be certain whether it was a result of her inflections or a property of the language itself. Darrio then wondered whether or not such a tongue could be translated.

There had always been barriers of understanding between the nations, but one of Salia's artisans created a script capable of diluting the language barrier. It functioned by translating the words of the speaker into something the listener would understand using an illusionary technique. The script itself was usually inscribed on a band and counted as a collar item that was placed around the rim of the neck. Salian ambassadors used the item, called the Speaker's Band, in their appeals to leaders of the Outer Realms, and soldiers used them to communicate with the local populous of an enemy territory under occupation. Still, it was far from perfect. There were occasional slips into the speaker's native language, particularly when under duress, and this particular flaw was deemed unacceptable when it came to negotiations. Later revisions of the script eliminated the defect, but the only apparent exception to this was Darrio.

No one understood why, but scripted items, even when perfectly written, would malfunction or warp when used by Darrio. Even his presence seemed to disrupt their normal function, but the anomaly itself was inconsistent. Darrio held a long-noted bias against scripted items and an even stronger one against the Speaker's Band. He also had a bad habit of projecting his disdain through manipulation magic, an unconscious effort that was responsible for many damages including the curvature of his blades. But even these things could not fully explain the irregularity.

Despite all of this, Darrio wondered if the band would allow him to understand her language. He already sampled the dialects of the Outer Realms and was fluent in one, but the language Elea used was so different that Darrio found no parallels between hers and the others, and this struck his curiosity. "What language is that?"

"What?"

"You cursed at me. At least, I think you did, but I didn't understand it. What language was that?"

"It's a dead language."

"Then why are you using it?"

"Because it's mine."

Darrio decided to leave the subject alone. He was not interested in her past.

Watching them from several yards away was the dark-haired man with the black glove. He was alone. "Won't this be a problem?" He was answered by a whisper on the wind, but it was nothing a third-party listener could understand. "Of course, I trust you. It's her I don't trust, never mind who she follows. What if he gets entangled with them?" Another gust passed over him, and the man lowered his head. "I know. I'm sorry, I just…." He sighed. "I just wish I could've done something." Darrio, Elea, and Saria all settled down to rest, and the man continued. "How's my brother?" Another breeze and the man nodded. "That's good. I know he's been wondering lately." The man chuckled. "I even remember lying on the ground, still hoping this whole thing would be over after the Cleansing. I guess I should've known better. I mean, I did know better but still. That guy. He really won't give up, will he?" Another breeze and the man smiled. "I know, and that makes it a little easier, but…I'm sorry. I guess I'm just tired right now. I'm sorry." There was a last, gentle rustle over the man's head, and afterward, the man took another look back at the camp. He then turned, was enshrouded by veils of darkness, and disappeared into the night.

The following morning, Darrio restarted the long march back to Ambrosia, but as they prepared to pass over Lumineth, he noticed a disturbance in the city. There were shouts, outcries, and a great commotion, but the adepts and casters were not present.

"What's happening there?" Elea asked.

"You mean you don't know?"

Elea shook her head.

"So your people aren't involved in this?"

"That's not what I said. I only said that I don't know what's happening."

"Are your people separated or something?"

"In a sense."

"Then how are you organized?"

"The master organizes us. Even if the left hand does not know what the right is doing, both still work towards the same goal. We trust him, and he cares for us."

"And who is your master?"

"I'm not stupid, Firestar. Don't ask me that question again."

Darrio rolled his eyes. "Well, either way, we're checking it out." He then stepped forward and suddenly stopped. "I almost forgot. This is your only warning. Don't try to slip away in the confusion."

Elea rolled her eyes in turn and asked, "And you feel the need to tell me this why?"

"I said it was a warning, didn't I? And just so you know, I'm still not above hurting you. A lot. Now come here, and get in front of me." Elea complied and proceeded in front while Darrio guided her steps as they entered Lumineth.

The citizens were standing around High Priest Derenger and a circular guard of acolytes. The people were confused and angry. One of them shouted, "How can you do this to us?"

"What's happening?" Darrio asked a local.

"The High Priest has closed the temple doors and won't allow anyone in to worship."

"Why?"

"He says it's a precautionary measure, something to do with their investigation. I think it's a bunch of crap."

"All these people are mad over a temple?"

"Magnus has many followers," Elea said. "There are many who revere him."

"Uh-huh."

"You sound unenthused."

"It's because I am. If this is all it is then we're wasting our time. Let's go."

"Aren't you concerned over what is happening inside the temple?"

"No. I'm concerned over getting Saria to Ambrosia. Besides that, it's crowded, and there're too many people here. Let's go."

Derenger noticed Darrio standing among the crowd and called out to him. "Firestar! So good of you to join me."

The people heard this and quieted. All eyes were on Darrio. "Shit," he mumbled.

"Would you please explain to the people here the seriousness of the investigation? They will not listen to me."

"If you hadn't been such an ass and actually treated them like people, they wouldn't have been against you," Darrio said. The people laughed at this and then cheered.

"You wound me, Firestar, but you are right. I apologize for my mistreatment. Nevertheless, I still cannot open the temple doors. We will continue services next week."

"But my business is suffering," one man complained. "I need a blessing today."

"And I need a word," said another.

"And I need to pray."

"You expect us to go another week without Magnus?"

"Consider it a test," Derenger urged. "If you are faithful, you will return, but we are in desperate need of the temple grounds and staff at the moment. Again, once a week has passed, you may return."

One of the citizens turned to Darrio. "Isn't there something you can do? Can't you make him open the door?"

Darrio shook his head. "This is a temple matter."

"But you're in the service of Magnus too, aren't you?"

"I'm sorry, but I really have to go." Darrio took hold of Elea and pulled her along with Saria out of the city.

Once they were clear, Elea said, "You were swift to leave there, Firestar. Why didn't you answer his question?"

"Too many people have decided to hate me once they find out who I am and what I think. I've got enough enemies as it is."

"I don't understand."

"I didn't want to give these people another reason to be suspicious of me, okay? Is that clear enough for you?"

It was not, but Elea said nothing. As the day wound down, Elea spoke. "Once we get there, what will they do to me?"

"They'll question you."

"Is that all?"

"No. They'll probably bind your magic and lock you up for a while too. After that, who knows? Torture, conscription, public execution, makes no difference to me."

"I see. Then you don't care at all what happens to me."

"You're an enemy. I don't care what happens to an enemy."

Elea looked away for a moment, her thoughts turned inward, but she soon returned her eyes to Darrio and quietly examined him as they walked. She was told many things about him, but curiosity concerning his true nature gnawed at her mind. "I need to ask you a question," she said. "Will you answer it?"

"Depends."

"Where are you from? You don't look like a native."

"Why do they do this?" he uttered. "Is that all people want to talk about lately? I wasn't born here if that's what you're asking."

"That's not it. I mean to ask if you're from this world."

"What…the hell kind of a question is that?"

"The master calls you the Wrath of Magnus, an embodiment of the fourth pillar."

"So?"

"That makes you a physical manifestation of a cardinal star."

"So…what? Are you asking whether I'm an ancient or whether I came from up there?"

"Both."

"Are you serious?"

Elea was offended by Darrio's reaction but answered, "Yes. I am."

"Then the answer is no on both counts, but even if I was, what the hell did you expect me to do as this so-called star?"

"As the Star of Wrath in the Order of Magnus, I would've expected you to cleanse the world."

"So, is that what this is all about? Is this a religious war?"

"Of course not."

"Then start making sense. What are you people after?"

Elea turned away and answered, "I can't say."

"Figures," Darrio mumbled. "Well, I'm sorry to disappoint you, but I don't even believe in Magnus."

"It makes no difference. You are his star, and you're using his magic. Whatever you believe is irrelevant."

Darrio looked up. "Is she actually trying to convert me?"

"You'll see the truth someday."

"Whatever. The sun's going down, and I'm tired of talking to you. Be quiet while I set up camp."

The night sky came and settled itself high over the fields, and once the camp was established, Darrio set his mind on testing the limits placed on him by the shackles. Their weakened hold over his will was continuing to deteriorate, but Darrio still could not ascertain why. He already considered his habit and history with scripted objects but started to wonder if his encounter with dark magic was the event that initiated the script's degeneration. There seemed to be few alternatives, but as he thought about these things and tested his manipulation skills on a summoned ball of fire, the sleeves of his cloak slid back, and the shackles were exposed.

Elea was the first to notice. "What are those?"

"What?" Darrio noticed the exposure and quickly dissipated the flame. "Shit." He covered his wrists. "Sorry, Saria."

"Huh?" Saria was half asleep, and her head was resting in Darrio's lap. "What?"

"Nothing. I was apologizing for....never mind. Go back to sleep."

Elea watched Saria fall back into rest with both sadness and jealousy. "Do you have someone, Firestar?"

"Like who?"

"A woman?"

Darrio shook his head. "I'm too busy."

"That's unfortunate."

Darrio gently set Saria aside and covered her.

"You take such care of her."

"What's it to you?"

"Even your guard of her is committed. Strange. Throughout the world, your name is synonymous with death and destruction, and yet here, you are gentle with a child who suffers an unfortunate malady." She paused. "Do you love her?"

"Shut your damn mouth, okay? It's none of your damn business."

Elea repositioned her arms and leaned back. "Very well. Why don't you tell me why they shackled you. Will you answer that?"

"What are you talking about?"

"I can read the scripts. It uses an old illusionist technique to suppress the will. They don't want you to use magic. Why?"

"Hell if I know."

"You know. You just don't want to talk about it." Darrio ignored her and went back to testing his limits with a summoned ball of flame, but Elea asked, "It's because they fear you, isn't it?"

The fire suddenly erupted into a blue pillar of flame in Darrio's hand and returned to its original form. "What do you think?"

Elea was silent for a moment while Darrio went back to his task. A few seconds later, she asked, "How many?"

"How many what?"

"In your battles. How many were killed by your hands?"

"Why does it sound like we're comparing numbers?" but Elea did not answer, and Darrio shrugged. "I wasn't counting."

"Do you have an estimate?"

"One million. Two million. Who knows?"

"Does it disturb you?"

"Should it?" Darrio snuffed out the flame with the closing of his fist and stood to his feet. "I'm the Firestar. You said so yourself."

As Darrio stepped away, Elea asked, "Where are you going?"

"I'm taking a walk. Watch Saria for me."

"How do you know I won't escape and take her with me?"

"Because you know what'll happen if you do."

Darrio did not stray far and maintained just enough distance so he could be alone and watch the camp at the same time. In truth, the numbers who had fallen as a result of his actions did bother him despite how often he would push it out of his mind. He remembered the agony, the screams, the cries for mercy, and even the backs of those who fled. He even recalled in detail the torment of those who were damaged and the empty eyes of those who died. There were hundreds, even thousands, of terrified faces of men who were forced to contend with death. But there were no names or histories in Darrio's mind that lingered to accompany those faces.

Darrio rationalized their ends as the necessary result of war, the part and parcel of yet another battle, but since the conflict ended, the weight of all the lives he took fell upon him. Darrio reminded himself that they were enemy combatants, and thus, he had no reason to feel guilty. It was the leaders of the seven realms who were ultimately responsible, but because of his pivotal influence concerning its outcome, Darrio found a sense of responsibility still rested with him. Had he been just another conscript contributing a small part to the greater whole, Darrio believed he would have felt differently, but his final role and influence were defined in his title as the Great Destroyer. It was something he never wanted to be.

The following morning, the three continued their journey with a final passing through the wilds. Not long after pushing through brush and bush did they hear a rustling in the distance ahead of them. It was a trio of men, two adepts and a caster from Ambrosia, and they were screaming with fear. "He's coming! He's coming!"

"Hey!" Darrio shouted. "Slow down! Who's coming?"

The men stopped short of Darrio and fell backward. "By the gods! He's here too?" One of the adepts then fled in the opposite direction. The other two remained still.

Darrio watched the first one leave, but glared at the other two, "Is anyone going to answer me?"

"Stay back, Firestar. Stay back!"

"What the hell are you—?" but the caster launched a stream of fire in Darrio's direction. Darrio sidestepped the attack and immediately drew his weapon. "Stupid bastard!"

The frightened caster fired another stream, but Darrio redirected the attack to burn the caster's hand.

"This is pointless," Elea said. "They're delusional and under the sway of illusion."

The second adept helped the caster to his feet and ran.

Darrio put away his weapon. "By who? Is it one of yours?" but Elea said nothing. "What the hell are you people doing? I already know you're after the light element, but why?"

Elea became cold. "How did you learn of that?"

"Don't worry about how I know. Just answer me."

"We need it for the Cleansing."

"Why, and who's this master you keep talking about?" but Elea narrowed her eyes and refused to speak. "Fine. Have it your way."

When they finally emerged on the other side, Ambrosia sat like a jewel on the distant horizon, but a sight caused Darrio to stop in his tracks, and his mouth cracked open with wonder. A battle had erupted inside of the city, and in the air were heavy arcs of fire, ice, and lightning.

As he watched this, Elea stood beside Darrio in solemn silence and said, "This is how it always begins, Firestar." She then turned to him and said, "Are you ready?"

CHAPTER 7
Omitted

OMINOUS FEELINGS AND scattered thoughts plagued the tortured minds of the capital city. A great delusion descended upon Ambrosia, and Darrio was the central figure. The eyes of the people were glazed over with fear, and in them was an apparition of the Firestar. It was unique to each person, as was the torment he provided, but though no physical harm was inflicted, the psychological horrors they suffered were all too real. Such was the strength of the delusion. Children fled, women screamed, and men fell out in terror. Adepts and casters roamed the streets in defensive packs and attacked anyone who dared to draw near at the perceived defense of their lives. Everyone unfamiliar to them appeared as the wrathful form of Darrio, and as a result, a great number of skirmishes broke out in the streets.

To escape the horrors of their visions, most of the citizens locked themselves inside of their homes. Confined and alone, these people and their families took to dark corners of the room and kept their eyes shut. Those unfortunate enough to remain outside were often happened upon by the ever-defensive soldiers. Even still, among the ranks there was division and fear as differing factions, having had little interaction before, met and clashed openly in Ambrosia's city streets. Each group perceived the other as incarnations of the Firestar, and each group suffered heavy losses as a result. Bound by duty and driven by hatred, neither side would back down from the other. Countless bodies littered the road.

The most unfortunate of those under the delusion, however, were the ones who suffered the tortures alone. Among them was a caster who collapsed in the middle of the road. The ghostly vision of his personal Firestar had been stalking him throughout the city while he ran, but when he fell, fear overtook the use of his legs, and there was nowhere left for him to go. "Mercy, Firestar!" he cried. "Please, have mercy on me!"

The apparition, saying nothing, stood over the caster as a tall, dark, and menacing figure. A black shadowed aura pulsed over his silhouette, and he slowly extended his open palm and closed his hand into a fist.

The caster felt a painful sensation course through his legs and watched as they deformed and twisted in place. "My god!" he screamed. "Stop! Stop!" but a heavy sweat came over him, and his skin shriveled and flaked away. The apparition smiled, and the tormented caster turned into a cadaver of flames, but in reality, the caster's body remained stationary and underwent no dramatic change at all. Nevertheless, the pain he experienced was by no means an illusion to his mind, and he fell into shock as he faded and pleaded, "Somebody! Help me! Help me…please…."

Amidst the chaos and frightened wails was a small population untouched by the delusion. Counted among them were Turil, Captain Palim, Seris, Abaddon, and the entire host of Shades. They went around the city quelling areas of dissent, and a team of illusionists awakened the minds of all they subdued. The citizens who were rescued sought shelter in their homes, but the soldiers were drafted and forced to aid in the recovery. In time, small groups were teamed with an illusionist and sent to perform similar operations in other areas of the city. Some of the recovery cells grew and succeeded while some were overwhelmed and crushed by the citizenry.

During a particularly heavy struggle, Palim complained. "This is a fine time for a rebellion." Palim then sidestepped the forward thrust of a delusional adept and his blazing sword.

Turil came to Palim's aid by striking the attacker with the blunt handle of his blade. "Be quiet, Captain. It's not their fault."

"This is some powerful magic to hold sway over an entire city. Are you sure your boy is not a part of this, Seris?"

"Darrio is not an illusionist," Seris replied after making a swift and nonlethal counterattack on an advancing caster. "And do not accuse him of this again."

"Or what?"

"Don't test him," Turil warned. A great commotion then erupted at the city's front gate, and the battle that had been raging there stopped as the people fell back. "Now what?"

Members of the crowd parted and fled and left behind a clear view of an angered Darrio. Both of his crescent-edged daggers were drawn and covered in an aura of flame. An even greater aura of power surrounded him, and the binds on his wrists trembled violently in place. The scripts etched in the metal were brilliantly lit, and Darrio's eyes flickered between their natural color and a veil of red. It then became all too apparent to Turil that Darrio was dangerously close to his state limit.

"Get away from her you bastards," Darrio warned. Saria was wounded and unconscious behind him, but Elea was with her and tended to the injuries.

In the meantime, the remaining casters and adepts surrounded Darrio. They were clearly frightened of what they faced but were gathered together by a mutual sense of duty and also by a collective disdain for Darrio. "Be still, Firestar."

Darrio twitched and clenched his weapons even tighter. "Be still?"

"If you give up now, the High Elders may have mercy on you, but if you insist on continuing, we'll be forced to destroy you."

Darrio was already in a defensive state. He hated the Elders and hated their accusations even more. But when he heard the murmurings of the forces around him, rage and indignation overtook him. "To hell with you."

"I think we should take him out now," someone whispered. "The High Elders aren't going to miss him. Nobody will."

Darrio's eyes then faded to red, his will was overcome, and he boldly declared, "If any of you approach me, that person will die, but if even one of you attacks me, all of you will die."

The once delusional adepts and casters were somewhat aware of the dangers they faced, but despite Darrio's threat, they converged on his position while casters provided streams of fire from the rear.

Darrio retaliated with a cold, canceling wind and summoned a high wall of earth to separate the adepts from the casters. This act also shielded the concerned Elea from viewing the slaughter that took place inside.

"Seris!" Turil called. "Seris! Come quickly!"

Seris, after subduing another caster on his own, turned and saw the rocky formation in the distance. He then heard and recognized Darrio's battle cries and said, "We must clear this area. Remove everyone from the site."

"But the men inside—."

"The men are lost."

Turil looked back at the furious arcs of fire and lighting being weaved in the air. The skirmish was small compared to the reports he read, but the sight and sounds still filled him with dread. "Retreat!" he ordered. "Fall back! Clear the area!"

Those who were free of the illusion did as ordered while those who succumbed to their hatred remained. Seris also stayed behind.

The intensity of battle and the sounds therein diminished within the enclosure, but a few casters, hoping to provide more direct assistance, ran to the outer edges of the stone wall and prepared to climb. At once, the slabs of earth fell over them and crushed them in the process, and the once obscured enclosure became an open ground of incinerated bodies and broken corpses. Darrio stood alone and unscathed, but the will of desire had not yet been met.

The remaining casters took shots at Darrio with streaming attacks from a distance, but his only response was skillful evasion accompanied by swift and brutal retaliation. Darrio opened a pit beneath three of them and caused the earth to swallow them whole. Torrents of fire were redirected and amplified at another five. When one attacked, three and five would fall. Where multiples were involved, the response was folded. Anger and rage fueled Darrio's movements, and no tactic or attack seemed capable of containing him.

When all of the casters had fallen, only seven adepts remained, but six of them, driven by the deaths of those around them, continued to press ahead. The leading adept was severed in half by a flaming swipe of Darrio's blade, and the second was decapitated by the motion of his second blade. The third and fourth were disoriented by rumblings in the ground, and when they fell, spikes of earth rose to meet and impale them. The fifth advanced ahead of the corpses in a hopeful effort to strike, but he fell after an icy blast froze him mid-stride, and his body shattered into pieces against the pavement. The sixth was the only one to reach Darrio's position, but as he raised his arms to strike, Darrio severed the hands, slashed his belly, and incinerated the body before blasting it into a cloud of ash.

Flakes of dead men still hung in the air when Darrio turned his attention to the last adept. The man in question had fallen to his back out of awe and terror of the things he had seen. Darrio advanced on the adept with a cold and silent stillness while empowering his right dagger with a biting mist of cold.

Seris interceded just as Darrio raised his blade to strike, and he came between the frightened adept and Darrio.

Darrio was first incensed by the interruption, but when his eyes fell on Seris' face, his struggle against Seris' sword eased.

"Darrio," Seris called. "Can you hear me?"

"S-Seris."

"Stand down."

Darrio's aura dissipated on command, and his eyes returned to normal. Shaken, Darrio dropped his weapon and surveyed the area around him. When he had seen the results of his wrath, limited as it was, against his city's fellow guardians, he grumbled against himself and held his heart in contempt.

Seris observed Darrio and took notice of his trouble. "Darrio," he said. "Be still."

Darrio's response was abject disbelief. "Be still?" and he shouted. "Be still? Did you see what I just did?"

"You were unable to control yourself."

"But I just—!"

"Enough, Darrio." Darrio silenced, and Seris sighed. "There is still work to be done, and the time for mourning is not now."

Darrio lowered his head and had in mind to protest further, but he remained quiet. He then turned his attention to Elea who had just finished tending to Saria. "I brought a prisoner," Darrio said with pangs of guilt. "She's a shadow caster, and…I captured her and brought her here."

"Bring her."

Darrio returned to Elea who assured him that Saria was okay. "She's bruised," she said, "but otherwise in stable condition. Her body will heal on its own."

"Good," Darrio answered, but the lack of enthusiasm and presence of remorse alerted Elea to his increasing level of discomfort.

"What is it?" Elea asked, and she peered ahead to see Seris waiting. He stood as one incensed by the happenings around him, in her eyes, and yet partially accepting of the whole matter. "That is your captain, isn't it?"

"Come on."

Elea placed Saria into Darrio's arms and walked with him. On the way, she prodded him. "Your tone has changed since last we spoke. I thought you did not care what happens to me."

"I don't."

"Then why did you hesitate?"

"You took care of her when you could have escaped."

"Are you thanking me?"

"I'm answering your damn question."

Elea smiled. "Then I will take it as it is."

When they reached Seris, he examined Elea. "This is the shadow caster?" Darrio nodded, and Seris turned to Elea. "You will be questioned on what you know, and if you do not cooperate, there will be repercussions."

"I understand."

"Then you will come with me."

"What should I do?" Darrio asked.

Seris looked first at Saria and then to Darrio who was clearly unsettled and seeking an opportunity to redeem himself. Even so, Seris replied, "Go to the Hall of Order and do not come out until the unrest has settled. Your presence will only make matters worse."

"But isn't there something I can—?"

"No. Rest and I will ask you about the girl later."

Darrio mournfully obeyed and retreated with Saria to the Hall of Order. On the way to his room, he took notice of the glaring and fearful expressions of those he passed. They knew the disastrous effects of state limits and the condition the fallen casters and adepts were under. They knew once that line was crossed, there was little, if anything, that could be done to alleviate the situation. Nevertheless, they blamed Darrio not only for the demise of their comrades but for every death and pain that resulted from the delusion. It was not an opinion formed of reason or rational thinking. They did not try to link his existence or actions to any particular event or speculated motivation on the part of the attacker. These things did not come until after the decision was made. Darrio was hated first, and the hatred was justified second, for it was not an unknown enemy that approached them in their nightmares. It was the Firestar. The image would be forever burned into their minds.

Later that day, Seris located Abaddon who quelled an uprising on the north end of the city with Tam. However, when Abaddon and Elea's eyes met, Elea turned away, and Abaddon's eyes narrowed. Seris saw their reactions as clear signs of recognition but hesitated to probe. Instead, he said, "I want you to interrogate her."

"Understood," Abaddon replied.

Seris then lingered a moment to see if he could ascertain the nature of their mutual recognition, but his observations were impeded by silence and stillness. Soon after, Seris left them and returned to the shades to undo the illusion placed on the city. By the time Talim and Eloi returned later in the day, most of the citizens and soldiers were free. Nevertheless, Talim's influence quickly boosted their efforts to restore the people who remained.

The Elders, who were the last to be saved, locked themselves within the audience chamber and refused to come out. They were arguing among themselves. Elder Tiberius shouted, "You see? I told you all this would happen! No one is safe as long as he exists!"

"We all knew that," Elder Judas said, "but it's your fault something was not done sooner!"

"We should have never lifted the ban on flesh scripts," argued the fifth. "Now look what has happened."

"We would have lost the war if we hadn't," said the sixth.

"So? At least our enemies would have given us a quick death, and in any case, I think we could have won without them."

"Oh? And you really want to say this now?" said the fourth. "Because as I recall, you were the most zealous supporter of amplification rights, you hypocrite! I say this is your fault!"

"How dare you!"

The shades breached the chamber and attempted to restore the minds of the Elders, but the Elders banded together in arms and fought against the shades. Their first strike burned the man closest to Seris, and Seris, in response, drew his sword.

Turil turned to him in surprise. "What are you doing, Seris? Put away your weapon."

Seris, in a brief moment of hesitation, looked at Turil and turned his attention again to the Elders, but even before he put away his blade, Turil recognized a glint in Seris' eye.

To everyone else, Seris' action seemed to be a simple and reasonable error in judgment, particularly given the circumstances. But Turil, having eyes into Seris like no one else, saw truly what the hesitation meant.

The spark in Seris' eye had been a familiar phenomenon even before the war, and it once stood out to Turil like a beacon as plain as the nose on Seris' face. Time and distance tempered Turil's recognition of his old friend's subtleties, but in that moment, long-held knowledge of Seris began to penetrate Turil's forethoughts. The spark was an indication of sight, a signal of opportunity or confirmation in whatever Seris had planned. Seris recognized something he could use to his advantage against the High Elders but clearly deferred his intended actions out of respect for Turil.

Turil was frightened by these realizations, for it meant Seris was scheming against them, and he knew Seris to be a patient man who ignored very little and was known for the success of his plans.

In the midst of these considerations, Seris turned to Turil and said, "You are staring at me, Turil."

Turil then heard Seris' voice in an altogether different tone and wondered what else he could have possibly missed. Nevertheless, he knew Seris could see just as well into him and tried to hide his unease with a smile. "I'm sorry, my friend." Turil then turned his face towards the Elders.

He shared no great respect for them, particularly in their delusional state, but insurrection and overt rebellion never entered his mind. He had never known Seris to be capable of such a thing, and Seris never expressed such things in the past. But as the flame of doubt continued to burn concerning his knowledge of the Firestar, so a new one was ignited regarding Seris, his loyalties, and his plans.

The Elders were subdued and freed from the illusion, and the day's long and tumultuous affair ended. However, in the dead of night, the Elders called for an immediate trial so they could condemn Darrio for the event, but Turil and Seris were quick to remind them of the fractured state of the city and advised that time be allowed for healing. Seris also informed them that, once again, Darrio was not in the vicinity when the delusion hit. Nevertheless, the High Elders, Tiberius and Judas in particular, expressed an unequivocal desire to see the Firestar when the period of mourning and healing passed.

A week passed as the streets were cleared away, and a mass funeral was held for those who died. During the eulogy, presided over by Elder Tiberius, a promise was made to strike back against the enemy responsible for the attack though no specific name was mentioned. Darrio was not allowed to attend.

In the meantime, Darrio tended to Saria within the Hall of Order, and in accordance with Seris' order, he did not leave the grounds, but the adepts and casters kept their distance from him and even shunned Saria in the process. No one would speak to them, either together or alone, and everywhere they went, their presence was met with silence and contentious tolerance. This became a source of turmoil for Darrio, especially as it related to Saria, but he kept his peace and said nothing in protest. His every movement and expression was being monitored, and he could not so much as open his mouth without a man standing ready to counterattack should the opportunity arise. The shades, while more accommodating by far, offered little in the way of better treatment. Saria's greetings were given short replies while Darrio's presence went unrecognized, but their collective indifference and spirit of apathy concerning Darrio were rooted in events that transpired during the Magic War. It had nothing to do with what happened in Ambrosia.

After the funeral, there was a small protest against the Hall of Order for their housing of the Firestar, but Seris had the protesters removed under threat of imprisonment for trespassing. Turil backed the order but kept an eye on Seris. When it appeared as if things finally settled, Darrio took Saria with him to roam the grounds. While doing this, he passed over the interrogation room where he heard Abaddon speaking with Elea. At first, Darrio thought little of it and was prepared to move on, but as he listened, he detected a heightened sense of emotion in Abaddon's voice which he counted as unusual. He told Saria to keep quiet and listened. Abaddon was speaking. "Is that all you have to say?"

"It is."

"Then perhaps what you have disrupted is of no concern to you, but you will note this. All of the people who surrounded you will be hunted and gathered like weeds to burn, and there will be no place to rest for them when it is done."

"What? How? You don't even know where we are."

"The people of the Saline Realm are resourceful and will do what is needed until your works are undone. The Shadow Casters and all who follow them will be wiped from the face of the earth. The High Elders themselves have determined it by decree. Until all of our enemies have perished, we will not rest."

Elea paused. "Those Elders can't do anything to us."

"Pride before fall," Abaddon answered. "To underestimate any target is to step first into failure. My interrogation is finished. Take her away." Elea was escorted to the exit by two adepts, but before they could reach the door, Abaddon spoke. "Firestar."

Darrio jumped and looked through the door. "What is it?"

"You mustn't eavesdrop. It is a bad habit."

Darrio left. Abaddon rarely spoke in such tones, and Darrio did not understand what it meant. He thought perhaps recent events had shaken Abaddon like no event prior. It had certainly shaken Darrio albeit for different reasons. He did find it interesting to see Abaddon actually upset by something. It made him seem more passionate and human.

More time passed, and Seris came to Darrio's room and knocked.

"It's open," Darrio answered.

When Seris entered, Darrio was in the process of trying to improve his improvised game on the floor while Saria kicked her feet and sat on the bed nearby. Instead of sticks, there was a line of utensils. Balled clumps of paper replaced the stones. Seris watched for a time but could not understand the purpose of it. He then asked, "What are you doing?"

"I'm working on a game," Darrio answered.

"What kind of game?"

Darrio looked over the pieces, pulled away from his work, and scattered the elements. He was fatigued. "It's nothing."

"Aw," Saria whined. "I was hoping you'd finish."

Seris had not seen Darrio in an artistic state for a while, and though curious, he neglected to ask what encouraged the creative outburst.

Darrio stood. "Did you need me for something?"

"I wanted to ask you about the girl."

"Oh. Come here, Saria." Saria did as told and stood in front of Darrio. "Her name is Saria. She was one of the people kidnapped by the Shadow Casters in Esea."

"She's blind?"

Darrio nodded. "But she can still see in a way."

"What of the others?"

"Gone."

"Then what can she tell us?"

"Not a whole lot. She and the others were put under a conscious dream. I think it might have been done by the one I chased into the Burning Realm, so I thought Talim and the other illusionists could try to read the emotional signature he might have left behind."

"And the shadow caster you brought back with you. She was not the illusionist?"

"She didn't show up until later."

"I'll need a full report of your experiences."

"I was already working on it," Darrio said pointing to a scattered set of papers on his desk. "I didn't have anything else to do, so…."

Seris smiled but took notice of another sheet that had been scrawled with multiple sketches of a single subject. It was an emblem that contained a central circle and a flame-like shape that surrounded it. These two elements remained the same in all of the drafted incarnations, and the variations between them were minor. "What is this?" Seris asked as he moved forward and picked up the paper.

"That?" Darrio said with embarrassment. "I don't know. It's been in my head lately, so I thought I'd put it down."

"Are you looking to express yourself again?"

Darrio did not answer.

"Your style has matured since last time."

"You really think so?"

Seris smiled and nodded. "And I'm glad you've prepared your

report so soon. You've done well, Darrio."

Darrio was not used to praise, even from Seris, and stuttered in his acceptance of it. "Thank you."

"May I speak with the girl?"

Saria pointed her face towards Darrio. She appeared worried, but Darrio reassured her and released her into Seris' custody. "What do you want me to do?" Darrio asked.

"Stay here," Seris replied.

After Seris left, Darrio returned to his desk, glanced once more at the emblem he made, and placed it in the upper drawer. He then reorganized his reports. He checked over his statements, read over them several times to be sure of their accuracy, and when that was done, Darrio reclined on his bed to relax. His first thoughts fell on Sam who he hoped was away on business during the time of the attack. Darrio had not developed as strong of an attachment to him as Saria, but he did not wish to see Sam harmed either. Darrio also thought about the reactions people had towards him since the delusion.

He thought he should have been used to being feared, but the idea provided him with no comfort. It was one thing to be hated by his enemies. It was another matter to be hated by the ones he was bound to protect, and whether he cared about them or not was irrelevant. He then wondered if this pattern of rejection would continue for the remainder of his life, but considering the possibility stung him all the more. Darrio wanted to believe there was something more for him, that people and circumstances could change, but as he reflected on his life up to the moment, all he could see was a progressive pattern of death and decay. He did not want this for Saria, and to that end, Darrio decided he would live even if for no other purpose than to see a better life for her.

While Darrio was thinking and considering these things, another mob gathered outside to heckle him in protest. At the peak of their discontent, a stone was thrown that crashed through Darrio's window and landed on the floor beside his bed. Squads of adepts were immediately dispatched to arrest the offenders while Darrio stood to his feet and watched. The people below caught a glimpse of him, spat, and cursed his name to his face. Darrio walked away from the window, picked up the stone, and placed it on his desk. He then turned to leave his room and mumbled, "Saria, I'll protect. To hell with the rest."

Seris had stressed to Darrio that it would not be in his best interests to leave the grounds. He even placed other shades on monitor duty to keep the Firestar within the boundaries. Darrio found little to do under the circumstances, and because Saria was away, he decided to hone his skills. He knew the Elders would still be against him whether he was found innocent or not, but their next course of action would largely depend on Talim and the evidence he uncovered.

Talim, as the greatest illusionist of the realm, excelled at reading the emotional signatures left behind by others. His knowledge of mental feints, traps, and strategies up to then was unsurpassed. Yet even he could find nothing concerning the illusionist who attacked Ambrosia. Every clue was a riddle and a puzzle to be deciphered whose answer only made sense within the context of yet another riddle. For every answer gained, a new mystery would present itself, and the answers were of such a kind as to mock the investigator. Even when they managed to follow a trail to its conclusion, the conclusion itself was sealed by a trace of dark magic. The illusionists essentially found themselves embroiled in a logical maze that led nowhere, and this was a source of great frustration. The sheer number of interlocking mysteries coupled with the devious nature of the traps that hid them made finding any definitive answers practically impossible. Talim never fared well with riddles, and it seemed to him as if the blockages were tailor-made for his weaknesses. Talim reported this to Seris in his office. "Whoever the man was, his mind was unlike anything I have seen. He took great pains to keep his true nature hidden though many of his traces were hidden in plain sight. I believe he took some enjoyment out of this or else enjoys mocking those who attempt to decipher his meanings."

"And the effects?"

"He was careful. Deliberate. There was no damage to the people's sanity, and their sense of self remains intact. Had he truly meant to destroy their minds and bring the city to ruin, he could have. But for what was done, the damage is irreparable."

"What damage?"

"The delusion has created an ingrained fear of the Firestar even to the point of physical sensation during his presence."

"What of the Elders?"

"It is the same," but Talim caught himself. "No, I correct myself. It is even more pronounced in them than in the others. Elder Tiberius in particular had two layers to his tampering, but this second layer was so subtle and obscured that I could not decipher it."

"I see."

"I knew their fear of the Firestar was great, but the delusion has pushed it beyond the depths of reason. There is no hope of reprieve from them."

"Then at the end of the trial?"

"They will most certainly condemn him."

Seris fell into thought and then asked, "What of the girl? Have you learned anything from her?"

Talim leaned back and grinned. "A different matter altogether. This so-called illusionist was careless."

"What did you find?"

"The man's name is Bacchus. He was a scientist of the second world, or so he believed."

"Scientist?"

"It was an ancient occupation devoted to the study of creation and all of its functions. He and the others with him were specifically involved with the study of magic, but he was disbarred by his superiors and continued his research with someone else. He apparently still resents this or it would not have been on his mind when he descended."

"Did you see who he worked for?"

Talim shook his head. "The name and form of his master was obscured. Whenever I sought to recall it, I was greeted with substitutions and gibberish."

"What else did you find?"

"The darkness they use is referred to as dark magic, but what he sought within the girl was the power of light."

"The light element?"

Talim shook his head. "No. There was no reference to it as light magic or the light element. That distinction was very clear. I have no idea what it means nor could I discover it without having the head of the illusionist here."

"And what of the woman Darrio captured?"

"Ah, Elea. Now that one has an interesting history! This woman, like the scientist, lived in the second world, but she used to be a warrior filled with passion and vigor. It was a controlled passion that befitted a soldier of her ranks, and she once held a position of leadership and lead in many glorious battles. There were also these flying vessels they traveled in called arks and an impassible barrier that divided the world and regions. I also saw twins, one light and one dark, and a mountain covered over in a cloud of darkness. There was also—."

"Talim."

"Yes?"

"Focus. Have you learned anything from her concerning the Shadow Casters?"

"My apologies. Unfortunately, I was unable to gather much in that area. Certain corners of her mind have been sealed."

"Sealed by what?"

"Dark magic, and there is nothing I can do to get past the barriers. It reduces and voids the effects of other magic by nature. Thus, my techniques have no effect on them."

"And who sealed these things in her?"

"Unknown. As was the situation with Bacchus, the name and form have been sealed away from conscious thought. This is ancient magic, Captain, far greater than what we know, and while I hate to admit it, the levels of mastery I've borne witness to are beyond even my level of understanding."

"I see. Thank you, Talim. I'll be sure to take what you've said to the trial."

"Then may I ask something of you, Captain?"

"You may."

"The Firestar. How does he fare?"

"You've seen him."

"I have. The boy is not well."

"Are you concerned?"

"Me? Ha!" Talim laughed.

"Concern for a comrade is no sign of weakness, Talim."

Talim's hearty bellow then trickled to a light and nervous chuckle. "Where is Eloi?"

"I do not know. He is always away."

"Is he concerned as well?"

"Why do you ask?"

"Darrio has not complained about him which means Eloi has not approached him."

"Then perhaps he is though absence is a strange way of showing it. Do you believe the man is capable of such feelings?"

"He is capable of many things even if he does not know it."

"Your sight and ability to inspire continues to evade me, sir. I wish I had these traits."

"Everyone has their talents, Talim. Do not discount what you have at the expense of what you do not. You are dismissed."

Talim smiled and humbly nodded. "Yes, sir."

When Talim left, Seris leaned back to deliberate over recent events and formed a ball of flame in his right hand. He often did this in moments of solitude since the heat provided him with a point of focus. Seris went through the motions of manipulating the shape and intensity of the fire as he thought about the Elders, Turil, and Darrio in sequence. Abaddon then entered through the door. Seris looked up with a degree of irritation and dissipated the flame. "Do you have something to say to me, Abaddon?"

"The woman has escaped."

"Heading?"

"Northeast." Seris fell silent, but Abaddon asked, "Do you want me to pursue her?"

Seris shook his head. "We have what we need." He then stood to his feet. "Come. We have work to do."

Abaddon followed Seris out of the office where they moved towards the Hall's Library of Law, but as they walked, Abaddon spoke. "I sense lamentation concerning the choices you have made."

"There is lamentation," Seris replied.

"Then I must say it again. The boy will be a hindrance to you."

Seris took only a brief moment to contemplate the full meaning of Abaddon's statement, but when he finished, he declared with finality, "It matters not."

"You know, then, what you are saying?"

"And I no longer care."

Abaddon glanced over at Seris, and after seeing his resolution, faced forward. "So be it."

Several days were spent preparing for the eventual hearing called for by the Elders on Darrio, his report, the delusion, Saria, and the Shadow Casters. Carsis and Lon returned during this time and added their report to the notes Seris gathered while Tam was sent away on another assignment. When Saria returned to Darrio, she spoke of Seris and the air of tension surrounding him. "He's probably nervous about what the Elders will tell him," Darrio said. "It doesn't happen much, but he can be like that sometimes."

"But I don't think it was about the trial, Sir Darrio. I think he was bothered about something else."

"Like what?"

"I don't know," Saria said, and she shook her head. "I don't want to know. I just don't want to be around him again."

"Did he really bother you that much?" Saria nodded, but Darrio could not understand it. He knew Seris could be demanding and even overbearing when the need arose, but he never saw him as a fear-inspiring figure. Someone to be feared if crossed, certainly, but not the kind of man who commanded it with presence. Darrio could only relate Saria's fear to her age, but Saria, detecting that Darrio did not believe her, huffed. "What?"

"You don't believe me."

"It's not that. It's just...I know him. He's not a bad guy."

"If you say so, Sir Darrio." Saria clearly did not agree.

When the time of preparation ended, Darrio stood before the Council of High Elders and High Generals in a hearing at the Grand Hall. Abaddon and Seris stood beside him while Saria was being cared for by Talim at the Hall of Order. General Turil was also present at the hearing. Elder Tiberius spoke first. "Captain Seris?"

"Yes?"

"You gave us the Firestar's report, but you did not include the results of Tam and Abaddon's investigation. Why?"

"They could find nothing of relevance."

"Then what of the other teams?"

"The same."

"You mean to say none of your shades could produce results?" Elder Judas asked.

"I mean to say only Darrio, sent alone and bound, returned with actionable information and a prisoner per your request. The others searched, but there was nothing to be gained at the sites they investigated."

"We all read the Firestar's account," the fourth said. "He was explicitly forbidden from the use of magic. The penalty was death."

"Then I will not argue this case, but we should first consider what he has brought us and what he alone is capable of."

"Firestar?"

"What?" Darrio replied.

"Why did you breach the trust of this council?"

Darrio shook his head to contain his provoked annoyance. He knew well that he never had their trust or else he would not have been standing there. "Magic was the only way I could capture the shadow caster and survive their attacks."

"What of this Ashtoreth person? You had no need of magic then."

"Ashtoreth was weak," Abaddon stated, "and the wall of darkness stripped what remained of the Firestar's limited power."

"What about the delusion?" asked the fifth. "Who caused it?"

"A shadow caster," Seris replied.

"And how do you know this?"

"Talim reported a heightened mastery of illusion, a mastery greater than his own, and there is no illusionist known who is greater than Talim. Traces of dark magic were also found within the minds of the people. These traces concealed certain portions of the emotional signature so nothing definitive could be gained concerning the illusionist's identity or motives."

"Then, Firestar," the sixth said. "Do you deny any and all involvement with that event?"

Darrio simply nodded. He had in mind to remind them that he was not an illusionist as well but grew tired of repeating this fact.

"We have learned much concerning the Shadow Casters and their intent," Seris stated. "It is only because of Darrio that we have the information concerning their motives and their search for the light."

"What are you talking about?" asked the third.

Seris turned the report over to Abaddon who spoke. "Before her escape, I interrogated the captured shadow caster and combined her testimony with Talim's report."

"What did you find?"

"They follow a set of four masters who are headed by another who preceded them. The latter four govern a single faction of which there are also four while the first controls them all. The Firestar has identified two of these factions as bearers of the fire and water pattern. The other two bear earth and wind patterns."

"How many of these shadow casters exist?"

"That is unknown. We cannot determine their numbers."

"Then who are they, exactly?"

"They are ancients with roots set in the first and second worlds. Their time predates your knowledge of magic, the war, this nation, and the seven realms as they are now known."

"You mean there are some who have been in existence from the beginning?"

Abaddon nodded. "Their goal is to initiate the Great Cleansing which has been foretold in the doctrines of Magnus and see the world ruled by him. They believe the combined use of light and dark magic is necessary to this goal and have involved certain high priests and priestesses in their search."

"But why? And why attack Salia?"

"Salia is seen as a corrupting influence on the state of magic, but she is not the only offender. The desire of their master is to see all seven of the realms subjected to the will of Magnus. If not, they too will be burned by the Great Cleansing."

"Then they have agents in the Outer Realms as well," Turil commented. "We still have enemies in those regions. The Shadow Casters could easily guide them across our borders or provide a moment for them to strike."

The Elders conversed among themselves with grumbling and trepidation. They wanted to simply receive the report and condemn the Firestar to death, but the circumstances presented to them changed their minds. They still had legal cause due to the forbidden use of magic, and there would have been no disagreement by the people. They too wished to see the Firestar away whether it was by exile or forceful expulsion from his mortal coil. However, the threat of action by the Outer Realms as a result of the Shadow Casters appeared a more pertinent concern. They were quite capable, after all, of placing Darrio into harmful situations as shown by events prior. They still moaned about his successes but figured, in either case, they would get what they want. The Firestar was bound to slip sooner or later, and if he did not, they could condemn him anyway. When they completed their deliberations, they turned again to Seris. "We want the Shadow Casters eliminated," Elder Tiberius stated. "Do whatever you must, but hunt them down. Do not leave a single one alive."

"What of Darrio?" Seris asked.

"His punishment will be delayed. For now, he is to be supervised at all times and his restraints reinforced."

Darrio lifted his head. "What?"

Seris warned Darrio with a glance not to retaliate, and Darrio kept his peace.

"Start with the shadow casters in this realm," Elder Judas continued. "We will send agents in secret to hunt in the Outer Realms as needed. Will the Council of High Generals confirm this decision?"

"We will confirm it," Turil answered as did the others.

"It has been decided."

"What of the Priesthood of Magnus?" Seris asked.

"Indeed," Abaddon said. "What will you do with them?"

"The priesthood is a sensitive matter," Elder Tiberius answered. "We will make decisions on a case-by-case basis."

"Very well."

"This hearing is adjourned. Dismissed."

As everyone filed out of the chamber, Abaddon said, "You have been spared, Firestar."

"Yeah," Darrio said, dismissive of the statement. "And when they don't need me anymore? When I'm no longer a concern?"

"That time has not yet come."

"And we still have work to do," Seris said.

After the hearing, speculation arose concerning Darrio's restraints and how he remained capable of performing strong feats of magic. There had never been a case in the past where such a weakening occurred, and they fitted Darrio with a second set of shackles to be sure his powers were completely suppressed. Some cited his past history with scripted items as the primary reason for the breach, and some others thought his exposure to dark magic had something to do with it. The rest considered it a combination of both, but even they felt something more was going on.

Tam returned from his task a few days later but was immediately sent on another by Seris. Tam was weary by this time and saddened by the news, but when he was given additional instructions to kill any shadow caster he found, his demeanor was lifted, and he left again with excitement in his steps.

Seris held a meeting with his shades so everyone would be current on the directives of the Elders. When he told them of their decree, Carsis responded by saying, "So they've finally decided to let us do something useful for a change. It's about damn time. I was starting to get bored."

"Gather what you can," Seris said, "but strike when you are able. Do not hold back."

"Could you find nothing more from the shadow caster woman?" Talim asked.

Abaddon replied, "The water bearers are the strongest faction in this realm, and the name of their master is Treos."

"They are the ones who orchestrated the initial attack on Ambrosia," Seris continued, "and are believed to have a tie to the unusual affairs that followed shortly afterward. We know of their involvement with the kidnappings in Esea. They may have ties to events in Allinea and the northern cliffs as well."

"We found nothing in the cliffs," Talim said. "There was only a field of the dead and no one among the living willing to speak on the matter. What did you find, Sir Abaddon?"

"The pillars of fire died before we arrived in Allinea, and there was no harm to the citizens or surrounding area. I believe it was a distraction to divide and divert our attention. A poorly conceived distraction."

"One that worked, apparently," Lon said with a glimmer in his eye.

Abaddon took notice. "Apparently."

Seris saw the exchange between Abaddon and Lon but continued nevertheless. "Then what remains are the northern dead."

"What about Ceria?" Darrio asked. "What happened there?"

Carsis and Lon glanced at Darrio but turned aside uncomfortably except for Lon who continued to stare.

"What? What happened?"

"It was…an unpleasant matter not meant for your eyes, Firestar," Lon said.

"Why not?"

"Because it was stupid, sick, and irrelevant," Carsis answered. "Just…no. I don't even want to think about it."

Carsis had an unusually high threshold for the dark and disturbing which rivaled even Tam's demented tolerance. Whatever turned the stomach of Carsis, then, was not something Darrio wanted to pursue. "Never mind, then."

"There will be two teams of three," Seris said once again looking at Lon and Abaddon. "Talim, Eloi, and Darrio will return to the valley of bandits."

"Curses," Talim said with respect to Eloi.

Eloi looked towards Darrio. "I will not hinder you, Firestar."

"Him? Ha!" Talim said. "You should worry about hindering me."

Eloi ignored him and kept his focus on Darrio. Darrio did not understand why Eloi was doing this. Darrio was dismissive and abrasive in the past and could not think of a single thing he had done to inspire a change in Eloi. However, given Eloi's incessant attention, Darrio could not think of how else to respond except to say, "Okay."

"Abaddon, Lon, and Carsis will return to Allinea."

"Why?" Carsis asked.

"We may yet uncover something Tam and I have missed," Abaddon answered. "Your eyes will be new to the situation."

"Is that all?" Lon prodded.

"For now."

"You may be working alongside adepts and casters," Seris said.

"Some of them have yet to make a full recovery. I say this especially for you, Darrio."

Darrio lifted his head.

"Be careful who you interact with." Darrio nodded, and Seris finished. "Dismissed. Abaddon. Lon. Carsis. Remain with me."

Darrio, Talim, and Eloi left to make their preparations. "Ah," Talim breathed. "It has been too long, Firestar."

"Too long for what?"

"Since we were last placed together for a mission."

"It was a disaster last time, that's why."

Talim dismissed the sentiment. "A single mission of many."

"What happened?" Eloi asked.

"It was a gathering and assassination assignment in the Hollow Realm," Darrio answered. "I had already marked the target, and Talim had to go and show off."

"Petty tricks!" Talim barked. "I could not abide their pitiful attempts at illusion."

"It was a show, you moron. Entertainment. The last thing we needed was five hunters chasing us out of the region. They didn't even rest until we were gone."

"And yet they never ascertained our identities."

"That's not the point."

Eloi tilted his head. "This still bothers you, Firestar? Why?"

"I don't want to talk about it."

"Why?"

"Because I don't want to talk about it," Darrio repeated with heightened agitation.

"Okay."

"We have time before our departure," Talim said. "Is there anything you need to do before we go?"

Darrio remembered Sam and Saria and took the moment to meet

them. First, he conferred with Saria who wanted to know where he was heading. "To the northern cliffs. We're trying to find out what happened. I shouldn't be gone for more than a couple of weeks."

"But you're coming back, right?" Darrio nodded, but because Saria could not see, he placed his hand on her head and caused hers to nod as well. Saria chuckled. "You promise?"

"I promise."

Darrio then returned to the streets to find Sam. On the way, he received a number of unwelcome, hostile, and fearful glares. Unlike before, the city was fully aware of Darrio's limitations, and the people were bold in their disapproval. When a piece of fruit struck Darrio in the back of the head, he turned to find a small boy who was then swept away by his father. "Fool!" the father chastised. "Come here," but Darrio said nothing and moved on.

Sam was at his stand and involved in an active sale when Darrio approached. The other merchants were sure to cover their wares, a sure sign they had no intention of doing business with the Firestar, but when Sam looked at Darrio, he jumped with fright. Darrio was immediately saddened by this and assumed Sam had been struck by the same delusion as the rest of the city, but Sam said, "Man, Darrio. You startled me. Didn't see you standing there. How's it going? I mean, how's it going these days? I mean…man, what do I mean? I mean, I know it's not good, but…you know what I mean, don't you?"

Darrio relaxed. "So you weren't here when it happened."

"Huh? No, I was away on business. Good thing too. Everyone around here's gotten all jittery all of a sudden. Less people too. Somebody said something bad happened and you were involved, but I don't believe it."

"Hey," said one of the other merchants. "Are you actually talking to this guy?"

"Yeah. So?"

"That's the Firestar. You can't talk to the Firestar."

Sam crossed his arms and furrowed his brow. "I know good and well who he is, and his name's Darrio. Besides, what's it to you?"

"The Firestar's bad for business." He then turned to Darrio. "You ain't welcome here. Go away. You're scaring my customers. Shoo!"

"Hey! That's my friend you're talking to!"

"Friend? I don't trade with friends of the Firestar."

"So what? I've got no business with you."

"You won't have any business in this city if you keep talking to him. Get me?"

Darrio stepped away, but Sam called out to him. "Where are you going? You don't have to listen to him."

"It doesn't matter," Darrio said.

Sam left his stand and stood in front of Darrio, barring his steps. "What are you doing?"

"You can't trade here if you're associated with me."

"So what? I'll find someplace else."

"You…idiot," Darrio sadly rasped. "You've got a debt to pay, don't you? You've got a family to worry about, right?"

"Yeah, but—."

"So do what you need to do," and Darrio stepped around him.

"Ha ha!" the arguing merchant laughed. "Go on! Go!"

"Go back and pay your debts," Darrio stated as he left.

Sam slowly returned to his stand. Soon after, the market was once again lined with customers, but few people were buying from Sam. "Why so glum?" the arguing merchant asked. "It's better this way."

Sam looked at the merchant and shook his head. "No. It's not."

When Darrio returned to Talim and Eloi who were waiting outside of Ambrosia's main entrance, Eloi took notice of Darrio's diminished disposition. "Firestar? What has happened?"

"Nothing."

"Are you ready then?" Talim asked.

Darrio nodded.

"Then let us go."

The three left the city and headed north, but a great distance east of their position stood a man in white. He was the same one Darrio saw at the temple of Magnus in Esea, and he watched the trio of shades with stillness. Darrio, sensing they were being observed, turned his sight toward the man's direction but saw nothing. The man in white was gone.

CHAPTER 8
Feared

FEAR, ANGER, AND a contentious form of tension had risen in Turil concerning Seris since Ambrosia's delusion. He knew reporting his suspicions to the High Elders would likely be less than fruitful. Nevertheless, he approached Elder Tiberius in the Grand Hall's upper chamber which was used for private meetings and discussions. The Elder was standing at the window but did not turn when Turil entered. "I saw you approaching. You look worried, General Turil."

"I am concerned."

"About the Firestar?"

"About Seris."

Elder Tiberius turned and motioned for Turil to have a seat at the council table. "What about Seris concerns you?"

"He is a changed man. He has always been, and still is, a cunning sort. Always calculating, figuring, and planning. If you had only known him as I know him, you would—," but Turil stopped and sighed. "Know him. I knew him."

"The Magic War has changed many of us."

"It is not just the war. Seris has always believed in change towards the greater good. He would accept convicts, criminals, people I would have otherwise deemed unfit for duty, and forged them into soldiers, officers, captains, and the like."

"You are still against this?"

Turil shook his head. "But you must understand. It was never his messages that I disagreed with. It was always his methods. He was too close with men of that sort, the Firestar in particular. I believe that is what changed him."

"And the Firestar's damage continues."

"Sir Elder. I do not trust Seris. I do, now, believe he is capable of treachery."

"You said he was duty-bound."

"He is. Even now, I can see his limitations, but Seris has always maintained a...flexible interpretation of his duties. He judges more by principle than by letter of law. He could not ask others to obey him and likewise disobey others. In that sense, he is still bound by duty but only by the principle of that duty. Outside of this, I know he has no inherent reverence or respect for authority of any kind."

"What are you trying to say then? Is he capable of rebellion or isn't he?"

"Not overt rebellion but...something. Elder, I know the man's patience. He can wait for opportunity, and if it should come at an inappropriate time, then he will wait for another, but he does not give up on what he has set his mind on doing. Even if it should take entire seasons from his life, he will wait."

"But do you believe he will raise his sword against us?"

In truth, Turil knew Seris had done so during the delusion and would likely do so again if the opportunity presented itself, but the circumstances had been extreme in that case. "No. At least, he will not do so directly. I don't know. I have no idea what he is planning, but he is planning. I have seen the look in his eye."

"What do you want to do then? Will you relieve him from duty?"

"He would then fall out of my sight, and doing so would give him greater room to act according to his own desires. No. If I do that, there is no telling what he will do."

"Then you are in a most difficult position, General. You have a subordinate and former friend who you do not trust and who may prove dangerous to the affairs of this realm."

Turil winced. "It is difficult. Yet, and pardon my presumption but, you do not seem as concerned about this as I."

"I am concerned, but it is not over Captain Seris. A man like that can be kept on enough detail to make opportunity for betrayal impossible."

"What is it then?"

"His influence and control of the Firestar. The boy does not agreeably answer to anyone but Seris. Even during the war, though he followed the orders of those above him, he did so only because of his captain. If you should cut him loose, what of the boy? Who will he regard then?"

Turil had no answer for this nor had he considered it.

"The Firestar is angry at us, the High Generals, and the whole world. If left to his own devices, I and the others fear he may very well end the world as we know it. We cannot allow that to happen, General."

"But the Firestar, Darrio, has learned to direct most of his anger."

"Indeed, and he directed that anger towards our enemies, but in times of peace when there is no enemy left to fight, who then can receive his wrath?"

"I don't believe he will strike without reason."

"Are you really so naive, Turil?"

Turil had not been accused of such a thing in years and never in that tone. Even though the question came from an Elder, Turil was insulted by it. "Excuse me?"

"He has enough reason to direct his anger towards the world. He is hated. Even if he does not do so soon, he will eventually. I understand your concern over Captain Seris, but the Firestar is the greater threat, and not only to us but to everyone. So long as he exists, the world remains in danger of his wrath. Do we have an understanding, General?"

Turil, despite resenting the dismissal, nodded after great hesitation.

"Good," Elder Tiberius said as he returned to his window. "I'm glad we had this discussion."

Turil stood. "What should I understand as your final recommendation concerning Seris?"

"You have already received my recommendation. And, General?"

"Yes?"

"Do not plan operations behind the back of the councils. We expect better of you."

"Sir?"

"It may be construed as an unnecessary act of aggression that would place this nation in even greater danger. Such actions could even be considered treasonous. Try to keep this in mind the next time you discuss secret incursions into the Outer Realms."

Turil stood trembling in place. He knew the consequences of his actions, if discovered, would likely be dire, but he did not expect them to be uncovered so soon. His heart skipped a beat as he considered who might have reported his plans, but after he calmed himself, a necessary exercise, his blood grew hot. He considered Seris as the most probable culprit, and this possibility angered him.

"That is all, General. You are dismissed."

Talim, Eloi, and Darrio were still continuing their trek in the days following Turil's meeting with the High Elder. They had moved across the dusty lands of Salia's northern canyons and cliffs unhindered, but they were far from being at ease. Darrio had grown tired of Talim's boasting and recollections of glory moments during the war. In fact, he even stressed on several occasions, "Nobody gives a damn, you idiot! Shut up!" Yet Talim would continue as if the sentiment was not heard. Darrio thought Talim, being an illusionist, had unconsciously summoned a world around him in which his every word was of great importance. Unlike Sam, who jumped from subject to subject, Talim appeared to think his stories were of such substance as to necessitate continuous recital of each tale. When he finished his tale of a single experience, he would retell it over and over again while adding a few new details and omitting others until Darrio once again argued his dissatisfaction. So far as Darrio was concerned, involuntary self-delusion was the only reasonable explanation for this behavior. "You've already told the same damn story seven damn times by now!"

"I have it memorized," Eloi added.

Talim scoffed. "You unseasoned miscreants could never appreciate a good tale."

"That's because nobody cares," Darrio said. "And half of your stories aren't even true."

Talim bellowed, "Which half is untrue?"

"The half where you make yourself look good."

Eloi snickered, and Talim noted the expression with astute attention followed by shock and awe. "Did you just laugh, Eloi?"

Eloi's expression quickly faded as he took a moment to consider the question. When he finished recalling the moment, he flatly replied, "I did."

"Firestar! Eloi just laughed!"

"So?"

"Eloi never laughs! He never cries or expresses pain. He has not exhibited the faintest expression of life before now, and even when he has smiled, it has been form without substance. He has always lacked heart, and now he laughs. Does this not surprise you?"

Talim was far more excited about the development than Darrio who only shrugged. "Why should I care what he does?"

Eloi looked towards Darrio, his expression once again devoid of feeling. "You do not care, Firestar?"

Darrio once again looked at Eloi and was unsure of what to say. "Why do you keep asking me stuff like that? You've been doing it ever since we started."

"You do not care?"

"It doesn't matter what I think. Why do you keep—? Damn it! Stop talking to me!"

"Okay," Eloi said as he proceeded forward.

Talim watched Eloi's quickened advance and recalled what Seris once told him. If there were traces of humanity still dormant in the heart of Eloi, it was surely a damaged one. It was difficult, however, for even Talim, the most humane of Seris' shades, to consider this given the total lack of presence. When he recalled his first encounter with Eloi, he shuddered, for he had never encountered a person with no readable emotions until then. This made him a complete unknown in Talim's eyes, a living puzzle with no clues to the solution. But then, as he began to finally see traces of Eloi's humanity, however faint they may have been, he began to feel a new thing for Eloi aside from uncertainty and fear. He pitied the man. "What has ruffled you, Firestar?" Talim asked. "Eloi has not said more than ten words to you, and you are already more angry at him than you are with me."

"What do you care?"

"He is a comrade, Firestar. He should be treated as such."

Darrio did not take well to Talim's rebuke though he knew it was rightly deserved. For some reason, seeing Eloi show even the faintest concern for how he thought only made the situation between them less bearable. Where before Eloi could be dismissed without worry of damaged feelings, he then became another potential casualty of Darrio's anger, and Darrio did not like this. So far as he was concerned, despite the past, Eloi was still an innocent.

"There is someone in the distance," Eloi said.

Darrio and Talim peered ahead to find a lone, black figure moving swiftly across the horizon. "Is it a shadow caster?" Darrio asked.

"I am uncertain."

"Who else would roam these forsaken lands?" Talim said. "Come! Let us catch him and see what he is doing here."

Talim and Eloi soared ahead using wind magic though Eloi was assisted by Talim, but after a significant advance, the two stopped and looked behind them. Darrio had not moved. "Firestar! Make haste, or we will lose him!"

Darrio put on an indignant expression and lifted his arms to expose his twin pair of irons. Talim's response was embarrassed laughter. Darrio's response was an utterance. "Moron." Talim continued ahead to retrieve the figure while Eloi walked quietly with Darrio. He almost resented such treatment but appreciated, at least to some degree, the company even if that company happened to be Eloi. Even so, he felt largely unnecessary without his magic and felt he had little to contribute to the mission without it. He was still a skilled fighter, but unlike the others who appeared to have talents deemed useful for any field, Darrio felt he had no other practical abilities. His only skill, so far as he could see, was killing people, and it seemed as if every other talent he had was tied to that end. "Eloi?"

"Yes?"

"I'm about to ask you a stupid question, and you can't tell anyone I asked you this. Understood?"

Eloi nodded. "What is your question?"

"How do you know me?"

"Clarify."

"I mean...how do you...look at me?"

"You are Firestar."

Darrio paused as he waited for a more thorough answer, but nothing came. "Is that all?"

"That is all."

Darrio felt he should have known better than to expect a great answer from Eloi. Nevertheless, the answer saddened him. "Thanks a lot."

Eloi looked at Darrio and once again took note of his diminished expression. "Have I said something wrong?"

Darrio shook his head. "No."

Talim's boastful laughter then echoed from the horizon. He approached with the figure bound and slung over his shoulder, and when he reached them, he threw his quarry to the ground. "He was a shadow caster, just as I said!"

The three stood in a circle around the frightened caster, a fire bearer who, by physical appearance, was not much older than Darrio. His hair was dark and at shoulder's length, and his eyes were young and unaccustomed to the possibility of death. His complexion was also darker than the Salian natives but of a different hue than Darrio's. "He is a foreigner," Eloi said.

"Yes," Talim confirmed, "but he is too light for the Hollow Realm," and while he said this, he looked at Darrio. Darrio noticed Talim's analytical gaze, but his only response was an indignant glare of his own. "What?" Talim responded.

Darrio shook his head and did not answer. "He's obviously from the Burning Realm which doesn't make any damn sense since there's no magic in the Burning Realm. And I thought the Shadow Casters were supposed to be ancients."

"Remove the bind," Eloi said.

Darrio did so and asked the foreigner, "Hey. Are you from the Burning Realm?"

"Y-yes?" he answered with his thick, native accent.

"What the hell are you doing here dressed like that?"

The young shadow caster looked at each of the three shades but said nothing.

"What's the matter?"

"The boy appears to be frightened of us!" Talim laughed.

"Is this unusual?" Eloi asked.

"Indeed. The people of Fira are known for their resilience. Fear is among the many words they do not know."

"They do not know fear? Then they are like me."

"No," Darrio said. "They only say that to make themselves sound good. It isn't true."

"Oh."

Darrio forced the caster to sit upright and twisted him about forcefully. "Hey! Are you listening? Can you understand what I'm saying?"

"Yes, yes! Please do not shake me!" the caster replied.

Darrio released him. "Good. Now you're going to tell us everything you know. Do you understand?"

The young caster nodded. "I understand, but I cannot tell."

"Then I hope your ancestors are happy with you."

"Are you going to torture me?"

Darrio stepped back. "No. I'm going to kill you."

"What? Why? What did I do?"

"You didn't do anything. You're just useless, and I don't feel like dragging you around with us if we can't get any answers. We're supposed to be killing you people anyway." Darrio turned to Talim. "You want to do this or should I?"

"You want me to do it?"

"You'll make less of a mess."

"Don't kill me!" the caster pleaded. "I do not want to die! I am not ready!"

"So your ancestors would be ashamed of you, huh? Too bad. Not my problem."

Eloi tilted his head with curiosity. "Why is he afraid of death?"

"Because he's too much of a damn coward to be accepted by his forefathers. The people of Fira have this big thing about honor and courage. It's a deal breaker for their version of paradise after death. It's why they're so tough to fight and stupid at the same time, except for this one. He's just weak."

"Weak?"

"I am not weak," the caster protested.

"Yes, you are," Darrio said. "You're soft. You've got no courage, no dignity, no self-respect, and you definitely don't have any honor. Your ancestors are probably sitting upstairs somewhere and shaking their heads. Or laughing."

At Darrio's taunt, the young man became incensed. "What would you know about me? What would you know of honor?"

"I know better than to get tied up by a man who doesn't even use the muscle he has."

"You tease too much," Talim said, "but you have done enough."

The shadow caster, curious to know what was meant, faced Talim and looked directly into his eyes. They were no longer Talim's actual eyes by the caster's sight but two glowing spaces of yellow light. Talim smiled. "Now let us see what secrets lie in that untempered mind of yours."

Darrio and Eloi waited for what seemed like a span of mere moments, but for Talim, the seconds stretched into minutes and the minutes into hours. There was no concept of time for an illusionist performing his craft especially as it pertained to descending as the act of entering a person's mind was known.

Descension was largely impossible for those who were both conscious and unwilling to go through with the act. However, when a subject's emotions were heightened, the spiritual will, it was thought, would give way to the will of desire. It was therefore important for the subject to be properly taunted, tortured, or else made to feel sad in order to open the way for descension. If this was not done, or if the subject was to regain a sense of their spiritual will, the illusionist could be ejected, trapped, or else harmed within the mind of the target. The illusionist always strove to remain in control of a person's mind and did this through the revelation of the subject's fears, insecurities, and doubts. In the most extreme of cases where a target allowed the descension and prevented escape, the illusionist was left at the mercy of the person he entered. Because of all the risks associated with descension, in addition to the illusionary school itself, there were few people in the realm who took up the art as a profession. With the exception of rogue illusionists who consistently met with a bitter end, Talim and three others were the only ones known who could competently perform a descension, and Talim was called the master.

The young shadow caster, then shrouded in the darkness of his own mind, was fearful and filled with insecurity. He knew nothing of descension, the techniques of illusionists, or how to defend against them and was unsure of what happened. He heard Talim's voice echo at him from all directions. "Boy!"

The frightened young man looked around in spirit. There was no sense of a body, and he called back. "Where are you?"

Talim laughed, the echo carrying his voice everywhere at once. "What a colorful mind you have. It is so full! Stories! Legends! Grand struggles of old! So many of others. So few of your own."

"How do you know this? What are you doing?"

"Hm? What is this?" The sound of a heart's beat then echoed like a forceful rumble of thunder. "Drat!"

"What have you done?" but Talim's silence only worried the young man further, and he screamed, "What have you done?"

Darrio and Eloi stood patiently as Talim and the young shadow caster remained still and motionless. "I bet he screwed something up," Darrio said.

"Talim does not do such things. He is careful with other minds."

"What do you mean?"

"He respects them and calls them precious. Only when the subject is an enemy will he inflict harm, and even then, only from inside. Do you not know this, Firestar? You have known him longer than me, have you not?"

"I just watched him do whatever it is he does. I didn't know he had rules for it. Or maybe he tried to tell me and I forgot. I don't know."

"Have you no rules for your actions?"

Darrio thought for a second and responded. "Kids."

"Kids?"

"I don't kill kids."

"Why?"

Darrio looked at Eloi unsure of why he had to answer the question, and then he remembered who he was speaking to. "Kids are innocent. They're too young to know what they're doing."

"What if you encounter an innocent adult? Would you kill him?"

"An adu—? No."

"Then it is not children only but anyone who is innocent. Yes?"

"Yeah. I guess."

Eloi looked forward, his blank eyes staring over the horizon. He then stated with empty words, "I will not kill innocents."

"Okay. Fine."

A moment of silence passed, but Talim had yet to ascend out of the shadow caster. Eloi spoke again. "Firestar?"

"What is it?"

"Who is innocent?"

Before Darrio could attempt an answer, Talim's body heaved a bitter sigh, and he was animated once again with life. The young shadow caster followed directly after but remained asleep. "What happened?" Darrio asked.

"I have isolated the boy," Talim replied, "but we must move."

"Why?"

Talim plucked the shadow caster from the ground and placed the unconscious body over his shoulder. "We were baited."

Darrio and Eloi followed Talim further north until they entered a local region of high cliffs. Night descended upon the landscape, and the three shades set their camp in between the deep fissure of two high precipices. Once settled, Darrio asked, "What's going on? Why did you isolate him?"

"Fear and insecurity traced his being, and these things were amplified within him. Someone has descended before me, or else some other force has multiplied his anxieties. I feared a full revelation would have killed him."

"It is our mission to kill him," Eloi said.

Talim groaned. "The boy has not yet come out of season. He is but a child."

"A child?" Eloi then turned to Darrio. "What does this mean?"

"What does what mean?"

"He is nearly an adult, but Talim says he is a child, but he is also a shadow caster. Does that mean he is not innocent, or is he innocent?"

"Innocent?" Talim chuckled. "Eloi, there is no one who is innocent."

"No one? Then everyone may be killed. Correct?"

Talim then stumbled over his previous expression and replied in haste. "No, no, no! There are exceptions, Eloi! Exceptions!"

"Who is exempt?"

"Ah," Talim sighed as he leaned back. He knew well of Eloi's method of interpretation. While he would naturally build upon previous lessons in some cases, in others he seemed to simply erase what he knew about a subject and substitute it with the new doctrine. Talim did not want to say something that, when taken to its furthest end, would do more harm than good. Explaining moderation to Eloi had been nearly impossible, so most simply told him to do as he was told. This had also been problematic. "Children," Talim finally said. "Anyone clear of criminal charges, women, those in need, friends, allies, all of these are people who you do not kill."

"What if there is a criminal who is an ally and a woman? She is not an innocent. She would be executed, would she not?"

"Well, of course she would."

"Why?"

"Allies don't hurt each other," Darrio said. "Besides, you can't just go around killing people. There has to be a reason."

"What is justified?"

Talim and Darrio both sighed. "Look," Darrio said. "You're a soldier. You can only kill people you're told to kill. If it's a target or an enemy, fine. If not, leave it alone. Okay?"

"Okay," and Eloi turned his attention to the shadow caster. "May I kill him now?"

Darrio and Talim both shouted, "No!"

"Leave the boy be, Eloi," Talim continued. "You will be told of what course to take as we move."

Eloi blinked twice but nodded. "Understood," and the other two shades sighed with relief.

Darrio then said, "Now you've made me tired. How long before the kid wakes up?"

"He will not wake unless I allow him to," Talim replied.

"Do we have time to rest?"

"Yes."

"Good." Darrio slumped against a precipice wall and slid to the ground. "You keep first watch, Eloi. I'll take second."

"Okay."

Darrio set his head to sleep, and Talim followed shortly after. Eloi was then left alone to watch the camp. His first thoughts were to examine the boy and ponder the meaning of innocence, but after a fruitless expedition into the subject, he turned his eyes towards Ambrosia.

Within the Hall of Order, Turil sat in his office as he waited impatiently for Seris' arrival. He was visibly upset as his hands were clasped, and his knee bobbed up and down in his seat.

When Seris finally arrived, Turil asked him to enter and forced the door shut behind him by force of magic. "Are you angry, Turil?" Seris asked.

"Have a seat," Turil answered. Seris calmly did as requested while Turil glared at him. When a moment of silence passed, Turil asked, "What have you done to me, Seris?"

Seris was quiet.

"Why did you betray me?"

"Who has told you of this?"

"I learned of it from Elder Tiberius, but that is not the point. I placed my trust in you."

"Your trust was misplaced."

"I can see that now."

Seris shook his head in disagreement. "I misspoke, and you misunderstood me, Turil. I did not tell the Elders of your plan. I would not. I could not."

"Then how did they find out?" Turil asked with a cynical look in his eye.

"One of your subordinates? Captain Palim is the one I would suspect."

"Palim has been loyal to me."

"Except in giving a full report concerning Arthis. I have heard his tone, Turil. His hatred for Darrio matches the Elders. Do you think he is above sacrificing your plans to refocus their attention on him? I say he is not."

Turil grumbled but kept his eye on Seris.

"But you suspect me of more than this, don't you?"

Turil's eyes turned to the framed picture sitting on his desk, the one depicting the two of them standing side by side as comrades. "We have all changed, Seris. My concern is over what you have become." He then looked directly into the eyes of his friend and said, "And I must know your intent. I saw the look in your eye after you drew your sword on the Elders that day. I know you are planning something."

"What do you want me to do?"

Turil unclasped his hands and placed his feet firmly on the ground. "Do not lie to me. Do not speak in riddles. Do not veil me with omissions and substituted details. Just tell me what it is, plainly and truthfully."

"If I tell you, you will think less of me."

"And if you lie to me, I will hate you."

Seris leaned back and took a moment to think. The hesitation and conflict were evident on his face.

Turil frowned. "I see you in a most uncomfortable position, old friend. If it takes you this long to answer, then I know something is wrong. Is it dire?"

Seris nodded.

"Does it involve the boy?"

Seris nodded.

"And are you…set to betray this nation, Seris?"

Seris replied firmly. "No."

"Then what is it? What are you doing that you are so unwilling to tell me? What do the Elders have to do with it?"

All questions were met with silence.

"Do you resent their treatment of Darrio that much?" but Seris turned away. "Seris. How can I say this? I know what the boy must mean to you, and you know I cannot produce children either, but—."

Seris, upset, pulled back and stood to his feet. "If you will hate me, Turil, you will hate me, but I can not tell you of my plans."

"Seris, I would go to the ends of the earth for you! If it's of any benefit, let me assist!"

Seris shook his head. "I do not want you involved."

"Why not?"

"Because you are innocent."

Turil sat in shock. "Do you think I have no shame to carry, Seris? Don't you know me?"

Seris said nothing. He had rarely shown himself vulnerable in the presence of others and was the stone by which many of his shades placed their confidence. Turil knew, by experience, that he would only speak plainly to those he deeply cared about. He also knew that this moment would be his only opportunity to get through to him. "Turil," Seris said.

"Yes, what is it?"

"You mustn't trust me."

"What do you mean?"

"You mustn't believe a word I say. Question my every move and action. Suspect my motives. Observe me in silence. View my movements as you would view the movements of an enemy, but I say to you again, do not trust me."

"You are hiding again, Seris. Do not do this to me."

"I am sorry, Turil." Seris turned and made his way to the door, but before leaving, he said, "Take care that you are not around when I have the opportunity to act."

Seris left the office leaving Turil dazed and winded. Turil once again looked at the picture, and in a fit of despair and rage, he swept it up and launched it against the wall above the fireplace. The frame shattered, and the glass trickled to the ground. The picture escaped and slowly descended until its form entered the flame. The caption on the picture was the first to burn away followed by Seris, his smile, and lastly, Turil.

When the morning came, Darrio stood over Talim and nudged him with his foot. "Hey. It's time to wake up."

Talim growled at first, he was not a morning person, but he rolled his massive form over and sat up. "Nothing to report?"

"Nothing."

Talim yawned and proceeded to awaken the young shadow caster. "Arise, boy. It is time we talked."

Darrio then turned to Eloi. "Get up, Eloi."

Eloi's eyes opened on command, and he promptly stood to his feet. "Good morning." He then greeted Talim and the young shadow caster in turn saying, "Talim. Prisoner who I may not yet kill."

"What?" the young man said nervously.

"Stop talking like that," Darrio said.

Talim leaned on the wall across from the shadow caster and crossed his arms. "Boy. Do you remember where you were going?"

"I was late."

"Who were you going to see?"

"I can not tell."

"Did you realize you were being used as a lure to keep us occupied?"

"A lure?"

"You have been used and disrespected by those around you. They cannot see you for what you are worth."

"You are lying. You are lying so I will talk."

"You have come to know something of me as I have come to know something of you. We have both left our impressions on each other. Answer me. When I speak in this manner to anyone, do I lie?"

The shadow caster searched within himself, and his eyes left Talim to do so. "No."

"Have I lied in the past in this manner?"

"No. You do not even mean to in your stories."

"I told you," Darrio said.

Talim dismissed the statement. "Then you know that I do not lie when I say you have been used." The shadow caster did not answer but instead broke into tears. "I know this is difficult for you. You have lost much, and in your attempt for gain, you have attained little, but the people you serve are no more honorable than the creature you chase. They do not have the best interests of you or your nation at heart. They have lied to you. I know what you sought by joining them, but this is not the way you should have gone."

The shadow caster was still unable to respond, and Darrio could not help but feel sorry for him. "What happened?"

"He joined their ranks in hopes it would grant him power and strength. He received his desire for power, but he has not attained the kind of strength he was looking for."

"Is he alone?"

Talim shook his head. "He is one of many from the Burning Realm. Many of their youth have joined them."

"But the people of Fira hate magic. What could have happened to make them join?"

Talim grumbled as he decided how best to frame his words in front of the caster but found he was unable to do so. Instead, he turned aside to face the shadow caster and said, "To sleep, boy." Talim snapped his fingers, and the young man quickly fell to rest. Talim then returned to Darrio and said, "Are you familiar with a village by the name of Bir?"

"Never heard of it."

"Are you sure? He has a memory related to an event there. You have not heard nor encountered such a village during the war? Not even in passing?"

Darrio shook his head. "If I remember right, the only battles I fought in the Burning Realm were against Legionnaires, and even that was usually in the field or in duels. We didn't scout many villages."

"Puzzling."

"Why?"

"He saw you, or a form of you, attack and burn his village. His siblings, a brother and sister, were destroyed."

"Is that why he joined? So he could avenge them?"

Talim nodded. "And his was not the only village. Bir, Heats, and many other villages were burned to the ground before the war ended."

"But the final battles of the Magic War were fought in the Hollow and Aural Realms."

"And I know you were in those regions at the time of the boy's recollection, but his image of you is still very clear."

"Then why didn't he recognize me?"

"He has no face to associate with the destruction, only eyes and a form of you without your cloak of shades. He knows of your titles as well. Deloran, Firestar, and besides this, he knows of your first name, but that is all. So long as we do not refer to you by title, he will not know. Do you hear me, Eloi?"

Eloi nodded.

"Wake him up," Darrio said. Talim snapped his fingers, and the shadow caster, still weary, arose. Darrio exchanged glances with Talim, affirming a decision the two had made in silence. "Pay attention."

"Are you going to kill me now?"

Darrio shook his head. "But you're going to tell us everything you know, understand? I know you think we're evil because we use magic, but the people you're with are even worse. If you want to go home, you've got to help us. Understand?"

"Home," the young man mused.

"We, unlike you, live long lives," Talim stated, "The span of your people is short. You remember in years and months. We remember in seasons. You must find something else to live for. Do not waste your time on revenge. Learn a craft in accordance with your abilities. Place your energies into something constructive. Build something. Do you understand what I am telling you?"

"Build...." The young man trailed into thought and then settled his mind with a nod of his head. "Okay. I understand. I will help you."

"Good," Darrio said. "You can start by telling us where you last met with them."

"I met them in the west. I was headed east. Master Sephor said he needed to meet with Master Treos."

"Sephor?" Talim asked. "Who is Sephor?"

"He is master of the Stars of Fire. Pillar of Magnus, he says."

"Stars of Fire," Darrio repeated. "They call themselves Firestars?"

The young man shook his head. "No. Not Firestars. Stars of Fire."

"Where's the meeting supposed to take place?"

"East. Two days. I did not want to be late."

"Alright. You're going home, and take that cloak off. If anyone else sees you, they won't ask questions. They'll just kill you."

"Okay."

At that moment, dust and stones fell from the surface above, and there was a low rumbling all around them. "The hell?" The walls of the crevice began shutting together in slabs on both ends. They were closing in towards the center. The ground around the young man also came up and held him at the ankles. "They're here."

Eloi scrambled up the wall face to the top while Talim placed his hands on the ground and caused the radius of their camp to rise on a slab of earth. The crevice closed completely by the time they reached the top, a narrow escape, but they were then surrounded by six shadow casters bearing the fire pattern, and each of them had the appearance of Burning Realm natives. "They must have come for the boy," Talim said.

Darrio drew his pair of crescent-edged daggers and sighed. "I'm really getting sick of this, and I hate using these things."

Eloi had a single short dagger, and Talim carried no weapon at all since he preferred to use the environment and his illusionary techniques against his enemies. "Then do not use them," he said.

"Do I look like an idiot to you?"

"It was a jest, boy. A jest."

"Stupid time for a joke."

When the first of the enemy shadow casters stepped forward, Talim summoned a fierce wind to stir up the dust around them and cover their actions. Eloi was the first to attack, and he leaped upon his first target and stabbed him repeatedly in the chest. The remainder fired blindly into the fog of dirt. Darrio met two. The one whose hand still held another shot of fire had it severed at the wrist before he could release while the other suffered decapitation. Talim, in the meantime, was accustomed to fighting without sight and picked up on the sounds of battle to detect his enemies. He positioned himself behind two others who huddled themselves together. He calmly placed his hands on their head, his eyes flashed yellow, and in the next moment, they fell dead. Eloi crawled across the field like an insect towards the final shadow caster and cut him down at the ankles before finishing him with a slash across his throat. Talim kept the dusty haze of debris circulated while he ordered his quarry to run. "Do not look back!"

The young man darted away from the cloud of dust and ran as fast as he could. He then slowed and began to turn his head to look but was interrupted by the thunderous sound of Talim's voice in his head. "No! Do not look back! Go, I said! Go!" The young man continued his run with increased vigor until he disappeared over a clearing of stones. He did not return.

When Talim could no longer detect the young man, and the link he established with him during the rise was broken due to the distance, he cleared the dust around them.

"You know," Darrio started, "when you said we were baited and told us to move, I thought we were moving to a place where they couldn't trap us."

"They must have been tracking him. Perhaps they were suspicious."

Darrio looked around. All six of the enemies, then dead, were only a little older than the one they released. "Damn kids."

Talim shook his head. "By their reckoning, they were adults."

"I don't care how they reckon. They could have been two hundred for all I care. They were kids. Just...stupid kids."

"Firestar," Eloi said.

"What?"

"Is this what you mean by exception?"

Darrio's eyes drifted to Eloi whose genuine innocence and ignorance were apparent. It was strange to see him as still young in mind, especially against the context of the moment, but Darrio's patience was exhausted and his tolerance for innocence was diminished. Had Eloi been anyone else, Darrio would have kept his peace, but in this case, his only response was to say, "Shut up, Eloi."

Talim sighed. "We are still no closer to discovering the cause of the dead bandits."

"What about the meeting?"

"The meeting?"

"We've still got two days, and you saw the location while you were in there, right?"

"Indeed."

"Then it's as good a place as any. We might even find out where the rest of them are."

"Then let us go."

The three shades left the site and headed east unaware that a shadow caster, the wind bearer who spoke with High Priest Derenger, had been watching them from a distant cliff. He was displeased. As they left the scene, he spotted another man dressed in white with white hair and a red collar. He too was observing the three and took notice of the shadow caster as well. "Meddler," the shadow caster noted. The man faded and vanished. The shadow caster then took a final look at the three and departed to the south.

The day came and went as Eloi, Talim, and Darrio moved across the landscape. As they settled into making their second camp, Eloi set out to hunt for food. In the meantime, Darrio and Talim were left alone to discuss the mission which then turned to a discussion on magic. "I must admit that sometimes I feel a sense of unease concerning the whole matter," Talim said.

"Why? Because of what's been happening or because of what the outsiders have said about it?"

"The latter, mainly. In fact, had it not been for Seris and the war, I may never have taken up illusionary practices."

"I don't remember being too excited about it either. I was curious, but this old man kept trying to push it on me."

"Old man? Who? When was this?"

"Before the war."

Talim leaned back. "I have just come to realize how little you speak of the past. I feel as if I am just beginning to know you."

Darrio's eyes shifted away from Talim. A deep-rooted sadness had emerged from behind them. "There's not much to tell."

Talim hummed. "Well, I have many seasons behind me, Firestar, and I even bear the memories of others. If there is something you would say to me, feel free to speak it."

"What are you? My counselor now?"

"If you would like me to be."

"You're an illusionist, and why would I tell you of all people?"

"You do not need to, Firestar. I am merely saying that I am here."

Darrio crossed his arms and continued to divert his attention while Talim proceeded to increase the campfire's intensity. It was a cold day, and the fire was slowly dying out. "You know," Darrio said. "I haven't said this to anyone."

"Said what?"

"How I still think about them. My parents, I mean. Sometimes. What happened, the past, things that just happened, you know?"

"Is there a reason?"

"It hurts too much."

"Your past?"

Darrio nodded, and Talim hummed. "I mean, I'm fine. I can take care of myself, and I'm fine. There's nothing wrong with me. It just hurts to think about it sometimes…you know?"

"I know."

Darrio was then stuck in a moment of hesitation and did not know how much he could afford to expose himself. To be vulnerable was to leave oneself open to attack or criticism. He then wondered whether or not Talim was using any of his techniques to relax him since he found the release to be somewhat calming. However, the question on Darrio's mind still ached to come out and not necessarily for the answer's sake. "Do you have any memories like that?"

Talim then became very solemn. His eyes cast themselves to the flame in front of him, and he answered, "I have many."

"Your own?"

"My own."

Darrio did not have the heart to ask for details and could see that his question had probed some ancient experiences. Talim, the normally boastful giant of a man, then seemed no greater in stature than the nearest pauper. In his eyes were many seasons of heartache and pain, doubt and transgression, worry and fear. Darrio had seen none of this during his previous tours with the man, and as Talim said shortly before, it seemed as if Darrio was seeing him for the first time. "I didn't mean to…I mean…."

"You do not have to apologize, Firestar. We have shared something." He then looked Darrio in the eye and smiled a wide and prideful smile. "I will not regret it if you do not."

"Regret what?" Eloi asked.

Talim and Darrio both jumped though Talim laughed afterward while Darrio, flustered and blushing intensely with embarrassment, asked, "How long were you standing there?"

"I have only just returned. See?" Eloi held up a string of gribbits that he captured. They were small and fuzzy creatures with long, wide ears and brown, fuzzy coats. They were regularly hunted for food. Eloi thought it strange for them to have forgotten his task and did not realize that his timing was less than desirable. "I was sent out to hunt. Do you not remember?"

"I remember," Talim chuckled.

"What's so damn funny?" Darrio asked.

"I have not seen you jump that high since our encounter with the Death Chaser of the Hollow Realm."

Darrio groaned. "Please don't remind me about that."

"Death Chaser?" Eloi asked. "What is a Death Chaser?"

Darrio groaned while Talim replied, "You shall love this, Eloi," and he recalled a tale that lasted for all of Darrio's renewed patience, and they retired to sleep that night.

The following day, the three came within viewing distance of a thick and unnatural fog. It sat like an impenetrable cloud on the surface of the dusty earth, and while Talim recognized it as a cover, he thought the environment they chose was an odd one to implement it.

"It does not rain often enough in these lands for this, and the air is quite dry. Their choice of concealment in the matter is poor."

"It could be a trap," Darrio said.

"Eloi."

"Yes?" Eloi answered.

"Scout ahead in the fog. If it is a trap, tell us, but if the enemy is present, remain quiet and report back when their business is finished."

"Yes."

Eloi moved ahead while the others stayed behind and took shelter behind a crop of boulders. "I hope it's not a trap," Darrio said. "Do you think he'll be okay in there?"

"Eloi? He will be fine."

"Good." Darrio then glanced ahead of him to find the man in white looking at him from afar. As soon as the man realized he had been discovered, however, he vanished. Darrio blinked several times to be sure that his eyes were not deceiving him.

Talim took notice. "What is wrong, Firestar? Have you seen something?"

"Somebody was watching us, but he just disappeared."

"Disappeared? It was not an illusion?"

"He was too far away to affect me, and there's nowhere to hide. It couldn't have been."

Talim was quiet for a moment. "Artisans and men more learned than I have repeatedly stated that the only method of disappearance in plain sight rests within the realm of light magic."

"I know what I saw."

"Then I do not like this."

"How do you think I feel? He was looking right at me."

"At you?"

Darrio nodded. "And I've seen him before. He was in Esea, and there was someone else who looked just like him but different."

"You said nothing about this."

"I didn't think it was important."

Talim grumbled. "Then we'll have to report this when we return."

Darrio turned towards the fog. "Hurry up, Eloi."

Eloi was slow, careful, and methodical in his advance. He had been a common pick for the scouting role due to his small size, mobility, and ability to evade detection, but his experience in stealth and silent maneuverings had been honed over many years and well before his conscription. The fog was thick and difficult to breathe in. This was no doubt purposeful to deter any would-be spies. However, Eloi gave no thought to his own comfort and regarded himself as the instrument of others in this case as in most cases. He was not aware of any other view to hold and considered himself no more and no less than a tool.

Eloi then came to a small region where the fog was thinner yet still present, and in the center were five men. Three were fire bearers, and one of them was Sephor who had been present at the Shadow Caster's gathering Darrio discovered. The other two were water bearers, Treos and an escort. Sephor was speaking. "Varis too?"

Treos nodded.

Sephor groaned in response. "Well, they have taken seven more of mine, but still, this is troubling news. With Bacchus missing, the search for light will be slowed."

"And I would search for him, but the master has forbidden it."

"You have spoken to him recently?"

Treos shook his head. "Elea gave me his words. They were… unkind."

"Where is she?"

"She has gone into the Hollow Realm with instructions to remain there and not return."

Sephor hung his head and sighed. "I warned you, Treos. I told you your actions would draw his rebuke."

"But he said it was…," but Treos shook his head. "It no longer matters. The master has punished me, and it is most severe."

"How so?"

"He has put the burden on us to finish our conflict with the Salians."

"Finish? He does not want you to flee?"

Treos shook his head. "And the Salians are hunting for us now."

"Then you will require assistance."

"Forbidden. The burden is ours alone to bear."

Sephor's eyes fell to the ground, and he quietly uttered, "I see."

"Sephor. I must ask you something."

"What is it?"

"I have received…many questions as of late pertaining to the direction of our tasks. I am beginning to wonder if…."

"If what?"

Treos quieted, and the muscles around his eyes and mouth twitched. It was a face lacking in peace and resolution and bordered on breaking. Treos then struggled to speak, but sadness choked off his words as if the terms he wished to speak were too painful to exit his throat. Treos then shook his head and turned his mind to something he could say. His throat was released from the grasp of that momentary despair, and he asked, "Have you heard what is happening in the Pillar of Wind?"

"No."

"No…I hear strange things, Sephor." Tears began to trickle down Treos' face. "Strange things indeed."

"What is wrong with you? What are you talking about?"

Treos continued to speak on in bursts of tears and feigned, unhappy smiles. "I meant no displeasure to the master. You know this, do you not?"

"I know this."

"He must know this too. Don't you think?"

"Treos, what is this? What bothers you so? What have you heard?"

"Nothing, Sephor," and Treos did his best to compose himself. "Nothing bothers me. I have simply heard that…that change is a strange thing."

"Change?"

"Pray for me, Sephor. You will pray for me, won't you?"

"Of course I will."

"For our master and our mission?"

"Yes, yes. I will pray."

"Good," Treos said as he smiled, and he raised an arm to wipe the tears from his face. "Good," and he placed his other hand on Sephor's shoulder. Sephor's initial reaction was to raise his own hand to the spot that Treos had touched, but Treos stopped him. "Then when it is over, we shall speak again."

When Treos released him, Eloi could detect a faint trace of smoke as if something had been burned into Sephor's cloak, but there was no way for him to distinguish what was burned into the area or why. The trail, however, was so quick and difficult to spot among the wisps of the fog that no one else among them appeared to notice.

Treos finished. "You have been good to me thus far. Take care of yourself, Sephor."

"I will," Sephor replied with a puzzled look. "You also take care, Treos."

"May the will of Magnus be with us."

"By his will."

Sephor and his fire bearers walked into the misty wall opposite Eloi's position while Treos and his escort approached. Eloi quickly and silently drew back choosing not to stir the air too much and give away his position, but even after they passed, Eloi remained among the fog. He returned back to the center to find that a single shadow caster had returned and was surveying the area to be certain that no one was watching him. He then shed his outer cloak which bore the flaming insignia. Underneath, he wore long, black pants which were tied off at his ankles with green and white wrappings. These same wrappings were tied around his waist and wrists, and for a shirt, he wore a sleeveless black ensemble and carried two shortened daggers on both sides of his waist. Emblazoned across his clothes and flesh were scripts arranged in a wind pattern. His first act was to stir the air and further clear the area of mist, but as he did so, Eloi's position was revealed, and when he took notice of the shade, he cursed.

Eloi drew his weapon and pounced toward the wind-bearing caster who swiftly hopped back and leaped forward over Eloi's follow-up attack. This one showed a far greater mastery over evasion and used the force of winds to effortlessly dance around Eloi's swift and lethal advances. When the caster managed to distance himself, he fled into the mist and swiftly leaped out of the fog only to land among Darrio and Talim.

"Ho!" Talim jumped with a laugh, and the caster cursed once more. Before he could leap again, however, Talim took hold of him and slammed his body to the ground. Darrio then leaped on top of him and clamped his hands over the caster's wrist. "Hold him!"

"What do you think I'm doing?"

Talim placed his hand on the caster's head, but try as he might to force him to sleep, the caster's will was too strong. "He is not like the others."

"Then I'll do it."

"You will?" Talim asked with surprise.

As an act of affirmation, Darrio pulled his arm back and delivered a swift and heavy blow to the caster's face. This promptly knocked the man unconscious.

Talim stood disappointed. "Your methods are crude, Firestar."

Darrio climbed off of the caster. "Well, it worked, didn't it?"

"You know what you lack?"

"What?"

"Grace. You should carry out your motions with style like I do."

"Style? I don't care about style."

"But it will display mastery in ease."

"No, it'll display that I'm an idiot and give someone else a better chance to kill me. You know better than that."

"Do you mean to say you do things the hard way every time?"

"I'm just saying illusionists and all you diplomatic types have the time to think about that stuff. People like me don't have that luxury."

"So you think my tasks are easy, is that it?"

"I'm not saying that at all."

"But you imply it in tone. You think less of what I do."

"What the hell? All I said was—."

"Luxury," Eloi interrupted.

"Huh?"

"You said Talim and those in his position have attained a luxury in relation to their craft, but you also have attained a luxury, Firestar. You are feared."

"Feared?" Darrio repeated. "You call fear a luxury?"

"It is the tool of powerful leaders, is it not? You have no need to worry about what others think of you because you already know, and there are fewer who would oppose you than would oppose a man like Talim or myself. You speak in open hostility towards me because there is no fear of me. However, Carsis, who is openly hostile towards you, minds his tongue even though he hates you. It is because he fears you whereas no one fears me."

Talim stood in awe and nodded. "You have such an astute eye, Eloi! I never knew you were watching us in this way."

"Great," Darrio said. "Just great. You're putting me under the damn looking glass when we've got an enemy to fight." He then leaned forward and hoisted the caster's unconscious body to its heels. "So are we going to take this bastard in for questioning, or do you want to stand here and talk about me all day?"

"Is this a valid option?" Talim smiled.

Darrio shook his head, "Moron," and dragged the body past them.

Eloi watched Darrio's shaken composure and looked toward Talim. "Was I wrong?"

"About what?"

"About fear."

"I do not think so, but it seems he regards the matter as more of a curse than a blessing."

"Could it not be used as one?"

"I suppose, but I imagine everyone has a different perspective on the matter."

Eloi blinked twice, and a spark ignited behind his large and empty eyes. "I would like to be feared."

Talim laughed. "And why is that, Eloi?"

"It is because you laughed. If I were feared, would I not be respected?"

Talim's composure then became very solemn, and he looked directly into Eloi's still-calculating eyes. There was no explanation Talim could conjure that would prove safe or satisfactory in his mind. In fact, given the way Eloi processed information, it seemed it would be better to say nothing at all than provide a broken rule which could be used for greater harm. Nonetheless, Talim could not bear to keep quiet and simply had to address the issue. "There is more to respect than fear, Eloi. You must also be trustworthy."

"Then is it greater to be feared or to be trusted?"

"There are dangers in both realms. In one, you can make yourself a slave to others while in the other, you enslave and oppress the ones around you. I am not prepared to give you an answer to this question."

Eloi was quiet while Talim awaited a response. He then said, "I will be both," and he left Talim and followed after Darrio.

Talim watched him and uttered, "God help the one who ignores his troubles, who sees and never acts on the plight of Eloi," and when Talim finished saying these things, he proceeded forward and reunited with the others.

CHAPTER 9
Solemn Justification

STANDING BEFORE TURIL was a reporting shade who answered, "Still no sign of him, sir."

"I want the man found," Turil ordered. "He has to be somewhere. Seek him out and bring him to me."

The shade standing before Turil bowed his head in response. "Yes, sir."

When the shade left the room, Turil sat back in his seat and sighed. Captain Palim had gone missing, and with Turil already under the Elder's scrutiny, his implied role in the affair seemed ominous. It was a situation that, in Turil's mind, appeared all too convenient for Seris, and he wondered whether or not it was engineered that way. After all, if he were to judge the case from an outsider's perspective, he would be the primary suspect of wrongdoing.

Turil set his mind to his paperwork, and the wind outside increased in intensity as a storm was coming in on the clouds. Turil thought very little of the rain and only hoped there would be no thunder and lightning. It then dawned on him as a contradiction in terms since this hope stemmed from a fear of uncontrolled elements. Turil then shook his head and attempted to return to his work.

A man's voice echoed to him from everywhere at once and said, "General Turil."

Turil raised his head and peered around only to find a canvas of empty space. "What's going on? Who is it?"

"Here." At this moment, the voice clearly originated from behind Turil, and he jumped from his seat and drew his weapon. Standing behind the desk was the prominent wind-bearing shadow caster who spoke with High Priest Derenger in the city of Lumineth. His long, dark hair still draped over his chest from the hidden features of his head that were shrouded in darkness underneath his hood.

"You're a terrible assassin," Turil sneered. "Guards!"

The caster shook his head. "I've isolated this room. No one can hear you."

"Then no one shall hear you either."

Turil advanced, but the caster bent backward to avoid the attack and sidestepped the forward kick which followed. "I have not come to kill you," he said in an agitated tone.

Turil attacked again, but each movement was met with indifferent evasions which frustrated him. "Be still, damn you!"

"General," the caster replied still dodging. "I have had the unfortunate task of ending men with lesser integrity for greater things than you." He then ended things with a forceful wave that hurled Turil's body against the wall and followed it with a multi-pronged arc of lightning that rendered his arms and legs immobile. "Do not try my patience now."

Turil groaned. The shock of the caster's attack was being sustained, and it circulated in Turil's joints. This made moving about too painful to bear. "What do you want then?" Turil asked. "I'm listening now."

"I came to offer you my assistance."

"Assistance?"

"We share a common foe."

Turil first smiled at the remark and then laughed despite the ever-present pain crawling just below the surface of his flesh. "Is insanity a common trait among your people?"

"You believe this is a joke?"

"Or a poorly conceived ploy. Do you honestly believe a man in my position would accept help from someone like you?"

"Only if it were justified."

"And what would justify this cooperation? Death? I tell you, I have been ready to die for a long time."

The caster shook his head. "If it were as simple as that, I would not even be here. No, the only thing you must worry about is the safety of your nation."

Turil remained quiet for a moment as his previous resolve slowly dissolved from his face. "You would hold this land hostage in exchange for cooperation?"

"I would not."

"Then why did you speak it?"

"It's not as you understand. The enemy has more in mind than your pathetic nation."

"Release me."

The caster obliged, and the shock which continued to hinder Turil dissipated providing him with a moment of relief. Turil stood to his feet to stretch and soothe his newly liberated muscles. "You have a strange way of offering assistance. You say you've come to help me and then insult my country."

"I apologize. It has become an ancient habit."

"I'm sure." Turil, then of the proper mind to use restoration magic, used the silence to heal his wounds.

The caster took notice and was dissatisfied. "Your restoration is inefficient."

"How so?"

"It is ignorant. Your body complies, but it does not agree. Will you allow?"

"I will not."

The caster shook his head. "As you wish."

"You must tell me, though. This action you're taking to enlist my help, won't this work against you and your master's cause?"

"His cause is no longer my cause."

"How so?"

"That is none of your concern."

"Then what benefit will you gain from this?"

"Also none of your concern."

"Then why should I help you?"

"You are looking for the five masters, are you not?"

"You would deliver them to us?"

The caster was silent. "It is not that simple. The one you would ultimately face is no one to be trifled with."

"The highest master of your group."

The caster nodded.

"But he is only one man."

"It was by the work of one man that this world was destroyed."

Turil returned to his seat, sighed, and peered at the ceiling. There were many thoughts racing through his mind, the most pertinent of which related to the shadow caster and how Turil could trust him. "You are still the allied enemy of my enemy."

"Then what is your choice?"

"You must provide me with insurance of your claims."

"I will retrieve your captain for you."

"Alive."

The caster nodded. "And unharmed."

"Good, but that will not be enough. I must learn about your people. Who they are, how they operate, and where."

"I will tell you only so much."

"And why is that?"

"I am still under watch."

"Give me your name, then."

The man hesitated. "If you should repeat this, either in word or in writing, I will be forced to silence you, and you will not be warned."

"You will not have to if anyone discovers this. Besides, you have me at a crossroads. There is no one else I can trust at the moment. I either take you on as an ally or sort through this mess on my own."

"So be it." The caster opened the office door where two guards sat unconsciously but otherwise unharmed. They were sleeping. "It is Asher," he said.

Turil nodded in response, and once Asher took his leave, Turil leaned back in his seat and sighed. He then stared at the ceiling while tracing the room with his eyes. With each area marked out, he could imagine the room as a tightly knit puzzle with each element interlocking with another. His mind then drifted to what he knew of the events and what he could see as far as the outcome. He then drifted to Saria, the blind girl that Darrio returned with, and recalled the defensiveness Darrio had shown in trying to protect her. "Enough," he thought aloud. Turil stood to his feet and walked to the door of his office where he nudged the sleeping soldiers with his foot. "Why are you sleeping? Get up you two."

The two soldiers were quickly roused, and they stood to their feet both embarrassed and fearful. "S-sorry sir! I don't know what happened. We were standing here, and we—."

Turil lifted a hand of silence. "I'm not concerned with that now."

"Was there an intruder, sir? Are you okay?"

"I'm fine, but I have a job for you."

"Yes, sir."

"Fetch the girl the Firestar brought back from Esea, and do not let Seris see you."

"Yes, sir."

"Be gentle."

"Gentle, sir?"

"I have heard the whispers among the ranks, but I expect better of those under my command. If she is harmed, that person will pay twice the penalty because she is only a child, but if I discover one of my own has caused her damage, the atonement will be multiplied ten times over. Is this understood?"

"Y-yes, sir."

"Then go."

The soldiers left while Turil shut the door behind them, and after returning to his seat, he pushed his paperwork aside and drew up a new sheet. On one half of the page, he marked down the names of everyone he knew involved in the case surrounding the Shadow Casters and drew lines with notes to show their connection. On the other half, he listed Darrio and Seris and everyone of significance who surrounded them. Saria was the only link. "Two separate cases," he mused though a feeling stirred inside of him indicating that this was not so. "One case?" Turil took a closer look at his notes and summarized in his mind everything he knew about each subject but still could see nothing else that would relate the two. As such, he was unable to determine whether or not the feeling was simply his imagination, the result of lost sleep, or something of a more divine nature. He then resolved to hold his notes, and he placed them in his drawer. "Later," he mumbled, and Turil returned to his paperwork.

As the night wore on, Talim, Darrio, and Eloi settled with their new captive near a cropping of stones. After Darrio released the body to the ground, Eloi gathered what little he could find to start a fire. As they sat, Talim kept the fire going while telling Eloi and Darrio tales of his achievements and his discoveries in illusion. "The mind is a complex thing," he finished. "I may never grow tired of probing its secrets."

"Yeah, yeah," Darrio said, waving him off. "Can we talk about something else now? Like what Eloi saw in that cloud back there?"

"There was a dispute," Eloi recalled, "but the water master said to the fire master that he would remain in the region to finish his fight."

"Foolishness!" Talim stated. "Do they not know that we are hunting them?"

Eloi nodded. "But it was an order from his master, a form of punishment."

Talim hummed. "This punishment will be their undoing, but that works well for us, doesn't it?"

"We still need to find out where they are," Darrio stated, and he nodded his head toward the captive. "Do you think he'll know?"

"Perhaps. Did you see anything else, Eloi?"

Eloi nodded. "The water master burned something into the fire master's fabric, but I could not see what it was, and no one noticed."

"He did this subtly?"

"Yes."

"Then it was not meant to be noticed. Perhaps it was a secret message to be shared only between them."

"Sounds like trouble in their ranks," Darrio said. "What do you think that's about?"

"We will have to ask our quarry."

"You think he'll talk?"

"There is only one way to find out."

The following morning was particularly dusty as the winds moved with greater urgency. "Wake up," Darrio said.

It was the first thing the captive shadow caster heard upon awakening. His eyes opened to an inverted view of the three standing around him in a circle. He then realized they had hung him upside down and bound him to a slab of risen rock. He was facing the winds. "What is this? Why have you fixed me like this?"

"Because the Firestar is cruel, and I believed it to be funny," Talim answered.

"Firestar." The caster turned his attention towards Darrio. "Then you are the one I hear so much about lately."

"Yeah? What of it?" Darrio asked.

"You have remained in a youthful stage. Why?"

Darrio crossed his arms. "I don't think that's any of your business. Besides, you're not in a position to ask questions."

"Yes. You intend to kill me when this is over."

"So you've heard," Talim stated.

"And it does not give me much of an incentive to speak."

"Who said anything about speaking?" Darrio said. "I was going to hurt you until Talim could get an opening. You suffer, and we take what we need. Or you could just make it easy."

"You'd rather I didn't?"

"I'm not in a good mood today, so no."

The caster shook his head. "Your tactics of fear will not work on me. I have been trained against all manners of torture, and my mind has been carefully sealed. You will get nothing from me."

"This sealing," Talim started. "Is this a normal practice among your people?"

"Among my own, it is mandatory."

"You speak for the Wind Bearers then."

"Wind Bearers," the caster said in a derisive breath. "Yes. I speak for us."

"I sense the title we have given you is not proper."

"No, and collectively? Neither is shadow caster. Yours is an imitation."

"What's an imitation?"

"It does not matter. Even if I told you, you would never believe me. You're all such fools anyway thinking yourself safe within the confines of your own reality. You do not know the truth, and you will never know the truth. You're all doomed."

"Safe?" Darrio said. "We just came out of a war, you moron. You think some of us know what safe is? Everybody dies in different ways. Some just go sooner than others."

"Is that so? And this is what the Firestar believes?"

"Did you expect something different?"

"I suppose not, but such rigidity is self-defeating. Change is among the only constants, my friend, and now I am curious as to what it would take to change your mind."

"Happy thoughts, a perfect world, and a city full of dead bastards like you."

The caster laughed. "A sense of humor. That's interesting."

"Uh-huh. Talim? We're wasting time. Let's get this over with."

"Indeed," Talim nodded, and he rotated the position of the caster until he was upright.

Darrio drew his weapon. "You can talk any time, you know, but I really don't care one way or the other."

"Spare me," the caster said.

"Suit yourself."

Darrio was never capable of deriving any real pleasure from the pain of others, especially in the realm of torture, and as he carried out his acts upon the caster, he did so with clear contempt. First, he asked, "Where's the rest of your party? Where do you gather?"

The caster did not answer, and Darrio began with a series of small cuts to the arms and legs of the caster who winced but otherwise reacted with indifference. "A waste of time," he finally said.

"Idiot." Darrio followed the statement with another inquiry into the Shadow Caster's whereabouts and questioned why they attacked the bandits. Again, the caster refused to speak, and Darrio followed with a series of quick and deeper cuts along with a few light perforations into the enemy's chest. After doing so, Darrio turned to Talim who, still seeking an opening, shook his head. Darrio returned to the caster. "Why won't you talk?"

The caster chuckled painfully. "Who is the one being tortured here? Is it the Firestar or the enemy?"

Darrio continued with even more severe perforations and even struck the caster's face with the handle of his weapon. "Quit being so damn stubborn! Talk!"

"But you said you were not in a good mood. Are you feeling better now?"

Darrio turned to Talim again who once more shook his head. Darrio then looked the bleeding caster over. "This isn't a game, you idiot. I really will kill you."

"That's funny. Wasn't that already your intention?"

Darrio struck the caster a few more times with severe blows to the head, chest, and limbs, and though the caster writhed in agony, his resolve never waned. Talim then ordered Darrio to stop. "That is enough, Firestar. He will not talk. He will not be opened."

By this time, the caster's body had been ravaged and bore numerous red ribbons of severed flesh. "Are you finished?" the caster gasped.

"We're finished," Darrio said, his eyes averted.

"Disappointing...and curious."

"What?"

"Salians....You are more physical, and yet...you are not the worst...when it comes to torture."

"Yeah," Darrio said with remembrance. "We have the Firans to thank for that."

"I expected...even worse...from the Firestar."

Darrio did not answer but crossed his arms and turned away.

"I would say something to you. I see in damaging me...you have also damaged yourself. I will also assume...that it has always been this way."

"Assume what you want," Darrio said without turning though his voice quavered.

"Perhaps he was right," the caster said. "Perhaps everything under the sun…is subject to the winds of change," and he chuckled. "Even with the best of intentions…with the worst of character, change is a dangerous thing." The caster's eyes then shifted in hue to yellow. He had suddenly transitioned into a state limit, but his body, damaged as it was, convulsed from the sudden shock. When it became still again, the three shades found him dead.

Darrio uncrossed his arms while he, Eloi, and Talim stood in silence for what appeared to be ages. "What just happened?"

"He invoked the call of oblivion," Talim answered.

"What?"

"It is a forbidden technique," Talim answered. "An amplification method of the illusionary school. I've seen it used among certain radical sects of Magnus. An illusionist well-versed in the craft of scripts will plant a command or phrase within the being of a willing ally. When the phrase is spoken, either by the host or the illusionist in front of the host, the will of desire, and by this I mean the desire of the illusionist, takes hold. But in order to induce this state and plant the command, the illusionist must leave a significant impression of himself, so much so that on commencement, the host gains all of the knowledge and experience of the illusionist."

"Is that why it is forbidden?" Eloi asked.

Talim shook his head. "When the phrase is spoken, the host takes on all attributes of the illusionist who implanted him and in turn loses his own identity. Thus, when the effect wears off and the will of desire has been satiated, the host, his identity then destroyed, dies in both mind and body. We illusionists associate a loss of identity with oblivion. It is why we give it that name."

"What kind of master uses his men like that?" Darrio asked.

"Either a madman or a desperate one. In any case, our captive is dead, and we have no other leads."

"But we have not checked the field of dead bandits," Eloi said.

"We might not find anything there," Darrio replied

"But it is the only place left to look," Talim said. "Let us go." Darrio and Eloi moved first while Talim prepared the caster's body for burial. While doing so, he repeatedly shook his head with pity. He detested torture, and seeing it troubled his heart every time. After removing the body and burying it, he uttered a silent prayer and returned to the others. "I do hope we are more fruitful in this endeavor. I grow tired of the dead."

"An enemy's an enemy," Darrio said.

"But still human."

"Human doesn't help me sleep at night."

"Then you would believe what you must. I will continue to say otherwise."

Their journey continued in relative silence without the recitation of tales or boasting from Talim and without questions from Eloi. Two of them were still in low spirits due to the events of the day and continued in such even when night fell. Eloi was curious about this but kept his peace until the following morning. Then, as they rose and prepared to go, he asked, "Why were you troubled yesterday, Firestar?"

"What?"

"When you tortured the shadow caster, you were troubled. Why?"

"Don't start with me, Eloi. It's too early."

"He does not wish to remember," Talim continued.

"The Firestar has been tortured?" Eloi asked.

Talim nodded and turned to Darrio. "Once in the Burning Realm and once in the Silent Realm. Correct?"

"Tauren bastards," Darrio groaned.

"Lon and I were together in rescuing him from the Silent Realm, but even to this day, no one knows how he escaped the Burning

Realm's camp. He has refused to talk on the matter but insists the Silent Realm was worse."

"What happened in the Burning Realm?" Eloi asked.

Darrio responded only by shaking his head.

"What is your opinion of torture, Talim?"

"I detest the practice!" and Talim sighed. "But I will admit that I have taken my part at times when I thought it could not be helped and could see no other way. Still, it is a detestable practice, Eloi. Pray you are never involved."

Eloi's body responded with a twitch, and his eyes blinked twice during the disturbance, but no one took notice.

They continued unimpeded for the next two days until they reached the field of bandits. It was west of a minor road and marked with brush, steep hills, and various obstructions for thieves to hide behind. Corpses dotted the area. "All this time and nobody's buried them," Darrio noted.

"Because they are too afraid to come here," Talim said. "All of these people came from a single camp. They were targeted."

"Why?"

"We do not know."

"And you went to the other camps?"

Talim nodded. "They would not speak."

"Think they'll speak to me?"

Talim hummed with thought. "Perhaps. Perhaps facing the Firestar will arouse a greater fear than whatever holds their tongues."

"What if they should test him?" Eloi asked.

Darrio and Talim exchanged glances, and Talim fell into thought. "We will just have to make a way," he replied.

There were a few scattered camps in the area made up of criminals, refugees, and other wanted and unwanted types who had banded together to make it on their own in the wilds. Even so, due to a perceived lack of resources and a general ignorance of practical crafts, they would often conduct raids on each other one week and then attempt trade the next. It was a precarious way of living the Elders paid no mind to. The citizens of the camps were sure to exasperate themselves with either worry or wine, and in either case, they would eventually destroy themselves or be destroyed by others. The only time there would be talks of action was if, and only if, one of their raids disrupted or disturbed one of the more protected territories. Besides this, the camps were left alone, a luxury they relished.

The nearest camp was only an hour's travel from the site and was composed of carts for holding goods and tents both great and small. Most people were in a state of either work or defense, and the newly noticed presence of three shades only agitated them. A man closest to them asked, "What do you guys want now? We said we don't know anything."

"Circumstances have changed," Talim said. "The information you contain is now even more valuable to us."

"We don't want any trouble."

"Then you will not have it but only if you tell us the truth, and I warn you. I will know if you are lying."

"Didn't you believe us last time?"

"We are here aren't we?"

The man looked over at Darrio. "Well, why did you bring a foreigner here? And why is he dressed like you?"

Darrio lowered his head and sighed.

"What?"

"The boy is no foreigner," Talim replied. "He is the Firestar."

"F-Firestar?" the man shouted, and the entire camp was alerted. "Why did you bring him here? We didn't do anything wrong!"

Talim laughed. "Have we entered a den of saints by mistake?"

"It's not fair!" a woman shouted. "All we want is to be left alone!"

"Why do you people hate us so much?" another man asked.

After this, another man approached them wearing a green vest with blue trim and dust-colored pants. His attire was also decorated with rags with another he wore around his head, and on his wrists were two irons, the same type which had been placed on Darrio. "Calm down folks. There's nothing to worry about." He then turned to Darrio. "I heard the Firestar was sealed anyway. He can't do anything to us."

"Is that true?" a man asked.

"He can't hurt us?" a woman followed.

"Why don't you show them?" the vested man asked.

"You sure you want that?" Darrio replied.

"Why wouldn't I?"

Darrio lifted his wrists to expose the twin pair of restraints, and on this particular note, the camp gasped and took note.

"Two pairs? Why?"

"Because the first one wasn't enough."

"And we'll remove them if need be," Talim added.

"Yeah right!" the vested man replied. "I spent a good year and a half hunting for the man who had the keys to mine and never could find him. You expect me to believe the Elders gave anyone the keys for unlocking the Firestar?"

"I don't give a damn what you believe," Darrio said as he lowered his arms. "It's not my problem what you think, but we came here for answers, and we're not leaving without them."

"I think you're bluffing."

"Fine. We'll do it the hard way then."

Darrio drew his weapons, and those around the vested man recoiled in terror. A few of them even ran for their tents. "Do something, Trevlin!" one of them cried.

The vested man, Trevlin, held his hands up in surrender. "Hey! Whoa! Wait a second!"

"We don't have all day! Are you going to talk or aren't you?"

"Fine, fine! We'll talk! Just…calm down! Be still!"

Darrio did as suggested though he felt an odd temptation to laugh as he remembered Eloi's comments on fear as a luxury. It had certainly proven useful in this case, and it took all he could to hold back a smile.

The camp, in the meantime, breathed a collective sigh of relief. "Shit. Is he always like this?"

"He is worse with his enemies," Talim replied.

"I'll bet. Guy's got a temper on him."

"Are you done?" Darrio asked.

"Uh, yeah. My tent's this way. Follow me."

Trevlin's tent was the largest one present and was decorated with trinkets of gold, weapons, and shields, all spoils of previous raids. Inside was a mat for sleeping in the corner, a table, a few chairs, and his possessions which sat in another corner. He asked the three to sit, and they did. "Alright. What do you want to know?"

"Why did you lie?" Talim asked.

"You're kidding, right?" Talim's stony silence said otherwise, and Trevlin excused his question. "We're not really on the best of terms with you guys, you know? We've got our secrets too."

"I'm sure."

"Look. Most of us just want to get away from what's happened, and it isn't easy trying to survive out here. It don't excuse what we did, but we're trying. You don't see us raiding the neighboring village, do you?"

"I suppose not."

"So, yeah. See? We're not so bad once you get to know us."

"Then you will tell us what you know and what you have seen. No more deceit."

Trevlin looked Talim up and down. "You know, I would have

never figured you for one, but you're an illusionist aren't you?"

"What brought that to mind?"

"I don't know. Probably something to do with your eyes. Looks like you're looking for a way inside my head or something."

Talim leaned back. "I did not know I had this look, but you are correct in assuming my profession."

"Figures. I hate illusionists."

"And I detest liars."

"And I hate listening to the two of you talk," Darrio said. "We didn't come here for this. Tell us what you know."

"Well," Trevlin started, "what I heard, heard mind you, was the people you're looking for were looking for something in the people of the Catalina camp."

"What was it?" Eloi asked.

"I don't know. I think I heard light or something. I didn't get it though."

"What else?" Talim asked.

"Well, ever since the camp was destroyed, we, the others and I, have been on the defensive. We never know when or if those people are ever going to come back."

"Have they approached you?"

"Why would you think that?"

"I have asked you a question. Have they approached you or not?"

"No."

Talim grumbled with annoyance. "I have warned you once not to lie to me. I will not warn you again."

"But I'm not—."

"Don't piss him off," Darrio said. "You're going to talk one way or the other, but if you let Talim in there, he's going to air every little dirty secret you've ever had. I'm sure you'd rather die than have to deal with that."

Trevlin sat in fearful silence as he pondered what he would say. "Listen, you've got to promise me something."

"What?"

"No matter what I say, you've got to promise not to get the Elders involved."

"They're already involved, idiot. That's why we're here."

"No, I mean…don't tell them about us. Don't tell them about what we did."

"What did you do?" Talim asked.

"You've got to promise first."

"Tell us the truth, and I promise that we will plead for you."

"And how long do we have to keep paying for what we did? For the rest of our lives? Even after serving our time? Things are strained enough as it is around here, and the people ain't friendly. I'm not asking for much here."

Trevlin's plea stoked a lingering desire in Darrio's heart which he had pushed to the far ends of his mind. There was a memory attached, but he was unwilling to face it. Still, he uttered, "We promise," to Talim's complete surprise. "But this is it. If you lie again, you'll get no protection from us."

"Okay," Trevlin sighed. "Alright. Listen. The people who attacked Catalina were scoping all the camps, and some of us were scoping them at the same time. Catalina was looking to change things around here, you know? Turn over a new leaf for us so we didn't have to go and loot each other all the time, and I was going to go with them on it, but then this happened."

"So did they kill the camp because of the reformation," Darrio asked, "or because they couldn't find what they were looking for?"

The man shrugged. "Both? And maybe because they knew too much or were too close. Catalina told us not to trust them. Even had half a mind to go to the Elders about it saying it might buy all the camps some security. They were seriously looking to legitimize things around here. I don't know what got into them, but considering what's been happening lately, I don't think I want it."

"What do you mean they warned you not to trust them? What did they say to you?"

"Did they make you an offer?" Talim asked.

"See? This is why I asked you to promise."

"What did they ask of you?"

"They asked us to keep a channel in the northern border open so they could sneak some of their people in. We used to go through it on rare occasions to steal food and supplies from the Silent Realm. It was always small stuff. Nothing to go to war over."

"Fools! There are organizations in the Outer Realms still plotting our downfall, and the people you have helped are no different!"

"We didn't know all that! They asked us a favor and said they'd give us something in return. More security, food, peace. That was stuff we actually needed around here and wasn't getting from the high and mighty Elders. I didn't know it would come with all this other stuff attached to it."

Talim shook his head while Darrio pressed on. "Is that channel still open?"

"No. We shut it down after Catalina was destroyed."

"Then they're getting their people in and out a different way."

"Fine by me so long as we aren't involved. What's going on with them anyway? What's this light thing they were looking for, and why did they kill Catalina for it? Why didn't they go after us too?"

"We don't know," Talim answered, and he stood. Darrio and Eloi followed suit.

"Do you think they'll come back?"

"I believe they have more important matters to consider."

"You'll keep your promise then, right? You won't tell the Elders about what we did?"

"We won't," Darrio answered.

"Thanks, and I'll remember this. I'll make sure everybody remembers this."

When the three shades exited the camp, Talim said, "I have witnessed yet another soft moment from you, Firestar. What was it this time?"

"I don't know. What he said reminded me of something."

"What was it?"

It was his mother, but Darrio shook his head. "I don't know."

"We should return to the city then and report what we have found. I do not believe investigating the other camps will be any more productive."

"We are going home?" Eloi asked.

"Was there something you wished to investigate?"

"No."

"Then let us go. We have much to tell."

As they walked, Darrio's mind fell back to his mother and a faint memory of her sad but smiling face. He was still only a boy when they found refuge in the village of Aria, a place just on the outskirts of the Saline Realm where they were treated well for a time. He remembered approaching her one day in a mood of excitement and yelling, "Momma! Momma! I'm a spirit!"

His mother, called Emelia, was astonished at her young son's self-realization, and she smiled warmly and said, "Yes, you are, honey."

"No, you don't understand. I'm a spirit!"

"I know, honey. I know." Darrio then remembered the sadness in his mother's eyes and the presence of something else which pressed her forward for his sake. He did not know what to make of it or what to call it though he was always aware of it. One day, he simply asked her what it was, and his mother answered, "It is faith," but Darrio did not understand.

The last thing he could remember about his mother without anger or sorrow was her comforting expressions. He would return home embittered and crying about what the other kids said against her. He often fought with them. Nevertheless, his mother would comfort him and calm him down and warn him not to fight because they were guests. Still, Darrio became more and more of an angry child, and his mother would look at him and say, "Don't be angry, Darrio." For a second, Darrio considered what his parents would have thought about the road he had been traveling since then, and the thought pained his heart. He quickly shifted his mind to Saria.

"Firestar," Talim interrupted.

"What?"

"You appear lost in thought. Is there something wrong?"

"No."

"Perhaps you are worried about the girl."

"A little."

"I am sure she is being taken care of."

Darrio could only hope, and not only for her sake, but for the sake of anyone who crossed him in harming her. Saria herself, however, had something else in mind.

She was sitting in Turil's office and kicking her feet over the edge of the chair in front of his desk. Turil's guards successfully extracted her from Darrio's room without notice, and while she was sleepy, she was still happy to be talking to someone. "I apologize for summoning you like this," Turil said. "I trust my men were gentle with you?"

"They were nice," she said.

"Then tell me, young lady. How have you been?"

"Fine."

"That's good. Good. Well, the reason I asked for you is because I have a few questions and a few concerns."

"What questions?"

"The Firestar."

"Sir Darrio?"

"Yes."

"He wants me to call him Sir Darrio. He doesn't want me to call him Firestar."

"Is that so?"

Saria nodded. "He doesn't like being called that because it makes him sad."

"How does it make him sad?"

"He doesn't want to be Firestar."

"And he's told you this?"

Saria shook her head.

"Then how do you know?"

"I can see it, and I can feel it with this," she said pointing to her heart. "See?"

"I'm afraid I don't, dear one."

"Well, I can see you're a nice man, and you like other people."

"I like some people, yes," Turil said with a chuckle.

"My sister used to tell me that people who like other people are nice people. I think Sir Darrio likes other people too even if he doesn't feel like liking them sometimes."

"Then perhaps he is like me and likes some people as well."

"But people make him mad too. How come nobody likes him? Maybe if more people liked him, he wouldn't be so mad all the time."

"You sense he is an angry person?"

Saria huffed and crossed her arms. "Only because nobody will let him be nice."

Turil marked Saria as an interesting child and could not help but ask more questions, but the more he asked, the more he found out about other people's feelings instead of hers. Their talks then fell on

Seris. "He scares me," she said.

"Why does he scare you?"

"He's always hiding something, and he won't let anyone see it, and I know it's not good because he doesn't even want to hide it."

"You received this from Seris the Unknowable?" It was an old title shared between Seris and Turil while the two were still captains during the war. Turil would sometimes call Seris by this name in jest though it was not without its truths. "What else have you seen?"

"I don't know."

"What do you mean?"

"He's mixed. He mixes a lot. He feels one way and then another way, and then he always has something else."

"Something else?"

Saria nodded. "It's the only thing that's always there. He's… he's…."

"He's what? What is it, child?"

"He's scared. I don't know. It's like there's something he doesn't want to do that he's worried about doing, and it's always there when he's thinking about something."

"Seris? Afraid? What does he have to be afraid of—?" But Turil caught himself at the end of his statement and sighed. "Oh. Oh no."

"You know what it is?"

"I know what it is."

"What is it?"

"I'm afraid it is a private matter, and I cannot tell you."

Saria leaned forward but then slowly leaned back. "It makes you sad too."

"Indeed, it does." The two shared an uncomfortable and solemn silence before Turil attempted to end their meeting. "You are a very special young lady, Saria. Your heart is something to be desired."

"Do you know when Sir Darrio is coming back?"

"I do not know."

"I hope it's soon."

"I'll have my men escort you back to your room. I am glad we had this talk."

"Me too. You're a nice man."

"You go on back to bed now, young one. You need to rest."

Saria took her leave, and when the door was shut, Turil leaned back and retrieved the diagram of the two cases he drew earlier from his desk. On it, he encircled both sides within a single shape and wrote, "One case." Afterward, he stood to his feet and looked out of his window towards the dark horizon. The sky was clear, the winds were still, and Turil could make out the stars that hung brilliantly overhead. Despite all this, Turil's eyes were saddened, and he shed a single tear. He then shut his eyes and reopened them with a sense of firm resolution which had not been seen since the final battles of the Magic War. "We shall do what we shall do," he said, and by force of magic, Turil extinguished all of the lights in his room.

CHAPTER 10
Heart Unmerited

HAD IT NOT been for the heat, Darrio thought he would have been able to think more clearly. Exhaustion, however, continued to express itself in his mind as he poured over the matter of recent events. He, Talim, and Eloi were nearing the end of their return trek to Ambrosia and were discussing among themselves the meaning of what transpired so far. Darrio was simply tired of the whole affair. "Too many secrets," he said. "Too much going on."

"But it will make for a grand tale when it is over," Talim said.

Darrio shook his head. "You and your stories."

"All of our lives are stories, Firestar, and each moment adds detail to the greater tale."

"You read too much."

"What will your story be?" Eloi asked Talim.

"Mine? Ha! Mine will be too complex to tell, for it is a tapestry of memories both of mine and of others."

"What if you exclude others? Could you not tell your story then?"

"I could not, Eloi, for every mind has had an impact on my own. If I separate them, there will be no context to my actions, and without context, my story would be meaningless."

"What of your story, Firestar?" Eloi asked.

Darrio shrugged. "I don't know."

"What do you want them to say?" Talim asked.

Again, Darrio shrugged and gave little thought to the matter. He did not know if he had much of a choice in its telling, for it seemed as if circumstances and others determined it for him. "What's it matter anyway?" Darrio finally said. "People are just going to say what they're going to say."

"You think you have no choice in the matter?"

Darrio could never understand how Talim was able to pick up on such insecurities. He thought perhaps it may have been an unconscious habit of Talim's to enter people's minds much like Darrio's own habit of destructive manipulation, but Darrio was not interested enough to explore it deeply. "I don't know."

"What do you think, Eloi?"

"I do not know."

Talim laughed. "Answers of the unseasoned! But the two of you will learn in time. Every good thing in time, I always say."

Talim's saying then reminded Darrio of his father, and this bothered him. He attempted to shake it off.

"Is something wrong, Firestar?"

"It's nothing."

Talim patted Darrio on the back with his broad and mighty hand. Darrio stumbled forward due to the gesture, but Talim smiled all the more. "Then be of good cheer! Soon enough, this will all be sorted out. So! What will be your primary activity upon returning home? Will you tend to the girl?"

Darrio nodded. "And then I'm going to bed."

"Bed?"

"I can't wrap my head around this with you talking all the time. I liked it better when you didn't talk so much."

Talim laughed. "And where will you go, Eloi?"

Eloi blinked but did not answer.

As they approached the city, they found General Turil standing at the entrance in wait. "What's he doing?" Darrio wondered.

"Perhaps the Elders have issued another trial."

"Great. I wonder what they'll accuse me of this time."

"The general is alone," Eloi said. "If it was a trial, he would be accompanied by others, would he not?"

"Then perhaps he waits for a scout," Talim surmised. "In any case, let us pass. I know Seris is not on good terms with the man."

Turil waited patiently as the three shades approached, but as they drew near, he smiled. "Welcome back. I trust the mission went well?

The three exchanged looks of confusion while Turil took special notice of Darrio's apprehension. "We got eight of them," Darrio answered.

"Good, good. What else? Have you learned anything else?"

Darrio did not know how to speak to Turil who was being strangely informal. He also knew the general and Seris were at odds with each other even if he did not know the details. As such, and given his relationship with the captain, Darrio was not at all comfortable speaking with Turil despite his duty and rank. It almost felt like a betrayal on his part.

"Speaking respectfully, Good General," Talim said, "we are all quite tired and will need to rest before giving our report."

"Of course. Carry on." As the three began to move, Turil spoke once more. "But, Firestar. When you are finished, I wish to speak with you in private. Come to my office as soon as you are able."

"Okay," Darrio replied cautious in his tone, and Turil left them. "What the hell was that all about?"

"I do not know," Talim replied, "but let us retreat to the Hall and make our report. We will ask Seris about the matter."

Abaddon was leaving the Hall in haste just as they were entering, but he neither acknowledged their presence nor looked at them as he passed. Talim opened his mouth to speak, but Abaddon, as if anticipating this, said, "No," and left them. Inside, the air was heavy and still. The shades, adepts, and casters went about their duties in solemn silence. A thick and palpable tension was in the air. Darrio, Talim, and Eloi erred on the side of caution and collectively decided not to ask anyone about the silence, but Darrio worried about Saria's well-being.

Seris sat alone at his desk when one of the shades informed him of the three's return. "Let them in," he said. Darrio, Talim, and Eloi, each one in turn, entered Seris' office, and the door was shut behind them. "Sit." The three did as told. "What did you find?"

"Do you wish to tell him, Firestar?" Talim asked.

Darrio shook his head, so Talim relayed their findings while Eloi and Darrio supported him with the finer details. Seris, in the meantime, sat and listened patiently, asked questions, and took in every detail no matter how minute it was. Darrio had not seen such attentiveness from Seris in a while and was not lost on its significance. When they finished, Darrio asked, "What's going on around here?"

"Did Turil speak with you?"

"He was at the gate."

"What did he want?"

"I don't know. He asked how the mission went and said he wanted to talk to me."

"In private?"

Darrio nodded, and the response drew moderate annoyance from Seris. "Did something happen?"

"No," Seris replied. "Nothing has happened."

"Then why is everyone so tense?"

"It is unimportant. Just take this time to rest and settle your affairs. We will be conducting a new set of operations in the coming weeks. Everyone must be at their best."

Talim's brow rose with curiosity, and Darrio asked, "What kind of new operations?"

"Rest. I will call for you when you are needed."

"Understood," Talim replied.

The three shades rose to leave, but Seris called on Darrio to stay. When Talim and Eloi were gone, and the door was closed behind them, Seris sighed. "What's wrong?" Darrio asked.

"Turil has made a nuisance of himself."

"What did he do?"

Seris looked at Darrio but did not answer the question. "Has he told you what he wishes to speak with you about?"

Darrio shook his head.

"Nothing?"

"I won't talk to him if that's what you want."

Seris shook his head. "I cannot ask this of you."

Darrio traced Seris' face and could see that something was wrong. He knew Seris well enough to interpret his mannerisms and could read between the implications of his words, at least to some measure. However, like Darrio, Seris would only allow people to come within a certain distance of his heart. This had been a source of great frustration for both of them. "You're hiding something again."

Seris' composure then eased, and his normally still and careful demeanor descended into vulnerable honesty. "I must know something, Darrio. Speak truthfully."

"What is it?"

"Do you trust me?"

Darrio searched within himself for an answer but was unsure of what to say and how to say it. Seris cared for Darrio when there was no one left for him to care about. This experience, combined with the experiences they shared during the war, compelled Darrio to comply with Seris' every order, but as things were at that moment, he did not know if he could call that trust. "I don't know."

It was a guarded response that Seris knew all too well. The fact that Darrio picked up on some of his interpersonal habits was among the many lingering regrets that still gnawed at his mind from time to time. "You need not guard yourself from me. If you do not trust me, say so."

"Tell me what you want."

"I want you to trust me."

"Okay. I trust you."

Seris sighed.

"What?"

"Darrio." The exchange was frustrating him. "You don't have to lie to me. I'm not your enemy, and I'm not a stranger."

"I said I trust you."

"You say that, and you follow me out of duty, but you don't really trust me."

"What else am I supposed to do?"

"What else?" Seris repeated with heightened tones.

"I've done everything you wanted me to do. I always do what you want me to do. What more do you want?"

"Do you think your obedience is the only thing I want?"

"How the hell should I know? It's not like you tell me anything. You never tell me anything! Just tell me what you want!"

"I want you to trust me!" The room shook, and the etchings on Darrio's bonds glowed faintly, but it was not Darrio's will that shook the room but Seris'. "I'm sorry."

Darrio recoiled in his seat and spoke solemnly. "You want me to trust you, and I want to, but...I don't think I can. I don't know if I can trust you. I don't know how."

"Why not?"

Darrio paused, and his eyes fell to the desk. He knew the answer, but he did not want to speak it. Nevertheless, "I just...I don't know you, Seris."

Seris winced, a rare occurrence, and he lowered his eyes to the desk. Hearing Darrio's words cut straight to his heart, and Darrio could see Seris mourning behind his eyes. A moment later, however, Seris' former composure returned to him as his softened face solidified and his once wavering voice hardened. "Go rest now, Darrio."

Darrio softened his tone. "I didn't mean to—."

"Rest."

Darrio's body protested, and his mind tried in vain to think of something comforting to say, but all words escaped him, and he was afraid of speaking further. Instead, Darrio stood to his feet, every movement fraught with distilled weariness, and he stiffly made his way to the door and exited. Everything within him wanted to apologize for his lack of understanding, for not knowing enough, for not seeing enough, but the pain was too much to formulate into words. He cursed himself and left the office in silence.

Saria was playing a solitary round of Darrio's game when he entered. After hearing his steps and recognizing his presence, she jumped to her feet and hugged him. "Sir Darrio!"

Darrio was pained and answered, "Saria."

Saria stepped back. "Why are you so sad?"

"It's nothing." Darrio forced a crooked smile to his face and knelt down. "How have you been?"

Saria placed her hands on Darrio's face which quivered beneath her fingers. It was hard for him to maintain his smile though he wondered why he was bothering. She was blind and could not see it anyway.

"You're crying, Sir Darrio," she said as she frowned, and Darrio sighed. "Why are you so sad?"

"It doesn't matter," he answered as he stood.

"But it does matter."

Darrio retreated to his bed where he fell and stared at the ceiling. "No, it doesn't."

"It matters to you, or else you wouldn't be like this."

Darrio shook his head. "It doesn't matter."

Saria crept to Darrio's bedside and looked at him as if he were a sick patient in need of immediate care. She placed her hands over Darrio's heart and asked, "Why do you do that?"

"Do what?"

"Why do you hurt yourself?"

Darrio did not have an answer. Although he was somewhat aware of his mental and emotional condition, he was unable to remember clearly when, why, and how it started. He remembered enjoying life at one point, but it was during a time which predated what he knew as reality. It was depressing to think such a thing could be outgrown. Darrio pushed it out of his mind and tried to steel himself. All of these feelings, he thought, were things he had to bury if he wanted to get anything done. There would be time to grieve when he was dead.

Saria slapped her hands on his chest. "Stop that! It hurts!"

But seeing her damaged by his pain only made things worse. He stifled his feelings, choked them, and pushed them as far away from him as he was able. Saria groaned, and Darrio apologized. "I'm sorry," but Saria tugged on him. "What?"

"Play with me."

"But I'm tired."

"Play with me!"

Darrio looked at her and could see she was trying her best to help, so he followed her and played games with her for the rest of the day.

Eloi listened to all this from behind their door and retreated to the Hall's library to find Talim standing before one of the many walls lined with books. "Talim," he said.

Talim was surprised by Eloi's sudden presence. "Eloi! You mustn't sneak up on me like that. Make your presence known."

"The girl is a sensate, is she not?"

"Girl? What girl?"

"The one Firestar protects."

"Ah, yes. Her. Yes, she is."

"She is able to feel and understand what others are feeling. Yes?"

"Yes."

"Is everyone capable of this?"

"To some degree. It comes naturally to some. Others must learn."

"How?"

"It is a form of sight, Eloi. Words, body language, tone, action, all of these reveal the state and heart of a man."

"May I ask you something?"

"Of course."

"If mind and body are separated and the one who is divided can no longer feel because of it, can he too become a sensate?"

Talim paused. "He must first unify himself before he can take on the feelings of others." While Eloi took a moment to contemplate Talim's words, Talim spoke again. "Has this been happening to you Eloi? Is this why you have been acting so strangely?"

"I do not know. I simply wish to understand."

"Does it hurt that you do not?"

Eloi blinked twice but did not answer the question.

"What troubles you, Eloi? While your heart expresses nothing, your body breaks silence. I do not understand the cause of it, but I am curious."

Eloi's empty eyes looked directly at Talim's. "I am broken, Talim. I do not understand, and I do not know what I do not understand."

"Then your ponderings, observations, and imitations...these are attempts at unification, to fix what has been severed within you."

Eloi nodded.

"And something has happened to further this process, or else we would not be speaking."

Eloi nodded again.

"May I ask what that something was?"

"I do not understand what it was, and until I understand, I cannot tell you."

Talim nodded. "I understand, Eloi."

"Do you?"

Talim nodded and another spark ignited behind Eloi's eyes. "Then you have just respected me, Talim. Thank you."

Eloi then left Talim who only stood in stunned silence. "The plight of Eloi," Talim uttered. He then tried unsuccessfully to return to his reading, but his mind was deterred by the recent exchange. He swiftly returned the book he was holding to the shelf and moved on to a section that held information about the healing techniques of illusionary magic. It was a subject he had not approached for quite some time, but he felt compelled to probe its secrets. Whether or not he could be of any help to Eloi was not a question to which he knew the answer, but Talim decided he would look into the matter for Eloi's sake wherever it took him.

Darrio awoke the following morning to a knock at his door. Saria slept soundly beside him and was guarded beneath his arm and close to his heart. "What is it?" he answered.

"I was sent by General Turil. He wishes to speak with you."

"Now?"

"Now."

Darrio groaned, and Saria awoke. "Sir Darrio?"

"I've got to go," and Darrio stood to his feet and prepared to leave. "Go back to sleep, Saria."

"Where are you going?"

"Somebody wants to talk to me."

"Is it Sir Turil?" she asked pleasantly.

"You like him?"

"He's a good man, and he's nice."

"You talked to him?" Saria nodded, and Darrio grew concerned. "What did he want?"

"Nothing. We just talked."

"You shouldn't talk to him."

"Why?"

Darrio did not know why. He only knew whatever opposed Seris was something he too would oppose. "I don't trust him."

Saria crossed her arms. "You don't trust anyone."

Though the statement struck a nerve with Darrio, he gritted his teeth and kept his silence. "I'm going to go see what he wants. Just… stay here."

The soldier on the other side of the door greeted Darrio and asked, "Are you ready?"

"I know where his office is."

"We're not going to his office."

"Where are we going then?"

"For your sake and mine, don't ask questions, Firestar."

Darrio was led to the Hall's lower chamber where the High Generals often met to conduct and coordinate their affairs. Those of lower rank were never allowed inside, and it seemed a strange place to conduct a meeting, especially something as simple as a brief talk. Darrio remained on guard, but the escorting soldier told him, "Stop that. You're making me tense."

"You're already tense. Everybody's tense."

"Well, you're making me even more tense. Cut it out."

"No."

"Cut it out!"

"No!"

Turil emerged from the Chamber of High Generals and addressed both Darrio and the escorting soldier. "I would appreciate it if you kept your noise levels to a minimum lest I remind you again in a more unpleasant fashion." The soldier quickly silenced and bit his tongue. "Thank you for coming, Firestar. Please. Inside."

The soldier left them, and Darrio cautiously entered. The room was empty save for a single round table in the center complimented by chairs on all sides. There were two ridges on the east and west walls and a large, painted map that showed the layout of the world and its seven regions on the north wall. Turil took a seat next to the map and invited Darrio to sit as well. He did so cautiously. "What do you want?"

"First of all, let me say that this is an informal meeting we are having. Do not think about my rank."

"Okay."

"And I wanted to speak with you about what's been happening so far. What do you think about all this?"

"What does it matter what I think?"

"I'm curious. Have you noticed anything unusual? Any patterns?"

"Even if I did, why would I tell you?"

"I know you have no reason to trust me, but you are still bound by duty, are you not? You and Seris both seem to share this."

Darrio crossed his arms. "What happened to disregarding rank?"

"My apologies. Let me try this again. How should I say this? I've been doing a lot of research lately. On you, especially, I must admit."

"Me?"

"I reread your Esea report and the trial statements several times. There's an obvious bias. The Elders are fixed on you. On your demise, I mean."

"So what? Just about half of everyone who's ever seen me wants me dead."

"What of the other half?"

"They're already dead."

Turil chuckled. "That sense of humor. I used to share it once."

"And if I were joking," Darrio said, "I'd be laughing."

"Of course."

Turil was a strange sort in Darrio's eyes, and he could not understand why he was even speaking with the man. "You didn't bring me here to make fun of me, did you?"

"No. I wanted to know how you felt."

"How do you think I feel?"

"I'm not prone to making such assumptions."

Darrio breathed a frustrated sigh and took only a short pause before giving his answer. "I'm pissed."

Turil clasped his hands together and nodded.

"I'm pissed, confused, and hungry."

"Hungry?"

"I haven't eaten yet."

Turil chuckled. "Then let's fill that empty belly of yours."

Turil stood to his feet and moved to the door. Darrio asked, "Where're you going?"

"I'm sending an order for food."

Turil left giving Darrio time to contemplate what was happening. He felt Turil was after something or else he would not be asking questions, but what and why still eluded him. Being a High General, he was within his right to order Darrio to give him the information he wanted, and Darrio would have to comply. Even so, Darrio wondered if he would still do so and thought about the potential consequences. Saria called Turil a good man. This only made the situation more difficult to assess. When Turil returned, Darrio was no closer to deciding whether or not he should regard Turil as another potential enemy or simply a man looking for answers. "What did you order?"

"Bread, eggs, and some tea."

"Oh."

"And they will take some to Saria as well."

Darrio watched Turil carefully and studied his expressions. He seemed relaxed enough and in a fairly pleasant mood, a sharp contrast to everyone else on the grounds. Darrio considered it a part of Turil's investigation, a method to get Darrio into a more relaxed and willing state for talks. "I know what you're doing."

"Do you?"

"You want to use me for something."

"I think you have me mistaken for someone else."

"Then why are you talking to me?"

"Wasn't I clear the first time? I wanted your opinion."

If Turil's question was bait, Darrio decided he would take it to see where it took him. "I don't have an opinion. They're after something, and we're trying to stop them. That's it."

Turil nodded. "That's true, but what of their motivations? Why show themselves now, and why hide in the first place?"

Darrio shrugged. "Maybe they had something to hide from, but we already know what they want. The power of light so they can put the world under some kind of religious rule until their god shows up."

"I take from your tone you think nothing of Magnus."

"No, I don't. Do you?"

"I have visited the temple several times, but something still eludes me, and I've yet to take a firm grasp of what that something is."

"What do you mean?"

"It just seems a bit…impersonal. As if the heart behind the story is a dark and vacant one. I sense no feeling except from the priesthood, but in the readings and teachings themselves, I sense nothing. Only words, but this is a personal feeling. I have no insights into its supposed truths. I am curious about this Great Cleansing, though. What do you believe that would entail, and why would they need the power of light to initiate it?"

"Hell if I know. I remember the woman I captured said something about a curse. Why don't you ask her?"

"You know I can't do that."

"Why not?"

"She escaped before your last trial started."

Darrio lowered his head.

"You were there when Abaddon mentioned it. Did you forget?"

"Guess I did. Must be this stupid room. Who was guarding her?"

"Hm?"

"She's not strong enough to have escaped by herself. Who was guarding her?"

"I don't know. You think someone let her escape?"

"It's not like she could've just walked out, not with these damn things on her," Darrio said exposing his wrists. The food arrived, and a plate was set before Darrio and Turil along with a cup of tea for each of them.

"You raise an interesting point. I'm currently missing a captain who has gone missing after a recent plan of mine was rendered inoperable. Perhaps he is the one, though I cannot imagine he would aid an enemy of the realm."

"What plan?"

"Some lingering elements from the war still remain in the Outer Realms, but the Elders refuse to look at them. I hoped to do something about it, but," Turil shrugged, "plans do not always go as expected."

"Seris says it's better to plan on opportunities than take risks on what isn't certain."

"He would say that." As the two ate, their conversation drifted toward their experiences, and Darrio found himself more and more relaxed. "It's the tea," Turil remarked with a smile. He then shared his stories surrounding the battle of Horus where he and Seris battled alongside each other in a small skirmish against militias who had taken refuge in the Silent Realm. "It was around that time we finally learned to trust one another."

"You didn't trust each other at first?"

"Quite the contrary. Our seasons were relatively few, and while he considered me too reckless for a captain, I regarded him as an impractical thinker. We were young. I was full of passion and zeal while he was full of ideals and dreams. It was a strange arrangement between the two of us," he chuckled. "Strange and fitting."

Turil continued reciting his tales, and Darrio listened. Unlike Talim, who spoke with boasting and exaggeration, Turil spoke with precision and was careful to neither overstate nor understate his details. As a result, it felt to Darrio like a clear telling of the story which he discovered he liked. It was a far better alternative to Talim's usual dramatizations.

"What else did you guys do?"

"Oh, we did many things. Did you know Seris used to criticize me for charging into battle? Battles that I would win! I told him, 'You worry too much,' but he would not hear it and chastised my hotheadedness. But he had faults as well. He would implement a plan and not tell me about it even when it required my participation! I was always trying to instill in him the practical matters. It seems we have both made our marks on each other."

Darrio was astounded at Turil's description. He had never heard anything concerning that side of Seris before. "I don't understand you guys. You were such good friends before the war, even during from what I saw. What happened?"

Turil leaned back. "We simply changed. We both made choices on the paths we would take, and now those paths have diverged."

"But that doesn't mean you have to be enemies."

Turil smiled. "Did the Firestar just make a statement of hope?"

Darrio crossed his arms and turned in a futile effort to hide the smile which appeared on his face.

"Perhaps you don't remember the first time we met."

"I remember. You made fun of me, so I kicked you."

Turil chuckled. "Seris told me your first encounter with him was even worse. I realize I never made an effort to understand you until now, but I think, perhaps, I am beginning to see less Firestar in you and more of the boy you used to be…and perhaps still are?"

"I think you need to get your eyes checked."

"Perhaps," Turil said with a smile.

They finished eating, and a moment of silence came and went. Darrio looked ahead at the map and remembered he had been called to the room for a reason. "So what are you really after? I know you talked to Saria, but now you're talking to me. Don't tell me you're lonely and looking for attention."

"I have my reasons even if I can't disclose them."

"So this is just a gathering for you."

"No. In essence, I seek people who I can trust and who are willing to trust me. I wanted you to trust me."

Darrio leaned back. "Seris said the same thing."

A curious eyebrow rose on Turil's face. "You don't trust him?"

"I do trust him."

"If you did, he would not have asked you to do so."

Darrio turned his head. "Well, I think I do. I mean, if he asked me to do something for him, I'd do it. But I don't know if that's enough. I don't know."

"What you describe may be the compulsion of duty. It does not necessarily mean that you trust him."

Darrio shrugged. "Maybe. What about you? Would you trust him? Now, I mean."

Turil crossed his arms. "In times like these, I do not know who I can trust. I think it would be best that I do not answer that question now, for your sake."

"My sake," Darrio repeated half-jokingly. "And what do you have against him?"

"Nothing. I do not hold grudges."

"Then what are you against him for?"

"Seris has been a dear friend to me, and I have loved the man like a brother, but when you love someone, you want what's best for them even if it is something they do not wish for themselves. Do you understand any of this?"

Darrio shook his head.

"Seris has involved himself in something that is detrimental not only to his own well-being but the well-being of those around him. I am bound, both by duty and by this love for him, to oppose his efforts. I don't expect you to understand the full measure of what I am saying, but it is the truth."

"But you've been friends for so long."

"This is true, but we are no longer what we once were. Surely you can understand that."

Darrio nodded, albeit hesitantly.

"Will you tell me what you know? Will you trust me?"

"I don't know. You're not going to ask me to do anything against Seris, are you? Because I won't. I won't do that to him."

Turil shook his head. "And I will not ask you to. I am only asking for your trust."

Darrio found such a thing difficult to consider. If he could not bring himself to trust Seris, how could he trust Turil? Nevertheless, Turil presented himself as a worthy candidate by exposing and sharing himself, but Darrio still felt his judgment was being clouded. His first thoughts were on the tea, but he settled on blaming the room again. "I need some time to think."

"I will give you two weeks."

"Two weeks?"

"There is a reason for this, but I cannot discuss it now. I need your answer before then." Darrio was unsure if it would be enough time and considered whether or not this exchange was a ploy on Turil's part to divide Seris from him. However, this consideration begged a reason that Darrio could not find based on the character Turil displayed thus far. "I do not mean to pressure you," Turil said, "but it's very important for me to know whether or not we can trust each other before then."

"What if I give you the wrong answer?"

"It is not that kind of a question, but I do hope you will come to view me as something other than a stranger and opposite an enemy."

"Maybe," Darrio answered.

"I look forward to your answer then." Turil stood. "Feel free to speak to me anytime you wish. My door is open to you."

Turil passed Darrio on his way to the door and took notice of the conflict evident on Darrio's face. He would be faced with a difficult decision and would not know all of the details. Turil pitied him having attained some idea of what Darrio had gone through in life, and he knew secrecy on his part would do nothing to alleviate the indwelt anguish. Turil asked Darrio to trust him while withholding at the same time. He remembered how frustrating it was when Seris asked the same thing of him in the battle of Horus. However, he had a greater responsibility to consider. It pained him that he could not disclose more, but he passed by nonetheless without a word through the chamber door.

After Turil left, Darrio stood to his feet and walked to the map to examine it. There he noted several locations which were marked and recalled his experiences, if any, that he had in those locations. Such places as Ember, capital of the Burning Realm, Oxus, Horus, two major centers in the Silent Realm, and Allure of the Hollow Realm were all marked. The map was quite old, though, and out of date. Darrio surmised that it was drafted during the early days of the campaign. There were towns and a few cities still listed that no longer existed. The most prominent of these was the formerly grand city of Cilica, the old capital of the Silent Realm. What was once the center of the Taurus nation's power and ingenuity was then a cold ruin that Darrio infiltrated, encased in ice, and brought crumbling to the ground in a frigid hail of stone and glass.

The last location of notice was Aria, a small village on the eastern outskirts of the Saline Realm. Such a place was negligible and was not marked, but it was no less significant to Darrio who marked the spot in his own mind with contempt. Seeing this conjured a most disturbing image in his mind of his mother tied to a stake. Darrio shook his head and cursed the memory before leaving the Chamber of High Generals.

When Darrio returned to his room, he found Saria eating. She heard him enter, turned, and smiled. "I told you he was nice."

Darrio sat beside her. "Do you trust him?"

Saria nodded. "Don't you?"

"I don't know. Seris doesn't, so I don't think I should either." Saria huffed at the mention of Seris' name. "Why don't you like him?"

"He scares me. Why do you like him, Sir Darrio?"

"I didn't have anything when I got here, and he took me in. He took care of me."

"Where did you come from?"

Darrio shook his head. "It doesn't matter," and he stood. "Come on."

"Where are we going?"

"You've been cooped up in the Hall the whole time I've been gone, haven't you? Let's go for a walk. There's a field on the west side of the city we can go to."

Saria leaped to her feet, and her small face beamed. "Okay!"

Darrio and Saria avoided the main road and instead took the back roads and side streets to the western exit. Darrio did not want to risk being attacked though he remained armed just in case. They stayed out the entire day and reclined in the grass when night fell. Darrio surveyed the stars while Saria experienced the breeze of the open air across her face. She then stirred and poked Darrio in the side.

"What?" Darrio asked.

"Do you think God is happy?"

"With what?"

Saria shrugged.

"I don't know."

Saria went back to her position and giggled suddenly.

"What's so funny?"

"I think He answered me."

Darrio hummed but did not think much of it.

"If you could ask Him anything, what would you ask Him?"

"I don't know. Why, I guess."

"Why what?"

"Why everything."

Saria was confused but returned to the breeze. Soon after, "Are you asking Him now?"

"No."

"When?"

"When I'm dead, Saria. It doesn't really matter right now."

"Oh...." After several moments of silence passed, Saria stirred again. "Sir Darrio?"

"Hm?"

"Can we go back now? I got to go."

The two rose and returned to the streets of Ambrosia. It was largely quiet as the stands were closed for the night, and the people slept soundly in their homes. Darrio, therefore, judged it safe for them to take the main road back to the Hall which was faster by far than the back roads they took in leaving. However, they were no more than a third of the way back when Darrio heard a familiar voice crying out for help.

Sam ran fearfully from his pursuing assailant who brandished a small, serrated dagger behind him. "Help!" he cried. "Somebody help me!" but no one emerged to answer his call. He then found Darrio standing alongside a small girl, and he pushed himself all the more to reach them. "Darrio!" he called.

"Sam." Darrio looked behind Sam, and when he saw the pursuer, his anger flashed.

Sam took refuge behind Darrio and pointed. "That guy's trying to kill me!"

Darrio drew his weapons, and the pursuer quickly slowed to a stop. "Stay here, Saria."

The pursuer, a man who bore no remarkable features, took one good look at Darrio and cursed his misfortune. "Shit." He immediately fled in the other direction.

"Get back here!"

The man ran with greater urgency away from what he recognized as the Firestar than he had towards his target. He knew the stories and the speculations of his power, but while he also knew the Elders had contained it, this knowledge made him no less fearful. The man pocketed his blade and ducked into a nearby alley where he hoped the Firestar would miss his presence running by, but as the man waited, he could see that his pursuer had not yet come. He cautiously peeked around the corner only to find Sam and a girl standing alone in the middle of the road. The Firestar was nowhere in sight. The man then recalled the Firestar's station as a shade and speculated he could be anywhere at any moment by then. When he spun around, he could see that no one was there. He looked above, and still, the Firestar was not to be found. He proceeded to the other end of the alley and saw no one. So far as he could discern, either the Firestar did not know where he was or was waiting for him to come out. He decided not to oblige the latter and took refuge in hopes that he could exceed his predator's patience. It was to his folly, for no sooner after he sat down and lowered his guard did his feared assailant leap down and land before him.

Darrio gave the man no chance to regain his composure and stabbed both shoulders and subsequently thrust his weapons through the man's legs, pinning him to the ground. The man screamed.

"I'm only going to ask you this once," Darrio said.

The man looked into Darrio's raging eyes, and his breaths became short, shallow, and hard. He contemplated that he was soon to die, and he started to weep and lamented the path he had taken in life.

Darrio spoke. "Where did you come from, who sent you, and why were you after Sam?"

"A j-j-job. M-m-my employers. His debts."

"His debts? He was paying his debts!"

The man shook his head. "Collateral! They saw you as c-c-collateral for p-protection in case he could not pay! They thought, m-m-maybe, he would not pay now s-so they sent me to s-s-stop him and m-make him pay in full."

"And who sent you? Where are they? Give me a name!"

"N-n-name? I don't know their names!"

Darrio leaned forward and took a firmer hold of his weapons.

"But they're in Silesia! Silesia! You can find them in Silesia!"

Darrio withdrew his blades, much to the man's anguish, and he cleansed them and replaced them beneath his cloak. "Don't let me see you again," and Darrio left the man quivering in the alley.

Darrio returned to a grateful Sam and a relieved Saria. "How'd it go?" Sam asked. "You didn't...you didn't do anything, did you?"

"He was going to kill you, Sam! The bastard's lucky I'm even in a good enough mood to not kill him."

"You're in a good mood? Never mind. I know what he was trying to do, but I've got a family to worry about too, you know? I can't have them taking out my debts on them."

"And you being dead is going to help them?"

"I'm not saying that. I'm just saying I don't want any trouble."

"It's a little too late for that, Sam."

Sam took a moment to think. "Hey, I know. We'll move! Someplace where they can't find us or get to like the Aural Realm or something."

"And how are you going to get your family out of Silesia? Your lenders are there too, aren't they?"

"Yeah, but...you don't think they'd try to stop me, do you?"

Darrio put a hand to his forehead. "How'd you live so long being this naive? Of course they'll try to stop you."

"Then I don't know how, but I've got to do something."

"Not by yourself you're not."

"You want to come with me?"

Saria tugged vigorously on Darrio's cloak. "Don't go. You only just came back."

"You can stay with Talim while I'm gone," Darrio said. "I won't be long."

"Please don't go."

"You don't have to do this," Sam said. "I can think of something."

"No. It's my fault they're after you, and I'm not leaving you alone." At these words, Sam attempted to think of something to say, but he was at a loss for words. Darrio continued, "Meet me at the eastern gate tomorrow morning. Alright?"

"Alright, but seriously. You don't have to do this."

"I've already made up my mind."

Sam shrugged. "Alright." He then took his leave but looked behind him several times as he did so.

Saria tugged on Darrio's cloak. "Don't leave me, Sir Darrio."

"I said you're staying with Talim. What are you worried about?"

"I'm worried I won't see you again."

"Nothing's going to stop me from coming back to you, Saria. Understand? Nothing."

Saria slowly nodded, but the worry remained evident on her face. Darrio pulled her closer and hoisted her onto his back. "See? Now how's that?"

Saria giggled as she wrapped her arms around Darrio's neck and set her head against his back. A single tear escaped her eye and fell upon him. The two then returned to the Hall of Order and rested.

The following day, Darrio set Saria with Talim who promised to take care of her. "I will guard her as if she were my own."

"Good, because if anything happens to her—."

Talim laughed. "Be still, boy! I know better than to trifle with what the Firestar holds dear. Just be sure to return promptly when your affairs are finished so the girl does not drown us all in perpetual weeping."

Saria struck Talim in the leg with her fist, but he looked down upon her and laughed. "Was that a strike? Such fire from the little one! She has already taken much from you, Firestar."

"Stop making fun of me," she protested.

The sight and thought disheartened Darrio as he watched Saria frown at Talim, but he pushed the image out of his mind and focused on the task at hand. Darrio met with Sam at Ambrosia's eastern gate, and the two set out for Silesia. Due to Darrio's hastening, the trip would only be a two-day affair as opposed to the three days it had taken them earlier. During the night of their first camp, Sam asked Darrio, "You really think this whole thing is your fault?"

"If you didn't know me, they wouldn't be after you."

"You think they're after me now because of you?"

"I know that's why they're after you."

"Oh."

When Darrio finished setting the fire, he leaned back and said, "You should've denied me, Sam."

"I couldn't do that."

"Why not?"

"I never learned how to lie."

"It's easy. You just say something is when it isn't. Instead of defending me like you did the last time I saw you, you should've kept your damn mouth shut or joined in."

"How could I do that? We're buddies, aren't we?"

"Your family comes first, Sam! Not me!" and Darrio leaned back. "Especially not me."

Sam looked into the fire and was quiet for a time before he spoke. "I love my family, you know. Don't get me wrong about that. I mean, I know I keep talking about them when I'm talking. It's always the wife this or boys that, and sometimes, maybe I talk about them too much, but that's only because I care so much, you know?"

"Then do whatever you have to do to keep them safe."

"I will. They'll always come first," and Sam glanced over in Darrio's direction. "But I don't abandon my friends either. Never have and never will."

Darrio shut his eyes and rolled to the side. "Go to sleep, Sam."

The following day, they continued their trek and entered Silesia in the dead of the night. Everyone had turned in to rest, and Darrio ushered Sam to his home to retrieve his family while he watched the streets for signs of danger. After several moments of searching and waiting, Sam returned only to say, "They're not here."

"Shit. Do you know where they might be?"

Sam shook his head. "But I doubt they'd be in town."

"Is there anybody here who would know?"

Sam lowered his head. "The guys I owe money to, but…."

"Where?" but Sam was hesitant. "Sam? Tell me where they are."

"You've got to promise you won't do anything too bad."

"Bad?" Darrio chuckled. "By the time I'm finished, they won't even remember what that means."

"Darrio, come on! This isn't a war zone! You've got to promise me, alright?"

"What the hell are you concerned about them for? They're the enemy here!"

"I don't care about that! You've got to promise me!"

Darrio huffed. "Fine. Fine, whatever. I promise."

Sam took a moment to think and then looked past Darrio to a house down the street.

Darrio followed his line of sight and looked back at Sam who confirmed it with a nod. "Stay here," Darrio ordered.

"Now you told me—."

"I know what I said. Stay here." Darrio advanced on the house and peered through the side window to find Sam's lender sleeping beside his wife. After this, he circled around to the back to look for another opening. In doing so, he drew his right dagger.

Sam's lender, in the meantime, was suddenly awakened by a heartfelt disturbance. His sudden rise then stirred his wife. "What is it, baby?"

"I think somebody's outside."

"This late at night?" A sudden crack was heard from the back of his house, and the sound of a door opening and closing followed right after. "What's that?"

"Stay here." The man rose and took hold of a knife which had been lying in wait beside his bed. The back end of his house was composed of a kitchen and dining room, but when he entered, he found nothing. The lock to the door, however, was damaged. Right after he observed this, he heard the front door get breached and his wife's scream. The man raced to the front door past his wife who was standing in the bedroom doorway, but he still saw no one. The man returned to his bedroom and drew a pair of scripted bangles from underneath his bed and gave one to his wife. "Get Dorothy and get out of here. Don't stop till you get to Fred's." The wife did as told and took their daughter through the back door while he cautiously exited through the front. "Who's out there?"

No answer.

"Is that you, Sam? Is it about the money you owe? You're going to pay up now, right?" There was still nothing, and the man turned sporadically just to be sure no one was behind him. In the meantime, Darrio watched him from the roof. "Your family's depending on that money, you know. You made us do this, Sam." The man then turned to find Sam watching the whole affair from down the road.

Sam was concerned about what was happening and inched closer to get a better look. When he saw his lender standing before him with a dagger and armed with a bangle of fire, he did not know what to think. "Where's my family, Mitch?"

"What did you say to him? Did you tell him anything? Were you going to?"

"I didn't say anything."

"Then how'd you get his protection, Sam? Did you promise him something? Were you going to tell him? Get the whole damn nation on us so you could clear up your father's debt? Is that what this was? Get us out of the way so you'd have nothing to worry about?"

"I didn't say anything, man. All I want is my family. We're going to go. You and Fred never have to see us again."

Mitch shook his head. "That isn't good enough, Sam. You know too much, and he's still with you. That makes you a huge liability, and we don't do liabilities. The first one should've got you, and the second one obviously botched the job. I don't know what got in your head to come back here, but if nobody else can fix you, I guess I'll have to." Mitch leveled his arm and opened his palm to face Sam's direction.

Sam lifted his hands in surrender. "Whoa! Hey! Why's it have to come to this? What did I do? I've been paying, haven't I?"

"You haven't paid enough."

"Son of a bitch!" Darrio yelled.

Mitch turned to see Darrio descending upon him from the rooftop with both weapons drawn, but he was only able to fire off a single stream of fire in Darrio's direction, a wild shot that narrowly missed Darrio's head. However, he was unable to avoid Darrio's counterattacks which severed his hand behind the edge of the bangle. Darrio followed up with a sweeping kick which caused Mitch to fall to the ground, and the third and final attack of Darrio's motion was to quickly stab Mitch's weapon hand with the point of his dagger. At the end of this, Mitch was laying on the ground, screaming. "You dirty bastard!"

Darrio sheathed his weapons and grabbed Mitch by the cuff of his shirt. "Where did you take them?"

The fear of death took a strong hold of Mitch, and he could hardly breathe while looking into Darrio's eyes. "The F-F-Firestar. Damn you, Sam. Damn you."

"Hey! You're talking to me now! Where's his family? Where'd you take them? Don't make me ask again you sorry piece of—."

"Darrio!" Sam pleaded. "Come on, man! Not like this!"

Darrio ignored Sam and shook Mitch with extreme violence. "Tell me where they are!"

A ball of fire then whizzed by Darrio's position. Behind him was Mitch's wife who also bore a bangle of fire. After realizing her obvious failure to hit the Firestar, she took aim again and fired. Darrio swung Mitch's body around him to absorb the attack just before its impact, and after doing so, he shoved the badly injured lender to the ground. Mitch's wife, horrified at her incalculable error, ran to the site of her husband who, against all odds, was still alive though his life was fleeting. The daughter, a young girl with a body no less mature than Darrio's, was left behind, and she looked upon the whole affair with burning hatred in her eyes. Darrio looked back at her and knew her contempt was aimed at him. Nonetheless, he returned his attention to Mitch and his wife. "This is your own damn fault. Now if you don't tell me where Sam's family is, I'll find somebody else who will."

"Fred, you bastard!" the wife replied. "Fred knows!"

"Where is he?"

She pointed down the road to a man who was beating a hasty retreat out of the town. Darrio immediately ran after him and called back to Sam. "Let's go."

Sam watched Mitch's wife and daughter tend to Mitch's wounds, and he pitied them. "Man. I'm really sorry about all this."

"Sam!" Darrio yelled.

Sam broke into a run behind Darrio, and the two of them chased Mitch's accomplice, Fred, into the forest east of the town. There, Darrio finally slowed as Fred did in an attempt to hide under the cover of darkness. As Darrio searched, Sam protested while trying to catch his breath. "Darrio, man, seriously! You can't go around doing stuff like that! He had a family too, you know!"

"Then he shouldn't have tried to kill you."

"How do you even know it was them, huh? That guy could've been some kind of a crazy thief or serial killer or something."

"Sam!" Darrio said as he spun around. "Stop being so damn dense! They went after you because you saw something and got associated with me thinking you would talk about whatever it is they're trying to hide! They even tried to kill you for it! Twice! Now I don't take kindly to anyone who tries to kill me or the people I care about, and as far as I'm concerned, they're no different from any other enemy I've faced, so shut up about trying to tell me how misunderstood they are because they're not! I don't feel sorry for them and neither should you! They don't deserve your pity, they deserve a hole in the ground, so stop giving it to them!" Darrio then picked up a stone and launched it ahead of him. The stone forcefully struck Fred who had been hiding in a nearby bush and nearly rendered him unconscious. Darrio marched upon his position, lifted him up, and pinned him to a tree. "Talk! What's going on between you two and Sam?"

"Ey, ouch, hey! Ease up already!" Darrio huffed and drew his weapon. "Hey, hey! What are you doing? Put that way!"

"I'm out of patience, moron. Either you answer me when I ask you, or I start cutting parts off."

"Alright, alright! We…we had a deal. His father was borrowing money, see? He borrowed too much, and we needed it back. But then the guy up and died, so we pegged the debt on Sam."

"And you tried to kill him for that?"

"No! He saw something! Something he wasn't supposed to see, and we couldn't let the secret get out so we had to do something to keep him on a short leash."

"What was it? What did he see?"

Fred writhed in place. "Ah, man. I don't want to talk about this. Not with you."

Darrio placed the edge of his blade just above Fred's left ear. "If you're not hard of hearing, idiot, you're going to be unless you tell me what I want to know."

"Alright, alright! Alright. Me and Mitch, we were talking. He arranged a deal through some contacts of his with people from the Burning Realm."

"What kind of deal?"

"Somebody needed clothes, information, some scripted items, but trade with the Outer Realms is banned, so if anybody found out, we'd become enemies of the realm. We couldn't let that get out so we had to make sure Sam wouldn't talk."

"By doing what?"

"By upping the interest to make him pay more."

"And then trying to kill him?"

"Hey! That was all Mitch's idea, and even he didn't have the balls or the money to up and hire some guy out of the blue, but then this guy came by. Said he'd take care of our problem in exchange for a favor."

"What guy? What favor?"

"I don't know. He never came back."

"He wasn't a shadow caster, was he?"

"He was dressed funny! Had long dark hair, spoke in monotone, called himself Sheol or something like that, but when he didn't come back, Mitch assumed the worst."

The name was only slightly familiar to Darrio as he recalled the shadow caster he killed during his escort mission with Sam. The name was mentioned at the meeting he disrupted in Ambrosia's western forest as well. "Okay," Darrio said, "so what did he want from you? What did he say?"

"I said I don't know. I didn't get the sense that it was a big deal though. Probably information or something."

"And the second assassin?"

"We heard Sam acquired some help from the Firestar and thought maybe he was buying himself some insurance."

"But I didn't even know about the first attack," Sam said.

Fred paused. "Are you kidding me?"

Sam shook his head. "I mean, I suspected the interest, and my wife said as much, but—."

Darrio shook his head. "It doesn't matter now. Where's his family? Where are you keeping them?"

"They're down there," Fred said pointing deeper into the forest. "Tied up beside the bog. You can't miss them."

Darrio motioned for Sam to go ahead, but Sam asked, "What are you going to do?"

"Nothing."

Sam went ahead while Darrio remained with Fred who he kept pinned to the tree. "So, uh," Fred started, "You're going to let me go now, right?"

"Not until Sam gets back."

Sam returned with his wife and two sons trailing behind him. "Hey, Darrio!"

"Are they safe?"

"They're fine."

"Good." He then returned his attention to Fred. "I've got half a mind to kill you." Nevertheless, Darrio shoved him back against the tree and released him.

"You're letting me go?"

"Only, and I mean only, out of respect for Sam, but you're an enemy of the realm as far as I'm concerned, and I'm reporting you as soon as I get back. With any luck, you'll be executed for treason within a week, but I bet you'll leave town before that happens which just means I'll get the chance to hunt you down. You're going to die in any case, so I really don't care at this point. Sam is safe and so is his family, but if I ever see you again, if I hear your name on somebody's lips, if I even feel like you might be chasing him again,

I'll end you, without questions, without warning, and without Sam to stop me."

Darrio left Fred shaking beside the tree as he made his way to Sam and his family. Sam smiled. "Thanks for the help, man. Can't say I agree with your methods, but, uh, yeah."

Sam's family was timid in their approach to the Firestar and said very little, but they waved and smiled nonetheless. "So everybody's okay?" Darrio asked. "Nobody's hurt?"

"Yeah. Everybody's fine."

"Good. Then…I guess you guys have a long trip ahead of you."

"Oh, yeah. I forgot about that."

"I know you'll be safe in the Aural Realm though. The people there are…nice. Stupid but…nice when they want to be."

"I'll take your word for it."

"You should get some clothes and supplies. You've got plenty of those at home, right?"

"Hey, man. I'm still a merchant. I'm always prepared for long trips. Never traveled that far, but I think we'll be alright. Besides," he continued while taking hold of his two sons, "with my own hunter and cook, we don't have anything to worry about. Right, boys?"

The sons smiled, but one of them looked behind Darrio and gasped. "Look out!"

Darrio turned to see a thin stream of fire headed in his direction at the center of which was a single, burning stone, but before he could react, he was shoved to the ground by Sam whose body took on the attack at the heart. Sam fell shortly after. "Sam!" Darrio cried. The two sons and wife gathered around Sam's body where they rolled him over. Darrio placed his hand over the wound in an attempt to heal it, but the bonds on his wrist made themselves evident in the motion, and he cursed. "Shit. Shit, shit! Shit!"

Sam, though barely alive, struggled to remain with them, but he was unable to breathe and unable to speak. The sons pleaded for their father to stay with them, and their mother wept. Darrio, however, stood to his feet and turned to find a still quivering Fred holding a fire shot staff which he had kept concealed on his person. Darrio's eyes began to shift, and the scripts on Darrio's upper set of bonds glowed intensely. Both sets rattled in place but proved themselves capable of keeping Darrio away from his state limit. They were ineffective, however, at containing his rage. "You're dead. Dead, do you hear me? Dead!" Darrio drew his weapons just as Sam watched him from behind, and though he extended a hand in a final attempt to plead with Darrio, the life in Sam's eyes faded away, and his hand fell lifeless.

Fred fled in terror at the Firestar's decree and dropped his only source of defense behind him. Darrio, however, pursued him with unmatched speed, and as soon as his target was within reach, he launched the first of his two daggers ahead of him. The weapon dug into Fred's back, and he fell to the ground while vainly reaching behind him to withdraw the blade. Darrio reached his position and obliged the sentiment violently but followed with a second slash to the chest of his prey. Though Fred tried his best to shield himself, it was all in vain as each of Darrio's attacks either met their target or severed the obstruction. Fred pleaded while Darrio screamed at him. "You killed him! He was innocent, and you killed him! You killed him!" Fred died under the Firestar's pressing, but Darrio did not stop attacking the corpse until all of his strength had been spent. Afterward, he fell to his back, and his bloody daggers fell in front of him. "You bastard," he cried. "You killed him. You killed him."

The body was no longer recognizable, and when Sam's family approached to find the weeping Firestar sitting before it, they shielded their eyes from the sight. Darrio looked back at them and tried his best to apologize. He could barely articulate the words, "I'm sorry," but the family passed over him without saying a word. They would gather their belongings, return to bury Sam's body, and begin their long trek to the Aural Realm.

Darrio sat in place for another hour before rising to his feet to return home. His thoughts were plagued by Sam's death and the circumstances surrounding it, but he was also haunted by a lingering element of blame. It took him four days to return home. He was too demoralized to move with any haste, and during that time, he contemplated what happened. When he finally returned to Ambrosia in the dead of night, he walked silently into the Hall of Order and retrieved Saria from Talim.

"How did it go?" Talim asked, but Darrio did not answer.

Saria, however, could sense the anger, regret, and anguish that resided in Darrio's heart. When they returned to his room, she asked, "What happened? Where's Sam?"

"He's dead," Darrio replied, and his face cracked with grief.

Saria was heartbroken by the news but was afraid to attempt her follow-up question. Nevertheless, she asked, "How did he die?"

Darrio sputtered. "I killed him," and he wept all through the night.

CHAPTER II
A Soul's Unrest

ALL SERIS COULD do was remain still and wonder as he listened to Talim's report on Darrio's condition. "The boy has not eaten for three days, and he has locked himself away in his room. From the moment he returned, he has spoken to no one, and all inquiries have been met with either silence or hostile irritation. I did not know what else to do, so I asked Eloi to travel to Silesia to find out what happened."

"And what did you find?"

"There are three men who are dead. One was a merchant, the same one Darrio was set to protect as one of the Elder's imposed missions."

"The mission where he was nearly assassinated," Seris recalled.

"Yes."

"Who were the other two?"

"The merchant's lenders. His father died without paying all of his dues, and these were passed on to the son. From what Eloi tells me, these same men were also approached by a shadow caster who offered them an exchange of services."

"How did he gain this information?"

"The daughter of one of the merchant's lenders is the one who spoke. Apparently, it was her bitter hope the information would bring about punitive measures against the Firestar."

"And what of these services?"

"The shadow caster would kill their merchant who supposedly was witness to something they held in secret, and they would in turn retrieve something for him. However, the shadow caster in question never returned, and as all of the men involved are no longer among the living, until the Firestar speaks, the secret of what bound them together is a mystery."

"That is unfortunate. Did you uncover why Darrio was there in the first place?"

"No, sir, and I understand the Elders will question you on this."

"They are incessant," Seris sighed, "but Darrio is unharmed."

"Perhaps someone should speak to him."

"I will in time."

"Then is there anything else you would ask, sir?"

"No. Thank you for your report, Talim."

"Yes, sir." Talim stood and turned to leave, but another subject had been nagging him for answers since he first entered Seris' office. Talim had passed a hurried Abaddon on the way to make his report, but when he caught Abaddon's eye, he was once again dismissed and denied an explanation. There was a great deal of reorganization going on among the ranks of Salia's military in preparation for the coming times which Talim and the rest of Seris' shades still knew little about. This was not what bothered him, however. "I apologize," he said. "I know I break from place in doing so, but I have a series of questions that have plagued me as of late. It is not good for a man of my position to ask them, but I do not want to assume."

"I have said before that I keep my door open for just such occasions, Talim. Do not think of your rank. Sit. Tell me what concerns you."

Talim reclaimed his seat. "Once again, I apologize. I do not wish to draw unsavory conclusions about comrades in arms. Nevertheless, I have noticed a great deal of things, and yet, I have never given voice to them out of concern for where the answers may lead me."

"Speak, Talim. There is no one here but you and I."

"We have all borne witness to many things and have experienced much, but no one, even among the High Generals and those who have survived great tragedy, no one is more seasoned than Abaddon."

"Agreed."

"And these Shadow Casters are a strange sort. They have gathered allies from the Burning Realm, and we must assume they have operations in the other realms as well."

"That is true, but why do you mention them?"

"This talk of ancients among them has brought to the fore of my mind certain…aspects of Sir Abaddon's character. Of all who serve with you, we know the least about him and his past. We have always lived in dangerous times, though these times are different indeed, and while I understand he aids us in their destruction, my mind still begs this question of suspicion. Perhaps you will think me another paranoid illusionist for calling attention to a matter which may very well not exist. Nevertheless, do you believe Sir Abaddon may have had a tie to these Shadow Casters even if in some improbable if not inane manner?"

"I do not think your opinions paranoid or frivolous, Talim, but tell me. What makes you think this?"

"It is his manner of being. He exposes so very little. Unlike Eloi, Abaddon has presence, but he does not reveal, purposefully I believe, the nature of that presence. Even the extent of his power, which we glimpsed only briefly during the war, has not been made known. The rest of us struggle to overcome our peaks. He has shown restraint from the beginning. Artisans and script makers work tirelessly to explore the fullest depths of magic, but Sir Abaddon does not train as the rest of us do in the magic arts. It is as if his knowledge of the craft is complete. I would have never believed such a thing to be possible, Captain, and I expose foolishness in saying this, but in the past, when I would attempt to probe his thoughts, to know his mind as I have come to know the minds of those I interrogate in silence or in peace talks, I am firmly and soundly obstructed. He has looked upon me in those moments, and when he did, he saw me as if I were a fledgling child attempting to learn and understand the contents of an ageless tome. The man even speaks and acts as an ancient even if he does not mean to."

Seris leaned back and clasped his hands together in silence.

"Sir. I will understand if my suspicions are dismissed. I do not wish to tarnish his name with empty hearsay. I have no proof in the matter, and if you will tell me to leave soundly, I will understand my error."

"No, Talim. Lon has told me the same thing."

Talim heaved a sigh of relief. "Then I was not the only one to notice. I know that both he and I have taken our sense of awareness from you. Is it then safe for me to assume that you have also seen this?"

Seris was quiet as he contemplated matters, but Talim could not be sure what matters Seris was contemplating. "Have you noticed anything else?" Seris asked.

"I have noticed that you speak to him in secret on more occasions now than before the war, thus, you are the only one who could answer these questions. Captain Seris. We have trusted you with our lives and our beings. If I am to disregard rank then please answer me. Are we correct in our assumptions? Is he an ancient as he seems to be, or do some of us simply suffer from a bout of stress-induced madness?"

Seris paused before returning his eyes to Talim. "It would seem a complicated matter, Talim. I have asked before if you would trust me as part of the group. I ask you again, now. Will you trust me?"

Talim could not be sure of what to say, and at first, he was hesitant. He had taken great pains to study the great men and women of the past, and he had seen greatness in Seris. Nevertheless, while the heroes and legends of old all had traits that he aspired to obtain, they also contained weaknesses he hoped to avoid. His admiration and respect for Seris, he soon realized, was one of his weaknesses. "You have cared for those under your command and shown strength beyond the measure of anyone else I have served with. Your cunning rescued me from destruction in Horus, and under your leadership, your shades have survived the fires of hell and war. Whatever your reasons, Captain, whatever the matter is, I will trust in your judgment."

"Then before I say anything on the matter, I must ask you to promise me this one thing."

"What is it?"

"You will not divulge anything I tell you to Darrio."

"Even if it should concern him?"

Seris nodded.

"Why?"

"What I intend to do, and what I will be asking you to do, is a burden I do not wish for him to share. He is soon to have his own addition of problems."

"And what is the nature of this burden?"

"Will you trust me, Talim?"

Talim nodded.

"Then close the door."

Talim slowly rose to his feet and placed his hands on the door. He felt the significance of his choice would be great, and as he stood in the moment of decision, he could not help but wonder if he would make the right one. He studied techniques, people, systems, and leaders, and he thought when his moment came, he would do better than those who failed. However, now in his own time of choice, he could not be so sure. It seemed as if history was the judge of those who came before him. Thus, Talim decided that he would let history be the judge of his actions as well. Talim closed the door to Seris' office, and beyond it, there was silence.

Darrio awoke later that day in poor spirits, and Saria tried her best to lift them, but all of her efforts were in vain. He was unresponsive, numb, and lacked the desire to do anything. He barely moved, and when he did, it was only to fulfill the most basic of necessities. Finally, there was a knock at the door, and Saria answered it.

It was Seris. "I wish to speak with Darrio. Please stand outside."

Saria turned back to Darrio but did as asked and closed the door behind her. Darrio looked vacantly toward Seris and turned away. "What do you want?"

"I wanted to speak with you. I'm told you will not eat."

"So what?" Darrio said with a diminished and unwavering tone. "I'm not hungry."

"I'm worried about you."

Darrio still kept his face turned away from Seris, and there was a long pause before he spoke. "Do you know how many people I've killed so far, Seris?"

Seris shook his head. "No."

"I don't either."

Seris took a seat at the side of Darrio's bed, but his long silver hair remained at his back. He did not turn or attempt to make eye contact with Darrio as he did not wish to stir up his pain. "I'm sorry I was not there for you."

"I just wanted to help people. All I wanted to do was help. Do you know how many people I've saved, Seris?"

Seris shook his head. "I do not."

Darrio turned, and his face quivered. "Not a damn one. I haven't been able to protect a single person so far, and I couldn't protect him. I killed him, Seris. I killed him, and it's my fault he's dead."

"What happened?"

"I killed him," Darrio said as he turned away in tears.

Seris placed a hand on Darrio's shoulder and at once felt the sensations of pain and anger coursing through Darrio's heart. This was yet another effect of the flesh scripts. It was said among a select few that as they took on the pattern and form of their host, the scripts would occasionally channel the overt and hidden feelings of the user. This usually happened during state limits when it was too dangerous to approach the user in any fashion, but it was also known to occur during moments of particular distress. Seris pulled his hand back and looked upon Darrio with pity. "Darrio. Tell me what happened."

Darrio relayed the story of how Sam befriended him and went on to detail the events surrounding Sam's eventual death. It was told with many pauses and tears, but when Darrio finished, he repeated, "If he never knew me, he'd be alive right now."

Seris shook his head. "That's not true. If not for you, his lenders would have succeeded, and that enemy would have attained whatever he was looking for. Sam's death is not your fault. It is theirs."

"But they killed him because of me."

"And evil men will do what they do out of the evil in their hearts. Darrio. They were decided in their choice to destroy your friend well before you knew his name. Your existence added to Sam's life. Take joy in this and stop torturing yourself over what those simple fools have done. Sam's death is on their hands, and they are the ones who have paid for it. There is no need for this. You did nothing wrong."

"But I wasn't strong enough, or fast enough, or—."

"You did your best. You tried to protect him, and you did not hold back. Even so, this does not mean you will succeed in what you set out to do. You must come to understand this. From what you tell me, Sam was a good man."

"He was."

"And you have added to his life. You may never know what good ultimately results from his friendship with you, but if you focus on the evil, you will never see it to begin with."

"I...guess," Darrio replied finally calm enough to wipe his eyes.

"But it still hurts. When I think about it, it still hurts."

"As it will, but time has a way of healing these wounds, most often by revealing the good in what was tragic."

Darrio's breathing slowed, and his once sorrowful breaths gradually reverted back to normal. "Seris? I want to ask you something, and don't laugh at me, okay?"

"What is it, Darrio?"

"Do you...think I'm a bad person?"

Seris smiled. "I do not. However, there is no one who is good." Darrio lowered his head, but seeing this, Seris called to his attention. "Look at me, Darrio," and when Seris had Darrio's attention, he continued. "So far as I'm concerned, there is nothing you have done that condemns you in my eyes. We have all made our mistakes, some greater than others, but it is how we choose to live with those mistakes and what we take away from them that defines who we are in this life."

"Survive today. Fight tomorrow," Darrio added, and Seris nodded. "Thanks, Seris...for, you know, making me feel better."

Seris smiled. "You're welcome, Darrio."

"I should probably take Saria out for a walk now."

"I'm sure she'd like that."

Seris stood and made his way to the door, but before he could exit, Darrio called out to him. "Seris?"

"Yes?"

"I think, I mean...no. What I'm trying to say is...I trust you. Just so...you know. Just so you know. I wanted you to know is what I'm saying, I guess."

Seris chuckled. "Thank you, Darrio," and there was a slight welling in Seris' eyes, but he opened the door to leave before anything could be seen by Darrio.

Saria rushed past him having listened to the whole thing and hugged Darrio with open tears in her eyes. "Sir Darrio!"

"Saria? What's wrong?"

"Nothing's wrong you big dummy," and she hugged him tighter.

Seris bore witness to this, and a tear ran down his cheek. He took notice of this, smiled, and departed in silence to his office where he remained for the rest of the day.

Two days later, Seris was brought before the High Elders to give an account of Darrio's happenings in Silesia. There, the Elders pelted the captain with questions though Seris described the event as a minor affair worthy of no great concern on their part. "He has killed two men in the dead of night," the third stated, "and there are complaints."

"The widow and daughter of one of the men demand justice," added the fourth.

"Justice?" Seris repeated. "The two men in question were enemies of the realm who attempted to work in collaboration with the Shadow Casters and engaged in trade with an unknown party of the Burning Realm. These are treasonous acts."

"We have no definitive proof of that."

"Eloi has never lied."

"But the Firestar cannot be trusted," Tiberius stated. Seris detected a slip in the Elder's countenance and reason. The two parties argued with no one gaining ground, and the meeting was brought to a close soon afterward. Seris appealed to Darrio's record of service, his unshakable determination to do what needed to be done during the war, and cited all he could recall of Darrio's moments of obedience and goodwill contributions to the nation. He even insinuated to the Elders, purposefully, that they were in need of good counsel and direction. Despite his best efforts, however, the High Elders would not listen. Instead, they simply took the incident as more evidence to justify their distrust of the Firestar. Seris left them on a bitter note but kept the contempt to himself.

The following day, Darrio roamed with Saria through the field where she picked sweet-smelling flowers and chased blindly after gribbits. Darrio shouted directions to her as she ran. However, later in the afternoon, Tam approached from the western forest exhausted and worn. Darrio hastened to him. "What happened?"

"Firestar?" Tam smiled. "I have been chased and beaten. I could not tell you the delight, but tell Seris I have succeeded in my mission." Tam then collapsed.

Darrio took hold of Tam's body and carried him back into the city where he was brought back to health. Tam was never capable of gaining a firm grasp of restoration magic, so healing for this particular shade was nothing extraordinary for those who knew him. With his bodily condition restored, Tam made his report to Seris. Darrio sent Saria back to his room as he was curious about what occurred with Tam, but as Tam finished his story with Darrio present, Darrio could only exclaim, "You did what?"

Tam frowned. "Are you not pleased, Firestar? I am, for I will once again hear the solemn songs of distress. I will see again the dances of fire and ice."

"Well, of course you'd be happy about it. You're sick. But you?" Darrio said addressing Seris. "You know what they'll do to you if they find out about this."

"I am not concerned about what they will do."

"Why are you so surprised, Firestar?" Tam asked. "I told you my task when I warned you about your pursuer. Do you not remember it? The night was cold and wonderfully dark, and you were escorting someone. A worm, I think?"

"Tam," Darrio said in a warning tone. "I'm going to hurt you."

"Wonderful."

"Tam," Seris repeated, "you've done enough. Thank you."

Tam stood, bowed respectfully to Seris, and cheerfully left the room to begin a new search for Lon.

Darrio, in the meantime, crossed his arms. "I still can't believe you did this."

"I thought you would be grateful."

"I would be if it didn't mean you'd get into more trouble. You know how the Elders feel about me. If they find out you've been sending Tam on missions to get the keys to my restraints then—."

"They will not find out."

"They'll execute you. The High Generals will call you a traitor, and you're on thin ice with them already. They don't like you, you know it, and so does everyone else, so why would you go and do something like this?"

"Is this something I must really take time to explain, Darrio? I have done what I have done, and I have no desire to undo it."

"You shouldn't have done it in the first place!"

"My mind has been made. The only thing that matters to me now, the only thing I care about, is that we have the means to free you even if we cannot do so yet."

"What are you talking about?"

"They would never approve of your release under the current circumstances, and we need you unrestrained if we are to eliminate the shadow casters in this region."

"Why? I didn't have much of a problem killing the ones I saw."

"Going forward, things will be different."

"How? How will it be different?"

"Have you spoken to Turil?"

"Yeah."

"What did he say?"

"He wanted to know what I thought about what was happening."

"And what did you tell him?"

"Nothing everybody doesn't already know."

"And you did not encounter anything else in your journeys? Nothing strange or out of place that you may not have listed in your reports?"

"There was this one guy. I think he's been following me."

"Who?"

"I saw him at the temple in Esea, and somebody who looked just like him pointed me towards the camp where Saria was being held. I never mentioned it because I didn't think it was a big deal, but I saw one of them looking at me while waiting with Talim, and then he just disappeared into thin air."

"Disappeared?"

Darrio nodded. "And I wasn't hallucinating, and it wasn't an illusion. He was just there one moment and then gone the next."

"The implication of such an action is difficult to accept, Darrio."

"I know what I saw, and Talim himself said the only area of magic where someone could do something like that is in the light element, so he was either a ghost, or he was using light magic, and I don't believe in ghosts."

"Neither do I," Seris mused.

"You think maybe they're really doing all of this to get to him? You think he's the power of light they're after?"

Seris shook his head. "It seems their focus is on attaining the power itself, not those who are capable of using it or else they would have taken the subjects of their experiments with them instead of leaving them for dead."

"Well, Saria doesn't use magic, and it looks like the people they were targeting didn't use it much either. You think there's something to that?"

"Perhaps, but if we knew more about the element and how it was originally bestowed, then perhaps we could determine their potential targets and how they intend to proceed."

"Has anybody tried talking to one of the priests? Maybe they would know."

Seris shook his head. "If they knew, the elements would not be lost, Darrio."

"Then we'd need to capture another shadow caster but one who's been around since one of the previous worlds. An ancient. Maybe one of the leaders?"

"Preferably someone who has existed from the beginning."

Darrio then lowered his head and snickered. "Yeah. That would be convenient. Without knowing who's an ancient and who isn't, what are the chances of that happening?"

Seris lowered his head, and Darrio could see that he was deep in thought. "What is it? What are you thinking about?"

Seris looked back at Darrio. "We need you at full strength for what will come. I will be looking for a way to convince the Elders of this. In the meantime, I believe you should spend your time in preparation."

"Well, can you tell me what's been happening around here? What's changed? Why is everybody on edge?"

"You will find out later. For now, let me to my thoughts. I have much to consider."

Darrio left the office confused. It was uncommon for Seris to require such time for heavy thinking, and he knew that Seris was planning something even if he did not know the context of these plans. Even so, Darrio was never one to probe too deeply. In the past, he simply went along with the schemes and things would turn out well in the end. As such, Darrio trusted the judgment of Seris and left all of the major planning to his superiors. With Seris at the helm of things, even if he was not a general, Darrio felt he would be ready for whatever was ahead.

The following day, Darrio was once again summoned late into the night in secret by Turil. This time, they met within the upper chamber of the Grand Hall as all deliberations for the day were settled, and everyone with tasks to perform within the structure retired for the night. The two were alone. "I understand there was an incident between you and a pair of lenders in Silesia," Turil said when Darrio entered. "I am sorry for your loss."

"It's late, and I'm tired," Darrio said wearily. "Get to the point. What do you want?"

"Have you considered what I asked?"

"Not yet. I'm still not sure about you."

"I can understand that, but I will be honest with you. I did not call you here only to see whether your mind has changed. I am in need of your help."

"For what?"

"My renegade captain, Palim, has been found. He was taking refuge in the city of Esea but is now under the guard and eye of the High Priestess."

"Why would that old hag be interested in him?"

"I don't know, but I need you to go there and retrieve him for me."

"No, you don't. You can send anyone for something like this."

Turil shook his head. "The Elders will not permit me to reclaim the man for various reasons. Aside from the usual implications of distrust, they said it was to preserve the barrier of separation we have maintained with the priesthood."

"So they don't even know you're asking me."

Turil smiled. "And if they should find out, I will be in even greater trouble."

Darrio paused to yawn and stretch, and in the process of doing so, a question entered his mind. "Okay," he continued. "So the Elders are on you, and they have all your people locked up in local duties."

"That's right."

"And you can't send anybody out of the city because it'll look suspicious."

There was a glimmer of suspicion in Turil's eye as he watched Darrio's looser-than-usual composure. "Are you coming to something, Firestar?"

"How did you find out he's in Esea if all of your soldiers are grounded here and there's no one you can trust?"

"What makes you think I have no one to trust?"

"You said you were looking for people, didn't you? And you're talking to me, aren't you? From the stories you've told me, I'm assuming it takes a while for you to trust people, so there's no way you found enough allies to do it for you. Not this soon."

"You really are Seris' boy, aren't you?"

Darrio yawned. "I'm tired. If I can't fight, I think. If I can't think, I fight. That's just how it goes with me. You want to make something of it?"

Turil shook his head. "Nothing at all."

"So who's helping you?"

"It isn't relevant now."

"Then what makes you think I'm going to agree to this? I could just as well say no and tell Seris about all this."

"I'm well aware of that."

"And you know the Elders are going to want a report from him on what I was doing. If he tells them he's sending me to Esea on your behalf, that's going to be bad for you too."

Turil nodded. "I am aware of this also."

"Well, if you know all this, what did you wake me up for?"

"The captain is not a willing guest of the High Priestess, and she will not speak to anyone but you."

"What? Why did that witchity old cow ask for me?"

"I don't know."

Darrio huffed. "Okay, then tell me this. What makes this captain of yours so important that you're willing to risk everything to get him back? Does he know something? Is there some sort of scandal?"

"The man is a simple captain. He knows nothing beyond the permission of his rank, and I do not take well to allegations of scandal, Firestar. I have always carried my position with integrity and will continue to do so despite the ramifications."

"So what you're saying is that it's not really about him. So, what is it then?"

"I have ignored intuitions in the past and have fortunately lived long enough to regret them. I will not continue making the same mistake, but rest assured, Firestar, if I were able to tell you, I would not need you for this."

Darrio did not understand what Turil meant by the words, but he shrugged. "What the hell. It's not like I have anything else to do, but I'm taking Saria with me."

"Are you sure you want to do that? You noted in your report that the woman was after her when you left."

"So? If she comes after Saria again, I'll kill her. That'll shut her up. Besides, if she really wants to talk to me like you said, I'm sure she won't do anything too stupid, and Saria's not going to like me going off again. I've left her by herself too many times already, and I can't keep doing that to her. Not again. She'll probably want to visit the guys who took care of her at the shrine of light anyway, so this is the perfect excuse."

"Your reasoning is…terrible, Firestar. Do you know what you sound like?"

"It's late. I never said I think well this late at night."

"Then you have fooled me. Perhaps you'll come to your senses in the morning."

Darrio shook his head. "No. I'm still going, and I'm still taking her even if I don't remember why."

"Are you always this strange at night?"

"I'm not strange, I'm tired. Stop acting like a moron. I've always been pissy when I'm tired." Darrio groaned. "And now I've got a headache. Can I go now? I can't think anymore, not like this. Jerk."

Turil nodded, and after Darrio left, Turil crossed his arms and stared at the door for a time. Afterward, he shook his head. "Seris' boy, indeed."

The following day, Saria awoke from her sleep before Darrio. This never happened since their return to Ambrosia, and while Darrio was still half dressed from having taken on a habit of sleeping in the clothes from the night before, his chest remained exposed due to a fit he had later in the night. Saria lifted her head and sensed something was in the room with her. "Who's there?" she whispered.

"You can sense me?" It was Eloi who once again clung to the roof. He had slipped in unnoticed after Darrio's return.

Saria heard the nonthreatening voice and was relieved. "What are you doing up there? Who are you?"

"I am Eloi. How did you sense me?"

Saria was not entirely sure as she was unable to detect any presence from the man. Nevertheless, she was receiving something from him like a faint beacon. "I don't know. I just…felt something from you."

"I was feeling?"

Saria crawled to the end of the bed and nearly stirred Darrio from his slumber, but when she looked back, he settled again.

"What did I feel?"

"You don't know?"

Eloi shook his head. "Talim says my body continues to express even if I do not."

"You were confused…and sad. Did somebody hurt you?"

"I do not know. I do not remember what happened before they found me."

"Found you?"

"I was discovered among a ruined household. There were three bodies close to me, but they were destroyed. I do not remember what occurred. I think what happened is what damaged me. I cannot feel what my body is feeling. We are separated. Broken. I tell it. It does not tell me."

"What are you doing up there?"

"I was watching you sleep. You two are peaceful when you sleep."

"Oh."

"And the scripts of Firestar have changed again."

"What scripts?"

"His flesh scripts. There is a soft formation on the chest. It has become larger since last I saw it." Among the rigid and pointed patterns on Darrio's person, the soft-edged shape which stood out near his heart grew in size and was exhibiting the beginnings of a residual surrounding pattern. Besides this, there were three pre-established focal points on which the patterns of Darrio's flesh scripts revolved. There were two on his back and one at the center of his chest. Even the smaller, seemingly self-contained patterns revolved around these three. The soft shape, however, sat just to the right of the focal formation on Darrio's chest. Saria crawled back to the head of Darrio's bed, and Darrio, disturbed by the movement, turned in his sleep, thus exposing his back. Saria lightly placed her hand over the surface but suddenly recoiled. "What is wrong?" Eloi asked.

"There's something on his back. What is it?"

"Those are his flesh scripts. They are all over. Have you not seen them?"

Saria looked towards Eloi and frowned. "I'm blind, remember?" She then turned back to Darrio. "But I can feel them though."

"Then you should not touch them."

"Why?"

"Talim warned us of their attributes before we were first engraved. They give us power but carry us within them. Our wills and emotions are transmitted through the lines. Such a thing is not to be shared commonly among men, and he said to never touch the flesh scripts of another without permission."

"What happens if you touch them?"

"I do not know, but I have only seen two touch Firestar. One of them is captain. The other is dead."

Saria looked back at Darrio's body and carefully maintained a slight space between her hands and his back. When she came to the first of the two focal shapes, the one to Darrio's left, she uttered, "This one is about his mother."

"You can sense this?"

Saria nodded. "She was…," but sadness swept over her, and she could not finish. Instead, she moved on to the second formation where she uttered, "His father," and began to cry. Darrio turned once again in a fit of disturbance, but when he settled, Saria held her palm over Darrio's chest and sobbed. "Sir Darrio?"

Darrio awoke with a start, and his first reaction was to take a fierce grasp of Saria's arms. Saria screamed and continued to cry, but when Darrio regained his bearings, he apologized. "Saria? Saria, I'm sorry. I'm sorry. I didn't mean to." Darrio then took notice of Eloi who continued to observe them. "What are you doing here?"

"I was watching."

"Get out."

Eloi dropped to his feet and took one more look at Saria. "Do take care of her in your journey, Firestar. She is rare. You will protect her, yes?"

Darrio nodded to Eloi's satisfaction, and Eloi left the room. Darrio did not know what prompted such a response, and his curiosity was short-lived. He returned his attention to Saria who he saw to be saddened and shaken but otherwise physically unharmed. As Darrio prepared himself for the day, Saria asked him, "Are you leaving me alone again?"

"No. I'm taking you with me."

"You are? Where are we going?"

"Esea."

"Esea? Why are we going back there?"

"You'll be safer that way."

"Does this have anything to do with Sir Turil?"

"No. It's just…every time I leave this place, something bad happens, and now Turil and Seris are talking like something big is coming. For all I know, Ambrosia could be buried by the time I come back again, and I don't want to risk losing you."

"Then why don't you stay home? I don't want to go to Esea."

"It's my job, Saria. Besides, I know the old woman is involved with the Shadow Casters in some way, and I want to know how. She must have had a reason for coming after you."

"But what'll we do when we get there?"

"We'll go to the shrine of light first. The priests should be able to take care of you while I take care of the, um…business. When it's over, we'll leave. Simple. See?"

"I guess."

"I'm not going to let anything happen to you. Do you hear me?"

Saria was doubtful but kept her fears to herself. The impression left by Darrio's flesh scripts still weighed heavily on her mind. She had received a truer sense of the feelings Darrio tried to keep hidden in his heart for so long, but more than this, she received a good sense of why.

Darrio proceeded to Seris' office soon after getting dressed to inform him of the eventual departure. "Did Turil request this service of you?" Seris asked.

Darrio nodded. "But I think it'll help. The Elders aren't going to do anything about the priesthood connection, and the old witch might know something we don't."

"I don't know that Turil has ever spoken deceitfully, and I know his intuitions to be a serious matter. I have no reason to doubt his intentions."

"So do you trust him?"

Seris nodded. "Even if I cannot permit him to trust me."

"I don't get it. Why can't you two just be like you were before the war ended?"

"It is a difficult and complex matter, Darrio. I do not wish to discuss it."

"He said you got involved with something." A sudden jolt of fear coursed through Seris' face which Darrio identified as exceedingly out of place. He continued on with caution. "He said it was serious."

Seris leveled his eyes with Darrio's, and in responding to him, Seris spoke slowly and solemnly. "What else has he told you?"

Seris' reaction shook Darrio's resolve to probe the affair as he was unsure of how best to proceed. There was a certain fear that arose in his heart over where such questions would take him. He certainly did not want to do anything that was in opposition to Seris though Darrio still, in some measure, wanted to do what was right. This was an age-old value instilled in him by his father, a value he still felt he failed to uphold. Nevertheless, Darrio remained concerned over the affair Turil mentioned and hoped to find out what it was. If it was something he could not help with, he thought perhaps he could steer Seris away from it. As he looked back, however, he could see Seris awaiting a response with calculating and analytical eyes. Darrio could not be sure what this meant for him, and he was equally unsure if he wanted to continue in the pursuit. "He didn't tell me anything. Not really. I'm not even sure he really knows what's going on."

Seris lowered his eyes to the desk. "Are you lying to me?"

"No. I wouldn't. He…he just suspects something. He thinks something is wrong, but he didn't give me any details. He wouldn't."

"Turil's intuition," he sighed. "To think someday that I would…no matter." Seris leaned back. "Even if you should ask, I can not tell you what I am planning, Darrio."

"Why not?"

"It would kill me to place this burden on you because I have known your pain. You have experienced enough. I will not tell you for your own sake." Darrio remained quiet while Seris rested his hands on the table. "As for Turil, neither will I allow him to harm himself on my account. These burdens are my own, and I wish to spare you both."

"Maybe we could help with whatever it is. Even if he won't, maybe I could—."

"No, Darrio. My answer is no."

"Is it really that bad?"

"It is enough."

Darrio diverted his eyes and tried to make sense of what he heard.

"I have not made these decisions lightly. If it were something I could share with you, I would. I will understand if you do not trust me, but I can not allow you to help me."

"Don't say that," Darrio said as he shook his head. "Not after everything we…not after everything that's happened. Not now."

"What would you have me say?"

Darrio shook his head. "I don't know. I don't even care what it is anymore. I don't care. If you can't talk about it, fine. If you want to leave me in the dark then fine. I said I'm going to trust you, and that's what I'm going to do."

"Then I'm glad."

"But don't lie to me, Seris. Don't you ever lie to me. If there's something going on or there's something wrong, you can either tell me if you want or keep it to yourself, but if you lie to me," Darrio warned with bated breath, "if you lie to me, I'll hate you."

Seris took in Darrio's words and nodded in agreement. "The Elders will want to know what you are doing in Esea."

Darrio calmed. "So what are you going to tell them?"

"I will tell them you left to give Saria an opportunity to visit her caretakers and will return before our operations go into effect. This is true of what you've already said to me, correct?"

Darrio nodded.

"They do not need to know about Turil's suspicions or his initiation of the gathering. I would prefer to send someone along with you, but it is best you go alone to maintain the integrity of what I report."

"Then I should finish getting Saria ready. Um…thanks, Seris, for, um…."

Seris lifted a hand in silence and shook his head apologetically. "No, Darrio. Thank you for trusting me."

Darrio returned to Saria after his meeting with Seris, and the two set out for Esea. Saria was largely silent which Darrio quickly noticed. "You're quiet today," he said.

Saria shrugged. "Nothing to say."

"You sure? No questions? No exploration of what's out there?"

"Not today," she sighed.

Darrio started to worry. "It's not about this morning is it?"

"No."

"Oh," but Darrio remained concerned.

The days passed in silence, the nights were uneventful, and Saria behaved wistfully for the duration of the journey. When Esea came within view, she broke her long silence by addressing Darrio in her usual manner, but her voice carried a heavy sadness. "Sir Darrio?"

"Hm?"

"Do you love me?"

Darrio had never been asked such a question before and did not know at first how to address it. "What? What did you just ask me?"

"Do you love me?"

"Well, of course I do," he stumbled.

"Would you be sad if I went away?"

"Sad?" Darrio surmised that he would be furious at anyone who attempted to take her from him. He became fixated on this thought and wondered if she was aware of anyone who would do her harm. "Did somebody say something to you?"

Saria shook her head. "No."

"Then what are you talking like this for?"

"Sir Sam went away, and you didn't say anything for three days. What would you do if I went away?"

"I'm not going to let anyone take you, Saria," but Saria sighed. "What's gotten into you? Did somebody say something? Did somebody threaten you? Who is it? He's a dead man."

Saria faced Darrio, and her blind eyes were heavy-laden. "Why do you have to be so mad all the time? Can't you let anything go?"

"I'm not ma—!" but Darrio quickly silenced and shook his head. "I'm not mad. I'm just tired of people always assuming things about me. It's frustrating."

"But don't you like people?"

"When there's a reason."

Saria shook her head but said nothing more.

As they entered, Darrio surveyed the area only to find business had gone as usual in the streets of the city. Merchants still peddled their wares on the road while the poor went about unnoticed by the affluent. "Miserable city," Darrio uttered, and the two made their way to the temple district.

The two priests of the light shrine were speaking among themselves when Darrio and Saria approached, but when they took notice of them, the two men smiled cheerfully. "You have returned, and little Saria remains safe I see!" the first of them said.

"I'm not little," Saria replied.

The second priest laughed. "Of course not. How can we make your acquaintance? Is there something you need from us?"

"I need you to watch her," Darrio replied. "It's just for a little while. I've got an errand to run and—."

"You just came to the city?"

"Yeah."

"Then nonsense!" shouted the first. "You two have come a long way, and now you speak of errands? No. You two shall rest first. Eat with us tonight, and you can complete your task in the morning."

"What? Eat? But I've got a job to do."

"It can wait until your belly is full. You Salians have such little regard for yourselves. You do not respect the little things in life. You lack zeal."

"Only the Taurens regard life with less appreciation," continued the second. "Perhaps for your people, it is because your lives are so long."

"Or perhaps it is because they do not eat enough."

"I can eat just fine," Darrio protested.

"Then eat with us. Rest. Then tomorrow, you may go."

Saria set her face towards Darrio and smiled. It was her silent but enthusiastic plea.

"If it'll make you happy," he sighed.

"Excellent!" said the first. "Come. I will set a place for you."

"And I will go prepare the food," said the second, and he left for the market.

Darrio looked at Saria whose youthful curiosity and happiness returned. Even so, he wondered what bothered her and whether or not he had anything to do with it.

The four ate on the grounds directly in front of the shrine where the two missionaries shared stories of their travels from the Aural Realm to the Saline Realm. Their talks then shifted to their experience so far within the region before crossing into matters of faith. "We do not understand this concept of multiple gods," the first said. "But the truth of one God confuses many of the people we speak to here. It is a shock for them."

"Things are different here," Darrio said wearily.

"What do you think?"

"It doesn't matter what I think."

"Surely you must have some sense? Some opinion?"

"He does," Saria said, "but he's mad at Him."

"Saria," Darrio said as he snapped to full consciousness. "I'm not mad at Him."

"You sound angry to me," said the second.

"I'm not. I'm just…you wouldn't understand."

"This is an uncomfortable subject for you," said the first. "I do not know you and have no business in asking this, but why this anger towards Him? Did something happen to you?"

"How long have you two been here?"

"Four years," the second replied, "and they have been long."

"Have you ever heard the Firestar's story?"

The two shook their heads. "All we hear is rumor," said the first. "Words spread on the lips of others."

"Well, this isn't a rumor. This actually happened."

"Then please, go on."

"When the Firestar was a kid, he lost both of his parents to two groups of idiots. His father was killed protecting his mother from one, and his mother died on conspiracy charges from the other."

"That is tragic."

"Yeah. And after his mother died, the kid left the village he was in and eventually settled in Ambrosia where everybody ignored him. So he was alone and went from place to place looking for food, getting into trouble, and just going wherever his curiosity took him. Then the kid ran into this captain who felt sorry for him and took him in, and this made the kid happy again, but it couldn't fix what already happened, and he couldn't forget. After that, he was forced into military service where nobody liked him because he was a foreigner, and they put him in harm's way, forced him into duels, and hoped the enemies they were fighting would do him in, but no matter what happened, no matter what was thrown at him, the kid just kept on surviving and kept on living."

"What happened then?"

"The war happened. He killed people, leveled cities, buried armies, assassinated leaders, and he fought and did everything his commanding officers told him to do. But he was attacked, threatened, taunted, tortured, beaten, hated, and feared. When the war ended and the leaders heard what he did, they decided he was too dangerous and plotted to kill him. They acted just like some of the enemies the kid fought, the same ones he destroyed, even for their sakes."

"Did they succeed?"

Darrio shook his head. "No, but they're still trying. Even to this day, they're still trying."

"No one has ever spoken of this story."

"That's because nobody's interested in hearing the Firestar's story. They're only going to see what they want to see or whatever's the most convenient for them. They don't want a hurt little boy. They don't want an angry young man. They want a monster they can hate."

"That is not true," stated the second. "There are always people who are willing to see the truth. Perhaps there may not be as many of them as we would like, but they do exist."

"Do you know how many lies I've seen growing up? I don't even know if what I know is true."

"And we have seen our fair share of atrocities over the years as well, and while we can attest that, yes, the world is full of deceit and foolishness, it is not without the truth. I realize, still, that this is a sensitive subject for you, but we believe in a God of truth and light and purpose."

Darrio shook his head and repeated, "Purpose?"

"Yes, purpose, even in places where we see no purpose."

"You're beginning to sound like those Tauren bastards of the Silent Realm."

"Except we do not regard life as a simple matter of function. Please, listen for a moment. We do not believe in a fearful God. Whatever your quarrel is with Him, if you are so mad, why do you not tell Him? If you pray, perhaps He will give you some answers."

"Are you kidding me?" Darrio said as he recoiled from the table. "He doesn't want to talk to me! He'd rather kill me!"

"Peace, my friend! Peace! Be still. It was only a suggestion."

It was a suggestion that jostled Darrio with intense fear and self-loathing, and though the answer as to why was within his sight, it was something he could not bring his heart to grasp. The pain was simply too great. "I can't stay up like this. I've got something to do tomorrow." Darrio rose to his feet. "Thanks for the food and everything, but I should be going. I'll come back for Saria tomorrow."

"Sir Firestar," addressed the first.

"What?"

"I thought I should say before you go that we also believe God to be one of mercy and reconciliation. He can forgive anyone for anything. This includes anything you have done."

It did not occur to Darrio why was told such a statement until he settled down to rest within one of Esea's inns. The missionary referred to Darrio by his title, but he was too flustered to pick up on this at the time. "Idiot," he mumbled to himself, and he soon sighed and set his feet over the end of his bed.

The room was dark, and the only source of light came from the moon outside which hung in the night sky. While nervously running his hands through his hair, Darrio's eyes darted about the room. In his heart, he was searching for something, words to express his true feelings on the matter, but for all that he was sensing and for all the interference, his mind could only settle on a question. "Don't you hate me?" he whispered, but there was no answer, and he fell back to consider the question which pained his heart to ask. He felt lost because he did not know the answer, not by any definitive measure, but despite what he remembered hearing about Him, he thought in his heart, "Not me. He couldn't feel that way about me." However, the question still hung in the air, and though unable to see Him, Darrio felt exposed. He turned his body over and covered his head with the bed sheet. He wrapped himself even tighter in it, but it was a futile effort that he knew he only did out of compulsion. While decidedly frustrated, angry, and depressed all at once, Darrio spoke again, this time in closing. "I'm not mad," he whispered. "I'm pissed."

CHAPTER 12
Drawn

DISPOSED TO DEBATE, and with little else to do, two acolytes stood on the front stoop of the temple of Magnus. They had been posted there for the past week and took it upon themselves to discuss the doctrines of Magnus and the inner workings of magic to pass the time. Their subject at that moment was the Firestar. One of them, a fearful man, asked, "Do you believe it's true, and if it is, how do you think he does it? I mean, all that power we heard about during the war. It doesn't seem like such a thing should be possible."

"Flesh scripts they say, but I haven't seen it," responded the second. "I think they were exaggerating things."

"They say he boiled a host of forces in the Frozen Realm alive and refroze the ice on top of them. There are now ten thousand souls suspended in agony just below the surface of the ice."

"Don't believe it."

"And in the Stony Realm, in the midst of a fight, he lifted the earth around him, a two to three-mile radius they say, maybe more, and he took the men under during the rise. Then he collapsed the earth down on top of them forming the Crater of Bones."

"Lies."

"And the Ash Dunes of the Burning Realm? They say they're made from the charred remains of at least five hundred thousand. Even so, I think some of it may be made of soot from the region, but can you imagine ash made from the bodies of five hundred thousand men and—?"

"For the love of Magnus, man! I tell you, there is no way any one man can be capable of such things! These are simply the kinds of tales told to frighten children. The Firestar has become a fable of sorts now."

"But for the Elders to find it necessary to bind him twice is significant, wouldn't you say? Only a single pair has ever been needed for anyone. Ever."

"Then the artisan who prepared the first pair was a fool who did not do his job properly."

"Perhaps he employs some kind of amplification technique we do not yet know about."

"Or perhaps the people who have told you these tales have let their imaginations run wild. Of the many legends in the world, do you honestly believe any of them happened just as they say or in the grandness of how they were told? These are stories. Some are made to inspire and some are to instill fear, but they're stories nonetheless."

"Well, I for one believe in these stories. I am glad he is bound."

"And I do not think him to be any more special than anyone else. He lives, he bleeds, and he may eventually die. The world will have one more legend, and that will be the end of it."

"I think you're pessimistic."

"He's not pessimistic," Darrio said. "He's an asshole."

The two men jumped. "F-f-f...f-f-f-f...."

"Be still. I'm tired and not in a good mood. Is Valeria in there?"

"Sh-sh...sh-sh-sh-she...."

"She will speak to no one else," the other finished. "The temple has been closed for a few weeks now, and the people are getting agitated. Rather than come here, they've been directed to Lumineth for the blessings and services."

"Why?" Darrio asked.

"High Priestess Valeria is...not well, and she will not permit anyone to take her place until she has spoken with you."

"Th-th-there's a sh-sh-shade inside too," added the fearful acolyte.

"You idiot! We're not supposed to tell him that!"

"Why? He was going to find out anyway."

Darrio sighed. "I already knew about the shade."

"You see? I told you this would happen! And now they've sent the Firestar! It's just as the prophet of light said! He's come to bring retribution! We're doomed, I tell you! Doomed!"

"Shut up!" Darrio barked which he soon followed with a groan. "You're making my headache worse. You said Palim's inside?"

"Y-yes."

"Let me through."

The two acolytes parted ways and allowed Darrio passage through the tall, twin doors. Once he was inside, the frightened acolyte was struck by the other. "You're an idiot, you know that? You were just about to tell him everything, weren't you?"

"So what? I'm more afraid of him than I am of you and Valeria. Who knows? Maybe he'll kill you all and spare me in the process. I heard he has a merciful side too."

The cynical acolyte shook his head in disgrace, and while the two continued their conversation outside, Darrio proceeded carefully down the aisle and took in what he was seeing.

The interior was dimly lit, dusty from neglect, and the pews were all empty. The greatest source of light stemmed from the sun streaming through the stained glass window at the far end of the main hall. Valeria was stooped over a pedestal on the stage as she scribbled furiously on an open scroll and mumbled incoherently. Her hair was frayed and strewn about her face. A layer of worry-induced sweat moistened her pallid skin, and her countenance was fractured by moments of fear, confusion, and despair.

Palim sat beside her gagged and bound to a chair, and though he was in his own world of sorrow, when he saw Darrio, his grief multiplied. He groaned, shook his head, and pleaded with his eyes for

Darrio to stay away, but these actions did not befit his station, and Darrio counted them as strange.

Valeria took notice of Palim's reactions and looked forward. "Firestar! Firestar, thank God. I'm so glad you came." Palim continued to shake his head and cry out from his stifled state, but Valeria frowned. "Oh, be quiet you big buffoon. Nobody's going to hurt you."

"What's going on here?" Darrio asked.

"What's going on here? What's going on is I cannot trust anyone. Everyone, Firestar, everyone! They're all against me. I can see the demons inside of them. I had one too before I cast it out of me, but he went and told the others. Now they're all against me. Against me, I tell you! And now I see curses. Curses in the night. It waits for me. The Curse of Shades. The Curse of Night. I am afflicted, Firestar!" and she began to weep. "Oh, how I have become so darkened. Looking for sight, and now I can see. I have become so sad. So lonely. Look at me, Firestar. I have become so broken. Now I can see, but at what cost? I have forfeited my soul. What I wanted to see has blinded me. Oh, how I've learned. So much and so little. All of my gain, Firestar. All of my gain is loss."

"Calm down," Darrio said. "Just tell me what happened to you."

"What happened to me?" she asked with genuine confusion. "Nothing happened to me. I'm fine, Firestar. Can't you see? I'm fine. By the will of Magnus, there's nothing wrong with me…oh god. Did I just say Magnus?"

"Yeah. You're a priestess. Did you forget or something?"

"Priestess? Priestess of what? Of fools? Of heretics? Blasphemies. No, no, no, Firestar. I am the priestess of nothing and the greatest nothing. All of it is a lie. A great, dark, and shady lie. That emotionless bastard. He's a liar, I tell you."

"Who's a liar?"

"The liar is a liar," Valeria replied with indignation. "Have you become dense since your return?"

Palim wept.

"Oh, be quiet you big baby. He's been like this ever since he got here, you know. Or was it ever since I touched him? Maybe I told him. Touched him? Told him? Oh, now I remember. I gave him something. It was a gift."

Valeria reminded Darrio of an early version of Tam which Seris had long since tamed during the war. He displayed a similar though significantly more violent style of dementia which Darrio found to be equally disturbing. Had it not been for Seris, in fact, Darrio would have killed him. Darrio lifted his hands in a non-threatening manner. "Be still, okay?"

"You don't have to tell me to be still, Firestar. I already told you. I'm fine."

Darrio did not regard Valeria as much of a threat, but he remained wary of her and approached cautiously. Palim, in the meantime, became even more upset and kicked away from Darrio until he fell on his side. Darrio ignored him to see what Valeria scribbled, but he only saw it for a second before Valeria snatched it up and held it to her chest in defense. "You can't have this, Firestar. It's mine."

"I only want to look at it. I promise I won't take it."

"You promise? Seriously?" Darrio nodded, and Valeria slowly relinquished the scroll from her grasp to set it on the pedestal. When it was unfurled, she closed it again and asked once more, "Do you seriously promise not to take this from me?"

Darrio nodded again, and Valeria opened the scroll.

Written on the paper were strings of nonsensical handwritten scripts, a crude drawing of a dancing pig, and the words God, Power, Magic, Shade, Day, Night, and Curse. These etchings, however, sat on top of a highly organized set of scripts that were etched into the paper in gold-colored ink. "The hell is this?" Darrio uttered. "I've never seen scripts like this before."

"Wonderful, isn't it? Aren't they unique? There's power in these words, Firestar. Power like you wouldn't believe."

"What do you mean?"

"These are special scripts. Personal scripts. It is not enough for them to remain on the page like normal scripts. These must be accepted and pronounced. They're useless just sitting there, and they cannot function on their own."

"So they're like the sound scripts we use to make traps with."

"Didn't you hear me, Firestar? These words have to be read. From your heart. You can't just make little clapping noises and expect something to happen, no, no, no, no, no. Hear them. Read them. Speak them, aloud. Then, only then, will the real magic begin to happen."

Darrio looked once again at the scripts on the scroll and realized the language was indecipherable, but he recognized the phonetics which were similar in sound to the ones used by Elea when she spoke in her native tongue. "I've never read this language before, and I've only heard it once. It's a dead tongue, isn't it?"

Valeria nodded. "A dead and ancient one. Would you like to know why it's dead?"

"Why?"

"It's because the language itself is cursed."

Darrio looked once again at the page, and as he stared, the golden etchings appeared to glow and whisper to him. He saw past the hastily written black lines constructed by Valeria and saw simply the words which seemed to almost writhe with lively vigor.

"If you read it, Firestar, you too can gain this power."

Darrio was entranced and could not bring himself to understand why. It seemed, by mere appearance, to be familiar to him, but he also felt there was something foreign about the scroll's call, and the sensation brought to mind the word, "illegitimate." Whatever he was looking at was an imperfect copy, a forgery of whatever had been the true source of inspiration. Nevertheless, he could not tear his eyes away from it, and his mind, curious as it was, began to try and decipher the cryptic words on the page.

"Stop!"

Darrio was rattled by the emboldened command and looked up to find the white-haired man who he had seen in the valleys and at the temple grounds. He was dressed just the same as Darrio had seen him before with the same white shirt and red collar. However, he lacked the peaceful tone of the past sightings, and the look in his eye was a stern one.

"Light Bearer!" Valeria cried. By virtue of utter terror, she fell to her back and retreated to a corner of the room where she turned to hide her face in shame. Palim crawled in similar a style, bound as he was, to the opposite corner where he shuddered. Darrio, however, remained suspended in silence.

The Light Bearer, as Valeria called him, promptly took the scroll from the podium where it burned in a flash of white flame and sparks of lightning. So total was the scroll's destruction that not even a speck of ash was left to fall to the ground. "You're not ready," he said calmly. "And you of all people should know a counterfeit when you see one."

Darrio could not determine what had become of him. He found it hard to speak, and after several failed attempts, he finally rasped, "How did you get in here, and how do you know me? Were you following me?"

The Light Bearer looked past Darrio to Valeria and Palim, and without answering Darrio's question, he sighed. He then leveled his eyes at Darrio. "I will warn you only once. Never, under any circumstances, endeavor to seek this power. You are not ready for it, and there are more pressing matters ahead of you."

"Ready for what? What power?" and Darrio paused. "What was on that scroll?"

The man continued to shake his head, and his body faded slowly.

"Was it dark magic? Is that what it was?"

"Leave it alone. You're not ready," and when the Light Bearer's body was no longer visible, there was silence. He was gone.

"Come back!" Darrio shouted. "You didn't tell me who you were!" Darrio's pace of breath quickened to rapid panting. He did not believe in ghosts. He refused to, but the fear he felt stemmed from the uncertainty of what happened and the possibility that the Light Bearer had just saved him from something dire. With this in mind, Darrio turned angrily to Valeria and spun her around. "What the hell was on that scroll?"

Valeria wept. "You promised not to take it from me, Firestar."

"Answer me!" he ordered while shaking Valeria in anger. "What was on it? Were you trying to give me the powers of dark magic?"

Valeria hesitated but nodded.

"You idiot!" Darrio shouted as he released her. "So that's what happened to you! And you gave the same thing to Palim?"

"Yes," she replied in distress.

"What the hell were you thinking? You didn't think what happened to you was bad enough? And then you tried to get me into it! You stupid old hag! I ought to kill you!"

"But you're the Firestar! What better vessel for the powers of light and darkness than you? And then," she said clambering to her knees, "and then when the time comes, you can do what you were always meant to do."

"Which is what?"

"What?" she repeated, taking offense to the question. "Are you daft? Hasn't anyone told you yet?"

"What is it?" Darrio shouted.

"You're supposed to destroy this world and usher in the next. You will bring about the Great Catastrophe."

"What the hell?"

"I saw it, Firestar. You don't believe me, but I saw it. It was as clear as day, and I must admit, when I first heard of it, I thought it the talk of heretics; feeble minds whittling away in the dark. And now look at me. But now I've seen the truth, and it's true! You are the one. You are the one who will bring to pass the end of Magnus, and you will usher in the dawn of the new world."

"What the hell are you talking about? You told me something different before."

"I know what I told you, but I wasn't right then. The Firestar is wrath, that is you, and one of the four cardinal stars of Magnus, and it is written, in that liar's theology book by the way, that he will come and destroy the enemies of Magnus to make way for his coming. I don't know whether he's found his Magnus or not, and quite frankly, I don't care at this point, but all of that? No. That is not God's plan. Oh no. What a man has written will not come to be. Instead, it will be your shadow that destroys the old world, and you, Firestar, will bring to bear the end of what comes and herald the fruition of a new and wonderful world which will be as it was in the beginning."

"You're not making any sense! Why are you telling me this?"

Palim managed to ply the gag from his mouth at that moment and shouted, "She's insane and speaks lies! All lies!"

Valeria retorted. "You dare call me a liar? The one who first spoke mistruths about me and told me the Firestar would not come?"

"I will speak now, witch, and to the Firestar only."

"You see now why I gagged him, don't you? He's a big baby and a blabbermouth."

"I will tell you the truth!"

Darrio turned to face Palim whose eyes were just as clouded as Valeria's and even less trustworthy.

Palim continued. "You will receive power, Firestar. Power far beyond what you have known, and on your very hands, even in them, you will bear the elements of creation! The Shadow Casters will be a mere footnote in the grandest story ever told in the history of this world, and you will trample them, all of them, under your feet on your way to power and your ascension to glory!"

"Power and glory?" Valeria retorted. "There's no glory for him, not from men. He will be tried and tortured. The shadow will turn on him and be a torment to his heart. He's a sorrowful figure."

"No! With ambition, he will overcome and face a decision held to the face of those who once existed in the beginning. Imagine it, Firestar. You will hold powers held by no one before you and never to be held by anyone again. You will be a god among men! All you must do is seize it and at the earliest opportunity!"

"He must receive it you demon-possessed fool, and he will not become a god but a man, one who will be faced with the most difficult decision of his life! For the sake of them all, Firestar, don't make the wrong choice, and don't listen to him. He's insane, I fear."

"Do not speak to me as if you are full of light and truth, witch! I have seen you too, and your days are numbered!"

"Shut up!" Darrio shouted. "Shut up! Both of you! Be quiet! Stop talking!"

"Let me prove it to you, Firestar," Valeria pleaded. "Take me to Lumineth. Derenger will be there, and when we find him, then you will see."

"No you won't because he is not there," Palim said. "Don't go to Lumineth. You'll only be wasting your time."

"Come now, Firestar. Who are you going to believe? The dolt who betrayed his own general or me?"

Darrio crossed his arms and glared in response. "You think that's going to make the decision any easier?"

"Well…I suppose not, except, yes. Yes, it should make the decision easier."

Darrio shook his head. "I didn't even come here for all of this. All I wanted to do was to find out what happened, go home, make my report, and go to bed."

"Well, if you ask me, Firestar, that sounds rather boring. Are you always this dull?"

"I wasn't asking you!"

Valeria settled back and lifted her hands in surrender. "Never mind me then. My lips are sealed. You could go and spend the rest of your days in obscurity, wasting your life away on mundane tasks in service to simple men instead of embracing your destiny, but who am I to say such things? High priestess of a cult. But you see? I'm shutting up now. You'll hear no more words from the likes of me."

There was something discomforting about Valeria's demeanor. Darrio expected more of a fight, but she was strangely pliant in addition to the other mental deficiencies she exhibited. Had he known she would be this easy, he thought, he might even have decided to take Saria with him. As he considered it further, however, he decided he had indeed made the right decision in leaving her with the light shrine priests. Darrio shook his head and cursed. "Get up."

"Are we going?"

Darrio nodded. "But you've still got a lot of explaining to do on the way."

"Oh, this is wonderful. Wonderful!" she laughed. "Perhaps… perhaps I can redeem myself. Yes? No? What do you think, Firestar? Oh, it doesn't matter what you think. Let me make my preparations. I cannot travel with such a disheveled appearance. It's unfeminine!"

Where are those acolytes of mine? Boys? Boys!"

Valeria stormed towards the entrance and blew open the doors by force of wind magic, and this surprised the two acolytes who were still arguing beyond it before her arrival. "M-mistress!" the fearful one responded.

"How could you let me go insane like this? My hair is in disarray, and the two of you are just standing here?"

"But you told us to stand here."

"I told you no such thing. I said stand here and guard the entrance, not engage in idle chit-chat. Now come in here and help me. The Firestar and I are going on a trip."

Darrio shook his head as he witnessed this, and Palim called out from the corner. "Firestar. You have come to rescue me, have you not? Did General Turil send you?" Palim had regained his natural senses. His eyes were no longer darkened, and he appeared oblivious to all of his prior behavior.

Darrio responded by saying, "Yeah, he sent me."

"Ha, ha! I knew he would rescue me from this witch!"

"What did you come here for?"

"I did not come here. I was brought here."

"What do you mean?"

"Somebody kidnapped me in the middle of the night and dropped me off here. Me! A captain of the Shades bound up and carried on the winds like a defenseless leaf."

Darrio faced Palim in total disbelief. "I thought you ran here after telling the Elders of Turil's plan."

"How could the general think such a thing? I am no coward."

"Are you saying you didn't tell them?"

Palim shook his head. "I overheard Captain Seris discussing the plan with Abaddon, so yes. I told them."

"Why?"

"Because the Shadow Casters are something we can deal with, on our own, without your dangerous influences. You are the single greatest threat to this realm right now, and if you can't realize that, you're either too simple or too stupid to understand."

Darrio stepped forward and forced Palim to his feet all while keeping a firm grasp of his cuff. "You're going to regret saying that to me."

Palim laughed. "Have you forgotten your rank, Firestar? I'm the captain here. Show some respect."

"There's only one person in this world that I respect, and he isn't here right now to stop me. Neither is your general. Understand?"

"So what? Are you going to kill me?"

"I don't have to kill you to make you suffer." Darrio then released the man and shoved him backward. "Now get ready. You're coming with us too."

"Why?"

"Because I don't trust you and because I said so. You're not in the position to give orders around here, and I've still got a job to do, so when I tell you to do something, I expect you to do it."

"Now see here, Firestar. My mind may have been clouded a bit by this dark magic phenomenon, but you are in no position to usurp my authority."

"What authority? Your general sent me after you, remember? Until this mission is over, his is the only authority I even remotely give a damn about, so shut up, do as I say, and stop pissing me off!"

Palim opened his mouth again to speak, but there were no words left to say, and he closed it again in silence. "Whatever you say, Firestar," he grumbled, and his eyes darkened once more.

Darrio anticipated such sudden shifts in mood were going to be a regular occurrence in the journey to Lumineth although he was somewhat used to it thanks to Tam. "Damn it, Tam," Darrio mumbled as he came to realize some practical use for Tam's madness. It desensitized him.

Darrio and Palim waited an additional thirty minutes before leaving the temple of Magnus where Valeria left the acolytes with explicit instructions to carry on with appearances until her return. She also told them to burn all of her writings when the night came.

The three of them then made their way to the shrine of light where Saria sat with the two priests who were laughing. When they saw Darrio with the priestess, however, their heartiness turned to concern. "Isn't that the priestess of the Magnus temple?" the second one noted.

"Come on, Saria," Darrio said.

Saria ran to Darrio's side but slowed while in Valeria's vicinity and completely avoided Palim's sphere of presence.

"Thanks for taking care of her," Darrio said.

"She is a sensitive child," said the first. "I hope you will not expose her to unsavory influences."

"They're not my friends," Darrio assured them, "and if they cross me…they know better. They won't."

"I am glad to hear that. I think."

"Anyway, thanks."

Saria also thanked them with a bow, and the four left Esea.

Darrio and Saria walked in the lead while Palim and Valeria trailed behind them silently. Palim merely observed the surroundings as they passed while Valeria, who was uncomfortable with the silence, tried to distract herself with whatever she could find. After a while, Saria tugged on Darrio's cloak and whispered, "Why are they with us?"

"Did the child say something?" Valeria asked with interest. "What did she say?"

"None of your business," Darrio answered.

"Oh, please, Firestar, this silence is killing me! Someone, say something."

"I would like to say something," Palim said.

"I don't care what you have to say," Darrio replied. "Both of you. Shut up."

Valeria huffed, and Palim peered away despondent.

Another while passed, and Saria whispered again. "What's wrong with them?"

"They're sick," Darrio whispered back.

"Oh. Okay."

On the night of their first camp, the four of them sat around the fire. Saria and Darrio were on one side while Valeria and Palim, who were spaced further apart, sat on the other. Darrio spoke. "Alright. I've got some questions for you."

"Finally!" Valeria cried. "Seriously, Firestar, I'll tell you anything even if only to end this dreadful silence. Are you always this quiet on your journeys, because I've found the whole ordeal to be rather dull."

"Are you done?" Darrio asked.

It was a rhetorical question, a fact that was lost to Valeria. "I think so. Yes. I just needed to get that out of my system I guess. Go ahead, Firestar. Ask me anything."

Darrio sighed and shook his head. "First, what were you doing with the Shadow Casters, and why were you working with them?"

"That's two questions, Firestar."

"Would you just answer the damn...answer it!"

"Alright. The what. Well, what I was doing was aiding them in the search for light."

"Which is what?"

"What? Don't be so dense. You already know what the light is." Valeria's eyes then lit up. "Oh, I see! This is one of those review sessions to make sure everyone knows what's happening, isn't it?"

"Damn it, woman!"

"There's no need to be huffy. Patience is a virtue, you know, or so they say. I don't believe in it. Anyway, you know about the seven elements of magic. There's fire, earth, wind, water, thunder, light, and dark, but two of those elements, light and dark, are known as lost elements because no one can control them."

"Can we skip past the history lesson?" Palim complained.

"Oh, be quiet. The Firestar asked a question, and I'm answering it." Palim groaned while Valeria continued. "Now, the Shadow Casters have somehow acquired the dark element, and they're now in search of the light so they can bring about the second Cleansing."

"And the Cleansing is supposed to bring a new age of magic," Darrio finished.

"Right. As for the why. Well, quite simply, I was just as interested in seeing the results of the cleansing as anyone. A paradise of magic had a very great appeal for me being a high priestess and all you understand."

"And the fact that they were killing a bunch of people to get there didn't bother you?"

Valeria shrugged. "I felt they were necessary sacrifices for the greater good, but come now, Firestar. You're a soldier. Surely, you could have understood this."

"I wasn't made a soldier by choice, and the Magic War was about survival. It wasn't some ideological struggle."

"Is that what you think? Consider the nature of the High Elders for a moment. They're politicians, all of them. Do you think their primary concerns are of life and death or rather of policy, procedure, and ideals made by men?"

"Who knows? I don't care. All I know is that the Outer Realms all came together and tried to destroy one nation, and that's us. We survived, they lost."

"Yes, and that's all well and good, but I believe there were larger forces at work during the war, and even before the war, to bring us to this moment. Mind you, I'm quite happy to be alive right now, but I am not at all ignorant of how and why. I don't think so anyway. I hope I'm not."

"Whatever. Let's just get to my next question."

"What is it?"

"Saria." Saria perked up at the mention of her name, and Darrio continued. "What did you want with her?"

"The child? Oh, I suppose nothing in particular. I simply wanted to know what she knew, is all. She was the only survivor, wasn't she? I thought perhaps she might know something. It wasn't personal."

"Are you kidding me?"

"Are you surprised?"

"You mean to tell me that you chased us halfway through Esea just so you could satisfy your curiosity?"

"Curiosity? The elements of light and dark are the highest forms of power that exist in our world. We are talking about the elements of creation! All of the other elements, fire, earth, wind, all of them are products of light and darkness. Seriously, Firestar! Please tell me you are not so dull as to miss something as important as this!"

Darrio crossed his arms. "From what I've seen so far, I don't see a reason to care."

"You're impossible, Firestar. Simply impossible. We are talking about powers that could ruffle the very fabric of creation. Absolute control."

"Ha!" Palim interrupted with darkened eyes. "The witch's true heart reveals itself."

"Be silent, demon!"

"Or what? Shall you exorcise me? You have not the authority."

"Shut up," Darrio said before returning to Valeria. "I thought magic was already an exercise over creation."

"Well, it is, partially. We're capable of manipulating the elements of creation, sure, but it's not as if we can do anything to its fabric."

"What fabric?"

"You really don't know anything, do you? Look." Valeria then scooped up several pebbles and scattered them across the dirt ahead of her. "With magic, I can take one of these stones and move it here, you see?" She then followed her words by moving one stone towards the other. "I can move this stone here and this one here, you see? With higher forms of magic, I can arrange these stones to whatever pattern I please, and with even higher forms I can create constructs, complex structures, systemic hierarchies, and the like."

"With even higher forms, you could create life," Palim noted.

"I have never heard of creating life with magic, demon. Be quiet."

"Only because you have not lived long enough to understand the practice, witch."

"Is that so? Then I'm sure whatever magic created in the past was just a meaningless series of monstrous abominations."

"At least on this, you would be accurate."

Darrio looked at Palim and then back at Valeria. "Is he really possessed by a demon?"

"You don't believe in demons, Firestar?"

"I don't know," Darrio said as he looked back at Palim. "I never met one."

The darkness in Palim's eyes faded, and when he noticed Darrio watching him, he frowned. "Stop gawking at me, boy."

"Idiot."

"Anyway," Valeria continued, "getting back to my illustration. I can do all of these things to the stones by using magic, but the medium upon which they rest," she said as she tapped the dirt, "I can do nothing about. At least, not to the same degree as the stones."

"But with light and dark magic, you could. So…what would it look like?"

"I don't really know for certain, but it would be a wonderful thing to discover, don't you think?" Valeria yawned. "Oh dear. I believe I'm all talked out. That's unusual. I thought I'd have more to say on the subject of magic. Hm. It must be that accursed curse. It's drained the life out of me. And the sense it seems. Do I seem crazy to you, Firestar? I don't feel at all like myself. Have I become insane again? My mind is drifting."

"You're fine, I think."

Valeria laughed. "Oh, you're such a delightful character, Firestar! Fine, he says," and her laughter continued. Her laughing then descended into chuckling and her chuckling to giggles before she finally fell to sleep.

Palim simply huffed and rolled over, and he fell asleep as well.

Saria tugged on Darrio's cloak. "Are they going to be like this the whole way?"

Darrio nodded and hummed his acknowledgment to her.

Saria set her head in Darrio's lap and sighed. "Sir Darrio?"

"Hm?"

"Will you tell me a story?"

"I don't think I have anything for kids, Saria."

"Can you tell me what you were like?"

"What I was like? Me?"

Saria nodded. "Before the war. Before your daddy died."

"How did you know about my—?"

"Please, Sir Darrio? Please, tell me. Please?"

Darrio sighed as he struggled to remember. In the process, he set his right hand to Saria's hair and stroked it back. "I was…young, I guess. Innocent. Naive."

"And? What else were you?"

"I guess…I was curious. I was always wondering how things worked, you know?"

Saria hummed as she drew in Darrio's feelings. "Your father was a carpenter?"

"And a clockmaker, but how did you know?"

"Please don't stop. Keep going."

Darrio hesitated but revisited the old memory nonetheless. "He wanted to make clocks for a living, but people were always asking him to fix things for them. He was really good at stuff like that."

"Did your mother help him?"

"Yeah."

"And they taught you things?"

"Yeah. My dad. He said...he said one day, I'd understand what he was doing. He said...one day, just like his clocks, it would all come together, but today, all we could work on were the pieces. Just pieces...one at a time."

"You loved your dad?"

"I looked up to him. I wanted to be just like him," and Darrio started to choke on the sentiments he was feeling. "I wanted to be. I wanted to," and he cried.

"Sir Darrio?"

"I'm sorry, Saria. I can't. I can't think about this anymore."

Saria crept to her knees and wrapped her small arms around Darrio's neck. "I'm sorry, Sir Darrio. I'm sorry."

"Don't," Darrio said through the tears. "Don't apologize to me."

"I'm sorry." It was a weary moment for the two souls, and they slept with heavy hearts that night.

The following day, the four continued their journey towards Lumineth, and Darrio suffered the voices of Valeria and Palim who were arguing back and forth. Their eyes were darkened. "You're a dolt!" she said.

"Witch!" Palim retorted.

"Demon!"

"Hag!"

"Brute!"

"Troll!"

"Shut up!" Darrio finished. "Please! Shut up!"

"But he insulted me," Valeria complained.

"How many times do I have to tell you to stop talking? Be quiet!"

"Oh, you be quiet."

"I've had it," Darrio uttered. "I've had it," and he turned around with the intent to bind the both of them, but he was interrupted by a commotion further down the road.

"Artemis!" Forum cried. Artemis fell dead with his body awash in fire as six pursuing acolytes gave chase along with a seventh figure who carried a pointed staff.

"Damn it all!" Deco shouted. As the remaining five ran, three of them were grievously stricken and finished by the pursuers as they passed. A bolt of cold snaked across the road and connected with Deco's legs. They were immediately frozen, and to Deco's misfortune and momentum, they snapped and crumbled at the knees. His top half fell to the ground. "Forum!"

Forum spun around. "Deco!" He started to return for Deco, but his intent was promptly dejected by the fallen comrade.

"Go! Go!" The acolytes reached Deco's position, and the man with the staff thrust it through Deco's back. Deco was incinerated.

Forum turned once again in a fearful sprint, and as he proceeded down the road, he caught sight of Darrio. "Firestar! Firestar, help!"

Darrio peered ahead as Forum ascended over a hill followed by the pursing acolytes of Magnus. "The hell is he doing?"

"Is that Forum?" Valeria questioned.

"You know him?"

"He's my brother. Of course I know him."

Forum was confused by the sight of his sister standing beside the

Firestar, and he did not know what to make of the little girl or the disturbed-looking man behind her. Nevertheless, he proceeded to take shelter behind them and plead for his life. "You've got to help me. They've already killed Deco and Artemis."

"What?" Darrio said. "I told you to get out of here!"

"Tried to, but when we went back, they caught us. Tried to escape. Now this."

The acolytes stopped several yards away from Darrio's position to size up the situation. One of them recognized Darrio from the previous visit and informed the one who led them. The man was a tall and imposing figure known as a predicant, a designation among the Order of Magnus just below the High Priest. Predicants had the ability to exercise edicts and services on behalf of the High Priest, but there were few among the temples of Magnus and were usually employed during ceremonies, large gatherings, or where the population of laymen was substantially larger than the High Priest could manage alone. "Please," the predicant said. "Hand him over."

"What's his crime?" Darrio asked.

"Heresy, blasphemy, and the forbidden practice of geo magia."

"You were practicing geo magia?" Valeria said speaking to Forum. "What for?"

"You wouldn't understand," he replied.

"Is that High Priestess Valeria?" the predicant asked. "I heard she was unwell."

"We've come to speak with Derenger," Valeria answered.

"Master Derenger is busy."

"Then we'll wait for him. I'm sure he wouldn't mind that."

"Now is not the best time, Mistress."

Valeria pushed her hands to her hips and huffed. "Now look. We traveled a long way to get here, and you mean to tell me we can't even wait? You must be joking."

"I'm afraid not."

"Then I'm afraid we're going whether you like it or not. Whatever silly business you have with my brother can wait."

"They're going to kill me, Valeria," Forum said.

"Well, it serves you right for being so stupid." Valeria then turned to the predicant. "Well, don't just stand there. Are you going to escort us or not?"

The predicant was clearly disjointed by Valeria's demeanor and seemed to forget his previous task. "Very well, Mistress. This way."

One of the acolytes whispered, "But we're under Derenger's command. Not hers."

"Quiet, fool."

As the group continued their trek to Lumineth, Valeria proceeded to pelt the predicant with questions concerning Derenger's state of affairs and was met with uneasy and evasive answers. When she was fed up, she turned her attention to the acolytes and talked through a range of subjects from the highest details of doctrine and magic to the mundane order of sticks and twigs. It then became apparent to everyone there was something wrong with her, but due to her position as a high priestess, the members of Magnus were too afraid to say anything on the matter.

They arrived in Lumineth two days later slowed somewhat by the fatigue induced by Valeria's questioning, and Darrio found himself among a throng of enthusiastic and eager faces. "They've returned!" said a man among the crowd. "Is it over now?"

The predicant pulled Forum to the front. "He is the last and shall die at dawn." The crowd cheered, and Forum was hauled away to a holding cell located above a stage not far from the temple. Darrio, in the meantime, struggled to make sense of what was happening. The doors to the temple were still closed, and acolytes were barring the way. "Follow me, please," the predicant said. The acolytes dispersed to perform other duties within the city while Valeria, Palim, Darrio, and Saria proceeded to the interior of the temple. "Wait here."

The predicant left the building, and the four were alone.

"Well, that's odd," Valeria thought aloud.

"Everything about this is odd," Palim said.

The air was heavy, and something about it nagged on Darrio's senses. He felt a sensation coming from the bonds on his wrists, and when he took a brief moment to examine them, out of sight of Valeria and Palim, he found the scripts were glowing faintly and flickered from time to time. Saria tugged on Darrio. "I'm scared."

"I won't let anyone hurt you," Darrio replied. "What's going on around here?"

Valeria shrugged. "Your guess is as good as mine."

The front doors of the temple opened once again, and High Priest Derenger entered the room. "I was told I had guests, but I did not expect to be graced by the presence of High Priestess Valeria and the Firestar."

"Stop flattering yourself, Derenger. It's unbecoming of you."

"And what can I do for you, Valeria? Surely you did not come to witness your brother's execution. I heard you were not well."

"Not well? You're mistaken, I'm afraid. As you can see, I'm quite fine."

"As I can see."

"And I received your message."

In the presence of Darrio and Palim, Derenger became uncomfortable with the mention. "Message? What message?"

"Don't be so modest, Derenger, there's no need for it now. They already know."

"And what do they know, Valeria?"

"I know about your connection with the Shadow Casters," Darrio said. "I know you've been working with them to find the power of light, and lastly," Darrio continued as he drew his left blade, "I know this isn't a temple matter, and you're going to cooperate this time."

Derenger's attention shifted between Darrio and Valeria before finally resting with the priestess in anger. "Did you tell him everything?"

"Not quite. He already knew most of it. I just helped him fill in the gaps."

"Why?"

"That scroll you sent me contained a template for dark magic. Are you aware of what dark magic does to a person, Derenger?"

"Valeria, I assure you. I did not know the contents of that scroll. Is that what made you so ill?"

"Why does everyone keep talking as if I'm sick? I'm not sick!"

"We're both sick," Palim said.

"Be quiet. You're the one who's sick, demon."

"Witch."

"Blasphemer."

"Hag."

Darrio tightened the grip on his blade in annoyance. "Both of you? Be quiet!" There was a dangerous influx of power within Darrio's body that came with his anger, a sensation he knew all too well, but it just as quickly passed over as he calmed. He was unsure of what was happening, but as Derenger watched him, Darrio returned his attention to the priest. "They've been annoying me like this the whole way here, and it's getting on my nerves. Now if you don't tell me something I want to hear soon, I'm taking all of my frustrations out on you."

"We're cursed," Derenger said suddenly. "That's why I had the temple closed."

"Cursed?"

"I had just released the scroll to Esea when a heaviness descended upon the temple. We could not perform the usual rites, and my acolytes, disciples, and laymen became ill. My predicant suggested it was the work of Magnus punishing us for not bringing the heretics to justice, and when they arrived to reclaim their families, I became convinced that he was giving us another chance."

"So you thought killing them would end the curse."

"Yes, I did, and I still believe it's the solution. You haven't come to interfere with this have you?"

"No, but I don't think your curse has anything to do with them."

"What do you mean?"

"This temple is filled with dark magic. I can feel it, and I'm starting to react."

"I don't feel anything," Valeria said.

"That's because we're consumed by it, witch," Palim stated.

Saria became even more fearful. Her palms were clammy, and she was beginning to sweat. She tugged once more on Darrio and said, "Can we get out of here? Please? I'm really, really, scared."

"What's wrong with her?" Derenger asked.

"Oh, god," Valeria said as her eyes darkened, and she moaned as if under the duress of a severe headache. "That girl. Is that what this is about? Is that how it works?"

"What's happening?" Darrio asked. "What's wrong with you?"

"Me? It isn't me you imbecile, it's her they want. That's what this is about. People like her, all of them. They're conduits." Valeria stood erect. "Yes. It's all so clear to me now. Now it makes sense!" she laughed. "It's what they've always wanted, like casts to the mold. It's indwelt, locked up in the center of their little spirits, lining the walls of their room. The details of light. Impressions. Imprints. I understand it now! I can see!" and she paused. "I must have those plans. Little girl? Come here. Come to me."

Saria shook her head vigorously and took shelter behind Darrio.

"Sir Darrio," she whispered fearfully.

"Stay back," Darrio warned. "I won't say it again."

"But you don't understand. I need her, Firestar! I need her light! I can't take this anymore! The curse, it's driven me! I'm paralyzed by it! Even here, it haunts me. Even here, it whispers for me." Derenger silently backed away in an attempt to head for the door, but Valeria caught sight of his movement and sealed the exit by force of manipulation. "Where do you think you're going?"

Derenger searched the doors for a point he could exploit, but to his own dismay, he was unable to reopen them. "Have you gone mad?"

"Why does everyone think I'm mad? I'm not mad. I'm not! All I want is what's mine."

"For once," Palim said, "I believe I agree with the witch. If that girl holds the secret to the light, then it is something the Elders will need to fight against the Shadow Casters."

"Derenger?" Valeria cooed. "You realize what attaining the powers of light would mean for the Priesthood, don't you? Aren't you curious?"

"It is what we've been searching for," he admitted.

Darrio drew his second blade. "I don't care what your reasons are for wanting her. I'm not giving her to any of you." He then whispered to Saria, "Don't move."

"But this is bigger than her, Firestar," Valeria pleaded. "This is bigger than all of us!"

"Did you hear me, Saria? I said don't move."

"I hear you," Saria replied as she wept.

"Her sacrifice could change the world," Derenger noted.

"I don't care," Darrio replied.

"You could become a god," Palim added.

It then became clear what was happening within the darkened space of that temple. The air of dark magic not only diminished the ability of everyone present to use magic, with the exception of Palim and Valeria, but it also weakened the bonds on Darrio's wrists. He had been regularly pushed to anger since the binding but did not readjust his reactions for a lower threshold. The terrible effect of this error in judgment was then able to manifest itself within the temple walls. Darrio shouted a final time, "I don't care!" and his eyes vanished behind a veil of red. The scripts on Darrio's wrist were illuminated by a brilliant glow and rotated in the aura of his power. Saria remained behind him, huddled to herself with arms held tightly to her body, but in staying true to Darrio's command, she did not move and did not run. Darrio reversed the direction of his daggers and spoke. "Stay back. Move forward, and I'll kill you." Saria was the only person in the room of concern to Darrio even in the midst of his diminished state limit, but everyone else was an enemy and would be treated to that end.

Palim made the first move and advanced with a bolt of fire aimed at Darrio's feet. In response, Darrio swept his left foot apart from his right, and his body pivoted around Saria's position. In doing this, he raised a slab of stone that rose just above his head to block the shot, and at its height, he shattered it and forced the pieces towards Palim's position like a sheet of earthen shrapnel. Palim countered with a similar movement and shielded his body from Darrio's counterattack. As they fought, Darrio pivoted around Saria and defended their position against attack after attack which included the occasional support bolt from Derenger.

Valeria shifted around the battle's outer perimeter and looked for an opening while Darrio, Palim, and Derenger continued their exchange. When Palim initiated an ice attack aimed at Darrio's arm, Valeria shifted the ground underneath Darrio's position in hopes of throwing him off balance. However, Darrio used this loss of ground to duck Palim's attack, and he further caused the ground beneath him and Saria to recess into a pit. Derenger then successfully sealed the hole with a covering slab of earth though he did so with great difficulty. There was a slight lull in the fight afterward, but the three underestimated the Firestar's resourcefulness. The ground surrounding Darrio hardened, and the outer shell was made to compress into an impenetrable shield of rock. Palim and Valeria both doused the covering in fire and ice to no avail, and the shell was made to rise out of the ground. The outer wall suddenly splintered with uniform cracks due to no effort on the part of the attackers, and the eyes of Palim and Valeria widened in unison. Each raised another barrier of earth to shield themselves, but Derenger did not realize what was to occur and was late in his attempt of protection which cost him dearly. Darrio scattered the shell around him with such tremendous force as to impale every exposed thing in the destructive shield's spherical line of sight. Derenger was pinned to the door where he died in immeasurable pain while several shards pierced through the softer barriers of Valeria and Palim. The two were wounded severely, and both tried as best as they could to recover by use of restoration magic, but Palim was stopped short when his body was encased in ice and shattered by a strike of lightning.

Valeria heaved in panic as Darrio's eyes settled upon her. "No, Firestar! Please!" Darrio raised his right hand and leveled his arm in Valeria's direction. "Firestar!" she pleaded, but whatever mercy she could have appealed to prior to Darrio's transformation was gone.

Forum was sitting dejected in his cell which hung over the stage on which the citizens hoped to see him executed, but the commotion coming from the temple gave him a glimmer of hope. Even the predicant could not discern what was happening as he was still tending to the cell when the noises first began to emanate. Suddenly, an impermeable cascade of fire erupted from every opening of the building, and the roof was completely blown off. A hail of stone and debris fell from the sky, and a cloud of smoke and soot rose out of the burning foundation. The people screamed and scattered for shelter. The force of the eruption shook Forum's cell free of its tether, and the cage crashed to the ground and opened. Emerging through the splintered remains of the front door were Darrio and Saria who kept her head buried in his chest. There was no remorse in Darrio's countenance, and he gave the destruction around him no mind. His eyes were set on Saria, and his arms carried her defensively. They left the city without impediment and without word from anyone around them. Forum, in the meantime, beheld this but did not attempt to make contact. He instead extracted his weeping wife from their home and fled the city. The two never looked back.

Lon and Carsis were just approaching Lumineth when they witnessed the explosion that brought them to a stop. When they found Darrio walking out of the city with Saria held tightly in his arms, they approached. "Who pissed you off?" Carsis asked, but when his eyes fell on Saria, he winced. "Oh. Right."

"You should mind your tone," Lon warned. "The Firestar is in a transitory state. You would not wish to upset him now, would you?"

Carsis huffed. "I guess not."

The bonds on Darrio's wrists finally relented and dulled. His eyes softened, and his posture relaxed. When he was fully himself, Darrio asked, "What the hell are you doing here?"

"We were going to ask you the same thing, stupid."

"Indeed," Lon continued. "Have you executed your affairs here, Firestar, or should we wait further and see what else you burn?"

"What do you guys want?"

"We were sent to recover you. General Turil and the other High Generals have been given orders to mobilize."

"But they're going to be pissed when they find out about whatever happened here," Carsis said.

Darrio examined Saria once more to be sure she was safe.

"Is she asleep?" Lon asked.

"She's safe," Darrio said with satisfaction. "And who cares? Let them be pissed."

"Are you ready then?"

Darrio nodded, and the four departed for Ambrosia. To hasten the return, Lon and Carsis were careful to eject Darrio forward on the winds as they leaped across the landscape by force of manipulation and wind magic. Darrio hated relying on their support for movement, but expediency was of greater concern to him. He wanted to get Saria home, and travel took only half a day.

Seris and Abaddon were standing in wait when the three shades returned, but Seris could not help but notice the soot and dirt covering Darrio's uniform. "What happened to you?"

"Nothing."

"How is the girl?" Abaddon asked.

"She's fine, but it's been a rough day for her."

"I will take her inside."

Darrio relinquished Saria to Abaddon and watched as the two proceeded inside the Hall of Order. Once inside, Darrio sighed. "You wouldn't believe what I just went through."

"You encountered complications?"

"Complications? I'm more confused now than I was before I left! First dark magic and light bearers and conduits and none of it makes any sense! None of it!"

"Be still, Darrio, and slow down. Tell me what happened."

Darrio opened his mouth to speak, but there was a sudden crack in the distance followed by a thunderous roar. Seris and Darrio looked aside and bore witness to a massive form of burning stone and ice which blazed a thick trail of black smoke and ash in its trajectory towards the city. "What the hell is that?" Darrio shouted, but the deafening noise of the projectile overshadowed his voice. The flaming object then cracked at the center and began to trail a stream of dark magic. Abaddon had only just emerged from the Hall's front gate when Darrio realized the arc of the foreign object would cause it to land directly on the Hall of Order. "Saria," he gasped. Darrio immediately burst into a sprint where he pushed himself desperately to outrun the projectile, but it was moving at a much faster pace than him by far. The situation was hopeless.

Abaddon looked skyward and glared at the incoming obstruction. His eyes calculated its trajectory, and his mind grew aware of the intended target. It was too late to move naturally. "Foolishness," he uttered, and the air around him became distorted as he prepared for the oncoming collision.

The mass of ice, stone, fire, and darkness then crashed into the hall, obliterated the structure, and smothered it in a morass of black destruction. The cold shock which resulted from the impact ripped through the city of Ambrosia like a frigid gale. A dark cloud of vapor, dust, and debris rose like a storm from the site with peals of lightning and thunder. The sheer power of the blast shattered all glass in the vicinity and shook the foundation of nearby buildings. The cloud finally peaked out high above the city, and its contents fell back to the earth as black snow.

Darrio was forced to the ground by the shock wave, but when he recovered, he felt his life escaping him. He was quickly losing his breath and will to go forward. Nevertheless, he pushed his body until his strength was gone, somehow trying to imagine Saria's survival, but as the vivid image of total destruction burned itself into his mind's eye, his body locked up, and his movements became stiff. He fell to his knees and gasped for breath. Tears galloped down the side of his face. His heart collapsed in the midst of his grief, and he was beside himself with frustration. Darrio cried uncontrollably, and his body trembled with violent convulsion. "Saria," he sobbed, but after a familiar element of the rubble landed beside him, torn sketches of the emblem he had placed in his desk, his grief quickly turned to anger, and he screamed with an inconsolable rage into the sky.

The Magic War had done much to shred Darrio's resilient sense of hope even to a point where it was scarcely recognizable, and yet he managed to preserve some semblance of it to remain human. With Saria gone, his hope slipped into an abyss of despair where it was choked by anger and held down by pessimistic reason. It was not long before Darrio's own mind was consumed by dark thoughts though not as a result of dark magic alone but as the result of his own hatred. His hope had died leaving behind a void in the pit of his heart, and there was nothing left to fill in that void but a great and terrible wrath.

CHAPTER 13
Ominous Horizons

ORBITING THE ATMOSPHERE of Ambrosia was a heavy sense of hopelessness. All was lost, and this was the fear permeating the minds of Ambrosia's citizenry. A man wandered aimlessly through the streets, and a wounded woman crawled after him. The daughter the two left behind cried alone in the home they abandoned. There was another woman in a different part of the city who glared endlessly at her image in the mirror. A man stood in watch just outside of her window. Even still in another part of the city, two neighbors waged war with each other as they threw various obstructions and objects into the other person's property. Such was the state of the city enveloped in a fog of dark magic.

Turil emerged panic-stricken from one of the buildings that had been shaken apart, and he struggled in desperation to calm himself. "Be still," he breathed in repetition. "Be still. Be still." His eyes flashed briefly behind a veil of green but returned to normal as he became calm and composed. No one knew Turil was capable of reaching a state limit for generals and captains were never inscribed with flesh scripts. It was not permitted for them out of fear of its potentially disastrous effects upon the chain of command. Turil took one in secret, but of all the people he worked with, only Seris came close to discovering it. Even so, not even Seris would have surmised Turil's trigger as being one of fear nor would he have considered Turil's stubborn disposition towards charging into acts as intentional methods he employed towards overcoming his fear. Turil swore and endeavored to never reach his own state limit after seeing the effect it had on others, and these things were closely guarded secrets that Turil kept as near to him as his own heart.

After Turil sufficiently calmed himself, his eyes fell upon the state of the city, and he gasped. The air was thick and heavy. Glass, remains, and soot covered the streets. The sky was hardly visible through the darkened canopy that hung overhead. The once-white city was beset by shades of gray, and Turil felt his powers over magic were diminished, a sure result of the darkness, but they were not totally lost.

He suffered some minor injuries while straining to protect himself from the collapse, and he took a moment to heal them. The people he had been questioning inside, however, were crushed underneath the rubble. Turil then went on to check the city gates where thick walls of purest black barred the exit. A man attempted to traverse past, but when he crossed over, he fell upon the ground in a fit of madness and tore upon himself in violence. "What is this?" Turil uttered, and out of the corner of his eye, he spotted a familiar form. "Seris!"

Seris turned, his attention momentarily taken away from Darrio, and he called back. "Who else has survived?"

"I was not in the building," and Turil moved closer.

"The city is in shambles."

"And it will tear itself apart if we do not do something." Seris' eyes returned to Darrio, but Turil took hold of Seris and shook him. "Seris, listen to me. The boy cannot stay here." Seris struggled to break away and return to Darrio, but Turil tightened his hold all the more and said, "With the state this city is in, everyone will be a danger to him and he to everyone else!"

"I know," Seris replied. "I know." Their eyes met once again as friends, and Turil eased his grip. "Release me," Seris said.

Turil did as requested, and Seris moved to Darrio who remained on his knees. His teeth and hands were clenched, and his breaths were short and hard. "Darrio," Seris gently called.

"I'll kill them," Darrio said with vengeful tears, and he shook his head over and over. "I'll kill them. Every last one. Everyone I see. Everyone!" The effects of dark magic were bearing down on Darrio's mind, and Seris feared that it would only be a matter of time before the situation got out of hand. He took a firmer tone and said, "Come with me, Darrio, and do not open your eyes. Keep them shut, and do not look."

"They killed her!"

"Keep them shut."

Darrio struggled between the compulsion to obey and his desire for destruction, but one of his eyelids began to rise, and the burning veil of his limit emanated from beneath.

Seris spoke forcefully. "Shut them, Darrio!"

Darrio complied, but he could not contain his heart. He wept bitterly and released periodic elements of his frustration upon the environment. Sparks of lightning flew from his being and struck the ground causing small craters to develop. Arcs of fire also flew from him, and particles of debris were incinerated in his presence. Seris, however, was unmoved by this, and he guided Darrio unharmed back to Turil. It was not within Darrio's will to harm Seris.

Turil was waiting at the city's entrance gate and was astonished by the sight but not surprised. He also knew better than to approach Darrio's sphere of being. "He cannot go through here," Turil said, and he pointed towards the height of the city wall. "That is the thinnest section of this canopy of darkness. If we put him through quickly enough, he should be fine."

"What of the citizens?"

"We don't have the strength for it." Turil then peered through the barrier blocking the gate. "Do what you can to push him over, and I will try to cushion his fall from here."

Seris nodded. "Brace yourself, Darrio."

Though Darrio heard, he remained unprepared and was surprised to find himself hurtling through the air. Seris used what power he had to throw Darrio's body into the sky with a forceful and angular rise of rock. Darrio cleared the wall and passed through the barrier, but as he did, he felt a sharp burden upon his mind and heard the sound of a woman's scream, a man's cry, and a boy's painful wail.

Turil manipulated the ground on the other side to rise and turn in a gentle slope in accord with Darrio's trajectory. When he was caught, Turil returned the ground to a normal level. He then shut his eyes to calm himself with regular breathing. "I cannot do that again," he said.

At first, Darrio did not move, and his two superiors wondered whether or not he had fallen unconscious, but his stationary demeanor was in fact due to a lack of desire on Darrio's part. For a brief moment, he wondered as to the point of his getting up again, but as he remembered Saria's face, his anger returned to him, and he rose.

Seris called out to him. "Go to the western forest and wait for my call. I will send for you as soon as it is safe."

Darrio dusted the earth from his cloak and repeated, "Safe," to himself in contempt.

"Did you hear me, Darrio?"

"I heard you," he replied, but Seris sighed.

As Darrio headed west, Turil asked Seris, "Do you think he will return prematurely?"

"I can only hope not, but that is not what concerns me."

"Then why did you sigh?"

"He will be alone."

Turil knew no comforting words for the situation. He could only say, "Come, Seris. We have work to do."

The two set out to find who else survived the catastrophic attack with the intention of restoring order to the city, but their task would prove to be a daunting one. Over the course of the day, most of the populous either fell ill or turned on each other. The former pleaded with the clerics for relief, but the clerics were already overwhelmed by an influx of weeping laymen. Doctors especially were inundated with the newfound flood of the dying and unstable. Such a disaster only reminded the two groups of their prior petition to the High Elders to lift the ban on geo magia for the health field. They argued such a thing would be necessary for extreme emergencies and to heal the soldiers who were dying on the field in mass. They were denied this despite the ravages of the war. Frustrations in the medical community were also combined with the stresses of dark magic, and those whose minds remained intact feared the inevitable collapse of structure. People deemed hazardous or insane were isolated. Others exhibited symptoms that ranged from heart pain and guilt to boils and sores. The phenomenon was noted in greater detail later on by a prominent cleric who discovered the body had been turned on itself in most of the cases, but while healing minds tried to find an explanation for the odd reactions, those whose professions led to harm furthered their craft.

Those who once conducted their operations at night became ambitious and attempted to spread their influence into the day. Though diminished in their magical prowess, they were empowered in the darkened state of their minds to advance and take the streets for themselves. However, there was contention among them, and bloody conflicts broke out on once peaceful roads. Allegiances were formed out of fear and lack of security. The various factions fought each other for survival and control of resources. Post-attack casualties rose sharply in the wake of these miniature wars, and with the underlying civility of Ambrosia's citizens unhinged by dark magic, incubating grievances were quick to reach fruition. Where once there was tolerance between the separate groups, there was then open hostility and arguments. Where once there was apathetic indifference, there was then total abandonment of empathy. Parents left their children. Lovers became strangers. Enemies waged war, and with every hour, there came to pass a new nightmare to unfold. It was like this for the entire time the darkness hovered over the city, and that darkness remained heavy for three hellish days.

During this period, Seris and Turil examined the site of the attack and its surrounding area and found that of those killed, none were among the Shades of Seris. Abaddon's body, however, was nowhere to be found. Lon and Carsis were sent out to gather intelligence on the new state of the city while Talim and Eloi were found to have narrowly escaped the destruction. "What's more," Talim reported, "while I gave my all towards combating the mental effects of dark magic, I saw Eloi awash in the cloud. He emerged unscathed."

"He what?" Turil asked.

"I was unharmed," Eloi replied. "It has no effect on me."

"Seris. He may be capable of traversing past the wall."

Seris nodded and told Eloi, "Go south and see if you can identify who attacked us. If you find them, follow, but do not let yourself be seen. When you have gathered all you can, return to us."

Eloi nodded, scurried off, and passed through the gates of darkness as if they were not there. In the meantime, Seris, his shades, and Turil managed to form a small force composed primarily of shades with a supporting force of adepts and casters. With this, they tasked themselves with attaining order in the surrounding area and acquiring survivors to help. Turil noted the juxtaposition with humor, but no one laughed. Instead, they continued in their endeavors and carved for themselves a circle of protection within the chaos. With many of the other captains and generals dead, there was little order they could find outside of their own, and when night fell, they defended their site until morning. This was the first day.

On the second day of Ambrosia's week of sorrow, Turil and Seris ventured to the Grand Hall to find more soldiers and a few surviving officers. Like Turil and Seris, they created a temporary haven of safety within the building while they tried to work out how to restore order to the rest of the city. The High Elders were safe, much to Turil's relief, but were reportedly frightened and unsure of how to proceed. "Foolishness," Seris uttered.

"What do you think we should do?" a soldier asked.

"We secure the city. I already have Lon and Carsis gathering information on the city's state. They should be here soon with a report."

"We are here now," Lon said. The two shades had only just come through the door.

"What have you found?"

Carsis shook his head. "This place has gone to hell." The two reported everything they saw which included the state of the medical community and the aggressive factions which formed to take control of the city.

"It's my estimation," Lon continued, "that if this latter complication is not mortally pacified, it will only entrench itself and become a knife in the side of lasting order."

One of the captains protested. "Our forces are too small for a task of that magnitude. Are you suggesting we abandon everything else to tackle these factions?"

Lon laughed. "Of course not! A task such as this, to be resolved quickly, requires a large degree of subtlety. Captain Seris? If I may, I would propose a plan of action."

"What is it, Lon?"

"All of the involved parties have darkened minds and are easily susceptible to volatile suggestions of circumstance. With your permission, I would turn this to our advantage."

Seris replied without the slightest hesitation. "Granted."

"Seris," Turil said with surprise. "Turning the people against each other will only exasperate the problem."

"We talk of turning our enemies against each other, Turil."

"But there will be casualties. Many of them."

"There will be more in time if we allow the situation to go unresolved."

Turil whispered. "Then please do not put that man in charge of the operation."

"I have no one greater for this than Lon."

"But he enjoys his task too much."

"Agreed, but what he lacks in compassion, he compensates in precision." Seris then turned to Lon and ordered, "Do it, and take whatever you need."

"I will need five volunteers," Lon said, and five men hesitantly stepped to the fore.

After this, Seris said, "Be sure to minimize civilian casualties, Lon, and take Carsis with you. Send word if you require further support."

"It should not be necessary," Lon said with a grin, but he humbly bowed, and his group left. Turil was still astonished by Seris' action, but Seris replied to him by saying, "I do not send swords where a dagger will do."

After this, Turil and Seris met with the Elders. They were clearly shaken and confused, but as the two officers talked with them and informed them of the steps taken so far to regain order, the composure of the Elders solidified. "We should declare a temporary state of martial law," Seris suggested.

Turil agreed though with hesitation due to the speed in which Seris proposed it. "It may very well go ignored by those who no longer recognize our authority, but it will give us the right to act in whatever capacity is needed to deal with the situation."

"To be dissolved as soon as there is order," Seris again appended in haste.

"Very well," Elder Tiberius replied. "Let it be known. Do what you must."

The two left the chamber, and Turil was suspicious of Seris. "Are you planning something, Seris?"

"Order," Seris replied. "It is the only thing I am planning."

"I am no stranger to your double speak. I will find out what you mean someday."

"I pray that you do not."

When night fell, Lon's planning came to fruition and brought turmoil to the streets of Ambrosia. The criminal and immoral leaders of the city's dissident factions heard of the coming imposition of martial law and felt their opportunity for control was timed and soon to disappear. Through suggestion and manipulation by Lon and his agents, these leaders overestimated the strength of the standing military and the strength of their own forces. Many of the groups coalesced until only a few were left, and as they were unwilling to form further unions, they fought each other for control of the other. During their bloody conflict, Turil looked and did not see how the plan would work. For a time, he even felt a loss of hope for the city. Seris, however, remained still in his own thoughts and in his confidence in Lon's ability. He strengthened Turil, and the two kept a vigilant watch over their ordered camps.

The fighting carried on into the third day, and the veil of deceit had yet to fall. Then, when the leaders were exposed, they were each lured into carefully devised traps and eliminated by Carsis as a display of the military's dominance. Their deaths caused their groups to fall into confusion, and though others rose to take their place, they too were swiftly eliminated so as not to strengthen their respective parties. Martial law filled in the void of power, and the factions dispersed. Many of those who survived returned to their homes while some assisted and even joined the Shades, Casters, and Adepts. In a day, the city was simultaneously eased of its criminal burden and strengthened in its military. Turil was again astonished at the outcome though he continued to question the means by which this order was gained. Nevertheless, the sight of a quiet city filled him with relief, and the third day ended.

On the fourth day, there came a wind from the east, and this wind began to clear up and disperse the canopy of darkness from the city. The gates of darkness lost their integrity and dissolved. Still, no one left the city out of fear.

On the fifth day, the populous started to show signs of recovery. The medical officers, doctors, and clerics reported diminishing numbers. What remained of Ambrosia's criminal element retreated into the twilight of darkness, and by the sixth day, everyone returned to their pre-attack state.

Ambrosia's week of sorrow culminated on the seventh day when the people realized that with all of their grievances, there had been no steps towards reconstruction or even burying the dead. Thus, a horrible stench rose into the air as the sun heated the corpses left behind by the ruin. There was mourning as they picked up the pieces and as they identified the bodies and buried them. There was mourning as they recounted events and realized what occurred and who they lost. Finally, there was mourning all day and through the night as the people wept over the horrors that befell them.

Reconstruction did not begin in full until the eighth day since Ambrosia's dreadful attack, and though the Hall of Order remained in ruins and would take time to rebuild, in large part due to artisan bickering, the staff it housed would take even longer. After a round of field promotions, one of which was denied by Lon, the Elders convened with what remained of the High Generals, Turil, Seris, and the remaining captains to consider what should be done. Some suggested taking on a defensive stance by act of rebuilding and fortifying the city. Others advised continuing the nationwide hunt for the Shadow Casters. It was during these deliberations that Seris thought to propose freeing Darrio from his bonds, but before he had an opportunity to speak, Turil opened his mouth. "Elders. It is my belief that now would be a good time to consider a different set of options in dealing with our enemies."

"What options?" Elder Tiberius asked.

"I am in agreement with General Hammond on taking a defensive posture with our forces, but, as suggested by Captain Mako, not with our foes."

"But we cannot divide our forces," General Hammond said. "The chain of command is weakened. We require unification."

Turil nodded. "You are right, and I would not suggest division."

"But we should stay on the offensive," Captain Mako said. "At the very least, it will keep the enemy under pressure. If we relent now, it will only embolden them to further action."

"Then let us put them under pressure but of a different kind."

"Do not speak two minds, General," Elder Judas said with impatience. "What is your suggestion? Attack or defend?"

"Both. We should concentrate most of our forces in the region towards defending our major cities, and the rest on reconstructing and fortifying Ambrosia. In the process, we must draw more into the service to regain what we have lost, but as we do this, let us set aside a portion of shades towards mass gatherings."

"And our offensive would come in the form of what?"

"The Firestar."

The room was silenced, and Seris could not help but look at Turil with surprise. Turil looked back at him with a smirk.

"You cannot be serious, General," Elder Tiberius said.

"I am, sir. The boy would need time to readjust, but his recovery will be far quicker than ours, and his destructive powers have already proven themselves to be greater than any militia. If supported by the rest of Seris' unit, I believe—."

"No, General. The answer is no."

"No?"

The rest of the High Elders nodded in agreement.

"Why?"

"The Firestar is too dangerous of an asset to release unrestrained. He has already shown himself to be a destructive entity when left to his own devices. His journey to Silesia only proved to be a disaster, and we have yet to receive a report on his trip to Esea. This may very well be the opportunity he wants. What if the Firestar decides to turn his wrath and fury against the nation?"

"I understand the charges of fear championed by General Chorus, but the Firestar has never attacked without cause."

"But he has refused to strike, even when ordered to, without one. You were present for the final confrontation in the Aural Realm, and he has set nothing but dangerous precedents since that event."

"Honestly," continued Elder Judas. "This is the kind of suggestion we may have expected from Captain Seris but not you. You were once in agreement with our assessments."

"With all due respect," Turil replied, "these are different times in need of different solutions. But if you will not grant this request, then I will take my seat and instead suggest as Hammond has."

"Thank you, General."

Turil returned to his seat and noticed Seris was watching him. As the others continued to debate, Turil spoke to Seris beneath the tones in the room. "You were going to suggest the same thing, I assume."

"I was, but why did you?"

"Because I know what you have obtained."

"And how did you obtain this knowledge?"

"You are not the only one capable of gathering the loyalty of others." Seris once again found himself examining Turil in an effort to ascertain what was on the general's mind, but Turil only looked back, smiled, and said, "You are staring at me, old friend."

While this was happening, Darrio was focused on a self-imposed fit of exercise and survival training in the western forest. For the entire week, he fixed himself on various tasks designed to strengthen both his resolve and his destructive ability. Limited as he was by the bonds on his wrists and unable to use magic, he instead practiced attack motions. In doing this, he further refined what he knew and experimented with new offensive and defensive formations. Even more, though he loathed using them, he practiced and refined his skill with the blades by attacking his surroundings and shifting from one imagined target to the other. Most of the objects in Darrio's vicinity were scarred by the end of his sessions, but while his body was permitted time to rest, there was none given to his soul.

Much of this training was done in a bid to gain temporary relief from the conflicting anguish still residing within him. Saria's face still hung clearly in the frame of Darrio's mind and served as a constant reminder of what he lost. He cited two sources of blame for the matter, but when he remembered this, he was roused to restlessness and further pursued his training. Even so, when his body was spent and unable to obey, he could do nothing else but remember. The first blame, though secondary in his motivations, rested on the evil men of the world. The second one, however, fell upon his incompetence as a guardian. He first pondered this during his entry into the forest and decided then he would work towards finding a remedy to the situations in the order of whichever came first. His exercises were extensions of this endeavor.

Despite all of this, Darrio would still take time each day to emerge from his isolation to check on the state of the city from a distance. He cursed the sight of it but eagerly anticipated any word from Seris. On the fourth day of the week since the attack, he saw that the canopy was lifting and hoped he would be called back soon, but by the seventh day, he started to believe it would never be safe for him to return. On the evening of the eighth day, well after Turil gave his proposal to the Elders, Darrio rested, and Abaddon approached silently from behind.

Darrio knew there was someone behind him. The isolation heightened his sense of the area. Nevertheless, he did not turn his head to look. He did not care to. "Who is it?"

Abaddon was quiet for a while as he took a moment to examine Darrio's current state and the state of his environment. "You have lost something, and now you take this loss out upon the world. Answer me, Darrio. Are you well?"

Darrio briefly peered behind him to confirm the identity of the voice he heard. When he saw that it was Abaddon, he huffed and faced forward again. "I thought you were dead."

The response did little to satisfy Abaddon's inquiry, and he said, "You have not answered my question. I say again, are you well?"

"What the hell, Abbadon? No, I'm not well. I've been sitting in the same damn spot for the past week, and nobody's talked to me, and I'm out here all by myself. How do you think I feel?"

"But it has been over three days since the mist dispersed. Why have you not returned?"

"Are you serious? And what are you asking me all of these questions for? Did Seris send you?"

"He did not."

Darrio huffed and thrust his weapons into the ground. "Then I'm here because I'm here and because nobody's called for me yet."

"Then you are not injured."

"Bullshit," Darrio mumbled without thinking. He shook his head.

"I mean I'm not dead if that's what you're asking."

Darrio's responses seemed to satisfy Abaddon though Darrio could not understand it. He was clearly there to check on Darrio's status, but Darrio then questioned why. If Abaddon had not been sent by Seris, why was he there? "Do they even know you're still alive?"

"No."

"Then what are you doing here?"

"I saw your body pass through the barrier. It concerned me, and I returned to be sure you were unchanged by the passage."

Darrio turned his head and answered, "You're not my guardian anymore and haven't been for a while. You know that, right?" Abaddon nodded, and Darrio calmed. He had not spoken to anyone for a week, and it felt nice to have someone to talk to even if it was Abaddon. Darrio then turned his entire body to face him and asked, "So how did you survive it? And how did you get out?"

"I made a way."

"But there was dark magic in that attack and then all over the city. You may be a master of everything, but there's something you're not telling me."

"Nor do I care to."

"There you go again."

"Excuse me?"

"You're always so damn cryptic when I ask about how you do things. You taught me all of these high-level techniques that Seris and nobody else even knew about, and you never told me where it came from or how you got them."

"Haven't we spoken on this before?"

"Yeah, and you didn't give me a straight answer back then either. You've trained me once before the war and two more times after that. Why did you teach me this stuff, and where did you get it from?"

"If I had not taught you, you would not have survived."

"Yeah, and I already know there's more to it than that. You didn't train anyone else like this, so when am I going to get a straight answer from you? Am I ever going to get a straight answer from you?"

Abaddon paused for a moment and entered into thought. When he finished, he said, "I will make you this deal. If you discover who I am, I will tell you what you wish to know, and I will speak to you as plainly as I am doing now. But until that time, it will be as it has always been. My past, like yours, is not something I wish to discuss."

"And how am I supposed to do that? You're older than dust."

"Then ask the dust."

Darrio smirked. "Did you just make a joke?" but Abaddon was silent and did not respond. "Okay, fine. Deal."

"There is one more thing I would ask."

"What is it?"

"Do you remember what I taught you about your emotions?"

"It was a long time ago, but no, I didn't forget."

"Then repeat to me what I told you."

"Why?"

"So I may be sure."

Darrio rolled his eyes and leaned his head back. "You said my feelings were an asset, not an enemy."

"And an uncontrolled asset can become the most dangerous. Take note of what I'm about to say. The men who control their own assets may be capable of great things and yet fail to achieve glory and be destroyed. Even the passions and zeal of these men can be turned against them to their own ruin."

"So what are you trying to say? That I've been too pissed off lately? That I should relearn to control my emotions and use them like I did before?"

Abaddon shook his head. "You misunderstood what I was telling you then, and you still treated your emotions as an enemy. What I am saying is simply this. You must not allow your emotions to control you. Let nothing control you. Not one thing."

Darrio lowered his head to contemplate though he suspected Abaddon was not simply speaking about his emotions. "What about the Elders?" he asked.

"I will leave the Elders to you. I am glad to see your memory has not been altered by the darkness, but now I must depart. I have an investigation to continue."

"Well, why do you think they attacked the Hall like that? If they only wanted to destroy the building, they could have done it without the mess, but if they wanted to destroy the whole city, then they could have, but they didn't. It doesn't make sense."

Abaddon turned and said, "The Hall was not their target."

Darrio opened his mouth to ask more questions, but Abaddon swiftly flew off and headed south. Darrio grumbled, "Bastard," and continued in thought. If Ambrosia's Hall of Order was not the true target of the Shadow Caster's attack, it remained to be seen why they attacked in the first place. Darrio could not think of any other strategic targets in the general area though the damage done seemed to be enough. Darrio then began to wonder whether it was a person they meant to destroy. Such a surprising and destructive blow had likely been infused with dark magic to guarantee the certain destruction of its recipient. But who could be so dangerous to the Shadow Casters as to warrant such a move? Was the Light Bearer present? Were they after Saria? Was there someone else or perhaps a group of people? Darrio pondered on these questions, but his inquiries were getting him nowhere, and as they fell on Saria, he only became more frustrated.

Darrio removed his blades from the forest floor and retired them to his sheaths. He then breathed deeply and began his return trek to Ambrosia despite prior orders to the contrary. He figured, if need be, he would simply return to isolation until called though he loathed the idea. He found the experience for a week stressful enough. Though he would never admit to such a thing, he actually welcomed Abaddon's company to some degree. He thought it safe to assume, though, that his company would not be welcomed by the demoralized populous. Even in this, however, Darrio underestimated the reaction.

There was a man just past the western gate gathering flowers to place at the grave of his wife and two children. As he was searching, he looked up and saw the Firestar approaching on the horizon. He dropped what he gathered, and his blood grew hot in anger. "Firestar!" he shouted, and he retreated to the city. "The Firestar is coming! He's returning to the city!"

As Darrio drew closer to the city, he could see an angry crowd collecting at the gate. They were barring his entry and shouting at him. "Stay away from us!"

"We don't want you here!"

"Get lost!"

Darrio considered turning back but pressed on nonetheless, but when he was within throwing distance of the mob, several of the citizens picked up stones and threw them. Darrio evaded the projectiles and replied, "What the hell?"

"Go away!"

"What did I do?"

"You brought this on us!" a woman said.

"I didn't do anything!"

"Bullshit!" said another man, and he picked up another stone to throw. He was followed by others, and they slowly advanced forward with the clear intention of killing the Firestar.

Darrio stepped back. "I didn't do anything!" but his words fell on deaf ears.

"Kill him!" the crowd chanted. "Kill him!" They further jeered and tore upon the Firestar with their words.

Darrio's resolve weakened. "But I didn't do anything!" he cried. Still, no one listened, and the men raised their stones.

There was then a sudden rumbling, and the ground beneath the mob shifted and tumbled. The men fell to the grass, and the crowd drew apart. Behind them were Seris and Turil who were actively manipulating the earth. After they settled the tremor, Seris shouted, "Whosoever attacks the Firestar will be found guilty of treason and executed on sight!"

"Go back to your homes!" Turil continued, and he turned his attention to Darrio. "Come here, boy. They will not harm you."

Darrio was shaken though he moved through the parting crowd. He could feel the hatred in their eyes, their contempt for his existence, but he could not bring himself to blame them. It was an ever-present conflict. They were the people. He hated them, but he would not raise his hands against them. Part of him desired their acceptance. The rest despised their treatment. He would not see them as enemies. Such a view would bring him towards violent retaliation, but neither would he see them as allies. It had nearly become an exercise for Darrio to reaffirm his position and feelings on matters concerning the people. He knew he cared in some small if not untraceable measure, but he did not want to. Like so many things, it was painful. Just as Darrio was reaching his destination, several men took the opportunity to spit on him.

"Go home!" Turil shouted, and he raised his hand above his head and caused a flare of intense fire to rise and burn those in the area. The mob quickly retreated from the heat and dispersed. They had made their point.

"Darrio," Seris said. "Are you alright?"

Darrio was trembling. He sputtered, "I'm fine. To hell with them. I don't care about them. I'm fine." Seris sighed and put his arm around Darrio, and the motion caused a stream of tears to fall from his eyes.

Still, Darrio fought the urge to cry and gritted his teeth. "To hell with them," he repeated.

Darrio was taken to what was once a commerce building but was then serving as a temporary Hall of Order. Reconstruction of the old Hall had not yet begun, but the artisans ceased fighting and were drawing up new plans. News spread quickly of the Firestar's return, and thus Darrio was guarded by his superiors during the entire trek to the site. Once they were inside, Seris told Darrio to wait while he and Turil spoke in private in an adjacent room. Darrio then took the time to clear his head and compose himself. He tried not to think of what had just happened and pushed the matter out of his mind. He instead focused his thoughts on what he would do next. "The next mission," he thought aloud as he shook his head. "That's it. That's all." His heart was pained by the idea, and he again gritted his teeth to fight the grief welling up in his heart. He would not allow himself to consider the implications for too long. He was lost without a direction, but he had settled on one, and that was it. "The next mission," he repeated again with a sigh, and he felt his heart harden. He knew he would likely grow colder as a result of his decision, but he tried not to care. He was failing, but Darrio felt it necessary. He did not know what else to live for.

"Darrio," Seris called. "Come here, please."

Darrio stood and entered the room where Seris and Turil waited with Lon and Talim.

"How are you feeling?" Turil asked.

"I'm fine."

"Are you sure?"

Darrio nodded, and though Turil remained skeptical, he let Darrio's answer pass. "We were talking about the new operation and thought you should hear this."

"Hear what?"

"Turil proposed freeing you to the Elders," Seris said, "but they have rejected the thought."

"They do not trust you," Turil continued, "and we have been thinking of ways in which you could earn that trust."

"Why should I care what they want?" Darrio asked. "They've treated me like the unwanted bastard ever since the war ended. I don't give a damn about their trust."

"This is not simply for your sake, Firestar. Our forces have been weakened. We cannot expend much on furthering operations against the Shadow Casters, and we need your power, or we cannot win."

Darrio crossed his arms. "Okay. So what do you want me to do?"

"We're developing an operation which we think may work. I do not like it, but I see little else that we can do."

"What is it?"

Turil sighed and passed the question to Lon. Lon answered, "We're going to stage a rebellion."

"What?"

"Rather, I should say, a carefully incited…disagreement. There has been dissidence within what remains of our military. You have many enemies, Firestar, and some blame you for the misfortune."

"So I've noticed."

"Much of the tension which you and the others previously noted was a result of conflicting interests. There are those who would seek to destroy you given the opportunity and those who seek to reserve you as an asset. Both have petitioned the High Elders on the matter."

Darrio looked at Turil. "I thought it had something to do with you and Seris?"

"There are many details to the matter, Firestar, some of which are secretive. We don't have time to discuss them here."

"Okay. So what's the plan?"

"The plan," Lon smiled, "is to draw those who seek to destroy you into a position of open conflict with the High Elders. The past week has greatly enhanced their irrational malice toward you. This makes them easier to manipulate. Indeed, for such an event to occur at a time where we could take advantage is fortunate for us."

"There was nothing fortunate about it," Turil stated. "Don't ever talk of the event in such a manner again."

"My apologies, but more to the point, Firestar, when they have risen to this point, we shall put them down, so to speak, and prominently place you as the ideal defender of the realm."

"Turil will speak for the allied position," Seris continued, "and will repeat the proposition of freeing you to the High Elders."

"Why him?"

"I have defended you from the beginning, and they will not listen to me."

"And who else knows about this?"

"No one," Lon answered. "It is only the five of us, or else there would be other repercussions to consider."

Darrio looked towards Talim who had been unusually silent the whole time. He appeared to be deep in thought. "Talim?"

Talim quickly withdrew from his state of contemplation and replied, "Yes? What is it?"

"You're involved in this too?"

Talim nodded. "I can hear your surprise, Firestar, but I gave myself over to serving more interests than my own."

"And you're okay with this?"

Talim looked away at first but soon after returned his face to Darrio and smiled. "Let us do what must be done."

"Are you with us, Darrio?" Seris asked.

Darrio tried to consider the meaning of such an act. Both Talim and Turil were hesitant, and he considered both of them to be better men than himself by far. Even so, if it was something even they were willing to undertake, then Darrio would not argue. He uncrossed his arms. "Just tell me what I need to do."

"Excellent," Lon replied. "Now be attentive. I will say this only once to minimize our risk of exposure." Lon then proceeded to explain the details of his plan and the roles everyone would play therein. It was divided into five stages.

During the first stage, General Turil would act as the diplomatic conduit and would initially attempt to persuade the High Elders that Darrio's hindrance was a hindrance for the nation. Two sides would then be identified. Turil's would be referred to as the allied party, and the other side would be known as the enemy party. "I do not like this naming convention," Turil protested. "We are still one body."

"It is only for the purposes of the plan," Lon assured, and he continued his explanation. The second stage would consist of a progression of the two agendas to ascertain how the enemy would work and what their weaknesses were. The third stage, which Lon called the stage of conflict, would see more forceful action taken by both parties.

"What kind of force?" Turil questioned.

"Strategically tactful diplomacy. You must become bold but remain restrained. They will hurl barbs at you and those who follow you, but you will remain resilient. The Elders will see this, and the enemy party will fall out of favor."

Stage four would be marked by a trigger event which Lon carefully explained would be initiated by the enemy party. "When a group remains in a frenzied state for too long, there are bound to be… troublesome complications that arise."

"You do not mean violence, do you?"

"Why of course not, General! We will not actively draw the enemy party to violence, but they will be likely to do something rash which will both shame themselves and provide us with an opening that we will need."

"For strategically tactful diplomacy, correct?"

"Correct," Lon replied with a grin.

Turil, however, did not like the sound of the plan nor the tone in which Lon was carrying it. Nevertheless, Turil let him finish. The final stage, curiously dubbed the execution stage, would find the enemy party completely out of favor with the High Elders. The allied party would then have all the leverage needed to push through the desired agenda. The Firestar would be released, and a new campaign could be drawn against the Shadow Casters.

When Lon finished explaining all of this, Darrio shook his head as he tried to grasp everything which would be happening at once. "It's too complicated," he said.

Lon smiled in response and said, "If a plan is too simple, even the simple will uncover it, but plans formulated with the highest of understandings will be hidden from even the greatest of mortal minds."

Darrio groaned as he considered what he heard, and it suddenly dawned on him like a still, small voice in his heart that Lon, with all of his plans and high-mindedness, was evil. It was not a surprising revelation to Darrio, but it did give him pause if even for a brief moment. He was uncertain of where the message came from and why it came to him then, but he pushed the matter out of his mind. He did not wish to consider the implications of it.

The five conspirators departed after the briefing, but Seris and Darrio walked together on the streets of the city after all of the legitimate affairs of the day were handled. A curfew had been imposed since the initiation of martial law which had yet to be lifted. Thus, the two were free to move about without fear of attack. With the moon, stars, and the canopy of the night overhead, Seris spoke. "Darrio. I wish to speak with you about something."

"What is it?"

"You once spoke of your parents in passing. I understand they died while you were very young, but you still remember them."

Darrio nodded but said nothing.

"What was your father like?"

Darrio shook his head. "I don't want to talk about it."

"What about your mother?"

"Seris, please."

"Very well," and the two were silent for a while. "Darrio?"

"Hm?"

"Do you still trust me?"

Darrio contemplated for a moment and answered, "Yes."

"And my judgments. Do you trust in them also?" Darrio nodded, and Seris quieted for a while longer. "Tell me what happened to you in Esea."

Darrio explained everything he could recall from the moment he entered the city to the moments following his leave of Lumineth. He made little mention of Saria. In every case where her person would have been mentioned, Darrio gritted his teeth and shook his head.

Seris tried to comfort him and purposely changed the topic to a narrower subject, the Light Bearer. "The High Priestess identified the man as such?"

"Yeah. I mean, she was crazy, but she seemed to know what she was talking about. But she said Palim was possessed by a demon too, so I don't know."

"And you're sure it was the same man you saw earlier?"

Darrio nodded. "I've never seen the guy in my life, so it doesn't make sense that he should know me. He seemed to know something about my future too. Him, Valeria, even Palim. Everybody seemed to know something. Maybe it has something to do with dark magic."

"What did they say?"

"I don't know. They said I'd have something. Something like...," but Darrio trailed off. "It doesn't matter what they said. It didn't make any sense anyway."

"Are you sure?"

"No. I just don't want to think about it. There's enough going on right now."

Seris nodded. "You're right. There are many things happening right now."

"It got me thinking about who the Shadow Casters might have been after when they attacked us."

"Who? You believe they were after a person?"

"Maybe. I was thinking the Light Bearer might have been in the city, and we just didn't know it. Abaddon said they weren't aiming for the Hall, so that's the only thing I can think of."

"You spoke to Abaddon? He is alive then." Darrio nodded, and Seris asked, "When did this happen?"

"Just before I got back. He said he was investigating."

"Why has he not returned?"

Darrio shrugged. "Maybe he wants it to be a surprise. I don't know. I'm just wondering why the Shadow Casters had to attack like that, and if it was a person they were after, who was it, did he survive, and whose side is he on?"

"If only we had omnipotence."

"Are you joking, Seris?"

Seris smiled and then became very solemn. "Darrio. I have a confession to make."

"What confession?"

"It is a grave thing, but I want you to understand that what I have done and what I am doing is geared towards your best interests."

Seris' change in tone unnerved Darrio. "Don't talk like that, and don't tell me. I don't want to hear it."

"Why?"

"I don't want to know." Darrio saw a reemerging closeness with Seris that was in time with the regular rhythm of their relationship. However, Darrio did not feel he could take another loss after the recent deaths of Sam and Saria. There had been enough people, good people so far as Darrio could see, that came only to die or push him away. Pain and heartache, it seemed, were the only rewards he would receive in intimacy. Nevertheless, Darrio always found that a better side marked by sentimentality and occasional loneliness would get the better of him. He saw it as a reoccurring curse. In every case that he could recall, the risk outweighed the benefits, and the past two hundred years of his life gave him little reason to hope for change. Of everyone he could remember, he recalled five who he thought of as anchors to his sense of being and purpose. The first was God who he did not know. The next two were his parents, both deceased. The fourth he hated, and Seris was the fifth. If the trend were to continue, Darrio did not want to think about how it would result. "I don't want to know anything," he said again. "Just do what you need to do."

"But it concerns you."

"I don't care! Seris. I'm sorry. I just don't care. Don't tell me anything. Please. Just don't."

"Are you afraid something will happen to me if I do?"

There was more than Darrio could tell. In addition to his own history with people, he did not want his image of Seris to become tarnished. Seris was the only anchor he knew and was not afraid of. There was no one else in his eyes. "Don't tell me," he said once more. It pained him to think about these things.

Seris complied with hesitation and a heavy heart. "So be it, Darrio." He then leaned in to whisper something into Darrio's ear, and when he finished he said, "Do so only when absolutely necessary. Understood?"

Darrio nodded, and the two continued walking until duty forced their departure.

The following day, Darrio was confined to limited duties on the outskirts of the city to avoid confrontation with the citizenry. The adepts and casters on guard duty said nothing to him. He then found Talim standing just past the entrance gate. He was looking out over the horizon. "What are you doing?" Darrio asked.

"Boy!" Talim replied with a jump. "Why does it appear a habit of those around me to sneak around and surprise me lately?"

Darrio apologized but asked again, "What are you doing?"

"I am waiting for Eloi. He was sent away after the attack, but he has not returned. I fear something may have happened to him."

"Well, that's different."

"Indeed. I did not think much of the man before all of this. A testament to my keen sense of sight and judgment, eh?"

"You're just a loudmouth."

"I speak in jest, Firestar!" Talim laughed. "You are like Eloi to take everything I say so seriously. This is unbecoming of you."

"Don't say that," Darrio groaned. "I'm sure Eloi's fine anyway. He's probably just trying to figure out when to come home."

"Perhaps." As Darrio turned to return to his duties, Talim spoke. "One thing, Firestar, before you go."

"What is it?"

"Let us say the end of all things, for us I should say, is unfavorable. If the Shades of Seris were to become as devils, do you believe there would be meaning for us in this?"

"Who says we're devils? We're just shades with jobs to do."

"But beyond our professions, Firestar. When it comes to our actions and how history will remember us, even if what we do is wrong, do you believe there will be meaning in it?"

Darrio thought and remembered the words of his father. He then replied, "I was taught that there's a meaning for everything that happens even if we don't understand it yet."

"Do you think a devil can enter heaven then?"

Darrio shook his head. "Devils don't belong in heaven, and the only ones who get in are former ones. That's how I understand it at least. She was always fuzzy on the details."

"She?"

Darrio was referring to his mother, but the slip caused him to shake his head. "It's nothing. Nevermind."

Talim smiled and sighed. "Then it seems you were taught wisely, Firestar. I hope you will carry those words with you."

"Yeah. And if I live long enough to trust in them, I'll let you know." Darrio then left Talim to wait.

Talim sighed and waited a while longer before returning to the city to prepare for what was ahead. His mind was burdened by what he knew, and though he had given his commitment, his heart remained troubled. Before returning to the makeshift quarters assigned to him in a building near the substitute Hall site, Talim set his mind on a single train of thought. "Devils in heaven," he pondered aloud. "Devils and heaven. Devils or heaven." He placed a heavy hand on the door to his room and settled the matter. His heart was stilled, but the burden remained. He then turned the knob and entered the room. "So be it," he uttered, and Talim slept soon after.

CHAPTER 14
Wake of Silence

WHISPERS ELEVATED TENSIONS in the room to a palatable level, but after they were compelled to silence, Chorus spoke. "When Deloran, the Firestar, acts, and he will act, he will prove too dangerous to contain. I go so far as to say he is even too volatile of an asset to let live."

"He is too much of an asset to let die," Turil answered.

The two High Generals, Chorus and Turil, petitioned the High Elders in a secret meeting held late into the night. There were others present as well though Turil and Chorus acted as the primary speakers for their respective parties. Chorus continued. "The people are unsettled by him. We have had two violent demonstrations in the past week all on account of his mere presence in the city."

"And the Firestar has not retaliated."

"Only because he is kept on a leash by your captain. I seem to recall that when Seris was injured during the last stages of the war, the boy entered the Hollow Realm and set fire to their forests. One-third of the entire region was burned to the ground."

"Are you decrying an attack made against an enemy nation during a time of war? The Hunters of the Hollow Realm were our greatest threat."

"I am decrying that he did so despite express orders to the contrary. Do not twist the truth to your liking, General Turil. It is unbecoming of you."

"I am only making the point that while he did do so of his own accord and for his own reasons, the result was still beneficial to us. He has not expressly acted in a manner that would pose a threat to this nation. Even during the delusion, his limit was prompted as a defense response. He was trying to protect the girl. He may share no love for the people or even we who are his superiors, but if there is one positive trait he has shown, it is the discipline to act in accord with his station despite where his feelings may take him."

"Your sentimentality, I believe, clouds your judgment. What reports did Seris make of the Firestar's prowess with magic? He was classified a master of destruction and manipulation even before the release of flesh scripts. He gained knowledge of higher techniques only the gods or Magnus could know about. He has yet to show limit in his potential."

"And this troubles everyone, I know, but don't you think it remarkable how even with what he is capable of, he has yet to let the power control him? I have seen men with lesser strengths go wild with abuse."

"Just because it has not happened yet does not mean it will not happen at all."

"Were the Firestar as treacherous and dangerous as you think, he would not have allowed himself to be shackled in the first place or a second time for that matter."

"And I tell you it is only a matter of time before the monster that lies beneath reveals itself again. Only then it will be in our midst and on our land."

"Considering what has come to pass since the war ended, I am relieved and even reassured by the fact he hasn't retaliated already."

"I believe that is enough, General," Elder Tiberius said with discomfort. "As stated before, we will continue to deliberate on the matter."

General Chorus slammed his fist on the table. "How long must we deliberate? We know what he's capable of, and we know what he's done!"

Tiberius stared coldly at General Chorus. "Be still, General Chorus, or mind your tone. This council would prefer both."

Chorus recoiled, and his eyes retreated into himself.

"We will deliberate, as stated, and continue to consider the most prudent course of action. If there are any more petitions, speak them now," but there were none. "Then this meeting is adjourned."

As everyone left, Turil took another look at General Chorus who continued to shake his head with disbelief. Lon, Seris, and Talim were waiting outside of the entrance. Turil uttered silently, "Was that really necessary?"

"Explicitly," Lon replied. "Impatience is no virtue to any man."

Turil then looked at Talim. "I do hope in good faith you have never done such a thing among the council or me before."

"Of course not," Seris answered.

"In all seriousness," Talim started, "you are no enemy." He then smiled. "But even if I had, you would not have known it."

Turil smirked. "I find that greatly reassuring. I will say again, however, that I do not like this plan of yours nor the fact that you head it, Lon."

Lon smiled. "I don't believe there has ever been a target who has liked my plans."

Lon's statement put Turil on guard, and Seris saw this. "Lon," Seris warned. "Do not scare him."

"I spoke only in jest," but this statement did little to alleviate Turil's state. Lon had a terrible reputation born from his actions during and even prior to the war. After he was released from confinement to serve as a shade, Lon encountered other officers and superiors who ultimately displeased him. These subjects invariably found themselves placed in harm's way, and while there were no fatalities, there were many injuries. When the High Generals saw this trend, they placed him under Seris' command. Lon initially thought little of the captain and formulated a plot to test him. Seris, however, saw through Lon's manipulations and turned the scheme against him. It was no small feat, and he had gained Lon's allegiance ever since.

It was thus troubling to Turil's ears to hear himself referred to as a target in Lon's scheme. It was believed that he always meant what he said even if he was being deceitful. He always spoke with purpose, and he rarely erred. If there were exceptions in the world, there were none known by any among the living. Furthermore, since his pattern of speech was often sprinkled with connotations of death, his words were often scrutinized by those around him when he spoke. Fortunately, he never enacted a plan without Seris' say-so while serving under him. This troubled Turil also. Had it been a slip, Turil had every reason to worry.

Over the course of the following week, Turil was met by a number of other generals and officers who voiced favorable opinions of Turil's stance. Many of them, however, were worried about just how far the other side would be willing to go. Turil reassured each of them in turn and sent them on their way. He was gaining many allies, and among them was General Hammond. The opposing camp, likewise, saw growth in their support as dissenting officers rallied around General Chrous and Captain Mako. Thus far, everything was going according to Lon's plan, but Turil's heart stirred with misgivings. The people who visited him were already sympathetic to his cause but were made more so in their sleep by Talim's illusionary techniques. Those supporting the opposing side were likewise influenced to action in a similar manner. For Turil, it seemed a deceptive tactic to acquire aid by such a means. They would have likely helped their respective parties without the intervention though it may have been done with less fervor. Unfortunately, fervor was another necessity to Lon's plot.

As Turil made his rounds to check on the posts, he passed by the site where the reconstruction of the Hall was to take place. The rubble had been removed, but a new foundation had not yet been put into place. When he inquired as to its progress, the head artisan assured the general that progress was being made. They were only finalizing the design and settling on what scripts to place in and around the building. Turil sighed as he could never understand why it took the artisans so long to start on a task, but he took consolation in the fact that it never took them as long to create as it did to plan.

After leaving the site, Turil happened upon Darrio's position which was in a secluded corner of the city. "How are you holding up?"

Darrio shrugged. "Fine, I guess. No one's thrown anything at me today. How's the bullshit going? I mean, the politics?"

"It goes, same as always."

"Thought so."

"I wonder if I might be so blunt as to ask you a question, though."

"What is it?"

"When and where did you learn to swear?"

"Huh?"

"I do not remember hearing you curse before recently."

"You haven't been around me that much, but I don't know. I guess it started in the Burning Realm. While I was stuck in that prison camp, you know?"

"Why haven't you stopped?"

"Does it bother you?"

"I think it's improper for soldiers to swear. It sets a terrible example for military decency. Control is to be exercised over all areas including the tongue."

Darrio lowered his head to think. "What if I substituted? What if instead of saying, 'You son of a bitch,' I say, 'You moron?' Would that be okay?"

"I'd rather you say nothing of the sort, but if you feel compelled to open your mouth, I suppose that will suffice."

"I'll try that then. Moron."

"Excuse me?"

"Not you. I'm practicing. Don't pay any attention to me. Moron. You moron. You sorry son of a…moron."

Turil left Darrio to pursue his linguistic challenge, and when he had advanced to a safe distance, he shook his head. "Even awake, the boy is strange."

The following night, Turil entered his office and sat at his desk to review potential cases related to the Shadow Casters. One of them was a report from one of a handful of spies Turil commissioned in secret. Like Seris had done early in the Magic War, Turil had been screening potential candidates he could trust to carry out secret missions for him. He told no one about this nor did he record their names and locations on anything traceable. He committed everything about them and their operations to memory. There were four of them. One moved into the Burning Realm, the second into the Hollow Realm, the third was in the Silent Realm, and the fourth remained local. It was this fourth agent of Turil's that relayed news of Tam's mission objective and success to the general. In his last report, he wrote of the experience gained and of the near-fatal conflicts with Seris' shade of madness. Communication was done by way of a carrier bird.

These birds, while common to avoid suspicion, bore a single carrier script that would activate in the proximity of a second target script. The carrier script would then guide the bird to its destination. Turil had the target script inscribed on a bird feeder which he placed outside of his office window. He took good care of the creatures who aided him.

The prior evening's carrier had already been sent back, but Turil had not taken the time to look over what was delivered to him. It was a report from the Burning Realm, and as Turil read through it, he saw two names that piqued his interest and curiosity. Those names were Deloran and Bacchus.

"General."

The voice was familiar and provoked feelings of agitation in Turil. His train of thought was broken, but when he looked up from his desk, he saw nothing. "Step forward so I can see you." Asher approached from the right of Turil's desk, and after he had done so, Turil leaned back. "The captain you assured would be returned to me alive is dead. My city nearly tore itself apart in a devastating attack, and now I find myself involved in a deceitful plot I do not like in order to gain the Elder's trust. If irony were steel, I would have the finest blade on earth and the presence of mind to slay you with it. So please explain to me why I should not share my knowledge of you with everyone else."

"There were unforeseen complications."

"Complications?" Turil replied half chuckling in contempt. "Of all the things I have come to brave, complications have proven to be the most trying."

"Then our experiences are similar, but I assure you, my original plan never called for this."

"Then you mustn't lay schemes if you are not prepared for them to change."

Asher was quiet, and Turil sighed. It seemed strange to be arguing as an equal with an ancient enemy. Turil pushed it out of his mind. "You came to me. You sought my help, but I have received nothing from you in pledge. Please. If you will call yourself an ally then simply tell me, and tell me plainly, who attacked us and why."

"I cannot say."

"You mean you will not say," Turil said with elevated tones, but he remained cautious. It was likely Asher once again isolated the room, but Turil did not want to take any unnecessary chances. "I cannot help someone I cannot trust. Answer me or this alliance is dissolved."

"I warned you of what would happen if you spoke my name."

"And I have not so ignorantly entered a contract with a potential enemy without making preparations. Even if you should kill me, I have seen to it that your ghost falls not far behind."

"I did not believe you capable of such things."

"I am not naturally inclined to scheme, but necessity has taught me, and I have learned."

Asher's eyes darted about the room as he searched for a solution. He then said, "Give me assurance that you will neither report nor act on what I am about to tell you. Let events go as they will, but say and do nothing to change them."

Turil shook his head with disbelief. "Pardon my…hesitation, but why would I agree to such a thing?"

"Because if you do not, there will be no one to oppose him. If you do not, you will have no chance to overcome his plan."

"If it is as grave as I fear, may I also gain from you assurance that you will give me your full cooperation from this point forward?"

"As much as I can spare without betraying my concealment."

Turil mulled over the consequences of the arrangement and dreaded what he was soon to hear. Nevertheless, he replied, "Speak."

Asher hesitated all the more and anticipated the worst. Turil, however, thought it strange given their positions. Asher then answered, "It was I."

Turil nearly choked on his rage, but he clenched his fists and gritted his teeth to contain the anger within him. "How…could you?"

"Feel free to shout, General," Asher said as he lowered his head. "This room is sealed. No one can hear you."

Turil obliged. "Do you know how many people you've killed? Do you know who they were? There were good men working within those halls! Good men, and now they are dead because of you! How could you ask for my help and destroy the very agency I needed to do so?"

Asher stepped back into the darkness, but before Turil could ask about this, the office door swung open. A soldier was panting. "Are you alright, sir? I heard you screaming and ran as fast as I could."

Turil was dumbfounded and stammered as he tried to explain. He quickly collected himself and answered, "No, soldier. I'm fine. A terrible nightmare is all. I was having…recollections of that week. It is nothing. A phantom dream. Nothing more."

"Very well, sir," and the soldier left.

Asher stepped forward once again. "I will volunteer this one thing to you as a token of goodwill. I am one of the five masters you seek and the one who oversees the wind clans of change. What did you say about schemes only a moment ago?"

"You have made your point," Turil groaned. "We still hold each other by the throat, but mind you, my displeasure of you has now turned to hatred. Why did you attack us?"

"I was not attacking your city. I was trying to achieve our goal."

"What goal?"

"The master of masters was among you."

"Then who is he?" Turil said as he leaned forward with a hand on his sword. "Tell me his name so that I may approach him in his sleep and kill him." Asher shook his head, and Turil shouted, "Why not?"

"If it were that simple, the attack would have succeeded, and if I should tell you now, he will know it was me. As it is, his suspicions are on another, and I wish for it to stay that way."

Turil leaned back and sighed with frustration. "May I assume the Great Delusion was caused by you as well?"

"It was, but not of my own will. I was ordered to do so."

"To what end? To instill in the people fear of the Firestar? Because if that was his aim, then he has succeeded."

"I could not tell you what he intends because I no longer know."

"Then it seems to me he wishes to make the boy a destroyer agent for his god. Perhaps his plan is to make this place so inhospitable that he may recruit and turn the Firestar against the nation."

"And what would be the point of that? You believe he wishes to destroy this realm?"

"Is he not?"

"When your nation came under duress, he fought to preserve it."

"Then why does he endeavor to tear it apart along with the rest of the world? Why does he seek the power of light? Won't this Great Cleansing you seek destroy everything?"

"It may."

"Then on one hand, there is talk of subjecting the whole world to Magnus and on the other of destroying the world through this cleansing. The objectives are at odds. Is your master mad or are there reasons yet unseen for his actions?"

Asher shook his head with disbelief. "Excuse me, but how did you come to learn of these details?"

"We held a member of your other clans captive for a time, but she escaped soon after."

"She? What was her name?"

"Elea, I believe."

"Elea?"

"You know this woman?"

"And she told you everything about us? She told you our aim was to subject the world under Magnus?"

"Not everything and not willingly. We have been piecing together intelligence as we get them, but much of it has come from what the Firestar has gathered."

Asher was silent for a moment. "Something has changed. This is not in accord with what he told us."

"What isn't? Which part?"

"Subjection. His original plan did not include control of the seven realms nor placement of those realms under Magnus."

"Then what was his original plan? I need specifics if we are to work in unison." Three taps on the glass drew both of their attention. A carrier bird had just landed bearing a message. Turil opened the window and retrieved the rolled-up paper attached to the bird's legs and placed it on his desk. After making a quick glance, he remarked, "It is from the Silent Realm."

Asher took note of the bird. "I will give you specifics but not here and not in person. When you see me, it will only be for matters of grave importance to the both of us."

"Then why did you come to me now? To tell me of your guilt?"

"No. I only came to warn you."

"Of what?"

"Of the master's designs on you. He has seen you and will see to it that your end is not well. Stay on your guard."

"It would be easier if I knew who I was guarding myself from. Your reckless decision has not exactly filled me with confidence. You nearly killed me as well, and as it is, I do not know who to fear more. Seris, the Elders, the rest of the Shadow Casters, or you."

"I have done what I have done for a reason, General. My reckless action, as you call it, may have been a desperate one and poorly timed, but it was not without its reasons or its fruit."

"Then I'll hope you'll forgive me even if I cannot forgive you."

"I can only offer you my condolences. I will take my leave now."

"Please do." After Asher departed, Turil could not help his feelings of frustration, and he kicked the end of his desk. He barely slept through the night.

Another day passed with rising support for both sides, and just as it was reaching its peak, Seris, Turil, and Lon met again. "Stage one is complete," Lon declared. "Are you ready for stage two?"

Turil sighed. "I am ready."

Seris saw the general's fatigue and knew it was due to lack of sleep which was unusual. While they were still captains, Seris prodded Turil for his ability to sleep through loud commotions with subtle humor, but it was often lost on his friend. "What is wrong, Turil?" Seris asked. "I know you are troubled."

"I am fine, Seris. It is nothing. Go on with the plan, Lon. Speak."

Lon looked to Seris for permission, and it was granted with a nod of the captain's head. "Talim has noted few peculiarities with General Chorus. Both he and Captain Mako are of relatively sound mind. It would do us well to take advantage of the weaknesses of those below them, but support such as they can be easily replaced."

"What are you suggesting?"

"There are not enough weaknesses to properly exploit our enemy into doing what we want. This is something we will have to remedy."

"Are you suggesting we intentionally plant a weakness where there is none? In one of own generals?"

"Your perception is acute, but yes. That is exactly what I am implying."

Turil turned his attention to Seris. "My friend, this is beyond devious. This borders on treachery. I understood the plan to be a war of words, of diplomacy."

Seris answered, "It is a war of words, Turil, but a war nonetheless. Darrio is our only viable option in combating the Shadow Casters, and there is no telling when they may strike again as they did."

"I somehow do not think it likely any time soon."

"That is not a chance we can afford to take."

"If this will help also," Lon started, "these actions will put you in greater standing with the Elders. I understand they do not trust you these days. This may be your only opportunity to earn that trust. If your forces are freed, you would be able to act at a greater capacity for the nation, would you not?"

"I would," Turil answered cautiously. "I just do not think this is the best way to go about it. If something is worth doing, it should be worth doing through more legitimate channels."

"Like the plans you made for your secret incursions?"

Turil looked at Seris with surprise. "You told him?"

"My apologies, General," Lon replied, "but my eyes and ears detect many things. It was by no fault of the captain that I learned of your transgression, nor do I hold it against you. You were only trying to act in the best interests of the nation."

"I know that."

"But this plan is also in the best interests of the nation."

"Turil," Seris spoke. "Everything will be okay after this, but if it disturbs you so much, perhaps you should not be a part of this."

"And leave this plot to go unchecked while it is still being performed under my name? I will not."

"Then put this fear out of your mind. We still have much to do."

Turil felt a play had been made on his motivations but could not be sure from looking at the two. Seris appeared genuinely concerned for Turil's well-being while Lon only examined and planned, but his eyes always relayed such things. "We'll continue," Turil said, "but do them no harm. I want your word."

"You have it," Seris answered.

"And mine as well," Lon said with a grin. Turil hated the way Lon smiled, but he let the words assuage his fears, and the three departed to continue into the second stage.

Deliberations continued, but petitions concerning the Firestar became more frequent. The Elders shared a unified fear and hatred of Darrio which everyone was aware of. This made Turil's position all the more difficult to defend and the work of Lon and Talim all the more troublesome. Natural outbursts from General Chorus notwithstanding, the Elders still favored the position of eliminating Darrio as soon as the most imminent threat had been dealt with. Turil, by Lon's curious but purposeful suggestion, then attempted to downplay the extent of Darrio's level of power. It was a risky motion, and those who heard him initially thought he was mad. "But allow me to explain myself," he pleaded. "I have never borne personal witness to the Firestar's feats. I, like nearly all of you here, have acquired knowledge of his most infamous deeds by means of report and hearsay."

"That does not discredit the truth of what he has done," Captain Mako replied.

"Indeed, it does not, but I urge you to consider this. When the Firestar performed the most infamous of his deeds, he did so under the sway of desire. He was pushed beyond the reasonable boundaries of magic use on the fields of the Burning Realm to make the Ash Dunes of that nation's barren wastelands. On the soil where the Crater of Bones was created, our enemies captured a significant portion of our number and held them hostage to bait the Firestar. When he arrived, they were killed, and he was ambushed. This act no doubt pushed him towards destruction."

"What about the destruction of Cilica or the Wastes of the Frozen Realm? He was not under the sway of desire then, was he?"

Turil turned to Seris who shook his head and answered, "He was not nor did he need to be under those conditions. He was, however, more purposeful and disciplined in his actions. He knew his motions and the consequences of those motions."

"Are you saying the Firestar is of two minds?"

"I am saying the one who wrought the Crater of Bones was not the same who brought down the city of Cilica. The person the Outer Realms identified as the Great Destroyer, and who everyone now calls

Firestar, is not the Darrio who you are condemning. Time and again he has put his life in jeopardy and continued to survive for a single moment of acceptance from the fearful and ungrateful hypocrites who forced him into service. He bears a burden none of you have ever known and will never know for as long as you draw breath."

"Seris," Turil interrupted. "Please."

"I have said my peace. I will say no more."

A lot of time had passed since Turil last saw an outburst from Seris who usually kept his feelings and intentions a secret. Either the captain was relaxing his formerly restrained state or the stress of recent events had caught up with him. In either case, Turil empathized with Seris. "In bringing to bear the point," Turil continued, "the Firestar has typically demonstrated mastery at a degree far short of what we know he is capable of. Whether this is by choice or limitation, we do not know, but while in an impassive state, he shows himself vulnerable to the same weaknesses as the rest of us. Mind you, he has been captured twice and was nearly killed multiple times."

General Chorus sighed. "So what, General Turil?"

"So the boy is not the imminently dangerous and near invincible monster that you make him out to be. He has his limitations, his weaknesses, and his faults. Even you must admit he has not been able to so much as heat a glass of water with his bonds."

"That is why he is bound in the first place."

"And without practice, his skills will fall into disrepair. It is for reasons like this that the Elders should at least consider the Firestar's release from his needless restraints."

"Are you finished?" Elder Tiberius asked.

"I have said my peace," Turil answered. He returned to his seat.

"General Chorus. It is now your turn to speak."

General Chorus stood to his feet and took his position before the

Council of Elders and Generals. Turil and Seris were careful to examine his state and his choice of words while Talim and Lon, listening just outside the door, listened for signs and moments of weakness. Chorus addressed the council and spoke. "General Turil and I are the last of the High Generals to survive not only the entire term of the Magic War but also the most recent attack by this new threat of Shadow Casters. We both have witnessed many things, some of which I dare not speak on. It thus pains me to so strongly disagree with this longstanding ally in arms. I have seen no greater threat, no greater danger, than the ones which remain hidden in one's own camp. The traitor, the spy, and the undisciplined soldier are three agents who can bring down an entire unit. Perhaps Turil has had the great fortune of consistently meeting people he can trust. I, however, have not, but I have learned from my errors in judgment. I can say now, with great confidence, that it is easy for me to spot men of questionable commitment, and I have found the Firestar to be of such a kind. His place of origin is unknown. He will not speak of it and refuses to answer any and all questions related to it or of any time before his arrival here. He shares no sense of national pride. He bears the scripts of Saline magic and yet pays no homage to the god of this force. He instead chooses to remain associated with a foreign and unknown god. He keeps himself apart from the customs of our people. He even keeps himself separated from the very ideals by which our nation was formed. He is by all means a stranger to us even after two hundred years of service."

"Isn't it unfair to make such assessments about his character?" Turil questioned. "Particularly when the boy is not here to defend himself?"

"I believe these are fair and well-documented assessments drawn from those who served beside him."

"I'm aware of those records, and the men in question had an

unfavorable predisposition to foreigners, particularly those whose skin tones and physical features bore similarity to people from the Hollow Realm."

"The Hollow Realm and its hunters were the deadliest enemies of the Outer Realms. The men of those reports lost close friends to them. Could you blame them?"

"For the mistreatment of a brother in arms, I could. Yes."

"But the Firestar is not and has never been a brother to those he served with. He was merely an agent of the mission. His concern was not with the needs or survival of the nation and its people. He shared no discernible love for the realm or its inhabitants. No, he only composed himself as a soldier of the task, and when it was done, he would wait for the next one. He was not moved by the same ideals that motivated the rest of those who served. He moved only on the whim of those who commanded him and with a few notable exceptions. Captain Seris has stated himself, just now, that the Firestar's motivations were, in large part, selfish by nature. Such selfishness does no good among the military forces of any realm. For it to reside in the most powerful and destructive figure of our time is especially worrisome. Whatever the boy's…humanity, whatever his reasons, the fact still remains that he has shown and even stated that he owes no allegiance to anyone save himself and perhaps his captain."

Turil sighed and leaned back in his seat as the newer generals whispered among themselves.

"Now, we know nothing of his ambitions. He's stated that he has none, but life and war have funny ways of changing people's minds. I understand he's suffered a significant loss lately."

"Her name was Saria," Turil stated.

Chorus nodded. "Need I remind anyone here what the pain of loss can do to a man? Suppose the Firestar comes to the conclusion that her loss was not only the blame of the Shadow Casters but of this council? What if he comes to think of us generals and the High Elders as culpable accessories to her destruction? What then?"

"You talk again of speculation."

"But it is a viable speculation. Seris says he has fought in part for acceptance but has not received it. When a man feels rejected by the world, he comes to one of three decisions. To reject the world and live in isolation, to remain in the world as an agent of change, by whatever motivation and emotion drives him towards that change, or to simply fade away and die. I have yet to see him dig his own grave. I have seen that he keeps to himself, and I fear a dreadful fear that he may attempt a change which only he is capable of. A single moment, a single loss, is all that stands between our continued survival as a nation and destruction. We have no way of knowing how and when this event may occur, and given recent events, it seems a sure thing to happen. We as a people and a nation do not believe in leaving things to chance. The Firestar, his ambitions, and what possible courses of action he may choose to take, based on his history, is not something we should leave to chance either, not when the health and survival of the nation depend on his choice."

"Are you finished, General?" Elder Tiberius asked.

"I have said my peace," and Chorus took his seat.

"Is there anything else anyone would like to add?" There were whispers in the room but no definitive statements. "Very well. Then I would like to announce that these deliberations will soon be coming to a close. There will be two more of these meetings held. The first at an hour much like the one held tonight and another earlier in the day so the decision may be heard by the people. Is this understood?" The room acknowledged the decision, and the Elder responded, "Then this meeting is adjourned. Dismissed."

Turil and Seris filed out of the room and met with Lon and Talim.

"Their will is to condemn him," Talim stated. "The deliberations are a farce which they have only entertained to lull the Firestar into a false sense of security."

"Then my suggestion is working," Lon said. "By lowering expectations of his strengths and raising awareness of his weaknesses, they have entered into their own false sense of security."

"How is this working?" Turil asked. "The boy remains partially defenseless in an isolated portion of the city where he remains vulnerable to attack, and we only have two weeks left to change a decision the Elders have already made."

"Yes, but they are speculating on weaknesses the Firestar does not actually have."

"What do you mean?"

"I have given Darrio what he needs," Seris answered.

Turil at first did not understand what Seris meant, but as the realization of what he just heard dawned on him, his eyes widened. "Seris. Are you serious?"

Seris nodded. "It is a minor key and only for the second reinforcing set. I have advised him not to use it until absolutely necessary." The restraints created by Salia's artisans were scripted in such a manner as to require a set of three key phrases before removal. The first phrase, known as the minor key, stopped the first level of the scripts from working. The second, referred to as the major key, removed the second level, and the final key removed the effects of the third. These keys had to be spoken in a certain tonal range to work, and their details were known only to the artisans who crafted them. They would often record such information in a document held on their person, but the artisan responsible for Darrio's restraints had only committed them to memory.

Turil lowered the volume of his voice. "Why did you give the boy a key phrase to one his own restraints? It is not yet time for that."

"What precedents have I made in regards to Darrio that you are so surprised, Turil? Did you really believe I would allow him to remain here without means of defense? General Chorus was right to say we are a people who do not leave things to chance. I am especially so."

"And when did you do this?"

"The night he reentered the city."

"That was reckless of you, Seris."

Seris shook his head. "I did so with understanding, Turil. My judgment is sound."

Talim interrupted. "General. Someone approaches."

Turil turned to see a lone caster approaching in anger. "What do you want, soldier?"

"Traitor!" the man answered, and he fired a pointed bolt of flame without warning.

Seris interceded with a forceful dissipation of the bolt which swirled and scattered before reaching Turil's position. Seris then extended his hand just as the soldier turned to flee. At once, the caster was seized with rigidity in his muscles, and his heart was clutched by a combination of restoration and manipulation magic. This combination of the two schools allowed for direct control of another person and whatever area the user was focused on without regard for the person's will. It was also a difficult combination to employ and used to lesser effect by clerics and doctors. It had proven too difficult, and therefore impractical, to put into military use. Seris, however, employed it often enough for it to be recognized as one of his signature techniques.

Seris held the caster with cold indifference for his life. The captive struggled to breathe, and his face turned blue. When Turil pleaded for Seris to let the man go, Seris only turned to face the general. At that moment, Turil saw in his old friend's eyes a fierce protectiveness that had spurred the action. He again requested that Seris release the man, and Seris complied. The body fell to the ground.

As Turil examined it, Seris said, "He is alive. I did not kill him."

The caster was a captain, and Turil waved Talim over and had him carry the man to the nearest clinic. He was to be examined and then imprisoned for treason. Turil then answered Seris by saying, "But you nearly did so."

"It would have been lawful."

"But would it have been right?"

"Lon?"

"Yes, sir?" Lon replied.

"We are finished here. Please return."

"Yes, sir."

After Lon was gone, Seris sighed. "I did not want to see you hurt."

"And I see that you were only trying to protect me, but…Seris. I fear you have not been asking yourself these kinds of questions lately. I know we have spoken of this before, but the company you keep, they have already changed you. You no longer seem to know right from wrong, and it was you who first guided me in this."

"I have not lost this sense, Turil."

"Then it has changed into something I no longer recognize."

"And what do you see, Turil? What do you see in me?"

"What do I see?" Turil repeated as he crossed his arms. "I see an old friend who has lost his way, who has let his heart for change and goodwill be turned against him. I see a man who has become too attached to his subjects, a man who has allowed his connections to cloud his better judgment."

"You think my judgment is unsound."

"More your methods, but I remember what you've told me. I remember that this has always been your greatest fear." Seris was silent and did not respond, but Turil continued. "What troubles the judgment of Seris troubles me. I know by the look of you that whatever plots you have schemed weigh heavily upon your shoulders. I will ask you again, Seris, to ease this burden. Tell me what you are doing. To what end are your intentions taking you? What are you seeking? What do you want?"

"I have already told you what I want, Turil."

"Then repeat it to me."

"Order," Seris replied. "That is the end of my devices. That is the goal of my schemes. Order. This is what I seek."

Turil was quiet after Seris said this, and a shadow of possible meaning entered his mind. He responded slowly, "And of what kind, Seris?" Seris did not answer immediately, but in the short span of time which passed between Turil's question and the response, Turil saw another spark ignite behind Seris' eyes.

Seris answered, "Do not ask me that question again."

"Will you plot against me also?"

"I will try to protect you, but do not interfere, and do not pursue me in this. I will not speak on this matter again."

"Very well, but if I see that your schemes move us towards objectionable places, know that I will not hesitate to oppose you."

The two examined each other for weaknesses in resolve but none could be found. The spark in Seris' eyes faded, and the two relaxed. "We still have work to do. I will see you again tomorrow."

Turil nodded, and the two parted ways.

Eloi returned to Ambrosia the following day, and Talim was the first to greet him. "You have been gone too long, my friend! Look." Talim pointed to the site of the new Hall of Order. The artisans had completed construction and were in the process of completing the detail work which included the placement of scripts. "It will not be the same as it was, but the artisans say it will be better. We will be returning to it in a few days."

"It is bigger," Eloi remarked.

Talim nodded. "I do not know why, but why is the mystery of artisans. I assume your mission was a success."

Eloi nodded. "Where is Seris? I must tell him what I know."

"I believe he is with the Firestar at the moment. You will find them in the northeastern corner."

"Thank you, Talim."

Seris was indeed with Darrio and spoke with him at length about the progression of Lon's plan and the decision of the Elders. "Can't say I'm surprised," Darrio replied.

"Have you used the key I gave you?"

Darrio produced a spark of flame as a quick demonstration so as not to draw attention. "There was this party of self-righteous foreign idiots who came by and thought it'd be a good idea to take me out."

"You fought them inside the city?"

Darrio shook his head. "No. It was in the fields west of the city, and it was pretty late. They just walked up to me, said something I couldn't understand because I don't speak the damn language, and when I tried to answer, they attacked me."

"And they were strong enough to require the use of your key?"

"They're lucky they survived, but it looks like word is getting into the Outer Realms about what's happening to me. If foreigners are sneaking through the border just to get a crack at me then what's going to happen when the Elders are done with me?"

"I don't know."

"Well, I'm not going to lay down and die just so the Elders can feel like they're doing the nation some good. I said I'm not a threat, and I'm not. Why can't they leave me alone?"

"They're afraid, and fear drives men to do foolish things."

Darrio crossed his arms. "This whole thing is just stupid." As Darrio glanced to the side, he spotted Eloi watching them from a short distance away.

Seris traced Darrio's line of sight to the standing shade and told Eloi to come closer. "What have you learned?"

"The Water Bearers have been ordered by their master to gather. They are planning to destroy the realm."

"Where?" Darrio asked. "Where are they gathering?" The haste of his question drew Seris' attention, but Seris did not respond.

"They will make camp in a valley north of here. The master of water will be there to give them their duties, and they will spread to all locations within the realm. After this, they intend to strike simultaneously on a predetermined day. Their gathering is in three weeks."

Darrio returned his attention to Seris. "They have to let me go."

Seris looked back at Darrio knowing his eager intention was to avenge Saria's death. "Would you destroy them, Darrio?"

Darrio narrowed his eyes. "Every last one."

Seris paused before responding. "Then I will tell Turil of this and urge him to wait until the next deliberation before informing the Elders."

"Why?"

"I do not believe the Elders would be willing to release you fully even with this knowledge. We will wait for Lon's plot to come to greater fruition."

"I hope…I mean, you know what you're doing, right?"

Seris nodded and turned to Eloi again. "Did you happen to see Abaddon during your gathering?"

Eloi blinked twice but replied, "He is working."

"Then rest."

Eloi faced Darrio who did not understand the reason for the attention nor the following statement. "I am sorry, Firestar."

"Sorry for what?"

Eloi did not answer. He instead turned and left to find his

temporary quarters in compliance with Seris' order. When he was gone, Darrio shook his head. "He still bugs me."

"Leave him be. I must go. Be safe, Darrio."

"I will." After Seris left, Darrio contemplated what he would do to the enemy if given the chance, and his anger began to get the best of him. He stopped to clear his mind and pace his breathing. Darrio abhorred the loss of control taken by the desire of his state limit. Whenever it occurred, he could feel himself being pushed aside as a familiar but dark persona took hold. He saw it as a separate but conjoined entity that was given no formal reference by anyone around him. He thus had no definitive name for it. It was a part of him, and yet it was not him. Darrio then remembered Abaddon's words and considered taking control of this other nature to suit his purposes, but a familiar voice in his heart said, "No."

"I thought you hated me," Darrio said aloud, but the intentions of the voice continued to resonate through Darrio's being for a time. Whatever this other nature was, it was too dangerous of a thing to tamper with. To attempt control of it would prove to be exceedingly costly. "Fine," Darrio mumbled. "Fine. I won't touch it." The resonance within Darrio's spirit ceased, and Darrio grew sad. "But I still don't understand."

Lon's plan progressed over the following days as Talim played terrible dreams of the Firestar inside the minds of General Chorus, Captain Mako, and other key officers as they slept. These nightmares consisted of Darrio laying waste to Ambrosia's citizenry while simultaneously depicting the Elder's approval in the background. The dreamers were made helpless to do anything about the destruction. Fear concerning the Elder's final decision rapidly spread through Chorus' followers. Some raised questions of loyalty against any and all who appeared the least bit sympathetic to the Firestar. "He's a monster," the whispers went. "He'll destroy us all if the Elders free him." Calmer minds seceded themselves from the increasingly radical camp of General Chorus, and some were harassed as traitors. Lon rewarded their courage by seeding their dreams with reassuring suggestions of Turil's trustworthiness and the coming times. Thus, when they complained to the Elders, they also mentioned Turil's name with praise. Turil, however, was unaware any of this was happening.

The day before the first of the final two deliberations, some of those who defected approached Turil to tell him of what was happening. "They're going mad over there," an adept captain said in confidence. "I mean, I don't like the idea of leaving the Firestar to his own devices either, but I know the Shades order things differently. Hell, the idea of a loose Firestar still scares the hell out of me. That delusion burned an image in my mind so bad that I can't even think straight when I look at him."

"But their talks are crossing into the open realms of rebellion," said an accompanying caster general.

"Rebellion?" Turil inquired.

The captain nodded. "If the Elders decide unfavorably, there are rumors that some will go to the Firestar and kill the boy themselves."

"That would be…most unwise."

"I'll say. The last general in history to cross a High Elder was demoted to the lowest rank and sent to the front lines to die a horrible death. Now there's a lot to be said about this bunch of Elders but soft and easy isn't one of them."

"My fear," the caster general said, "concerns High Elder Tiberius. I remember how he talked about certain issues during the war. Do you think he is above assassinating citizens of the realm he deems to be a threat?"

The adept captain shrugged. "What do you think, General Turil?"

Turil was hesitant to answer. "I wouldn't know," he lied.

"Well, if he isn't, General Chorus and Captain Mako are going to have to watch their backs. The Firestar, monster or not, isn't worth getting killed over."

"Thank you for alerting me to this."

"No problem, General. As I said, I was concerned and thought you should know."

"As was I," the caster general said.

Turil nodded, and Lon's sinister smile entered his mind. "I'm sure it will be sorted out soon." Shortly after the discussion had taken place, Turil went in search of Seris. He could not be absolutely certain the escalation in fear was Lon's doing, but he knew Seris would be the one to know. There did not seem to be an alternative. The fact that he could see this, however, upset him as insulting. If Seris truly intended something objectionable from the beginning, Turil thought the least he could do was make sure it was clever enough to where Turil could not detect it. He found the captain sitting in his new office in the rebuilt Hall of Order. Turil did not bother to knock. "Seris."

Seris peered up from his paperwork. He was annoyed at having been disturbed. "What is it, Turil?"

"Have you heard of what is happening in the opposing camp?"

"I have."

"Have you any idea why this is happening?"

Seris pulled back from his work. "What are you accusing me of, Turil?"

"The situation seems to bear the mark of Lon upon it, and I know he does nothing without your prior knowledge or else you would have disciplined him already. I know you can see through his methods. I know you can. Your mind is above his."

"What is your point?"

Seris did not appear to be avoiding blame, and this made Turil all the more upset. "My point is that these actions are going too far, and you know it. We spoke of strategically tactful diplomacy, and I gave both of you the benefit of the doubt that this is what we were practicing."

"Then you were once again showing your recklessness, Turil. I told you not to trust me."

Turil slammed his palms to the desk. "Seris! This isn't a game or some high concept we are talking about! People are likely to die as a result of this. You know the temperament of Elder Tiberius. Do you now seek blood from your schemes? Is this something you really want to bear again?"

Turil's words struck a nerve with the captain, and Seris narrowed his eyes. "What did you say to me, Turil?"

"Did you think I would remain silent forever? You made one mistake, Seris. One mistake out of a hundred successful schemes! I know you've been doubting your judgment ever since then, and I know you've suffered silently ever since that day. You are now set to intentionally repeat the results of that mistake, so I am asking you now to tell Lon to stop his meddling!"

Seris hardened his tone and replied, "It is too late, Turil."

"What do you mean, too late? Do you think I will not tell the Elders what you're doing? Of what you've done?"

"You would be jeopardizing your position if you did so."

Turil pulled back. "Seris. I do not know what you are thinking or what you meant by that statement, and know that I would continue to defend the Firestar, but I will not do so like this. I am now ordering you to stop."

"I will not."

"You would continue in this foolishness?"

"Foolishness? You think so little of me now that you call my actions foolish?"

"What else is there to say of them, Seris?"

Seris stood to his feet. "Know this of my foolishness, Turil. When war is waged, there are few survivors. Even fewer go unchanged after touching its crest. I have seen what war and disorder has done and what it will continue to do so long as it exists among men."

"And yet there has always been and there will always be war, Seris. It is not something to be tried out in thought and theory. War and conflict is unavoidable!"

Seris shook his head. "It is not unavoidable, but it can only be deterred with a sufficient amount of violence."

"And what war do you hope to avoid by this scheme?" Turil saw another spark appear in Seris' eye, but he could not be certain what it pertained to. "Do not give me that look."

"Listen to me, Turil. I do not want you involved in what I have in mind. I do not want you to come to any harm."

"If that is what you seek then cease what you are doing."

"It is not that simple."

"Damn it, Seris! These infernal complications of yours will be the death of you!"

Seris thought ahead in the context of Turil's words and Abaddon's also when he said, "The boy will be a hindrance to you." He also remembered his response to the charge. "Listen to me, Turil," Seris said. "We must put our differences aside at the moment."

"This isn't a matter of differences."

"But there is something more important which you must know. I have learned of the Shadow Caster's latest movement. The Water Bearers, their entire number in the realm, will be gathering in the north in a valley not far from here. From there, they intend to spread throughout the region."

"To what end?"

"To coordinate a last and surprising motion that will destroy all we have sought to protect including the order we have only just gained since the war ended."

"And how did you come to learn of all this?"

"Eloi returned and reported it to me."

"Then why did you not tell me?"

"I was in the middle of preparing my report when you barged through my—."

"Sooner, Seris! Why did you not tell me sooner?"

"Because you would have rashly called for an emergency meeting to alert the Elders who, given enough time to prepare, would still condemn Darrio and risk facing the Shadow Casters with insufficient forces. We do not know their numbers, Turil, and they are armed with dark magic that no one, save Darrio, has faced in open combat. This is not the time to take unnecessary risks on impractical notions of right and wrong. I will not tell Lon to stop, and I will allow his plan to continue until the Elder's decision is assured in our favor."

Turil was stunned and hesitant to speak. After a moment of quiet contemplation, he asked, "Then what is this all about, Seris? If it isn't about theory, the one mistake, the Shadow Casters, or even the High Elders, then that only leaves…the boy?"

Seris returned to his seat. "You are as blind as you are reckless, Turil."

"You mean to tell me that you would risk plunging the entire realm into chaos for the life and safety of the boy?"

"For what this world has done to him, I would scheme no other scheme. I would even damn it twice to see it remade."

Turil had nothing else to say as there were no more arguments to be made. He instead turned and silently left Seris' office. The two would not speak to each other informally for many weeks.

The following day, deliberations continued as scheduled though Chorus spoke with greater passion than before. He vigorously urged the Elders against releasing the Firestar, and Turil defended his position though with less vigor than before. The Elders once again closed the meeting by saying they were still considering both sides, but Turil could see on their faces that the decision was already made.

Two days before the Elder's announcement, Turil arranged to speak with Elder Tiberius on the upper level of the Grand Hall. The Elder was once again gazing out of the window, and Turil was struck by a sense of familiarity with the moment. The Elder spoke. "How long has it been since last you've requested such a talk?"

"I do not remember. So much has happened since then."

"Indeed. And what did you wish to discuss with me, General? I assume it has something to do with the Firestar and Captain Seris."

"Less so with the Firestar and more with Captain Seris, sir."

"Go on."

Turil sighed as he considered for the final time what he was doing and its likely potential consequences. When he finished, Turil steeled himself and opened his mouth to speak, "Captain Seris has betrayed us all."

Tiberius paused but did not change his facing. "Do explain."

"He is employing his subordinates, Lon and Talim, into driving General Chorus, Captain Mako, and those allied with them into a state of madness."

"And why would he do that?"

"To ensure your favor with their side is withdrawn so the Firestar may be freed." Tiberius chuckled, but Turil assumed it was simply the Elder's way of coping with the situation. It had not been the first time. "He has used me in this as well, I'm afraid. I'm ashamed of my part, but I wish to make it right."

"Have a seat, General." Turil sat and maintained his facing of the Elder. "And what else have you learned?"

"I know Seris has attained the keys to the Firestar's bonds and has been waiting for the opportunity to release them. I know his obsession…his love for the boy has irrevocably clouded his judgment.

He tells me the Shadow Casters are preparing another attack, and on this, I believe he is telling the truth, but he times and controls the release of such information for his own purposes, all to protect the boy." The Elder chuckled again, but this time, Turil saw no reason for laughter. "I'm sorry, sir, but did I just say something funny?"

"You have, Turil, but in your way, you just haven't realized it yet."

"Then do not let the joke be at my expense. Tell me. Why did you laugh?"

Elder Tiberius turned and greeted General Turil with a smile. "As it is, quite frankly, I have more reasons to trust Captain Seris than I have to trust you."

"Excuse me?"

"Everyone knows of his attachment to the Firestar. He's made few strides in trying to hide this, but he has not let this attachment cloud his judgment to the severity of which you are speaking."

"But how can you know this? What has he said to you?"

"Do you remember the Firestar's first trial after the city was shaken and we were beset by the hail of fire and ice? Seris told us of the Firestar's retention with magic shortly before that event occurred. He also told us of his ill feelings towards the council and in fact, suggested to us that we keep a reserve of men specifically trained to combat the Firestar should the need arise. You, on the other hand, have gone behind the back of this council to engage with minor and distant threats and endeavored to train our sights away from the more imminent matters. Even Seris has agreed with us in secret that the Shadow Caster's threat to the realm is secondary when cast in the light of Darrio's combination of power and discontent."

"Seris said this? Captain Seris?"

"There is only one man with that name to which we are both referring, General. This call to free the Firestar was your idea, and now you come to me and tell me his captain's judgment is so severely impaired as to connect his name with treason? Have you thought about this accusation?"

Turil had not, and he had forgotten what this would have said about Darrio given their close association.

"Did you know that Seris arranged a meeting with me only yesterday and told me of General Chorus' mad intentions to revolt in violence when we announce our temporary release of the Firestar?"

"Release?" Turil repeated, and he shook his head with disbelief. "I thought you decided not to do so."

"And who gave you insight into our decision, General? It seems to me that if anyone's judgment has been impaired, it is yours."

Turil fell back in his seat, and his mind spun with a dizzying recollection of all that occurred since the war. Every word he received from Seris raced through his mind to make deposits of once-hidden meanings. Every event was recalled and supplemented by the details given to him by Elder Tiberius. All that he could remember was at once brought to mind, all that he understood torn apart, and when the debris of details coalesced in Turil's mind, it painted a singular and frightening image. In it, he saw Seris focusing the Elder's attention on Darrio and reassuring them of his commitment to the realm, but behind them stood the shadow of the Firestar whose arm was poised to destroy them with fire. "It's a trap," he mumbled. "He intends to… he lied to me."

Elder Tiberius tried to regain Turil's attention, but the call was lost. Turil was consumed by his thoughts, and his mind could not help but settle on the terrible consequences he was sure to see from Seris' actions. He had tried to see, to know what Seris was planning behind the glimmer in his eye, but Turil's understanding and strength failed him. Fear concerning the future began to rise within him, and Turil quickly set himself to his breathing exercises. The Elder tried again. "General Turil."

Turil leaned forward and shut his eyes to hide the developing emergence of his state limit. He placed his hands upon his head, his breathing slowed, and when he felt he had gained sufficient control of his senses, he muttered, "It is not over. There is still time."

"General!"

Turil looked up. "You said you will release the Firestar. Has Seris told you about the Shadow Caster's plot?"

"He has."

"And what will you do?"

"We will go and see them destroyed by the Firestar."

"Personally?"

"Is this a problem?"

"Why? Your presence is unnecessary."

"That is none of your concern."

"Then allow me and my men to come with you."

Tiberius laughed. "We are not taking you with us. You and your men are to remain here, in the city, in case of another attack."

"Did Seris recommend this also?"

"He did, actually. He's concerned about you, and quite frankly, so am I at the moment. You need rest, General, and time to clear these fanciful depictions of treason from your mind."

"Then may I make a request?"

Tiberius sighed. "What is it?"

"I ask you. Please. Do not attack the Firestar."

"I beg your pardon?"

"He is not the one you should be worried about. He is no threat to you so long as you do not provoke him."

"And I am to take your assessment of the Firestar over Seris', the one who has been with the boy since the beginning?"

"I know it sounds like madness, and having considered only what you've seen in this matter, I know I may appear…unhinged, but I am telling you the truth. I place my collective judgment as a High General upon this. The Firestar is not your enemy. Please, do not do what I think, and perhaps Seris knows, you are going to do."

"I will make no promises, General. At the Shadow Caster's destruction, we will see what the Firestar is capable of, and we will make our final judgment then," but this was exactly what Turil feared most. "You are dismissed, General Turil. Get some rest."

Turil left the chamber a shaken man, and he spent the rest of the day in relative isolation as he came to grips with what he had just learned. There was a time he remembered when Seris' loyalties were unquestioned, where accusations of ambition would have enraged Turil. Then, however, as Turil considered matters, it seemed as if fate had something else in mind. The following day, he happened to pass by Seris on his way to a routine check, and his heart was seized with anguish. Turil's eyes waned, and Seris could see the pain of betrayal evident in them. He looked away, and the two did not speak a word to each other.

On the day of the last deliberation, General Chorus, Captain Mako, and two hundred of their closest followers stood in wait outside of the Grand Hall. General Turil was also present and was assisted by a company of four hundred shades, casters, and adepts. The two faced each other, and Chorus spoke. "I've received word on the exceedingly foolish inclinations of the High Elders."

"No doubt brought to you by the onset of ominous dreams and copious whispers," Turil responded. His tone was flat and unenthused. "Though your madness was incited by another, it stemmed from the preexisting condition of your own heart and mind. It remains to be seen what he will gain from this, but I will stop him where I can."

"And you speak to me of madness. Do you even know what you are talking about?"

"Unfortunately, I do." The door swung open, and the greeter

welcomed all of the officers. "Now to see to the end of these things."

Once inside, the meeting began as usual, and Chorus made several statements concerning the danger of a released Firestar and attempted to reassure the Elders that, even in light of the new plot by the Shadow Casters, Salia's forces would be enough to eliminate the threat. His passion resonated with everyone who was already in accord with him, but it wore on the patience of those who were not. General Chorus was long-winded, and it was apparent that he was stalling for time. Elder Judas cut him off the moment the general started to repeat himself. When he finished, Elder Tiberius turned to Turil for his closing statements, but Turil declined to comment.

"You have nothing to say?" the Elder asked.

"I have said my peace," Turil answered. "There is nothing more to be said."

"Then after hearing both arguments and considering all, and most importantly, the most recent, of circumstances, this council has decided to release the Firestar from his bonds and reinstate his privileges with magic." A collective groan was heard from the camp of Chorus while a sigh of relief stemmed from Turil's side, but after this, there was tension. Both sides knew the result of the decision was sure to result in violence that day, but the question of who would strike first was on everyone's mind.

The Elder continued, "It will not be done here, however. The Firestar will only be released upon encountering the Shadow Caster's camp in the short time to follow, and it will be a tentative release. This council will be overseeing the affair personally."

"This is ridiculous!" Chorus roared. "We stand on the cusp of destruction, and you risk our existence on the supposed goodwill of that destroyer?"

"And what will you do, General Chorus?" Turil asked.

Chorus glared at Turil but did not answer. Instead, he and his men angrily filed out of the room.

"General Turil," Tiberius said.

"Yes?"

"General Chorus, Captain Mako, and the rest by virtue of being a military body make themselves traitors and a serious threat to the realm by defying this council. Follow them, and do what you must." It was then that the true intent of Lon's plot came to fruition. The end result of his schemes, fully sanctioned and furthered by Seris, was the destruction of Darrio's enemies with the Elder's blessing. A reduction in capable military personnel with the heart and ambition to face the Firestar meant Darrio's safety would be guaranteed further. Seris also stood to face less opposition from those who stood against him as a result of their close affiliation. When Turil saw this, he was saddened, and his men left to follow after Chorus.

Darrio, in the meantime, stood in wait on the fields just east of the city. He was surrounded by shades, adepts, and casters. Seris was with him as were the others of his unit with the exception of Abaddon who had yet to return. Despite this, Darrio was despondent, and Seris asked him, "What's wrong?"

"To be honest? I feel useless."

"Why?"

"Because I need all these people to defend me when I should be able to defend myself. Half of them don't even want to be here. I can tell just by looking at them."

"You cannot always rely on your own strength, Darrio."

"Why not?" Darrio mumbled. "Everyone else seems to."

Seris shushed him, and Eloi spotted someone approaching from the south. "It is Abaddon," he stated.

All of Seris' shades took notice except for Darrio who only rolled his eyes at the news. When Abaddon drew near the camp, Talim hailed him. "It does not surprise me that you have survived since you are full of so many secrets, but where have you been all of these days?"

"I was busy, Talim." Abaddon then turned his attention to Seris. "Has Eloi told you of the water clan's motions?"

"He has," Seris replied.

"Then what is happening? Why are you still here?" No sooner had Abaddon asked the question did Chrous and his men cautiously approach the camp. "Will no one speak?"

"They have come to take Firestar," Eloi answered.

Abaddon looked at Darrio who only looked back in return. "Don't look at me like that," Darrio said. "It's not my fault. Not this time."

General Chorus spoke. "Hand over the Firestar so we may strike him down while we are still able."

"That would not be in compliance with the Elder's directives," Lon answered.

"They've ordered him to dance," Tam said. "They also said if you come to remove him that we are allowed to eliminate you. Have you come to remove the Firestar? Please say yes."

"Tam," Seris warned.

Chorus' men drew their weapons, and everyone prepared themselves for battle, but Chorus raised his arm to ease the tensions. "We did not come here for violence. We do not want a struggle. All we want is the Firestar."

"The answer is no," Turil said as he approached from behind with his men. "And do what is right for those who follow you, General. You are surrounded."

"The Elders are sending this nation to its death, and I am to sit idly by and accept it?"

"If not, then the wisest thing to do would be to bide your time."

"We do not have the luxury of time, Turil. If the Firestar is victorious, he will surely turn upon us. And even if he is not and he dies in battle, I am not willing to take that risk."

"You would take these men with you to destruction."

"They volunteer of their own free will."

Turil shifted his attention to Captain Mako and the others. "This is your last chance to surrender. If you persist, the Elders have ordered us to destroy you. Give up this reckless charge or perish." There was no response, but there were many exchanged glances. "I take no pleasure in this. Will none of you concede? Answer now."

"I will concede," said a caster from Mako's ranks.

"So will I!" said another, and there were seven men who withdrew and behaved as if scales had been pulled from their eyes. Three of them were shades, two were adepts, and two were casters. These men threw their weapons to the ground and moved away from those who remained. Turil ordered those men to their homes. Those who stayed with General Chorus, however, were resolute.

"Is that all?"

"You have damned us all," Chorus remarked.

Turil drew his sword in response. "I'm sorry," he said, and the two parties engaged.

Most of the shades of both parties fanned out to the perimeter while the adepts fought near the center. Casters supplemented the combat, and arcs of fire and lightning streamed from all sides. Darrio was pushed to the rear of Seris' camp since he was the target and most vulnerable to attacks by magic. Despite this, he was still met in combat by the occasional shade who survived his leap into the midst of the Firestar's circle of protection. Darrio fared well enough during these moments, and the limited release of his bonds due to the use of the first key allowed him to fight with greater efficiency. He was still not battling at full capacity, however, and he felt as if his arsenal of techniques was limited. Even so, isolation in the western forest where he continued to practice his motions had trained him well for such conditions. The battleground was turned over, burned, and frozen in places as a result of the conflict, and General Chorus, Captain Mako, and all those who followed them fell in combat. Darrio nearly fell as well due to the vigorous struggle of the enemy members who fought to reach and strike him, but with the aid of Seris' shades, Darrio was kept safe from lasting harm. He suffered only a single injury when an enemy caster pierced his left shoulder with a bolt of thunder, and Seris himself killed the man.

When the conflict was over, the wounded were quickly treated, and the dead were buried. Seris tended to Darrio, and Turil glanced at the two briefly before taking his men back into the city. The day ended in bloodshed, but no one was given time to mourn due to the preparations made to immediately disembark north.

The following morning Darrio was placed among a standing army led by General Hammond. Darrio detected something strange about the men, but when he questioned Seris about it, he was told not to worry. "But they're looking at me like they expect me to do something," Darrio said.

"Ignore them, and focus your energies on the task at hand."

The High Elders were the last to leave the city, and Turil took it upon himself to see them off, but as they were leaving, he drew Elder Tiberius aside for a final petition. "Have you considered what I asked of you?"

"Your worry is misplaced, General. You must learn to better trust the council."

"But the Firestar. If you will not give me your word then at least tell me you have seriously considered it."

Tiberius nodded. "Fine, General, fine. If it will make you feel better, I will even speak to the boy personally. I give you my word on this, but rest assured, whatever decision we make will be in the best interests of everyone, and once the dust has settled, there will be nothing left to worry about."

Turil was still far from satisfied, and worry remained evident on his face. "Very well," he said, "but if I sense trouble, I will come."

"General."

"I will not leave the city defenseless, but despite your punishment, I will come, and I will not apologize for it."

Tiberius smiled and shook his head. "Men like you are exactly what this nation needs. Expect word of our victory." Tiberius left to depart with the rest of the Elders, and the army moved north.

Turil returned to his office to gaze out of the open window. His bird feeder was without carriers, and he remained unsettled despite the calming breeze of the afternoon wind. There was no news to be gained from the day, and with little else to do, Turil set his body to menial and far-off tasks. He reviewed the status of stations throughout the city, examined equipment, settled complaints, prepared orders for his agents, and spoke with soldiers who expressed remorse about the previous day's event. When Turil rested his head that night, his mind wandered towards all of the potential consequences of all that he knew, and with the understanding of everything his mind's eye could see, his heart was filled with dread.

CHAPTER 15
Stillborn

SOFT TOUCHES OF wind passed over the dark boy's head, but the words from the native child in front of him pierced his heart like a knife. "So what? You think I care what you think? I still say you're weird."

The dark-skinned child was Darrio, and wrapped around his neck was a speaker's band. "No, I'm not."

"Yes, you are. You and your mom."

"Leave my mom alone!"

"You don't even know how to use magic! You and your mom. You're both weird."

Darrio punched the native boy and tackled his body to the dusty ground of the small village. "Shut up!" he cried as he pounded his fists against the older child. "Leave my mom alone!"

Several other boys in the vicinity saw this and came to assist the older native boy. Darrio was dragged off and kicked. "Take that you stupid foreigner!"

An arc of fire disrupted the scuffle as another man, one of the Base Elders of Aria, came and chastised the group. "Get off of him! Off! Away with you!" The children scattered, and Darrio was left bruised and angry. "Darrio," the man said as he knelt down to heal the wounds. "You mustn't let the other children anger you like that."

"It's not my fault. He made me."

"You were the one who threw the first punch."

Darrio's mother, Emelia, came running down the dusty road wearing a speaker's band around her neck as well. "Darrio? What happened to you?"

"He was in another fight," the elder answered.

Emelia examined her son and held him. "Why do you keep doing this to me? I tell you not to fight, and you keep fighting."

"They keep talking about you," Darrio replied.

"Emelia," the elder interjected. "You should reconsider allowing me to teach the child restoration. These scuffles are becoming more and more serious."

"No, Eros" she answered. "I said 'no more magic' after you gave us these bands, and I meant no more."

"Think of the boy."

"I am thinking of him," she said as she pressed Darrio's head to her bosom. "He is my responsibility, and I will take care of him."

"Mom," Darrio said through the muffled fabric. "I can't breath."

Emelia stood to her feet and took Darrio by the hand. "Stay with me, Darrio."

"Emelia," Eros pleaded. "Please. It is for his own good, especially if he is going to grow up and live in this region."

"No," Emelia said for the last time, and Darrio was led back to the small home at the edge of the village.

He looked back to find Elder Eros looking at him sadly, but as Darrio started to wake from this dream, a fire rose up and engulfed the scene. The silhouette of Emelia's burning form pressed itself against the flames and was coupled with her agonized screaming. In the foreground of the noise and scene of death was a faded image of Eros. Darrio was then kneeling on the ground in the dead of night, and his eyes were cast down. He was looking through his own tear-blurred vision, and the dusty road was illuminated by an orange glow behind him. In front of him was a dagger and the elder who stood only a short distance away. Darrio extended his small hand, took hold of the weapon, and lunged towards Eros. Darrio screamed, "I hate you!"

Darrio awoke with a start to find himself back in Salia's military camp. It was late, and the army had settled for the night. It would be two more days before they reached their destination. Talim was speaking with Eloi, and Seris was seated beside Darrio. "Is something wrong?" he asked.

"No," Darrio answered. "I just had a dream. It's nothing."

Seris peered over at Lon who took notice of Seris' glance and promptly defended himself by saying, "Not I."

"It was just a dream," Darrio repeated.

"And what did you dream about?" Seris asked.

"Nothing." Darrio stood to his feet. "I'm going to go stretch."

"Don't wander far."

"I won't." Darrio removed himself from the camp by several yards in a bid to get away from the weary eyes of its soldiers and commanders. He did not recognize any of them, and he overheard talk of their training being done in the fields away from the city. They seemed careful not to say too much around him. Darrio stretched his body, sat down in the grass, and peered into the heavens. After a long wait, which he used to settle himself, he whispered, "Why did you put me here?"

"To help people," reverberated in his heart.

Darrio was sure he heard from God since the voice was so familiar to his soul. He became uncertain, however, as he recounted his life's events. If God had placed him there for such a purpose, and He did not lie, then Darrio did not understand. He answered, "I'm not doing so well," and he started to become fearful.

"Am I interrupting something?" Elder Tiberius said behind him.

Darrio looked back and could not think of how else to address the Elder. "What do you want?" he asked nervously.

"I thought we might talk," he said as he gestured a hand to a spot in the grass beside Darrio. "May I?"

Darrio looked around, and many of the eyes from the camp were trained on him. The soldiers appeared ready to attack and defend at a moment's notice. "Do what you want," Darrio answered. He did not want to cross the Elder with a hostile army behind him.

"Do not mind them," Tiberius said as he took a seat. "They are edgy about what they may face in the coming days."

"They seem more worried about me than the Shadow Casters."

"They have been training away from the city for quite some time as a reserve unit. They have not seen the damages of the enemy."

"Why were they set aside?"

"For special occasions."

Darrio did not feel like pursuing the subject further since he did not feel the destination would be to his benefit. "Whatever."

"So, do you do this often?"

"What?"

"Sit here, alone, by yourself."

"It beats sitting in a crowd of people who don't even like me. And I just think better when I'm by myself."

"Why is that?"

"Less talking," Darrio replied, but in the following moment, he realized his callous error and looked back at the Elder to see what his response was. He was smiling. "I didn't mean...I mean. I'm not used to talking to people who, you know, actually want to talk to me."

"I understand. It was not long ago that you were on trial after all."

"Yeah," Darrio said as he turned away.

"So, you have said you have no ambition, no plans for the future. Is this still true?"

Darrio nodded.

"You have no dream for yourself?"

"I wanted to protect people, once, a long time ago. Just to help, you know? Now the whole world's just waiting for me to die, and all I want is for everybody to leave me alone. No friends, no enemies, no…kids. Just no one."

"I see. Such a life sounds empty, Firestar."

"It's Darrio," he protested. "My name is Darrio."

"Darrio then."

It was quiet between the two for a while, and as Darrio continued to gaze at the stars, he felt emboldened enough to ask a rather direct question. "Why do you want to kill me?"

The Elder paused. "What gave you that notion?"

"You sent me on dangerous missions while I was defenseless, you put me on trial, and Arthis said you were the ones who sent him after me. I may not say a whole lot about what I think and how I feel, but I'm not stupid, and I have a long memory, so if it's all the same to you, can we just cut the bullshit, please?"

Tiberius nodded. "Very well."

"Why do you want me dead?"

The Elder breathed deeply before answering. "As long as we are being honest with each other, I suppose it is because we fear you. Of what you will do, of what you will become, of what you can do to this realm."

"But I said I wasn't a threat to you. Seris said I wasn't a threat, and if Turil hasn't told you by now, I'll be disappointed."

"None of that matters, unfortunately. In the end, the only assessment that really matters to a man is his own. This world has more lives than just your own, and we must take theirs into consideration as well."

Darrio was quiet, and he closed his eyes. "You know, your assassin did something stupid before I killed him, and I took his attack personally because of it. Do you want to know what he did?"

The Elder glanced calmly at Darrio and asked, "What did he do?"

"He talked to me."

"And why did this bother you?"

"Because he wasn't attacking a target anymore. He was attacking me." Darrio then looked directly at Tiberius and stated, "I don't like it when people attack me."

Tiberius looked back. "Neither do I."

Darrio took a brief moment to examine the Elder. He was obviously not a man who could be easily intimidated, not that Darrio was trying, but there seemed to be a genuine desire to do what was right for the realm as well. Darrio could not tell whether or not this window of sincerity was real or not. He had been fooled before, and he did not wish to dwell on it. "I'm going back," he finally said.

"I'm glad we had this talk," Elder Tiberius said. "It was quite interesting."

Darrio did not respond, and he retook his place beside Seris.

"Yes," the Elder mumbled as he peered into the heavens. "Quite interesting indeed."

The army progressed forward over the course of the next two days and settled upon a wide land bridge that crossed between two plateaus. It was an unnatural structure that was erected to impede the progress of legionnaires during the Burning Realm's initial incursions into the territory before the war. There were many such structures dotting the region which gave the valley a maze-like quality. The Shadow Caster's camp was situated in the valley below, a little over a thousand in number, but they did not appear to be disturbed by the distant Saline presence. Instead, they signaled the army, and each side sent representatives of their leadership and strength. General Hammond was accompanied by Seris and Darrio while the clan of water sent Treos and two others. They met at the center of the expanse separating the two camps. General Hammond was the first to speak, "So you are the ones who have brought new misery to this nation."

"Yours was a miserable nation to begin with," Treos answered. "And this darkened figure must be the Firestar."

Darrio crossed his arms.

"Had I known who you were when you interrupted our gathering, I might have continued the chase."

"And if you couldn't tell by looking at me then you're an idiot," Darrio answered.

Hammond continued, "We are giving you this one chance to surrender. If you accept, we will take you whole as prisoners. If you do not, we will take only your bones and bury them."

"The wrath of Magnus is upon you, and our master has assured us of victory. On this day, you will be defeated and your nation brought to its knees where it belongs, the first of many to the judgment of Magnus. We have all assurances and no need to surrender."

"Then your grave has been made. You should prepare your men for death."

"As should you, General."

As the two parties parted ways, Darrio remarked on the formalities as a waste of time. "Why do we keep doing it?"

"These are the conventions," Hammond answered.

"You've been told several times," Seris continued.

Darrio huffed. "I still think it's stupid."

The two camps prepared for battle, but after everyone was checked for preparation, the Elders, Seris, and General Hammond turned to Darrio. "Are you ready to fight?" Tiberius asked.

Darrio looked back at them and asked, "What? Alone?"

"Yes."

"They're not coming?" and Seris shook his head in answer. "Then what are they here for?"

"To support you," Tiberius answered. "As the Firestar, surely you can handle them by yourself. You've handled even a hundred times their number."

"Those numbers didn't have dark magic."

"We did not give you this opportunity to redeem yourself lightly," Elder Judas stated. "If you will not fight in full, you will remain in your restraints."

"I can't believe this," Darrio said as he shook his head.

"Darrio," Seris said, and Darrio raised his eyes to his captain. "Remember what I told you. Do not give thought to what they will do to you. Think only of what you will do."

Darrio surveyed all of those standing before him and nodded. Seris then stepped forward and whispered the remaining keys into Darrio's ears. Darrio used what abilities with magic he had to safely slide down the steep embankment of the land bridge and proceeded forward. Seris then stated, "We shall do what we shall do."

The enemy camp of shadow casters stood at the ready, and barriers of darkness were made to encircle their formation. Darrio spoke the major key to his reinforcing restraints, and the second line of scripts that encircled them sparked to life and dimmed. He was still a great distance from the enemy, but from his palms, Darrio fired a single stream of flame that he maintained for the entire duration of its travel. When it met with the darkened obstruction, it dissipated. There was nothing to be felt by the enemy on the other side.

"What is he doing?" Elder Judas asked.

"He is testing them," Seris replied.

Darrio spoke the final key to his reinforcing bonds, and they promptly fell from his wrists to the ground. He lifted his hands and then fired two simultaneous streams of fire which were more powerful than his first and proved to be just as futile. Darrio then sent a shock through the earth to create a tremor beneath their formation, but the same line which stopped his burning streams caused the tremor to stop as well. Anything held and maintained by the power of magic simply fell apart upon contact with the darkness.

"It is not working," Elder Judas spoke again. "He must move

closer. Ranged attacks lose their strength at such distances."

"He knows this," Seris said. The Elder annoyed him.

When Darrio spoke the minor key to his original set of restraints, the air around him slowed, and the breeze of the wind was limited to a faint and gentle rustle. It seemed as if the earth had become quite content with his restraint and was no longer used to his original presence. Darrio initiated the next attack by spreading his arms further apart and firing two streams of opposing properties. One consisted of fire and the other of ice. The line of the two attacks arched outward and returned to intersect at the shadow caster's position. Each one hit opposing sides of the barrier which proved to be just as effective as the first. Darrio maintained the streams despite this and sent a burst of additional power through each one. The intensity carried through the twin lines and connected at the head where ice and fire met darkness. The effect, however, was minimal. A light breeze and a warm waft managed to sift to the other side, but it had no greater effect than to cool one of the shadow casters and warm another. Despite this, the enemy fortified their position and erected a second barrier of shadow beneath the first.

"This is futile," Judas commented.

"Be still," Seris said.

After Darrio spoke the major key to his bonds, the air and the winds became still. There was no draft, no waft, and no breeze to be felt by any living thing in the area. The world was captured by silence. Darrio then fired grand arcs of fire, ice, and lightning toward the enemy. He did this in rapid bursts and caused them to converge on all points of the barrier. The heavy rain of elements even maintained more of their original power despite the distance traveled, and they hurled themselves upon the enemy position as a thick hail of destruction. The shadow casters entrenched themselves and increased the effectiveness of both barriers. None of Darrio's attacks sifted through though he even caused the earth around them to buckle and bend. The shadow casters remained still, and their position was untouched. Darrio ceased and let his arms fall by his side.

Judas was astonished. "He just paralleled the combined destructive power of everyone present. Is this what you meant to describe in your reports?"

"No," Seris answered. "It is not."

Darrio recalled all that he could remember from his encounters with dark magic. The properties of the barrier, so far as he could see, were similar to the ones he had seen raised before. Like the shadow doubles created by Ashtoreth, it was a vaporous solid and likely fragile to the touch. To test this, Darrio raised a single stone in front of him and caused it to fly toward the height of the barriers at great speed. When it reached its destination, the stone passed through, and Darrio was no longer able to control it. Natural forces, however, continued to see the object arc back to the ground where it landed on the other side of the enemy camp.

"He is no fool," Treos commented, and he ordered his men to raise an additional barrier of hardened stone beneath the second layer of darkness. It was done and encircled the shadow casters like a shell. It was made porous and full of holes so they could see everything Darrio was doing, and as an extra precaution, a second layer was raised, and it was hardened along with the first. There was no shortage of earth to be found, and Treos was confident that Salia's Firestar had failed.

"Bastards," Darrio mumbled, but he then settled on his approach and sighed with resolution. As far as he was concerned, there was nothing to stop him from achieving his goal. The shadow casters had achieved nothing by erecting the barrier except to establish the final dimensions of their grave.

Judas, however, threw up his arms in defeat. "This is hopeless!

They have grounded themselves and reinforced their position. All they lack is the ability to move, and should they learn even this, then what shall we do?"

"Be quiet," Seris said.

"Excuse me?"

"I said be quiet. Darrio is not finished."

Darrio reached beneath his cloak and drew both of his daggers from their sheaths. He then spoke the final key of his restraints, and the winds responded with ghastly effect. As the irons fell from Darrio's wrists to collapse in a heap on the hot and dusty ground, the air around him shifted, and the winds parted as if to flee from his presence. Elder Judas, sensing the sudden changes in the winds said, "This was a mistake."

But Seris replied by saying, "Now you will see what your Firestar is capable of."

Darrio charged forward and advanced his pace with springs of earth to propel him on. Treos saw this and laughed. "What is he doing? Will he charge us head-on? He will be consumed with madness before he even touches the rock." All boasting became silent, however, when a rumble was felt from a short distance in front of them.

Darrio did not slow his advance, but he had caused a massive slab of earth to rise from the ground like a door swinging open on its side. It was as wide as the shadow caster's encampment, as long as the height of their shell, and three times as thick as the layers of darkness. As it rose, Darrio perched himself on its edge and caused the block to swing further on the hinge of his manipulative line.

"What is he doing?" a frightened shadow caster asked.

"I don't know," Treos remarked. "Brace yourselves!"

A third layer of hardened stone grew along the walls of the first two, and all of the holes were covered. Darrio, however, did not stop.

The slab of earth passed through the obstruction of darkness, and Darrio hardened it upon contact. This effect carried through the core and inner portions of the block, but the darkness was quickly eating away at its edges. When it connected with the barrier of stone, however, both formations shook, and the tremor caused could be felt by everyone present including the Saline army and the High Elders. Darrio then placed his hands upon the stone and through exercise of will could sense a connection with the shadow caster's three-layered shell. "Morons," he said.

Darrio pressed his will through the stone and into the shell raised by the shadow casters. The surface splintered, and a uniform pattern of sharp cracks cascaded through the shell. When Treos saw this, he gasped. "By the gods."

"Die." The shell was ruptured and imploded with great force upon the camp of shadow casters. Many were either impaled or shredded to pieces by the fast-moving hail of hardened shards. Those who survived only did so by protecting themselves with smaller barriers, but the ones maintaining the barrier of darkness could only perform their task, protect themselves, or die. The dual-layered dome of shadow fell away, but the attack was not yet complete.

The massive slab of earth, no longer impeded by the hardened dome, continued to fall, and those dead or alive were crushed underneath its weight. When it was over, only a tenth of the enemy's forces remained, and these were the ones who escaped to the sides to evade the destruction. Treos was among them. "Damn him!"

"Why isn't the master acting?" asked one of the survivors.

"I don't know. Attack. Attack him! Kill the Firestar!"

The High Elders saw all that had occurred from a distance and were astonished. "I did not know he was capable of this," Elder Tiberius said.

"He is not to be underestimated," Seris replied.

"Indeed…Ready the men, General Hammond."

The general nodded and ordered all present to prepare. Seris, however, looked back at Elder Tiberius. "What are you doing?"

"I told General Turil before I left that after the dust had settled, there would be nothing left to worry about. I intend to stay true to that statement."

"But you spoke to him, did you not?"

Tiberius looked back at Seris. "You do not seem the least bit surprised by my actions. I find that curious."

"I am not surprised. Only disappointed that you have not changed your mind, but you should not have spoken to Darrio."

"Why not?"

"For your own sake because if you should err, he will destroy everything you hold dear in his path to seek you, and when you are broken, only then will he kill you."

The remaining shadow casters scrambled towards Darrio to converge on his position, but when no less than ten of them were near, Darrio conjured a hedge of spikes to impale the men. The rest kept their distance and fired bolts and streams of fire, ice, and lightning, but what attacks were not defended were redirected to another target with even greater force. The shadow casters summoned shields of darkness to protect themselves from the elements and even fired bolts and streams of darkness at Darrio who was careful to evade them at all costs. The fighting was intense, and Darrio was surrounded by men well-versed in the arts of magic. However, there was little they could do to overcome the combination of ingenuity born from two centuries of combat experience and the sheer destructive power of his fluid techniques. He moved like a hunter and struck with forceful precision. He did not engage his foes as a warrior eager to exchange blows and gauge techniques. He fought only to kill.

Treos then sent a large swath of shadow to overcome Darrio's position. Darrio was late in detecting the incoming cloud of darkness and attempted to duck the attack, but his movement was poorly timed. While the rest of his body remained unharmed, his head and mind were touched by the darkness.

Vivid scenes of war-induced sufferings entered his mind as did the shadows of past hurts. His torture and time spent in imprisonment crashed upon his senses. Memories of those he attempted to help and those hurt raced through his mind. He saw an old friend and his severed head on the floor. He saw an image of Sam and the smoking wound he suffered. He saw Saria and the cold desolate rubble that buried her. All of this pressed upon his skull in an instant, and the pain of loss consumed him. Darrio screamed and took hold of his aching head and mind. The ground around his feet shifted violently, and the earth was turned over beneath him. A schism was created that extended a great distance in front and behind him, and its formation was like a freshly opened wound on Salia's landscape. The dust which had been raised as a result of the struggle was at first forced away and then suspended by the ever-extending aura of Darrio's power. A dark foreboding permeated the air, and it was felt by everyone present. Salia's army saw the dust at their feet slowly rise from its initial resting place and were frightened. Tam, however, was ecstatic, Carsis rolled his eyes, Talim lowered his head, and Lon smiled at what was to develop. Eloi kept his eyes on the field and the spot on which Darrio was standing, but Seris remained still, and Abaddon did the same.

When Darrio opened his eyes, they were not the same for they had shifted from his natural color to one of deepest red. His state limit had been reached, and the nature of his desire took hold. Darrio was no longer a calculating combatant. Instead, he became the ruthless essence of wrath hated and dreaded by the world around him. The Deloran, Great Destroyer, and Firestar emerged.

Time itself seemed to be struck by the Firestar's presence, and the Elders felt his transformation with fear and trembling. The sheer will for destruction could be felt all around them, and his rage penetrated their being. There had surely been no time in all of the world's history where such fury radiated from a single person to be felt by all. Five of the Elders fell to their knees due to the weakness of their stomachs while Tiberius stood alone. Even he trembled to his core at the sense of it all, and with great struggle, he uttered, "What is this thing we have unleashed?"

Darrio's first act as Firestar was to heat the wounded ground to unbearable levels. Those still standing in the midst of the land's wound fell out due to the heat, and their flesh sizzled and burned on contact with the surface. A few of the remaining shadow casters went on the offensive to strike the Firestar from behind, but as they advanced, the Destroyer heated the edge of his blade and turned forcefully. The first sets of attackers were severed at the mid-section by an extension of crackling lightning that stemmed from the edge of his weapons. Those unfortunate enough to be at the end of this were disemboweled. All crumbled into a heap, and before their lives even passed, the Firestar encased them in ice and shattered their remains. Several more shadow casters took to the sky to surprise the Destroyer with diving aerial attacks, but the Firestar deferred their trajectories by force of wind magic and quickly opened pits beneath each man's landing zone. As soon as the prey entered the traps, the bodies broken by the impact of the fall, they were promptly closed and spouts of blood signaled the demise of the victims. Others advanced and suffered similarly terrible fates, and as Treos bore witness to the Firestar's cruelty he cried, "Retreat, you fools! Run for your lives!"

The Firestar heard this and stomped his foot. A hedge of earthen thorns rose to encircle the perimeter, and those who ventured near were struck with lightning and split apart. The Destroyer's destructive will was worked so thoroughly into the earth by then that the land itself acted as a host for his anger. The shadow caster's executioner then made his rounds killing all he could find. A man's body was forced against a standing wall of stone and incinerated upon contact. Another was thrust to the ground where a spike of earth was summoned to pierce through his heart while the rest of the body was pulled below. Still, another man was launched into the air and struck by lightning mid-flight. His flesh burned away, and his bones were broken and used like pellets to kill another. Treos was the last to be caught though he fled from his destroyer. The Firestar, however, trapped his lower legs in stone as he ran and crushed them utterly. Treos fell and attempted to crawl away from his pursuer, but his left arm was frozen and shattered. He flipped over and saw his red-eyed executioner level his palm in his direction, and as he opened his mouth to scream, a stream of fire engulfed him.

The enemy was then scattered and broken across the field's surface, but to the Elder's horror, what remained began to wither, and the temperature in the region began to rise. Every organic thing on the field of battle smoldered and fell into flame. Every corpse and stain peeled away with the burning heat. Flakes of ash took to the air, towers of smoke rose up in formation, fire consumed the last remnants of life, and the Deloran stood in the center of it all unmoved. The standing sight of acrid death seared itself into the minds of all present, and Darrio's wrath as Firestar came to an end.

The air was unburdened, and the winds were given permission to move. Elder Tiberius gasped, "I have seen enough. Prepare the men to attack, General."

"Yes, sir," Hammond replied. "Ready!" The casters complied by stepping forward and taking their stances. "Aim!"

"Are you sure you want to do this?" Seris asked of the Elders.

"There is no other course of action for us to take," Tiberius replied.

On the battlefield, Darrio shook his head as he tried to recover his bearings, and he placed a hand on his head. "The hell," he uttered. "The hell did he do to me?" Darrio was then distracted from his self-examination by a faint and barely audible groan. Despite his injuries, Treos shielded himself as best he could, and though he still lingered in life as the only survivor among the dead, his was fleeting. His flesh was seared and scarred by the fires of battle, and the ends of his wounds were sealed by the burns. Nevertheless, and despite the excruciating sensations of pain, he extended his right hand towards the formation line on the horizon. Tears fell from his parched eyes, and with a charred and raspy voice, he cried, "Ma...master."

"What?" Darrio said.

"Master!" Treos wept.

Darrio quickly knelt before Treos and asked, "What master? Where?"

Treos ignored him, his eyes locked on a single figure among the formation, but the subject of his attention was too far away for Darrio to trace. "You have...forsaken us....Why?"

"What master? Who are you talking to?"

"Why?" The life of Treos was then extinguished, and his head fell like a weight to the charred and blackened earth.

"No!" Darrio shouted to the corpse. "Who were you talking to? Which one? Who is it?" but there was no response and no sound. The dead were still and remained silent. "Answer me, damn it!"

Elder Tiberius grimaced. "Fire."

The casters combined their wills to fire a volley of stone, fire, ice, and lightning which were set to converge on Darrio's position. Darrio, in the meantime, continued his futile attempts at questioning until the first wave of caster's fire was upon him. He turned, hearing the whistle and roaring approach of the attack. Darrio then reacted by shielding himself with a canceling wave to slow the combined trajectories and conjured a reinforced barrier of rock. The bodies behind him were obliterated, and the elements kicked up a cloud of dust and ash. The Elders peered closer hoping their assault had connected, but Darrio remained to summon a wind and clear the dust. He was at first confused over what happened and thought a mistake had been made. It was a consequence of genuine disbelief concerning just how far the Elders were willing to go, particularly with Seris in the vicinity, but his hatred for them and their ways was immediately rekindled and erupted into a wrathful flame. With no barriers to contain him, he fell into his state limit with even greater ease than before, but this time, he was silent and still. His eyes, shadowed in red, surveyed the horizon. All of his movements became slow and methodical. He carefully withdrew his weapons but did not advance a step, and as he did all these things, the air in the region became motionless once again.

"What is happening?" Elder Judas asked.

"You have set Firestar into motion," Eloi said, and Seris and his shades took collective steps to the rear.

"What does that mean?" asked the fourth Elder.

"It means he is deep within his state limit," Talim answered. "He cannot be called back from this."

"What should we do?" the third asked. "Should we run?"

Carsis, half chuckling, replied, "Did you see what he just did? You can't run from him when he's like this."

"What, then?" demanded the fifth. "What do you do in situations like this?"

"What everyone else has done when faced against him in this state," Lon said with a smile. "You die."

Darrio began his slow and steady advance which caused the Elders to panic. "Stop him!" Judas shouted. "Fire! Fire!"

Another wave of fire, lightning, and stone was fired toward Darrio, but with an enormous push of gale-force wind magic, the entire volley was deflected to the side. Another was set against him, and Darrio diverted the attack a second time into the ground. When they launched for a third time, Darrio broke into a full sprint and mediated his advance by launching himself ahead with quick-rising portions of the earth. The Elders shouted all the more demanding action, and the casters lowered their marks to strike ahead of Darrio and fired once more. Darrio then propelled himself high into the air. His bare weapons gleamed in the sun like a beacon to those below. The casters, thinking Darrio vulnerable, fired a fifth attack and all strikes were set to converge on the Firestar, but in this, they underestimated his power. Darrio set the lightning to scatter, striking the stones around them and breaking them into shards. After this, he set fire to the stones to heat them all in mid-flight. He then forced their trajectory in reverse as he positioned himself among them, and both he and their attacks were sent hurtling toward the attacking line. Elder Judas gasped. "By the gods, what have we done?"

The heated trajectories and Darrio crashed among the edge of the cliff wall, and it, along with a full half of the formation, was blasted apart in a hail of hot, earthen shards and a great explosion. Before the dust even had time to settle, an adept's body, seared and still burning away, flew out of the cloud and landed among the Elders. Then, the Firestar emerged, his weapons ablaze, and he proceeded to cut a swath through what remained. Many who approached were cast aside over the edge of the steep embankment, and some were skewered and shredded amidst a sheet of earthen spikes and edges. Still some were shattered in ice, some struck by thunder magic of such a kind as to burst apart, and most of the others were incinerated, but they were only the obstacle and not the goal. He had but one target in mind and those around him as accessories. They were the six High Elders and Elder Tiberius in particular.

Tiberius pleaded with Seris, "Do something, Captain. Calm him!"

"I cannot."

"But you have done so before."

"When he was limited, but as of now, it is too dangerous for even I to approach him now. There is nothing I can do, and there is nothing you can do." Twenty more adepts and seventeen casters were sent screaming into the valley below by a single motion. "You should not have spoken to him."

Darrio stood just outside of the vicinity of the Elders. Everyone behind him had either been shredded to pieces, tossed aside, or both. Tiberius and Judas retreated to the rear, but they remained in front of Seris and his shades. The third Elder was the first to attempt communication. "Firestar. You are upset, but I think we ca—," but his head jerked, and his words descended into bloodied sputtering as two thin pebbles of stone had been shot from the ground in front of Darrio's feet through the forehead and throat. The Elder fell to the side, and Darrio continued his advance. The fourth had no time to speak as a spike rose in front of him and entered through his chest. The fifth turned to run, but his legs were frozen and shattered. As he lay there screaming, he was launched into the distance and plummeted to his death. The sixth attempted to retaliate with twin streams of fire and lightning, but Darrio simply reflected the attacks, and just as he had done with the fifth, ejected the Elder from the cliff to meet his end. Judas, in a blind fit of madness, approached Darrio to strike him, but Darrio sidestepped and plunged a dagger deep into the heart. He then electrified the body until it burned before kicking it over the edge. His angry eyes then rested on Elder Tiberius.

It was a terrible silence for the Elder as he wondered just how he would meet his end. It was not enough, it seemed, to simply kill those who came before him but to make them suffer in the process. He realized then, despite how it fitted the figure, that they had given the title of Firestar in blindness. Deloran, as a last name, was bestowed in ignorance. He watched as the red-eyed destroyer approached and extended his open palm, a weapon by all means, which had been leveled against him. However, the effects of the state limit diminished, and standing before Tiberius was no longer the Firestar but Darrio. His eyes returned to normal and tears ran down his face. He spoke. "Why? If you couldn't accept me, why couldn't you just leave me alone? Why?"

"I...."

A ball of intense blue flame then appeared in front of Darrio's hand and pulsated violently. "Why?" he shouted.

Elder Tiberius looked at the flame in Darrio's hand, the flame of hatred burning in his eyes, and the devastation which was behind him. "You are the Firestar," he answered. "What else could we do?"

Darrio moved forward to press the attack, but his mother's image entered his mind along with all of its implications. Hesitation took over his body. Even as the heat of the flame neared the Elder's face all in preparation to burn away whatever it came in contact with, Darrio found himself unable to finish the motion. His sphere of incineration fizzled away and died, but rather than withdraw his hand, Darrio balled it into a fist and struck Tiberius across the face. The Elder fell unconscious, and Darrio shouted, "My name is Darrio you bastard!"

Seris looked at the Elder's unconscious form. He was surprised by the development though he did not show it. He then looked at the Elder's attacker. "Darrio," he said.

Darrio reacted to the call with surprise, and for reasons unknown to him at the moment, he was overcome with embarrassment. "You saw him," Darrio answered. "You know what they did. This is their fault," but Seris was quiet, and a fear came over Darrio as a result. "Why aren't you talking to me? Say something."

Seris turned his eyes to the unconscious Tiberius.

"Say something!" Darrio pleaded.

"Darrio," Seris started, struggling to speak. "You must...you must leave this place."

"What?"

"You must run."

"Run...? Why? Where would I go?"

"Away from here. You do not believe the Elder will free you from this, do you?"

"No, but—."

"Then you must leave."

Darrio turned his attention to the last Elder. He did not want to flee for doing so would separate him from Seris with no indication of reunion, but the only alternative, so far as he could see, was the Elder's death. The realm would likely be engulfed in chaos particularly if there was no one suitable to step into the vacuum of power and authority. However, Darrio was not sure if he could bear such a thing. Though he increasingly saw the Elder as an enemy worthy of no pity or remorse, performing the deed then would have been an act of murder. Darrio saw himself as carrying many despicable titles and killer was among them. However, he had never considered himself a murderer. There was a line between the two distinctions, one he would never cross.

Seris saw the spark of this conflict in Darrio's eyes, and he asked, "What are you thinking about, Darrio?"

Darrio glanced upward.

"Would you kill him?"

"I...shouldn't. Should. Shouldn't!" and Darrio groaned.

"Make up your mind."

Darrio again took another long look at the Elder who was slowly beginning to stir.

But Seris grew impatient. "Choose, Darrio."

Darrio slowly reset his hand to call again the blue flame of destruction, but the image of his mother's face flashed again within his mind's eye, and he heard his mother's words, "Don't be angry, Darrio," and his charge dissipated.

"I can't," he said. "I can't do this. I can't."

"Then run," Seris replied, and his eyes showed disappointment.

Darrio tried to speak. "But I—."

"Run!" Seris shouted. "Do not argue with me! Just run! Run!"

The order shook Darrio to his core, and it echoed like a painful beacon from his past. Darrio shifted back with compulsion to obey, and though he tried to speak, his words were choked off at the continued sight of Seris. "This is my fault," he thought to himself, and the grief was overwhelming. Darrio slid down the cliff face and ejected himself across the land. He peered behind him only once before he disappeared over the horizon, and he was followed by a glistening trail of tears.

When the Elder finally came to full consciousness, he looked around and examined himself. "I'm still alive."

"Yes," Seris replied as he quickly regained composure. "And you are fortunate to be so."

Elder Tiberius faced Seris and stood fully to his feet, and after this, he heard a voice call out to him from the distance.

Turil arrived in haste on the winds with an escort of shades beside him. When he landed near their position, his eyes widened with the full realization that he was far too late. "Elder Tiberius," he gasped. "I had a feeling things would go wrong, and we left as soon as we could. We felt the winds press against us, and then we felt the quake, but… what is this scar doing on the land? What happened to the men? Why is everyone dead?"

"The Firestar attacked us," the High Elder replied.

"What? Why?"

"Because of a disastrous error in judgment! I should have never considered your proposal, Turil!"

The rebuke caused Turil to recoil in silence. The Elder then turned his attention to Seris. "I can only assume you were the one to drive the Firestar away from here. I owe you my life, General Seris."

Turil grew fearful. "General?"

"I am hereby promoting Seris and tasking him with the apprehension and destruction of the Firestar. Lastly, I am holding you accountable for this disaster and placing him over you. You will still hold your title, and primarily in name only, but he will not serve as a subordinate or even an equal to you. He will be over you for his judgment and prudence have proven to be even greater than yours."

A new wave of fear came over Turil as he heard this declaration, and he watched Seris stand with newfound authority and feigned humility. However, behind the veil of Seris' eyes, Turil could only see a confirmation of calculation. Seris looked back at his old friend with a terrible glint in his eye. "You are staring at me, Turil."

"Seris."

"General Turil!" the Elder called.

"Yes…yes, sir. I will serve to the best of my ability."

"Good. I won't accept anything less in any capacity from either of you. Is this understood?"

Seris and Turil both nodded, and Elder Tibrerius, assisted by the remaining shades, began their return to the city.

When Turil and Seris were left alone, Turil faced Seris in anger and asked, "Did everything go as planned for you, Seris?"

Seris shook his head. "Nothing ever proceeds as planned, Turil."

"And yet you have always managed to capitalize on the opportunity left by others."

"You should have heeded my warning."

Turil shook his head. "No. I should have only opposed and fought you sooner."

"And what will you do now?"

Turil stood erect and calmed his nerves. "I will obey the Elder's order for now. I cannot do otherwise. Not yet."

"But when the opportunity comes, you will fight against me."

Turil crossed his arms, and a new spark made itself apparent in his eyes. "I may, but I have already failed to exercise proper judgment with you, Seris. I will not make the same mistake again."

The two watched each other for moments afterward, each evaluating the other for signs of weakness or lack of resolution. There was none to be found in either of them, and when their examinations were done, Seris smiled. "I look forward to working with you, brother Turil."

"As do I, old friend."

Seris stepped past Turil, and the two returned to Ambrosia to settle and make preparations. Their first order of business was to rebuild their forces which brought an influx of young and inexperienced soldiers who by necessity required training. Seris was put at the head of this effort, and Turil was forced to assist. Five new Elders were then elected to replace those who perished at the hands of the Firestar. Darrio was officially named an exile, a traitor, and an ever-present threat to the realm so long as he existed. Nearly all in the city and many throughout the realm gave their support to Tiberius and the new Elders, and the nation shared a unified hatred that propelled them to produce for the sake of his destruction. What affairs still lingered as a result of the Shadow Caster's efforts in other regions went ignored. Turil attempted to warn them of the dangers in this but was soundly harassed by the Elders and the people. He soon descended into silence and spoke of the matter no more.

While this happened, Darrio fled as far as he could to the western border of the region where he faced entry into the Burning Realm.

There was no doubt in his mind that he would be hated and hunted if discovered, but the pain of remaining in the Saline Realm was too great. Sam and Saria had been the latest victims of association with his existence. His new separation from Seris also weighed heavily on his mind, and his eyes were downcast. He remembered his hopes and how all of them were dashed to pieces, but his anger got the best of his sorrow when he remembered the remaining Elder and a lingering element who escaped him before. He recalled the name, Bacchus, and set his mind on seeking him out. If there was any chance at redeeming himself, it would have to involve the total destruction of all shadow casters and their plot to initiate the Great Cleansing. Darrio fixed this mission firmly in his mind and armed himself with the knowledge he gleaned. He was on his own, though this had not been the first time, and he knew he would be chased. Even so, he leveled his eyes with the horizon and crossed over into exile. He did not look back.

The day then faded, and the sun started to set. On the bordering woods between the Burning Realm and the Saline Realm were two contrasting figures. The Light Bearer, clad in white with a red collar and wearing a white glove, stood beside the lesser-seen Night Bearer who wore black and a black glove. They stood as twins on the height of a branch that oversaw the very same horizon which Darrio surveyed earlier. The Night Bearer had his arms crossed. "There he goes," he said.

"Are you sure he's the one?"

The Night Bearer looked back at his twin and smiled. "Come on, Shyoa. You know me better than to ask me that."

Shyoa smiled in return, and the two were at ease. Shyoa then spoke. "Shyo?"

"Hm?"

"Has He told you how long we will be like this?"

The Night Bearer, Shyo, turned his head. "It's going to be a while longer." He then turned his face to his brother. "But what did I keep telling you back then?"

The sun dipped even further, and the Light Bearer, Shyoa, was fading away. He answered and smiled, "Do not be afraid," and then he was gone.

"Do not be afraid," Shyo repeated to himself, and he chuckled. "I just realized how long I've been saying that." He looked up. "Now look at me." The Night Bearer was answered by a gentle gust and a whisper only he could hear. After receiving the message of encouragement, he uncrossed his arms and prepared himself with renewed confidence. "You're right. You're right." Shyo then girded himself and placed a hand on his weapon. "Let's get to it then," and he jumped. Darkness shrouded his form as he fell from the height of the trees, and his body vanished before touching the ground. There was nothing to be heard in the area after that and no sign the twins had ever been present.

Two weeks passed, and it was late when Abaddon entered Seris' office to find him seated with a ball of flame. Seris did not allow the fire to dissipate as he had done before, and he continued to manipulate it in Abaddon's presence. Abaddon spoke. "Everything is now in place. The men are ready, and your shades have been fully briefed on what is to come."

"Are they committed?"

"They are committed."

"Good."

A moment of silence passed, and Abaddon spoke again. "I am curious."

"What is it?"

"Darrio. Why do you value him so much?"

"You have asked me this before."

"I have, and once again, he is gone from you. Will you answer?"

Seris leaned back but retained the ball of fire. "He reminds me of a former self. A self that was young, unseasoned…and innocent."

Abaddon paused and then asked, "Is that all?"

Seris shook his head. "But we all have our passions, Abaddon. You have yours, and I have mine. There is nothing either of us can do to escape them."

Abaddon pondered and answered, "On this, we are agreed. I will take my leave."

Seris nodded, and Abaddon left the office. Seris then dimmed all lights within the room as an expression of his will so that his flame was the only prominent source of illumination left. His thoughts fell on the events which had transpired since the end of the war. Darrio, the Elders, the Shadow Casters, and every word he and Abaddon shared in secret was carefully parsed and studied in his mind. Seris later caused all other light sources but his to die, and he sat alone in near-total darkness. The wind outside of his window howled, and the sound it produced was like a cry of mourning. The beams of wood around him wailed and creaked like weary bones to a body. His office bore sounds of buckling and pain. Panes of glass shook in their place, but Seris remained still in his seat and hardened in his composure. He peered outside while paying the wind little mind and with even less respect. He then replied to the commotion with three carefully chosen words, "So be it," and his remaining light was extinguished.

Darrio sighed, and his heart conveyed,
"I will not be alone."

www.ingramcontent.com/pod-product-compliance
Lightning Source LLC
Chambersburg PA
CBHW020246030726

47499CB00001B/85

* 9 7 8 0 6 1 5 3 1 3 5 9 7 *